ASCENDANT
BOOK 2

ASCENDANT

BOOK 2

EmergencyComplaints

Podium

ASCENDANT
BOOK 2

CHAPTER ONE

Nym stood in silence while his friends all stared at Ophelia. She'd said she'd triple-checked her math, but the answer she'd gotten was impossible, wasn't it?

"How sure are you that you didn't make a mistake?" Bildar, the leader of the troupe of earth mages he was traveling with, asked.

"Obviously something is messed up here," Ophelia said. "But I cannot for the life of me figure out what I did wrong on these calculations. I expected it to be high just because it took four of us to hold the spell, but more in line with Analia's. She's already enough of an outlier as it is."

What had started as a fun little activity, just to see what his results would be on a standard Academy test, had gotten blown way out of proportion. For a normal person, ten or eleven was a fine result, nothing unexpected. Analia had already floored the group with her score of twenty-six, more than twice anyone else's.

Nym's test had been . . . irregular. It shouldn't have taken more than two of the other mages to administer it. The test was essentially a bubble of arcana that he pushed against with his own magic and that was sensitive enough to give the caster feedback. Then there was some math that converted that feedback to an easy-to-understand number, which might be at low as seven or as high as fifteen without anyone looking twice at it.

It had taken all four of the adult mages in their group working together to reinforce the bubble so that it was strong enough that Nym couldn't break through. If he was being honest, he'd stopped pushing when he felt it about to break again. There was no reason to mention that part though. The others were already freaked out about his score.

"Seventy-four is too far outside of human capabilities. It's obvious that Ermy, sorry, Nym is strong," Bildar said, accidentally calling him by the alias Nym had been going by when he'd first met the earth mages. "But nobody is that strong. Regardless of his strength, he lacks a thorough education. However, we were hoping you'd want to come, and I may have picked up something to help you out that I couldn't give you earlier on account of how buried it was in the wagon."

Bildar revealed a book he'd been holding behind his back and handed it to Nym. "I had Nomick pick it up for me just to make sure it was a recent edition. There's no telling what stuff was true back when I took the licensing exam but isn't today. This is a primer that goes over relevant laws for different parts of the world in relation to mage craft. It should tell you everything you need to know to pass that portion of the written exam."

"And I," Monick added, "will be tutoring you while we travel on the various spells we had to know to pass the practical portion a few years ago when I took it."

"He means we will be tutoring you," Nomick said. "There's not a lot to do on the road, so it's easy enough to lecture and walk."

The twins were the youngest of the adult mages in the group he and Analia had joined and had most recently passed their own licensing exam, something Nym had been quite eager to do once upon a time. With the use of magic strictly regulated in towns and cities, and the fines for violating those laws ruinously expensive, his ability to use magic had been sharply restricted. Now though, they were on the open road, and he could use magic whenever he wanted. It felt less important, but he was sure he'd change his mind in the next city when he had to start worrying about who was watching him do magic again.

"Wow, uh . . . thanks, guys. That's really kind of you. You don't have to do this," Nym said.

"It's fine. You need to get a license so you're not hobbled every time we go into a town. Plus, they give you one of these," Bildar said, displaying a leather band on his wrist. On the inside was a small disc with three concentric circles inscribed into it surrounding a solid core. A line started in the center and reached out through two of them but didn't quite touch the third.

"This looks familiar," Nym said. "I've seen it somewhere before."

"It's a common mage symbol. Anyone who's proven they can pull arcana from the Edge of the Horizon is legally allowed to use it, whether they can just barely do it or they're on the verge of pushing past that layer to the next," Bildar told him.

"Oh! Right. The magister in my old village had this on a plaque next to his door." He'd been a no-talent hack too, though Nym hadn't realized it at the time.

"That's . . . kind of tacky. It's generally considered to be in poor taste to use it for anything that's not identification purposes, but technically there's no rule against having it made into a plaque."

"He was that kind of person," Nym said, remembering the abrasive old man's accusations that Nym must be lying simply because he couldn't figure out what was causing Nym's memory loss.

"Anyway, like I said, once you get a license, you can commission something with the symbol on it showing you have it. It's not unusual to see rings or amulets. I think for a little while, there was a fad where women were getting the design on earrings?" Bildar looked to Ophelia for confirmation.

"Among other piercings. Not all of them were visible upon casual inspection."

"So that's kind of our group goal over the next few weeks. Get you, and Analia if she needs help, trained up as much as possible. Nobody's expecting you to be able to pass the exam with only a month or two of dedicated prep time, but if we can get you that much closer, we'll consider it a win. Plus since neither of you are technically our apprentices, there's really no better time than now, while we're traveling far away from towns and cities, to practice."

"That all sounds great," Nym said. "When do we start?"

"Tomorrow," Monick said. "I'm still writing down all the spells I can remember needing and trying to remember how to cast them. A few are quite worthless on their own and really only serve to easily prove that you've mastered some concept or another, so they're a bit hazy in my memory."

The conversation died down as dinner neared its completion, and everyone started settling down for the night. There was a brief flurry of postmeal activity as the earth mages worked together to raise a circular wall around their campsite, including a separate pen for the oxen. Ophelia and Nym scribed rune sequences to strengthen them, though she said it was very unlikely they'd need them. There was some debate about putting up a roof, but as the weather was clear, they opted to skip it.

It was a good night for Nym in a lot of ways. The earth mages reminded him a lot of Ciana, whom he found himself thinking about and missing more every day. Now that he had the magic to defend himself against a group of adults, he was a lot less anxious about the idea of going back to Palmara. He still had no plans to go into the town itself, but the thought of being near it no longer scared him.

Analia opened up her trunk while they were winding down and pulled a foldout screen made of some thin paper from it. She set it up and invited Ophelia to join her, and the two of them bid the rest of the group good night before disappearing behind it.

The screen started glowing in Nym's sight. Both silhouettes disappeared, and all sound from behind it cut off. Once Nym knew to look, he saw a tiny line of runes inscribed around the framework, which he was interested in reading but decided it would be in bad taste to do so after it had been activated. He made a mental note to ask Analia for a look in the morning.

One by one, other auras popped up around various items. Bildar had a sleeping bag that was enchanted in some way, and the twins each had pillows and blankets. Nym suspected there were probably other mundane items enchanted to be more effective hidden behind Analia's privacy screen but couldn't tell with it active.

Only he had nothing of the sort, but that was fine by Nym. He'd spent plenty of time sleeping outside with nothing over his head. Compared to the recent week of traveling to reach Thrakus, it was downright pleasant with both the fire and the relatively warm night air. Nym curled up in his cloak, the hood bunched up to act as his pillow, and went to sleep.

The next few days were a blur as Nym and Analia passed the little book of mage laws back and forth, discussing it and quizzing each other on the more esoteric rules of some regions. Some of them made no sense at all, but when Nym asked about the reasoning, nobody could give him a good answer. The important part was knowing the laws though, not why they were that way, so Nym studied diligently.

Practical training was a different matter. Monick scribbled down schematics for spell constructs to do things like create different colored lights or make phantom sounds that mimicked everything from bird cries to creaking timber to metal clanging against metal. There were spells to clean things, spells to mend small tears, spells to foretell cards being drawn, spells to hide the smell of things.

The problem was that while Monick knew the spells and could demonstrate them easily, his scribblings were not very accurate, and if Nym had to base his own casting on the scrawled diagrams of how the constructs were supposed to look, they would fail. This usually meant he had to cast the spell a dozen times the wrong way before he could convince Monick to demonstrate so he could "see what the outcome was supposed to look like" but in actuality to study a real construct.

The fact that he could see arcana when no one else seemed to be able to remained his greatest asset and his biggest secret. He'd told no one, ever, not even his closest friends. He'd actually gone to great lengths to keep that ability hidden, on the basis that if no one knew, no one would think to guard themselves from it. He'd picked up a great many tricks simply by observing other people's magics with them none the wiser.

It was worse in some ways for Analia. She already knew many of the spells Monick was trying to show them, but the ones she didn't, she struggled with. Nym took to noting down which spells she was having the most problems with and, after he'd reverse engineered them from Monick's demonstrations, made his own schematics. He was by no means a professional, but his drawings were far, far more accurate. She had little trouble casting the spell using his notes, which were structured similarly to the spells that had been stored in her family's library.

Oddly, many of the spells weren't even second circle. Nym found himself drawing from the first layer, Phase Shift, more during those few days of training than he ever had during his normal activities. There was a lot of depth there that he'd missed out on when he was scrambling to increase his strength. The spells weren't necessarily powerful, but being able to mend tears with magic would have saved him a lot of headaches.

He also found that other than it being marginally easier to stop his conduit in the first layer, the spells weren't necessarily any less complex. When he mentioned it, Monick said, "Yeah, that's probably because you're using the same mental construct for your conduit for both. A first-circle spell just needs a needle that can pierce reality to bring in arcana. You can do it basically instantly. Second-circle spells need a pipe that can hold against the pressure of pushing through the membrane between two levels of reality."

"So what about third-circle spells then? It can't just be bigger and stronger, or there'd be a lot more third-circle mages," Nym said.

"Ah, well . . . that's complicated. You know how the conduit goes so far into the second layer and then it just kind of hits a wall?"

"Yes."

"Right, well, that's not really a wall. Here, let me show you."

Monick cast a quick spell, and a patch of the road turned to sand. He drew a circle in it, then two more circles around it. "Here in the center is us, reality as we know it. To reach the first layer, we just have to poke through this membrane surrounding our reality. Easy enough. To reach the second layer, it's the same thing, except our reach has to be a little bit longer."

Then he scattered a handful of rocks inside the ring that represented the second layer. "These things are hard points in the arcana. We can't just power through them. We have to go around them. But since we can't see into the arcana, we're going in blind. So now the conduit doesn't just need to be strong, it needs to be flexible. We need to avoid obstacles."

Monick squatted down and drew a line out from the center, bisecting the first circle in a straight shot and then weaving back and forth through all the rocks he'd dumped in the sand. "And once we get to the end, then we can pierce this membrane and get to the third layer, what we call the Astral Sea. That arcana is far enough removed from reality to do all sorts of crazy stuff. But it's not easy to reach."

"Huh . . . So all I need to change to reach the third layer is make the conduit flexible enough to go around the rocks?"

"Easier said than done, my friend. There are a few points where people fail. The first is simply making a flexible conduit. It's not as easy as you might think. Most mages do eventually figure that part out, but then they just can't hold the conduit long enough to make it all the way through the second layer. And for the ones that do that, the hard fail at the end comes when they've got a conduit that wriggles like a streetwalker doing a lap around the docks, but it's not strong enough to pierce the membrane."

"Wriggles like a . . . what? Never mind, I don't want to know. So, in order to draw in Astral Sea arcana into your soul well, you need a strong, flexible conduit that can provide feedback so you know when you've run into a rock but still has a sharp tip for piercing the third layer. Wow, that's got to take a lot of practice."

"I wouldn't know. I can't do it myself. I don't know anyone who can outside a few of the older masters at the Academy," Monick told him.

"I met one once. They were crazy but also scary strong."

"Yes they are, my young friend." With a wave of his hand, Monick transmuted the sand back into road dirt. "Now, as I was saying, the key to this spell is that the construct has to be flexible to allow for the arcana to build up before it releases . . ."

CHAPTER TWO

Valcort proved to be just a brief stop on their trip. They topped off their supplies, inquired about any dangers roaming the local area that they should be aware of, and left. There was no work for a crew of earth mages to be had there, and nobody was much interested in hanging around for more than a single night's stay at an inn. Beds were nice, but all of them were eager to be on their way, each for their own reasons.

The Earth Shapers, as they called their crew, wanted work, and where there was none to be found, they didn't want to stay. Analia seemed almost eager to get to Ebalsan, though Nym wasn't sure what had changed her mind. She'd been hesitant to make the trip originally, afraid of running into some of the same family she'd run away from. As for him, the farther west they went, the closer they got to Palmara, and more than ever, he wanted to go see his adoptive sister again.

The next few weeks were more of the same. Two more towns came and went in a blur, with no work for the crew besides putting up a new silo for a farm that was on the way. That took a good portion of an afternoon since Bildar was the only one who knew the appropriate transmutation spells, and they all grumbled about the low pay after they left.

Nym was reading through a spell book he'd picked up from a general store for cheap. The shopkeeper knew what it was, but since there was no real call for something like that in a village so small, he'd let it go to Nym for far less than it was worth. Nym was sure the man could have saved it for the next trader who came through to get a better price, so he appreciated the gesture.

The book focused on information-gathering spells, collectively called divinations by the author, and Nym was hoping to modify his scrying spell or at least learn a different version that allowed him to see significantly farther from the spell anchor. Painful experience had shown him that scrying was not all that useful out in the open if it lacked the range to see things he couldn't see himself.

So far, integrating the spells with his own version was not going well. "Look here," he said to Analia, pointing at his own sketched-out scrying spell. "I think this part is what's limiting the range I can cast it out to. See how this version in the book does the construct completely different? But when I try to adapt mine, the whole spell fails."

"Of course it does. Look opposite of it. If you don't counterbalance this side of the construct, it'll fall out of alignment. When you swap out this chunk by itself, you're screwing up the whole thing."

"No, I tried that," Nym said. "The construct doesn't fall apart, but the spell itself doesn't work anymore."

They dissected the spells for another hour, trying to find a way to mesh Nym's version that let him see through solid objects with the range components of the one in the book. They would have kept working on it, but Ophelia dropped back to walk next to them and reminded Nym that it was time to continue the project the two of them had been working on instead.

Nym stowed away the book and got out the papers he and Ophelia had drawn for the construct schematic of another spell: the earth golem. Adapting his ice-golem version was not going great, but they had at least had some small successes. The biggest problem seemed to be that unlike ice and snow, there were a lot of different kinds of dirt. If they transmuted it all into one kind, they could build clay or sand golems and had varying degrees of success with other materials.

Even those were fragile, however. The one part they'd had no luck with at all translating from ice to earth was the regeneration part of the spell. Ice golems would draw more water, ice, or snow from the surrounding environment to repair themselves, given enough time to do so. If they could perfect the regeneration portion of the earth-golem variant, it would be a fantastic spell for fighting the undead that the army in Ebalsan was working to keep contained.

"*Fantastic* might be too strong of a word," Ophelia said. "I can barely keep one of these going. I imagine two would be the limit for most mages, and it would leave them vulnerable since they'd be devoting so much arcana to maintaining them."

"That's why I want to miniaturize them. I think a half-sized one would still take out an undead but would be significantly less taxing."

"We might as well start over from scratch if that's how you want to do it," she said.

"I did it with that soup once!"

"Yeah, and how many seconds did it last before it fell apart?"

Ophelia was right, of course. The earth-golem spell was a good idea, but it wasn't going to revolutionize the face of warfare. There was a reason every battle mage didn't go into combat with a golem or two. There were better, more efficient uses of arcana. Of course, most mages couldn't come close to channeling the amount of arcana Nym could. For him the spell only limited him slightly instead of requiring his full focus and effort to maintain. Seventy-four indeed.

They spent the rest of the afternoon working on it, and when they stopped for the evening, they decided it was time for another test run. Nym crafted the construct himself out of standard dirt. A chunk of it ripped itself out of the grass and floated up about three feet in the air, then started spinning slowly. It pulled up more and more dirt with each revolution, until Nym couldn't even see it anymore behind the body it was building for itself.

The golem finished forming after about thirty seconds. It was roughly Nym's proportions, about five feet in height, but its limbs were more than twice as thick as his. Nym felt the connection snap into place as soon as it was finished, and he mentally commanded it to raise an arm and wave at the group.

"You figured it out?" Monick asked, excited. "It works?"

"Seems to," Ophelia told him. "Nym? Any issues?"

"Nothing so far. It's holding together fine, pulling arcana at a steady pace. No issues with controlling it that I can see."

The earth mages crowded around Ophelia so they could get a look at the schematic she and Nym had put together. "We need to try this. I can't believe you finally got it working," Nomick said.

"Yes, and with this, finally, it's time," his brother added.

"I hesitate to even ask this, but time for what?" Bildar asked, looking between the two.

"Golem battles," they said in unison.

Two golems stood in the middle of a bowl-shaped depression, duking it out. They rained blows on each other, neither bothering to block, and chunks of dirt were ripped out and tossed into the air. As fast as they dismantled each other, more dirt was sucked up from the ground to replace the missing material.

"This . . . is kind of intense," one of the twins said, sweat beading on his face.

"You . . . could . . . surrender," the other said, panting as he spoke.

"Never!"

From over by the wagon, the rest of the group watched with amusement. "I'd say we finally figured out that regeneration problem," Ophelia commented. "It's working overtime, and I'm fairly confident the twins are going to give out before the golems do."

"It's impressive," Analia added. She was currently reviewing the schematic, but lacking the thorough grounding in earth magic that the rest of the crew possessed, she had a ways to go before she was ready to try the spell herself. "I think an air-golem version might be more useful to me though."

"How would that do any work if it's made of air?"

"Solid air isn't a problem. An invisible servant would be quite handy though, don't you think?"

"Would it really be less work than levitating and telekinesis though?" Nym asked.

"That depends on how dexterous we could make it and how well it can follow orders," Analia said.

"We just finished making this one work," Nym said. "I am taking a break from golem making."

"Oh fine. Something to consider in the future though."

Off to the side, both twins had collapsed from exertion, and their golems were slowly unraveling. No longer were they pulling in new earth to fix the damage, but neither were they still attacking each other. At this point, it was a coin toss which of the two earth mages would give out first.

"Draw?"

"Never!"

Another few seconds went by of the golems basically falling into each other. It was not an impressive fight.

"Fine, draw."

"No draw," Bildar protested. "We've got money riding on this."

"Screw your gambling."

"And the horse it rode in on!"

The golems collapsed into dirt at the same time. With synchronous groans, the twins dragged themselves to their feet and shuffled back over to the wagon. "Dinner ready?"

"What dinner? You two were supposed to cook tonight. All we've got is cold travel rations now."

"Come on, Ophelia. We're starving. We worked ourselves to the nub."

"Work? You mean goofing around with the new spell we came up with."

"We were stress testing it," Nomick protested.

"It's very important to know its limits," Monick added.

"I'm sure. Either way, it's your turn to cook, so you best get on that."

"This job is so unfair," Monick muttered.

The twins settled down to recover their strength while the rest of the group snacked and discussed the golems. Despite how much the two earth mages were screwing around, the golems truly were a sight to behold. Mages who specialized in earth magic often had defensive options for every scenario but rarely had strong methods to attack with. That wasn't to say they were helpless, just that a fire mage packed a lot more destructive magic into his arsenal.

Nym was of the opinion that it was better not to specialize in any one discipline, but he recognized that there were only so many hours in the day, and if he was looking for a type of magic to support himself with, the Earth Shapers had proven there was money to be made in magical construction.

"We should be in Ebalsan in the next two days or so," Bildar remarked. "You two think you're going to want to stick around still? If it's been converted over to a staging ground for the army like we were told, we can probably get to work without worrying about you needing to get your licenses. From what I heard, the situation is getting desperate."

"*Desperate* might be a strong word," Ophelia added. "But it's definitely proven to be more dangerous than anyone initially thought. We'll stay far away from the fighting though, so it should be safe enough for us."

"We'll stay," Analia said. "Unless there's something unexpected in Ebalsan, there's no reason to change our plans."

"We'll see when we get there," Bildar said. "But my guess is we'll end up somewhere between Ebalsan and the front line of the fighting, building fortifications for supply dumps and big, long walls so the army can keep advancing without worrying about getting cut off from behind. That's what earth mages always end up doing in these kinds of situations."

"You've worked with the army before?" Nym asked.

"Once or twice," Bildar said with a far-off look in his eyes. "It's . . . The money is good. As long as you don't get too involved."

"What's that mean?"

But Bildar wouldn't elaborate any more, and sensing he'd touched on a delicate topic, Nym didn't push for answers. Everyone was entitled to keep their own secrets, after all. The group went to bed early that night to better prepare for what would hopefully be the final push to Ebalsan in the morning.

CHAPTER THREE

Without the military presence, Ebalsan would have reminded Nym a lot of Zoskan. It was on the eastern border of the same forest instead of the north, and it was probably two or three times bigger, but the homes were constructed in the same style, and its people wore the same clothes. Ebalsan was what Zoskan could have been if it was more conveniently located on important trade routes.

That was before the undead showed up, which Nym was becoming more and more sure was related to what he'd discovered in the forest half a year ago. Though it was still over a hundred miles to Zoskan if he flew straight over the forest, he was sure it was less than half that to the place Leaf had wanted to look at.

Near the city, right in the middle of a few fields like it had grown out of the ground, was a fort made completely from earth and stone. It had its own walls, also earth make, and hundreds of tents surrounded it in a rigid grid pattern. A trail perhaps two hundred feet wide had been carved into the forest, leading directly away from the keep. More walls had been raised from the ground between the keep and the opening, and all of them were manned by hundreds of soldiers watching the forest for signs of undead.

Bildar steered their wagon toward the town and handed the reins off to Ophelia. "I'll go get the paperwork sorted for us all while you resupply," he said. "Try to get us a barrel of something nice, yeah? I have a feeling we're going to be here for a little while."

While their leader walked off by himself toward the keep, the rest of the group went up to Ebalsan's gates. They were wide-open but staffed by both local guards and professional soldiers. "Your business?" one of the soldiers asked as they approached.

"Earth-mage crew specializing in fortification construction. Our leader is heading to the keep now to get an assignment. We're going into town to restock our supplies."

"Go on through," the soldier said in a bored tone. "Make sure you clean up after the oxen if they leave any messes, or you'll be fined."

Ebalsan was almost exactly what Nym had expected. There were fewer locals than he'd thought there would be, but the soldiers more than made up for the numbers. They were everywhere, eating meals, shopping at stores, chatting with citizens, or even standing guard. None of them paid the group much attention, and Nym reminded himself that he was there to work with the army, not get arrested by them. No one knew who he was.

Other than the old familiar fear he felt every time he'd seen guards who ignored him, Nym found the town rather charming. The group split into three soon after entering, with Analia wanting to find a room at an inn where she could get a well-cooked meal and a bath, and Nym following after. Ophelia went toward the market district to find general supplies, and the twins disappeared, intent on being anywhere but near Ophelia so they wouldn't have to help her load those supplies.

"I'll remember this, you treacherous dogs!" Ophelia yelled at them, shaking a fist in the air.

"Um, do you want me to help?" Nym asked.

She looked momentarily surprised, but then shook her head with a laugh. "No, it's fine. It's not that hard to resupply a wagon by myself, but I'm going to use this as a justification to make them set up everything when it comes time to unload it. You may want to consider buying a weapon before we head out to the woods."

"A weapon? But we're mages," Nym said.

"You think undead care? Get something heavy and ram it into them at high speed with magic. Or something pointy or sharp. In my experience, heavy is better, but I'm an earth mage. Heavy fits my style."

"I'll keep that in mind," Nym said doubtfully. He didn't want to haul around ten or twenty pounds of metal, sharp or otherwise, everywhere he went. But he had to admit, Ophelia had given him a lot of good advice over the past few weeks, and he had certainly never been part of a military operation or even seen an undead monstrosity, let alone fought one.

They parted ways, and Nym followed Analia as she sought out an inn. He felt like the only reason he was along was to transport her luggage for her, which had somehow grown heavier over the past few weeks. Unlike the rest of them, she had no plans on going farther than Ebalsan. She wasn't an earth mage and wasn't going to fight on the front lines.

Nym wasn't an earth mage either, but he thought he could do a decent job helping them. He knew enough of the basic spells they used and could run a lot of arcana through his soul well in a day before he started hitting his limits. For now at least, he wanted to both earn a bit of extra money and get a closer look at this undead problem.

Once Analia was settled in at a place called the Silver Gilder, Nym left her to her bath and meal and other luxuries and went to find the market square. The more he walked around, the more nostalgic he got for Zoskan. Even the cobblestone patterns were the same. If he'd scattered in a few familiar faces from the other town, he would never have known he was somewhere else.

This proved to be helpful, as the same kind of logic had been used to lay out the streets, and it took very little effort to find what he was looking for. The sign hanging above the door simply read *Halder's* with a crossed sword and mace beneath it. There was no display window or even regular-sized windows.

The door itself was unlocked, so Nym pushed it open and walked into his first-ever weapon shop. It was a bit intimidating, if he was being honest with himself. There were probably a hundred different melee weapons mounted on pegs on walls. Axes, flails, swords, daggers, maces, and even more weapons he didn't have names for lined just about every available inch of space. Stands were set up regularly and contained spears by the dozens of various sizes with different-shaped heads.

A teenage boy sat in the corner, idly throwing knives at a target set up about ten feet away from him. One after another, they thunked into the wood, each one quivering. A faint aura of arcana surrounded the boy, maybe enough to account for a weak first-circle spell. He didn't get up from his game until all the knives had been released, and even then, it was only to go collect them from the target.

"Excuse me," Nym said.

"Yeah, need something?" the teenager asked. "Everything's got tags on it. We don't negotiate. Just pick out what you'd like and bring it over to me."

"Oh, I see." Nym looked around at the shop. "Got any advice?"

"If you don't know what you're doing, it doesn't much matter what I say. You're going to get yourself killed the first time you pick a fight regardless of which weapon you're holding."

"I'm not trying to pick a fight with anyone," Nym said.

The teenager stopped pulling the knives out and looked at Nym for the first time. "Then why are you here?" he asked.

"My group is going to build fortifications for the army, and they said I should have something to defend myself with."

"Oh, you're a mage?" the teenager asked. "You should have said so. Come with me. We've got some special mage weapons in the back room."

Nym followed him to a room that had a decidedly different theme going on. Instead of a thousand pounds of steel mounted on different-sized handles, the new room had display cases holding some truly bizarre items. The closest one looked something like the head of a sledgehammer, except with no handle and a bunch of ridges carved into it. The whole room was shaped like one long hallway with an extremely battered wooden target hung on the back wall.

"So most mages go one of two ways. Heavy and spiky or thin and pokey. This side of the room has the heavy things; that side has the light. Feel free to try some stuff out and let me know when you figure out what you want."

That was apparently all the explanation Nym was going to get. The teenager left him alone in the room and returned to the storefront. It didn't take long for the sound of knives thunking into wood to start up again. Nym's eye started twitching in time to the sound.

Poking his head back out through the door, Nym said, "I'm sorry, but I don't really know what I'm looking at here. Could you help me out?"

"No," the teenager told him in a bored, distracted tone. "I'm not a mage. No idea how mage weapons work. I just know you pick them up with magic and hit stuff with them."

That was both vague and annoying. Nym considered going to another shop, but he didn't know where to find any, and he wanted to get this chore taken care of in time to meet up with everyone else so they could get moving again. He ducked back into the room and telekinetically picked up the closest thing he could find out of the light display case.

It was a flat disc, sharpened all the way around. Nym telekinetically shoved it at the target wall as hard as he could and watched it bounce off. He shoved it in again. It penetrated maybe enough to hold its own weight if he let go, but Nym didn't want to test it. Instead, he moved the weapon back to its tray and tried again with one of the heavier blocks.

That made a loud crunching sound and definitely did some damage to the wood, but it was so heavy he already was sick of it. It went back onto the display case too. He tried a few other from the heavy weapons before writing the whole section off. The light weapons looked more interesting anyway.

After experimenting with a few, he found he liked the ones that looked like throwing knives without handles the best. Those made solid thunking sounds, similar to the ones coming from the front room, each time they hit, and with magic driving them in, his accuracy was more or less perfect. Pulling them back out, however, was a different matter.

He couldn't find a weapon he wanted. They were all too heavy, or too hard to use, or too hard to recover. As Nym worked his way down the hall, he found himself getting frustrated. There didn't seem to be anything here he couldn't do better with his magic, and he couldn't find a logical reason to part with good silver and copper in exchange for weapons he didn't need.

He knew Ophelia wanted him to be armed, but nothing here suited him. He put everything back in the display case, shook his head, and left. The teenager barely looked up as he walked by, and neither of them spoke a word to each other. Nym left the shop and turned deeper into the market district.

Weapons might not have been on the table, but there were plenty of other things he could stock up on. Though learning the mending spell had negated his need to replace his clothes so quickly, he still wanted a few other personal items, like soap, ink, and paper. Nym had a strict budget in mind, but there were a lot of stores, and he was hopeful that he'd find everything he wanted at reasonable prices.

Three hours later, he met up with the earth mages, his face twisted into a scowl, and he was in a foul mood. "Why is everything here so damn expensive?!" he snapped. Ophelia just laughed.

CHAPTER FOUR

It was actually kind of impressive just how deep the new road penetrated into the forest, but then again, Nym supposed a few thousand industrious soldiers could fell a lot of trees very quickly, especially if they needed that lumber. The wagon rumbled over the dirt, bouncing over various ruts that had already formed in it, but Nym bypassed all that discomfort by simply flying at a walking speed six inches off the ground next to it.

"Which weapon did you end up getting?" Ophelia asked, once they'd rejoined Bildar and made it through all the checkpoints. They'd been cleared to move up to the five-mile mark, where they'd receive further instructions on where their services were most needed.

"I couldn't find anything," he told her.

"Nym! This wasn't a hard job. Just go to the store, pick out something you can carry, and pay for it."

"But there were all these mage weapons that were just the sharp bits, and they were either too heavy or didn't do anything or were too hard to get back."

"Why were you looking at mage weapons? Those take months of practice to get any good with. You just needed a short sword or a mace or something. It's a weapon of last resort for when you can't pull any more arcana into your soul well."

"I've never had that problem," Nym said.

"You . . . I . . . Be that as it may!" Ophelia trailed off, grumbling under her breath. "We'll look into it later. I'll go with you next time."

"Sure," he said, having no intention of spending five or six shields on a chunk of metal he'd never use. "Next time."

Ophelia gave him a flat look, grumbled to herself some more, and returned to smoothing out the worst of the ruts in the road in front of them. The wagon kept bumping along, and after a few hours, they came upon a barricade blocking the road. It was manned by forty or fifty soldiers, and Bildar left them outside while he went in to talk to somebody.

Traveling through the forest this way was incredibly boring and tedious. "When do we start work?" Nym asked.

"Probably tomorrow," Ophelia told him. "We'll need to determine which job site we're most needed at, but if I had to guess, I would say we'll probably be extending this wall to encircle more of the perimeter and help keep the undead outbreak contained."

"Would the wall really stop them? The frost wraiths I saw could fly."

"Frost wraiths? No, no, this is a lot of ghouls, wights, and geists the army is dealing with. That's probably lucky for us in some ways. They're nasty but much easier to contain than a wraith or specter outbreak would be."

"I don't know what any of those things are," Nym admitted.

"Oh for the love of . . . Seriously?" Ophelia said. "It's like you're trying to get yourself killed. Did you do no research at all on undead before you signed on to help the army contain them? Between this and the lack of a weapon . . ."

The barb hurt, especially coming from Ophelia. She'd always been so nice to him before. Something must have shown on his face because she took a deep breath and said, "I'm sorry. I should have made sure you were better prepared for this. We had weeks to get here, and it never came up."

"We were busy making the golem spell," Nym said.

"Yes, but still, there was time. Well, we've still probably got some walking to do before we get to the jobsite. Let's go over stuff right now."

So they did. Ophelia lectured, and Nym's head was packed so full of random factoids about various undead that he was sure he'd forgotten half of it as soon as he learned it. Ghouls were canny ambushers who lurked in shadows and climbed up high to jump down on people. Wights were more straightforward and would come right at a person, but they were also significantly stronger and smarter and could easily overwhelm the average unarmed human thanks to the fact that they could use magic. Geists were something completely different, and other than a basic description and the advice to run away, they didn't get too deep into the subject.

As they walked, Ophelia pointed out different spots a ghoul could be hiding in to ambush them, though considering it was still late afternoon and it was far from dark, it was rare that the shadows were deep enough to hide a man-size undead monstrosity in them. It would be a very different story come nightfall, and it was more important than ever to make sure they had adequate shelter to sleep in.

Eventually, after much bureaucracy and much traveling, they reached a point where Bildar handed off the wagon to an officer and received a handful of crests in return. Most of the supplies went with it, but they kept a few packs and barrels for themselves. Nym didn't much mind the weight of his own stuff and the few packs he'd been assigned, but others were less fortunate.

"This sucks," Monick said. "Why are we building in the forest? Why not build a wall around the outside of it where other creatures can haul our belongings for us?"

"Bildar lives to torture us, brother," Nomick told him. "But more specifically, me. Why do I have the heaviest barrel while you have the small, light one?"

"Oh, shut it, both of you. Poor Nym is carrying twice the weight of anyone else, and he's just a kid," Ophelia told them.

"Wait, what? I am?" Nym looked back at the packs floating along behind him. They didn't feel that heavy.

"Well, if the weight is so negligible, feel free to carry my share too," Monick said. He held up the cask to Nym, who easily swept it up into his airborne parade of supplies. "Oh, I didn't mean—are you sure, Nym? It's fine, really. Here, give it back."

Instead, Nym plucked the rest of the supplies out of everyone else's hands. "At the speed we're walking, I think I can manage this for about an hour or so," he said. "If we're not there by then, you can have it all back, and my stuff too."

"Shouldn't be that long," Bildar said from the front, consulting a crudely drawn map he'd been given back at the last base. "Maybe half a mile ahead of us. Thanks, Nym."

The others mumbled thanks as well, the twins in a considerably better mood and Ophelia with pursed lips as she glared at them. "It's not fair making you carry it all," she told Nym. "Here, let me take some of it back."

Nym raised the luggage farther overhead. "It's fine, I said. You're really overestimating how much effort it takes to lift this."

"So you'll carry close to two hundred pounds of supplies without complaint but won't buy a three-pound sword to protect yourself with?"

"Well, that's different. I'd have to haul it around all the time and physically carry it. I don't want to do that. Plus it's not like I even know how to use it anyway."

Ophelia just sighed and shook her head again. "Thanks for carrying everything, Nym."

They reached the encampment about half an hour later and got settled into their site. The first order of business was to create a semipermanent structure to live in while they were working, since this would be a project that ran for weeks and weeks. They would move the camp every few days as the wall continued to grow, which meant there was no point in making anything elaborate.

But they were after all a crew of earth mages, plus Nym. It only took them an hour or so to put up a small hut made of six rooms. The outer room had a door leading outside, and five other rooms were arranged in a half circle around it, one for each of them. The rooms were small, barely enough to fit the folding cots they'd brought with them, but it protected Nym from the elements and rogue undead that might roam through the camp.

When it was time for bed, the door was sealed off completely. Nothing bigger than a bug was getting through the strategically placed air vents, and they'd made the outer walls of hard-packed earth almost a foot thick. Nym slept just fine, safe and secure inside his room.

The next day was when the real work began. An army overseer started handing out tasks, and the Earth Shapers ended up with exactly what Ophelia had predicted: building the wall up. That wasn't as easy as it sounded, since the army didn't actually want to clear away any trees, so the wall was the furthest thing from a straight line that it could possibly be.

They worked in a pattern, first transmuting the ground that was going to be shaped into loose sand so that they could sweep all the plant life out of it, then hardening it back up into thick, hard-packed earth, and finally raising it ten feet straight up. Ideally, there would be no trees near the front side that a canny undead might use as a ladder to climb the wall.

The army recognized the impossibility of this. They knew the wall wasn't going to contain all the undead and that there was no way to run a wall through a forest while making no effort whatsoever to clear trees. It was a net, designed to stop the majority of the stupid undead. Active patrol units with paired trackers scoured the forest, looking for signs of clever or strong undead who'd managed to slip past the growing defenses. Freelancers helped fill gaps in the patrol routes.

Nor was it perfect, given the sheer number of miles the wall would have to cover. If it helped funnel the majority of the undead to the fortified positions the army had set up, it was doing its job. Every few miles, there would be kill fields cleared that allowed soldiers to rain death down on the undead that crawled their way across the length of the wall, looking for an opening.

Nym understood the logic of it, but it was boring work. After the first three days, he was ready for anything else. The Earth Shapers, however, knew exactly what they were signing on for when they'd started the journey and, at nine shields a day, were in no hurry to run the contract out.

"How many feet of this wall have we raised?" Nym asked when they stopped for their lunch break on the third day.

"Honestly? Hard to say for sure. A few thousand maybe? We're probably losing better than half the distance weaving it between all these trees," Bildar answered. "Too bad a job like this pays by the day instead of by the foot. I'm sure we're doing more than a lot of other crews, but we're all getting paid the same for it. We'll be linking up with Sansom's group's section here in the next hour or so and probably moving the entire camp another mile into the woods this evening."

"I thought we'd be doing something to help hunt down the source of the problem," Nym said. "Instead . . . this."

Bildar laughed. "I told you earth mages are good for defensive fortifications. This is a nice, safe, easy job. The pay is good, and we'll provide fallback positions for those brave soldiers who are culling undead numbers on the north side of this wall. Make no mistake, this is as much a contribution as picking up an axe and going out there to chop down undead flesh."

"Undead incoming!" a voice yelled through the trees. "There are hundreds of them. Everyone get back to the outpost!"

"Safe, huh?" Ophelia said. "You just had to open your mouth."

Other earth mages streamed through the trees around them. Nym recognized most of them by sight now, if not by name, and he turned with the rest of his group to follow the stream of them retreating toward the camp and its defensible walls.

The ghoul leaped down from a tree overhand and landed on Nomick, sending the man sprawling with a pained scream. Nym staggered to a halt, his mind whirling as he tried desperately to think of what to do to save his friend.

CHAPTER FIVE

Nym tried to force his brain past the initial surge of revulsion he felt from seeing his first ghoul, but it was a hard thing to take in at a glance. It was human shaped but with mottled gray-and-green skin. Patchy strands of lank hair hung from its scalp, and it had unnaturally long arms and fingers. A prehensile tongue hung out of its mouth, which was filled with sharp teeth many sizes too big.

It was disgusting to look at it, and up close it had a rancid stink that was unlike anything Nym had ever smelled before. It had landed on Nomick feetfirst, pushing the earth mage to the ground, and its sharp fingers were eagerly reaching down to tear into the man's flesh. Nym froze, rooted with shock, and even though he knew he needed to do something, he just stood there.

An aura of arcana sprang up nearby, and pillars of earth shot up on either side of Nomick. They slammed into the ghoul, lifting it slightly into the air and allowing Nomick to scramble free. He pivoted in place once he was back on his feet and cast his own spell, causing the ground to tear itself open. The ghoul fell into it, and it slammed shut over top of it.

"Come on! That's not going to hold it for long," Nomick said, grabbing Nym's arm and tugging him along.

"I . . . I can't believe I just stood there. I'm so sorry," Nym said. "What is wrong with me?"

"Not the time for introspection, Nym!" Nomick tugged on his arm again. "We've got to keep running!"

Nym snapped out of it and pulled arcana into his soul well, then lifted himself into the air and took Nomick with him. Together, the two skimmed over the ground, easily twice as fast as the rest. Once they had a decent lead, he set Nomick down and said, "Keep going. I'm going to go look for stragglers."

"No, Nym. Wait—"

But Nym was already gone, determined to make up for his earlier error. He cast night vision as he flew, even though it was still daylight. Colors got harder to differentiate in the light, but at the same time, the dark patches in the boughs became easier to see into. The last thing he needed was some ghoul jumping on his back.

Nym saw a ghoul ahead, down on its hands and knees with its head near the ground. A man lay underneath it, his eyes glazed over in death, while the ghoul ripped chunks out of his abdomen. A part of Nym considered smiting it with a lightning bolt or setting it on fire, but the man was already dead, and there were still earth mages and soldiers fighting for their lives.

Nym's best spell was still flight, but elemental air manipulation was a close second. He was passing decent with water, and a novice with earth. Fire was . . . Well, he was pretty sure he still wasn't doing it correctly. He felt like he'd found a work-around but that someday he'd have to learn to do it properly. For now though, he stuck with air spells.

When he found ghouls pouncing on people, he used blasts of air to push them off course. When they already had someone pinned down, he lifted them up with his flight spell. The ghouls struggled, of course, and even his magic could only make air so solid. It was easy for them to escape and not worth the effort to form more cushions or thicker ones. He only had to distract the ghouls for a second or two. The victims staggered to their feet and ran under their own power, or Nym whisked them away and dropped them off near groups of soldiers who were engaged in fighting retreats.

He saw quite a few ghouls roaming the woods, looking for meat. Those he ignored if they were far enough away or tried to trap in the ground if they were too close. As Nomick had said, the ghouls were easily able to dig themselves out, but it still gave the workers fleeing from them an extra fifteen or twenty seconds. Sometimes that was the difference between life and death.

While his tactics worked fine on the encounters that involved just one ghoul, that wasn't always what he found. Several times, there were two or even three ghouls working together to bring down someone. Usually it was a soldier who was fighting back, but occasionally he'd find pockets where earth mages had thrown up stone walls around themselves and the ghouls were trying to physically break through to get to the meaty victim inside.

In those cases, Nym resorted to fire. It didn't work the best. Ghouls were slimy and didn't burn easily, but setting one on fire was enough to distract it from its victim. That was usually enough to get the earth mage free and moving again, but several times they'd completely frozen up and Nym had to break through their walls himself, then pull the earth mage free and fly them to safety.

His efforts were saving lives though, and he didn't feel like he was in any danger of giving himself arcana poisoning anytime soon, so he kept scouring the woods for more survivors. As five minutes turned into ten, and ten into half an hour, he found more and more corpses being consumed by ghouls and fewer and fewer survivors still trying to get away.

Nym was feeling pretty good about himself and his contributions to the sudden undead attack right up until something slammed into his back and rode him to the ground. He managed to keep the air cushion that he'd been cruising on from breaking apart, but it was nowhere near strong to support him and the added weight.

He didn't need to look to know what had happened. All the tree-bound ghouls he'd spotted had been between ten and twenty feet off the ground. They were primed to jump down on an unwitting target who'd passed below them. He'd flown too close to one who'd climbed a bit higher, one he hadn't noticed because he wasn't looking up.

This wasn't like the first ghoul he'd seen. He knew what to expect now, and though the stink was even worse when it was his turn and the ghoul had locked its legs in a painfully tight squeeze around Nym's hips, he had a pretty good idea of how to dislodge it.

New air cushions formed between the two of them, prying the ghoul's grip loose. It tried to squeeze anyway and clamp back down, and it would have succeeded in barely a second, but Nym timed it so that he skimmed just under a particularly large and thick branch an instant after he loosened the ghoul's hold on him. The creature struck the branch at speed and was lifted clear. Nym let out a little sigh of relief as he flew off.

"Maybe I should have gotten one of those mage weapons after all," he said regretfully.

It was thanks to Nym's work that a lot of people were able to flee the ghouls instead of becoming meals, but he hadn't actually killed a single one. However, now that he wasn't finding people anymore, he thought it was time to change that. Fire wasn't really working, and air just didn't have enough of a punch, but he hadn't spent weeks working with Ophelia for nothing.

The next ghoul Nym found, he spent the time to create an earth golem, then he knocked it out of the tree with an air blast. The ghoul tumbled to the ground, and the golem advanced on it, knocking it around with repeated heavy blows. The undead seemed confused at the attack but matched the golem's blows with ferocious swipes. Chunks of earth where ripped free, but the golem shuffled dirt around in its body to fill in the gaps while pulling up more material from the ground under its feet.

Ghouls apparently didn't understand advanced tactics like retreating, and it kept up its attack, unrelenting and implacable, until the blows from the golem weakened it enough that pieces of its body started falling off. Slowly, the ghoul fell apart until it was nothing but a scattered collection of wiggling limbs. Even that wasn't enough to actually kill it, but Nym poured on enough fire to reduce it to ash.

It was exhausting work, if only because the ghoul didn't want to burn and he had to feed a constant stream of arcana to the fire to keep it going. He also discovered that while ghouls smelled bad enough on their own, cremating them was a hundred times worse. Nym couldn't stop himself from throwing up while the ghoul burned.

The next ghoul he encountered, he didn't even bother with having his golem beat it into submission. It just tackled the ghoul and held it down while Nym slowly burned it to death. If the ghoul was in any sort of pain, it didn't show it. The golem, being a creation of dirt, was unaffected by the flames other than its outer layer blackening and cracking. It simply shed the burnt earth and pulled up new dirt to fill its form back out.

"There has to be a better way to do this," he said out loud. It was way too much work and took way too long to burn each one until there was nothing left but ash. He tried other spells on ghouls, but daze did nothing, kinetic cutting worked even worse than it did on people, entombing them in the ground only held them up for a minute at most, and dismembering them stopped them but didn't kill them.

If there was a better way, he couldn't find it. Apparently, neither could the soldiers, as he'd found several groups throwing the ghouls they'd dismembered onto bonfires they'd built. The smell of a dozen ghouls being incinerated at once was even worse than being up close to one while he worked on it. Somehow, every time he turned around, this day kept topping itself in the category of worst-smelling thing he'd ever found in his life.

Nym stopped bothering to burn them himself, instead letting his earth golem start dismembering them again and scooping up the pieces to ferry to the nearest bonfire. The soldiers were surprised at first, but once they figured out what was happening, they cheered every time he came in with another load.

Eventually the sun started going down, and one of the soldiers flagged him down. "We're retreating back behind walls now, sir mage," he told Nym. "Will you be coming with us?"

"Sir mage?" Nym echoed. That was a new one.

"Sorry, we did not have time for proper introductions. We've held out here as long as is reasonable, but the night will favor the ghouls too much, and I can't risk my men's lives to keep the fires burning for you."

"You . . . You're only here because I'm still here?" Nym asked. "I didn't know that. I'm sorry. We can go back now."

"Good man," the soldier said. He turned to the little camp and yelled, "Put it out. We're retreating to the fort."

The soldiers snapped hurried salutes and got to work. Nym helped by scooping up huge chunks of earth and dropping them onto the bonfire. The flames started to sputter and die down, but Nym got impatient and opened a fissure directly under the fire. The whole thing collapsed into the pit, and he closed it back over top of it. "Whew," he said. "That takes it out of me. Okay, ready to go?"

"Indeed," the soldier said, chewing on his mustache and regarding Nym. "Forgive me for asking, but how old are you?"

Nym shrugged. "I don't really know."

The soldiers started shouting in alarm and rushing into formation. "Enemy coming in!"

"We might have put that fire out a bit too soon," the soldier said grimly.

Nym peered out into the forest, his night vision showing no ghouls. "I don't see anything except . . . Oh! It's fine everyone. It's not an enemy. That's just my golem catching up with me!"

"Your . . . what?" the soldier asked.

"Here, I'll show you."

Nym cast a light spell over the earth golem, illuminating it fully. "It's just some dirt I animated to fight the ghouls for me."

The soldiers didn't look reassured, but when the golem made no threatening moves, they slowly relaxed. "So," Nym said. "We're going back to the main outpost?"

CHAPTER SIX

N ym! You're alive!"

He didn't see Ophelia until she crashed into him, hugging him. "Hey! Stop. What are you doing?" he yelped.

"You idiot!" she scolded, pushing him out to arm's length. "Are you hurt?"

"I'm fine. Stop, I said. Stop!" He wiggled out of her grip and took a step back. "What's wrong with you?"

"What's wrong with me?! What's wrong with *you*? Why didn't you come back to the outpost with the rest of us when the ghouls attacked?"

"Because there were other mages who were closer to the ambush, and they needed help getting away?" Nym was confused. What else was he supposed to do?

"That's the soldiers' job to save them! You are supposed to retreat with the rest of the builders."

"Excuse me, lady mage," the soldier captain he'd been talking to interjected. "Your . . . um . . . son? Brother? Friend? Regardless, your companion saved probably twenty earth mages from being killed today and helped us destroy twice that number of ghouls. His talents are wasted on the back line making walls. A prodigy like that should be on the front line, driving the undead back so breakouts like this don't happen."

Ophelia was taken aback by the captain's speech. "That's . . . Nym . . . Is that what you want to do? You're . . . You're young for it. We only brought you with us because we thought you'd be safe here at the back lines."

Nym hadn't really given it much thought. He'd mostly just wanted to stay with the Earth Shapers because he considered them his friends. At some point in time, he was going to go back to the coast to see Ciana, but he didn't have specific plans beyond that.

"I don't know. I kind of just came to help you with this and make some money. I figured we'd work together until all the undead were gone and they put a new patch on Ul'tuthik's prison so new ones couldn't keep getting out."

The captain flinched and looked around. "Where did you hear that name?" he hissed, his voice pitched low. "That's classified information."

"Oh, sorry, I didn't know. Don't worry, I won't tell anyone," Nym said.

The captain grimaced. "This is going to be a mess. You need to come with me to the forward command post. However you're involved with this, they'll sort it out."

"What? Why?"

"Because you're too many weird things wrapped up in one package. Your age. Your magic. What you know. Someone is going to need to sort through this, and it's way above my pay grade."

"Oh," Nym said. He took a second to think about it. "I guess that's fine. Are we going right now?"

The captain sighed. "We should, but it's getting dark. Goddamn these undead. There's no way we can risk a run like that in the dark. You'll stay here at this fort with us tonight, and first thing in the morning, we'll run you over to the forward command post. The guys in charge can figure this out then."

Nym shrugged. "Is that okay, Ophelia?"

She chewed her lip and looked back and forth from Nym to the soldier. "He's not in trouble?" she asked.

The captain shrugged. "I don't think so. It'll go better for everyone if he cooperates."

"Can he stay with our crew tonight?"

The captain looked like he wanted to say no. "I really . . . shouldn't allow it," he said slowly. "Damn. Fine. I'll assign a guard. Early tomorrow, we're all going up together, understand?"

Nym nodded. He wasn't entirely sure what the problem was, but so far the soldiers had been friendly, and he didn't think he'd have a problem getting away if they tried to capture him. He knew a lot more magic now than he had a few months ago.

The captain assigned two soldiers as guards outside the structure the Earth Shapers put up. When the others questioned Ophelia about it, she just said, "Nym is very important now. He's going to visit the people in charge in the morning."

The new shelter wasn't nearly as good as the old. It was a similar size, but with a few stone pillars holding up a roof and otherwise open everywhere. There was no privacy to be had, but it was only temporary. There had been a huge influx of refugees fleeing to whichever outpost was closest to them, and the ones the Earth Shapers had ended up in had a surplus. It had led to a flurry of rapid-fire construction projects as they extended the walls and put up more shelters.

Night fell, and the group made dinner over an open fire. Nomick and Monick both thanked Nym about a dozen times for helping, though Nym still felt guilty about freezing when the ghouls had first attacked. They brushed off his apologies without concern, and Nym slowly let himself relax. The awkwardness vanished, and by the time they were all ready for bed, it was just like it had always been.

The soldiers entered their shelter at the crack of dawn and woke Nym up. Since it had an open floor plan, that meant they woke everyone else up too. They ignored the chorus of groans, curses, and a thrown shoe as they escorted Nym out into the sun. He stumbled after them, stifling a yawn as he walked, still half-naked.

"Take your clothes with you," Ophelia said from behind, shoving a bundle into his arms when he turned to look at her.

"Whu . . . ? Oh. Thanks."

Nym got dressed and used hydrokinesis and terrakinesis to scrub himself as clean as he possibly could without access to a real bath, then followed the two soldiers to the captain's tent. He looked significantly worse than he had the night before, with bags under his eyes and a slouch that had been absent the last time Nym had seen him.

"Oh? You're here? Right, it's morning. Sorry, we've been repelling ghouls all night. Extending the walls out put us too close to a lot of trees the bastards are using like ladders to get in. Let me just . . . Derket, where the hell did you run off to?"

"Captain Tainer, sir," one the Nym's escorts said. "The lieutenant had to be taken back to the rear base for medical treatment. One of the ghouls tore his arm off two hours ago."

"Damn it! Why is this the first I'm hearing of this?" the captain snarled. He forced himself to stop and took a deep breath. "Okay, fine. It's fine. You two are this young mage's guard now. You take him to forward command and get him in front of Commander Seskrit. Tell him that Mage Nym here has classified information learned from a prior engagement with the enemy and what he's done for our forces here in the southeast sector."

"Sir!" Both men saluted, and they were off.

Nym had to lift all three of them over the wall, as it hadn't been built with any sort of gate. There was a lot of squinting up into trees and flinching at any sort of loud noises as they traveled, which Nym felt was perfectly reasonable after the day they'd all had yesterday.

"Do you think there are a lot more ghouls roaming around here still?" he asked.

"Don't know. It was a really big outbreak. No one's sure how they managed to gather in numbers like that. The forward units would usually break something like that up before it gets this close to the edge. So . . . either they went down for some reason, or it formed behind their lines."

Both soldiers shuddered. "It's bad news. If the forward units are dead, then we're losing control of the situation. If the ghouls massed behind the forward lines, then they're being directed by wights, which wasn't the case before, at least not this close to the wall."

"I suppose we'll find out pretty soon," the other soldier said. "We'll be right at the heart of the front line in a few hours."

Most of that time was spent forcing their way through the underbrush to reach the road running between Ebalsan and forward command. Nym offered twice to fly them over, but both times the soldiers declined. "We're not really supposed to do that," one of them said by way of explanation.

"If you're sure. I'm sick of this though, so I'll be overhead. Yell if you need me."

Then Nym flew up over the branches and drifted slowly through the sky, keeping an eye on both of the soldiers as they watched him. They seemed upset, but it wasn't like he didn't offer to fly them over too. After an hour of watching them struggle, he called down, "Change your minds yet?"

There was a brief discussion below as they argued about it, until finally one of them yelled back, "Yes. If you're sure you don't mind?"

He picked them both up and flew them the last mile or so over the forest to land on the road. They took a break then, since they were ahead of schedule now, and had a late breakfast. It was road food straight from Nym's pack, but he was happy to share.

"Don't take this the wrong way," one of the soldiers said, "but you've got to be the nicest, least pretentious and stuck-up mage I've ever met. Most of the time mages just stare down their noses at us soldiers."

"Really? Why's that?"

"It's because of the magic," the other soldier said. "It takes a lot of talent to use 'real magic' instead of soldier skills. We're all trained to forge conduits so we can do forced marches and increase our strength when we fight, but we can't do the kind of stuff you can do."

Nym thought about that for a second. "But that's almost everyone. Why would they look down on just soldiers?"

Both of them started laughing. "Mages do look down on everyone, but soldiers more so because we can use some magic but not real magic. It's like they think we're lazy and just not trying hard enough."

"But you're not like that. It's refreshing to be treated well. Don't lose that, huh? Maybe when you get a bit older, see about adjusting some of your colleagues' attitudes."

"Now don't go pitting the boy against the world," the first soldier said. He turned to Nym and added, "It's nice that you're so well-mannered was all I was trying to say."

"Well . . . Okay then."

Now that they'd alerted him to it, Nym watched the faint, almost translucent auras appear around them when they started drawing in arcana, and the trio started off deeper into the forest. He watched the spell structures they used but didn't find much new there. It was mostly just basic muscle reinforcement, using arcana to keep themselves fresh. Occasionally, one of them would pull in arcana to sharpen their senses and scan the trees bordering the road.

Nym spent the trip trying to look past the aura of arcana he always saw and make out the conduits they'd forged to reach the first layer. Once he thought to search the aura for it, it wasn't hard to find. What he saw confused him though. His own conduits were straight, rigid things, like sharpened reeds that punctured through reality and let arcana flow to him through its hollow core.

The soldiers' conduits were nothing like that. They were curled around themselves and scrunched up and reminded him uncomfortably of some of the gutted victims' intestines he'd seen yesterday. They didn't so much pierce the membrane between realities as just pile up on it until it was stretched and strained so much that arcana started to seep in around the floppy, bunched-up conduit and get absorbed through the surface.

It was no wonder the soldiers weren't able to draw in second-layer arcana. They weren't even really reaching the first layer with their technique. It was more like they were pushing on a wet cloth, then sucking their fingers dry. Nym wondered if it was just a lack of willpower that caused it, or poor training, or if some people were really just built that way.

He thought back to some of the things he'd read in Analia's father's journals and considered if it was possible to fix a conduit.

CHAPTER SEVEN

The problem with the limited knowledge Nym had on the subject was that it was all designed to be used on an infant under very specific conditions. Nym did not have an enchanted tank to put the test subject in, nor was he able to imprint his will on the target's to guide the process. The far more likely result was that he'd break the soldier's brain instead of fixing his conduit.

He wasn't sure how much to tell them about their conduits. His ability to see magic was the one thing he never, ever, ever told anyone. It was his hidden trump card, the secret to a substantial portion of his success as a mage. He did not want people to find out. If he started explaining to the soldiers that he could see their conduits and what they needed to do to fix them, they might ask how he could see them. Even if they didn't, they might tell someone else who knew enough to know it wasn't normally possible to see such a thing.

Keeping his ability to see magic hidden hadn't been much of an ethical question before. It didn't really affect anyone but him, as long as no one knew about it. Now, he'd identified a problem in someone else because he could see things other people couldn't. He wasn't sure if he needed to say something or if it was better to preserve his anonymity, at least as much as he could considering how often someone pointed out that he was too young to be good at magic.

That problem would probably disappear completely as he now looked like he was thirteen or fourteen, despite it having only been around seven months since he'd woken up to Ciana's voice on the beach. That professor friend of Bardin's had said he was aging rapidly but didn't seem to know if it was going to stop. Nym wondered if, in five years, he'd look middle-aged. Maybe he'd be dead in twenty.

That was a disturbing thought. He hadn't given much consideration to it before, since looking older benefited him, but the sudden realization that he couldn't make it stop and might age right into the grave in a handful of years brought him up short. He needed to stop screwing around and get serious, to recover his memories and break whatever curses had been placed on him. He needed to know who he was and why this had been done to him.

He didn't have a lot of time to reflect on this, as both soldiers were running at an arcana-empowered sprint the whole time while he flew behind them. The forward command post came into view in a matter of minutes, and their group was met by a squad of soldiers on the road. His escort spoke to the squad leader in muttered tones for a minute, explaining the situation. When they were let through, another two soldiers from the squad joined them.

This process repeated itself several times as they went through various checkpoints. Nym watched the surroundings change from an open road hacked through the forest to a gatehouse in a fortress wall to a checkpoint inside the main keep, and then several more times as he was guided through the interior.

Finally, after a lot of being handed off from one group of soldiers to the next, Nym found himself waiting in a room outside an office with his two original escorts, and waiting, and waiting . . .

"I'm bored," he said.

One of the soldiers snorted. "Comes with the job. Better bored than getting ripped apart by a ghoul."

"Even that's better than what a geist'll do if one catches you," the other replied. They both shuddered. "Just put an arrow in my eye if you ever see a geist hauling me away."

"What do geists do?" Nym asked.

"That's . . . not really something we would normally tell someone your age. I guess it's okay now because you're . . . you know . . . you."

"I think so. If he's going to fight, he needs to know what he's up against."

"Right, so the thing about geists is that a ghoul will eat you while you're still alive, but a geist will flay your skin off you, then hook itself into your body and become your new skin. You'll walk around with a geist-flesh wrapper, except it's not you controlling anything. It's the geist. They'll just ride you around for days while you die wrapped up in them, and once they get ahold of you, there's no saving you. Even if someone else kills the geist, you just die with it."

"That's horrifying."

"They're the real reason for the walls. Ghouls are bad, but it's the geists we're trying to keep contained. Geists can't really climb on their own, so as long as they don't get hosts, we can close off the area and keep them from spreading."

"What about the other type, wights?"

"They're . . . probably the least of our concerns most days. Ghouls will climb things and ambush. Geists are geists. Wights only rise up from the corpses of the recently deceased. They retain all that person's skills and knowledge from life, so they're way more dangerous than a ghoul, but there are so few of them, and it's easy to take precautions against more of them rising up. When they do pop up, they're a huge problem, but they're rare."

Nym was about to ask what changed between a living person and a wight of that person if they still had all the same stuff in their head, but the door to Commander Seskrit's office swung open and ended the conversation. The commander himself stood in it. He was an exceptionally tall man, wiry and long limbed. His face was thin and sharp, with dark eyes that regarded them all with cold, calculating calm.

"You're the boy mage?" he asked. His tone suggested that he already knew the answer.

"Yes, sir."

"I see. Come join me in my office. You two are dismissed back to your posts."

Nym followed the commander in. Rather than sit down at his desk, Seskrit walked over to a large map spread across a table. It showed the local area and gave Nym his first look at where exactly he was in relation to places he'd already been, but its real purpose was to keep track of troop positions. Little wooden figurines covered it, most painted blue and white, with a minority in black, and an even smaller percentage in yellow. Tiny wooden walls formed a quarter circle around a portion of the forest.

"Your name is Nym?"

"Yes, sir." He should have insisted everyone go back to calling him Ermy when they got close to Ebalsan, but it was too late now.

"According to the report I received from a Captain Tainer, you are aware of the source of the undead from a prior experience in the area involving Babkin the Berserker and Leaf Aeldson where you investigated the frost wraiths."

It was the first Nym had heard of the title berserker, but given Babkin's stature and how afraid of angering him people were, he supposed it wasn't a surprise. On the other hand, he'd never once seen the man actually lose his temper, even when Nym was arguing with him. It was hard to picture Babkin roaring across a battlefield, slaughtering everyone and everything in his path.

"I knew them as Babkin the innkeeper and Leaf the guy who lived in the woods, but yes."

Seskrit snorted. "Yes, I heard about Babkin's retirement project. Regardless, we do not want information about the source of this getting out. Information about a tear in the veil could attract new, unscrupulous necromancers with fewer brains than God gave a rock who'll pick at it and make everything worse. You are to keep this information to yourself."

That was actually a pretty solid reason not to spread around the source of the problem, to Nym's mind. Whatever protections they came up with once the undead were contained and destroyed, they would work better if no would-be villains ever showed up to test them.

"Understood," he said.

"Good man. Now, onto the second report I received. A knot of ghouls some-how popped up behind our front lines and hit our building crews hard. You were there assisting a crew, but when the ghouls showed up, you helped evacuate your companions, and then came back for others. You created some sort of dirt mon-ster, which you commanded to destroy ghouls, and ferried the body parts over to nearby bonfires to be immolated."

"That . . . Yes, I guess that's true."

"I'm going to be honest with you. This military does not have a place for you. You are too young, and you are untrained. I can't attach you to our scouting unit, and you're not a trained and licensed mage. You could be an asset but not in a way we're structured to take advantage of.

"This undead problem keeps getting bigger. We've called in reserves trying to keep up with it, but it's growing faster than we can contain it on our own. We had to start recruiting from nonmilitary personnel, had to form a company of troubleshooters who take on odd jobs. They go out and destroy undead if needed, but they also deal with the other problems and challenges the forest presents us. People get lost. Wild animals attack our outposts.

"Sometimes the standard army kit isn't the best solution for the job. When those kinds of situations come up, we have freelancers. We operate as a fallback and resupply point for them, and they get paid to use whatever unique skills they possess to help pacify this forest. You're young, but if you're interested, I think I could get you a position doing this work."

"Well, maybe that could work. I'll be honest with you, sir. It's not that I don't want to help, but I came here with an earth-mage crew to help them, practice my earth magic, and to earn some much-needed money."

"You'll earn at least as much money this way as you would building barri-cades and outposts. If you're any good at it, you'll earn more. If we consider last night your first job, you'll be owed nine shields for the work," Seskrit told him.

Nym was hesitant to take the offer. It didn't sound safe, and he knew the Earth Shapers wouldn't be happy about that. Ophelia especially worried after him. But it did sound exciting and, more importantly, profitable. He was going to need serious money if he planned on hiring experts to help him recover his memories. He'd probably need serious money just to find those experts. That wasn't even considering how much he could further his own studies with this job.

"I'll do it," he said.

The commander nodded. "I had my assistant get all the paperwork done to commission you. It's here on the desk. Take your time reading it. Once you've signed, someone will give you the quick tour of what facilities you'll have access to."

The paperwork wasn't that complex, barely two pages long. It basically stated that Nym would be attached to the military as a freelance unit that would be paid by the job, pay to vary per job and agreed upon by both him and the military prior to accepting it. He would have access to their armory and quartermaster to resupply as needed, and he would be responsible for purchasing those supplies himself, albeit at the army's price.

Nym signed it and handed it over the commander's assistant, who'd been waiting for him outside the office. The assistant gave it a once-over, nodded, and said, "Let's go get you registered."

It turned out the freelancer's facilities weren't part of the central keep itself but instead occupied a few buildings pushed up against the north wall of the command post. They had the same rough look as everything else, clearly made with magic and in a hurry. There was a framework of lumber they had been built around to give them some extra stability, but if anything, that made them even uglier.

Commander Seskrit's assistant led him into the main building and up to a counter with a bored-looking receptionist. "New one to file paperwork. Needs a badge and a quick tour."

The receptionist looked him over and said, "Bit young, isn't he?"

"The commander cleared him, so . . . I guess just do it?"

A shadow fell over Nym and the assistant. Nym turned in place to see a huge man wearing a lot of leather with steel plates attached to it in strategic places. An axe hung from a belt loop, with one hand resting on the head. Its blade was over a foot long and secured by a leather sheath.

"No," Babkin said. "This will not be happening."

CHAPTER EIGHT

O h, you have got to be kidding me," Nym said. "You're seriously going to do this again?"

Babkin blinked and looked down at him. "Nym? You have grown much in the last few months! What are you doing here?"

"I'm signing up to go out and fight undead for money. Please stay out of it."

"By yourself? That is very dangerous."

The hall had gone silent as Nym and Babkin argued. There were a lot of wide-eyed mercenaries shifting in their chairs, perhaps on the verge of fleeing. The aura of tension that had taken over was palpable, but both of them ignored it. He glared up at the innkeeper, or rather the berserker, defiantly.

"Yes," Babkin said. "I remember our last conversation. I would have thought you were enrolled in the Academy already."

"Turns out it's too expensive," Nym said, his voice clipped. "So here I am."

He turned back to the receptionist and gestured to the paperwork. "Please finish this up."

Rather than do that, the receptionist turned to Babkin. "Is . . . Is that okay?"

The berserker gave Nym an appraising look. "Yes," he said slowly. "Process this for our young friend. Nym, please join me in the training arena. I would like to see how much you've grown."

Babkin walked out through the door, and the entire hall let out its collective breath. "God's breath, that was the scariest thing I've ever seen in my life," someone muttered. "I thought he was going to tear the whole place apart. Kid, you're either the bravest person I've met or the stupidest."

Nym threw a scowl at him, then swept out through the door after Babkin. He only noticed as he followed down the hall that Commander Seskrit's assistant was scurrying after him. They arrived at the arena on Babkin's heels. The berserker strode in and walked over to a series of training dummies set up against the wall.

"Please attack this dummy. Show me that you can hold your own against a ghoul."

Annoyed, Nym snapped a lightning bolt construct into place. He wove it as fast as he ever had, and barely a second later, the entire building was shaking and the dummy was nothing more than a scorched and smoking wooden post while flaming clumps of straw rained down around it.

"Happy now?" Nym said.

"Damn," the assistant whispered.

Rather than answer, the big man took some time to examine the destroyed dummy. "Powerful, but this spell is difficult to aim. Can you strike a moving target with it?"

"Are you volunteering?" Nym asked.

Babkin nodded. He started unbuckling straps on his side and removed the armor covering his chest. It thumped as it hit the ground, and his axe went on top of it. "Let's see."

"Are . . . Are you sure?" Nym asked, taken aback. "This could kill you."

The berserker just laughed. "You are not the only one who is able to use magic. Come. Let us test your true capabilities."

The two of them took their places in a sand arena, twenty feet apart. Arcana started to flow around Babkin, forming a swirling aura, deep crimson streaked through with jagged lines of black. Nym had never seen an aura like that, or one that was as animated as Babkin's. Suddenly, he felt a lot less confident in his abilities.

"Please announce the start of the match," Babkin ordered Seskrit's assistant.

"Er, right. Yes. Then . . . If everyone is ready? Three, two, one . . . Go."

Somehow, Babkin appeared in front of Nym without seeming to cross the intervening distance. Huge hands descended like striking snakes to grab the boy, and it was only pure reflex that got Nym out of the way. He didn't even try to use his legs, knowing he'd never be as fast as Babkin. Instead, his flight spell kicked in and shot him backward. Even at his fastest speed, he felt one of Babkin's fingers hook his shirt.

Nym didn't stop, and the cloth tore. He didn't have time to process that though, since he slammed into the back wall of the arena at full speed. His head smacked against the stone, and his vision started to turn to black. Before he could recover, Babkin was in front of him again. His hand closed around Nym's throat and started squeezing.

He had seconds left before he blacked out, time enough for a single spell, maybe two quick ones. There wasn't time for anything fancy. He reached out to the sand below their feet and caused it to explode upward. It blinded both of them, but Babkin didn't need to see to maintain his hold. He didn't flinch back from the attack, just squeezed harder.

Nym started to put together a lightning bolt. He just . . . needed to . . . thread it . . .

With a gasp, he sat upright. He was back in the middle of the arena, with Babkin standing over him. "You've lost this match," the lumbering giant told him. "Would you like to try again?"

Nym flew up into the air and flicked the sand off him with a bit of terrakinesis. This was ridiculous. He'd killed a hive queen by himself but couldn't last ten seconds against a human? Admittedly, the arena itself was working against Nym's style, but he should have done better than that. He could do better than that. He would.

"Yes, rematch."

The attendant counted down again, and now Nym was ready for Babkin's insane speed. He was already moving, back and up, when the berserker started. This time he saw the movement, and while Babkin was insanely fast, it wasn't any sort of teleportation. It was just muscle enhanced by arcana. What that arcana was doing, Nym had no idea. He couldn't penetrate the berserker's roiling aura to see the spell work underneath it.

If Nym thought he was safe just by flying over Babkin's head, he soon found out he was wrong. The berserker looked up at him, eyes narrowed, and flung himself through the air. Nym reflexively tried to grab him with cushions of air to force him off course like he'd done to the ghouls, but Babkin broke through them like they weren't even there. Panicked, Nym dropped his own flight and fell to avoid being grabbed again.

He caught himself and skimmed across the sand to the far side of the arena, but Babkin was already coming at him again. Nym needed some way to keep some distance, but Babkin wasn't letting him have it. He had no time to do anything but evade, and he wasn't even doing that very well. The berserker's speed and precision were unreal.

He was hesitant to unleash it, but Babkin had assured him he could take it, so Nym sped through the construct for a lightning bolt and let it loose. It struck Babkin head-on, but the berserker barely stumbled. Arcs of electricity crawled across his aura and grounded themselves in the sand below without ever touching flesh, then the berserker was in front of him again.

"Oh da—" Nym said, eyes going wide.

Babkin didn't grab him this time. Instead, his hand curled into a fist and cracked into Nym's face, sending the boy into a literal spin down to the sand. Nym sat there, dazed and in pain, while blood dripped from his nose.

"Better," Babkin said. "If that is your strongest spell, you do not have anything that can stop me. Your reflexes are fast enough to deal with ghouls individually, but I worry for your safety if they outnumber you. Come, let us discuss the ways you may still improve."

It was hard to focus on the big man's words, but Nym shook the dizziness off, wiped the blood away, and forced himself to his feet. "Not yet," he said. "One more match."

Babkin frowned. "You are stubborn. I have your measure now. There is no need for another match."

"One. More." Nym gritted his teeth and pulled in arcana. He flew back to the starting point and spun to face the berserker.

"Very well."

Babkin took his starting spot, and the assistant counted down. Nym was already spinning out arcana when Babkin started moving, and the ground erupted around him, sending the berserker stumbling to his knees when the sand fell away in front of him. That wasn't enough to stop Babkin. He hit the ground and threw himself up through the air, coming right at Nym.

He hadn't wasted the brief window he'd gained with the spell. Before Babkin could close in on him, the sand swirled up and hardened into a golem nine feet tall. It was only vaguely humanoid but reacted fast enough that when Babkin crashed into it, he met the golem's arm stub, its approximation of a punch.

The berserker grunted as he bounced off. He eyed the golem warily, then tried to dart around it. Nym flew to keep the golem between them while mentally commanding it to advance. It lashed out, and Babkin responded in kind. He avoided obvious punches to get inside the golem's reach and started pummeling it with his bare fists. Great gouts of sand blew out of the back of the golem's body, but Nym poured more arcana into it, and it sucked up new sand.

The golem fell on Babkin, pounding back with just as much force. The berserker aura shredded sand as it came close, which did nothing to soften the blows after they pushed through but did strain the spell's regeneration component and drain arcana faster. Babkin gave up on outmaneuvering it and threw himself on the golem.

It was impossible to see how the battle was progressing due to the sand flying everywhere. Nym floated backward to give himself some distance and sent in a scry anchor, which he had marginally better success with. The sand was still blinding, but he was at least able to pick out the berserker's hulking form inside it.

Babkin ripped a limb off and sent it flying through the air, where it struck Nym and knocked him back. He cried out in pain, and that was all Babkin needed. Two more limbs came flying out of the sand cloud, both solid hits against the young mage. Babkin was dismembering the golem as fast as it could regenerate, and with an enraged roar, he hefted it over his head and ripped it into two pieces.

The legs went behind Babkin, and he grabbed the torso with both hands. Babkin put his whole body into the throw and sent it toward Nym. There was just enough time for him to dismiss the golem and let it turn into a cloud of sand instead of a solid object and to project a kinetic barrier between them. Nym weathered the attack unharmed.

And then Babkin was in front of him. And then the fight was over, again.

"Damn it," Nym swore.

The berserker said nothing. His breathing was ragged, and his fingers twitched at his side. With visible effort, he turned away and stomped across the arena to the far wall. Babkin took a minute to calm down before rejoining Nym and the assistant.

"I have underestimated you again," he said. "I still have concerns, but this has done a great deal to alleviate them. I will not stop you from taking on jobs, only caution you to be aware of your limits and work in a team whenever possible."

Nym wanted to throw it back at him, to tell the innkeeper turned berserker that he would do whatever he wanted. But he still had blood dripping from his nose, his shirt was still torn, and he was covered in bruises from where he'd been hit with the limbs of his own golem.

Instead of telling Babkin off, he just said, "Thanks for the advice. I'll do everything I can to stay safe."

"Good. Now, come, let's get you to the healer. I'll cover the cost to patch you up."

"Thanks. One second," Nym said, pinching his nose and holding his head back. He swept the arena with terrakinesis to grab all the sand and put it back into the pit. There was no sense in leaving a mess for someone else to clean up. "Okay, let's go."

CHAPTER NINE

Nym's first army job was a lot less exciting than he expected. No one wanted him to go out and fight ghouls. He didn't need to kill twenty of them or bring back a certain number of plants that grew in the local area. They didn't want him to escort anyone anywhere. The army didn't even need him to scout anything, as they had their own division of mages who were well trained in a specific spell list that included flight.

No, for his first job, they shoved a satchel into his hands with nine rolled-up parchments, each sealed with a dollop of wax, and a map showing the locations of outposts within ten miles of forward command. "So . . . I'm delivering the mail?" he asked the man at the administration desk.

"Essentially, yes. Your application claims you can fly over twenty miles a day, so this should be an easy job for you. Go to the outpost, drop off new orders, collect the daily reports, and bring them back."

"And for that . . . one shield five?"

"It'll be added to your account, yes. You'll report in here when you come back, and we'll add it to your balance. You can cash out small amounts here, but if you want big sums, you'll have to go to the quartermaster's office to get those."

"That sounds fair. Thanks!"

"You're welcome, young man. Be safe out there, and we'll see you back in a few hours."

Nym left the office and stepped outside, took a moment to orient himself in the right direction, and launched himself into the air. It was easy enough to find the first outpost on his list, which was officially called the fifth outpost for some reason, and which was little more than a manned supply depot with an attached barracks surrounded by a fifteen-foot-high wall that the trees had all been cut back from.

"Hey, got orders from the forward command post and instructions to pick up the daily reports," he said as he landed in the middle of the outpost, startling two soldiers. The outpost captain was summoned and exchanged paperwork with Nym, who then flew off to the next outpost. He repeated the process four more times until he found himself at the outpost his friends were working near.

Nym took a quick break to skim the length of the wall until he got to the end and found them all hard at work. He floated down to land next to Bildar, who straightened up from where he was hunched over a pile of dirt. "Unngh," the mage said. "I'm getting too old for this. Back's killing me. How's the new job?"

"Not bad," Nym told him. "Delivering the mail. Just came from our outpost and thought I'd stop to see how it's going here."

"Business as usual," Bildar told him. "Nothing glamorous, but no more ghoul attacks like yesterday. I heard they tripled patrols in the area."

"I have been seeing a lot of soldiers around this part of the wall. I wasn't sure if it was just because I was getting deeper into the forest though."

"I'm not sure either," Bildar said. He waved a hand over at Ophelia to catch her attention, and she came over.

"Everything alright?" she asked.

"Yeah, just stopped by to check in. I'm doing fine. Delivering the mail for the army right now."

"That's good. They paying you decent for that?"

"One shield five for the mail run. It wouldn't be worth it if I couldn't fly, but it should only take an hour or so to do the whole circuit," he said.

"That's good money then. Are you coming back to our camp tonight?"

Nym hesitated. "Can I? I don't really have anywhere else to sleep, but I'm not really helping with the wall anymore."

Bildar shrugged. "So what? It's our hut. We built it, and there's a room for you there."

"That's . . . Thanks." Nym felt a warmth in his chest, and worry he hadn't even realized was there melted away. Even though he wasn't going to work with them directly, they were still his friends, and there was still a place for him in their lives.

"I should get going," Nym told them. "You're busy, and I've got to finish delivering these. I'll see you tonight."

"Yep," Bildar said. "You can tell us all about your exciting mail-delivery mission over dinner."

Nym waved his goodbyes and flew back off into the air, a smile on his face.

* * *

He returned to the freelancer's main operating hall in a good mood. It had been an easy job, though annoying as a few of the officers hadn't had their reports ready and he'd had to wait for them to jot something down. It had significantly delayed his return, causing him to overshoot his one-hour estimate and end up taking closer to three.

He returned the satchel to the desk clerk, who pulled out the stack of reports and counted them. "Everything's here. Good speed too. Did they actually have everything ready for you when you got there?"

"Most of them," Nym said. "Two of them kept me there for almost an hour each because they hadn't even started them yet."

"They're supposed to have it done by the time this job posting goes up each day. Even if you teleported from outpost to outpost, you should be able to collect them immediately. Feel free to remind the officers of that next time you do this job," the clerk told him.

"Thanks, I will. Anything else on the board that I could do in the next hour or two?"

"Not that can be done that quickly. There's some postings for overnight watches or long-range patrols but nothing else that's not fighting."

"What's the fighting job?" Nym asked.

The clerk shook his head. "You don't have authorization to take those yet. I'm not supposed to give you any details on these kinds of jobs without clearance. They're basically what they sound like though. Scouts bring back reports of surging numbers, units deploy to outposts and bases nearby and organize into strike forces to cull the undead back down. Freelancers end up doing a lot of it because the soldiers are busy pushing forward to pacify and secure new areas."

Nym wasn't counting how many soldiers there were, but it sure seemed like an awful lot to him. Other than that one outbreak that had chased him and his friends away from the wall they were working on, he hadn't seen very many undead at all. He'd been looking while he was flying around, and even though the canopy hid most of the forest from casual inspection, he hadn't seen any ghouls during his mail run either.

It was tempting to fly closer to the center of the forest and see just how bad it was at the vanguard. He was imagining thousands upon thousands of undead crawling all over one another. It almost seemed like that had to be the case. Considering how extensive the army's presence was in the forest, there would have to be that many undead.

Or maybe he was underestimating the effectiveness of the stronger ones. He hadn't seen a wight or geist yet, and nobody had mentioned frost wraiths. He knew for a fact those had infested the forest, unless the army had somehow managed to kill them all. He wasn't even sure how to hurt them though. They didn't seem to like fire, but the logistics of holding one down to burn it up sounded complicated, let alone doing it while fifty more swarmed him.

"How do I get authorized for fighting jobs?" he asked.

"Keep doing the jobs you're doing. We're keeping track of your successes. As long as you prove reliable and consistent, you'll start getting access to more important and time-sensitive work. Of course that work pays much better. For now, I've got a supply-scouting job you can tag onto, but it's at least a six-hour run. You'd be doing circles around a supply wagon train with a few other scouts and making sure it isn't attacked by undead. It pays five shields."

It was tempting, but Nym already had dinner plans. He shook his head. "I have other stuff to take care of tonight. I don't have that much time right now. Maybe tomorrow?"

The clerk shrugged. "Sure. There's always work escorting supply wagons or collecting reports from outposts. Sometimes if we're really strapped for available army mages, we'll put up jobs for mage work too. That doesn't happen too often though. There's a high demand for mage work, but it has to be really time sensitive to assign it to freelancers instead of waiting for the army to take care of it."

The clerk fidgeted for a second, then leaned forward. "Between you and me, I think you should keep on top of courier jobs. They pay just so-so, but you're so fast that you could make good money with very little risk just flying pieces of paper around. But that's just my advice. You feel free to ask about any jobs that interest you."

"Thanks. I'll keep that in mind. I'm going to fly back to Ebalsan now though to take care of that other thing. Is there anything on the board that would take me that way?"

"Not that I recall. Let me double-check for you though."

The clerk hummed to himself as he flipped through a pile of parchment. "Nope, sorry. There's nothing going that way right now."

"That's fine. I was just kind of hoping. Thanks for checking for me," Nym said.

He got back in the air and started flying southeast as fast as he could. Once, it would have taken him at least three hours to make the trip and he would have needed to take frequent breaks every few minutes. Those days were behind him now, and he landed outside Ebalsan's west gate in less than fifteen minutes.

He would need to check on the map posted at forward command, but he thought he was within a two-day flight of Palmara. For some reason, it seemed like going back was on his mind more and more often lately. He kept finding himself thinking about it at random times, remembering Bloodfin Cove and the shark swimming its waters that followed him around whenever he was out on the water. Something in the water had called to him, but he hadn't been able to reach it half a year ago.

It would be different now. He had spells to look at it, spells to manipulate it, and if it came down to it, he could probably survive the dive into the water to fetch it by hand. He didn't much care for that idea, but if he needed to make a few golems to help him fend off predators while he descended, he could do it.

Then again, he wasn't sure if an ice golem would actually sink. It might just float around on the surface of the water and be useless. Generating lightning in the water also seemed like a bad idea, and he doubted he could ignite arcana into fire. The more he thought about it, the less confident he was that he could keep himself safe with pure hydrokinesis.

He passed through the gates without more than a cursory glance and made his way to the Silver Gilder absentmindedly, still thinking about the particular combination of magic that would get him down to the bottom of that cove. That spell he'd learned from Monick to hide his scent might help, but he wasn't sure if he'd need to modify it to work underwater first, or even if it was possible to do that.

Once he'd reached the inn, he went up to the bar and asked after Analia's whereabouts. A server from the kitchen was sent up to knock on her door, and she came down a few minutes later. "Good timing," she said, "Come with me!"

"Hi," he said. "What are we doing?"

She dragged him along by his arm, ignoring his protests as they went up the stairs. "You're going to like this," she told him, fishing a key out of her pocket.

"Like what?" he asked, bewildered.

"You'll see," was all she'd say as she pushed the door open.

Nym peered into her room, and his eyes went wide. "How?" he asked, his voice barely more than a whisper. "How did you do this?"

CHAPTER TEN

Analia's room was full to bursting with books. There were at least a hundred of them piled up on the floor, all over the bed, and stacked on her trunk in the corner. There were so many in fact that he wasn't sure how she managed to squeeze any space out for herself. Nym stepped past the door and picked up the nearest one, titled *Althor's Guide to Living Rune Sequences*.

"Where did you get the money for all of these?" Nym asked.

"Oh, who cares about that?! That's not what I'm talking about," she said, pushing past him. "Look here!"

She pointed at a wall that had twenty or thirty sheets of paper tacked up on it. Most of them were filled with illustrations of a complicated spell construct covered by scribbled notes to the point of near illegibility. The farther down the wall he went, the cleaner things got. It was clearly a spell of some sort Analia was working on, iterating it over and over again as she tried to get it working.

A lot of parts looked familiar, but there were whole sections that were completely new to Nym. He studied it intently for a minute while Analia watched, a smirk on her face. It was obviously a modification of his golem spell, but he couldn't figure out what it actually did. Then he clicked.

"You made an air golem?" he asked.

"Yes, I did." She was practically bouncing up and down with glee. "I just got the first one working half an hour ago. Watch."

She went through the spell, weaving it together quickly and precisely, and a thing that Nym could best describe as a human-shaped outline of blurry air popped into existence in the middle of the room. It lifted up into the air and flew a few laps before landing, picking up a book, and handing it to Analia.

"That's amazing," he said, matching her grin. "I'm not sure how practical it is, but you got it working in just a few days!"

"Oh, it's plenty practical," she told him. "I also solved that problem you were having with your scrying spell. I can use the golem as an anchor and see through it, even with a far-sight spell going."

"Really?" he asked, peering at the schematics for the spell again. "How did you . . . Oh, I see. That is clever. The golem is an intermediary, so you could use far sight on it and then just connect to its senses to see what it sees. But how does that work if it doesn't have eyes?"

"No clue, but it does. I was watching the shift change on the walls from a golem I had flying over the roof when you got here."

"Huh . . . How about that. That's really good. Can I study these?"

"Of course," she told him. "But not right now. For now, tell me how things are out in the forest. The army is keeping everything quiet, and this whole town has turned into a giant rumor mill."

"Mostly fine. We got hit by a ghoul attack yesterday while we were extending the wall. I guess it was just our bad luck, but we all made it out alive. I'm working out of the forward command post now doing freelancer jobs. Supposedly it pays better, but today was my first day, and there was a lot of paperwork before I got started. I only had time to do one job."

"You'll do better tomorrow. You're going to have to if you want my spells. I am an expensive and highly paid spell researcher now, you know?"

Nym laughed. "I don't want the spell that bad."

"You say that now, but as soon as you can cast your own air golem, you'll be back for more. And only the first sample is free. Oh! And also this book. I found it for you guys. It's spells designed specifically to counter undead. Please make sure everyone gets a chance to study it. I don't want any of you getting hurt."

Nym took the book and flipped through it. It was only thirty or so pages and had maybe ten spells related to dealing with undead pests, like Analia had said. "Oh, there's a spell in here to block your ability to smell them," he said. "I'm definitely learning that one. They smell just awful when you burn their bodies. But right now, I'm more interested in your insane book collection. Where did they all come from?"

"Ah, that. Well . . . You see, I may have used my family's line of credit." Analia's face started turning red as she stuttered out the explanation. "You see, my dad's here. Not here here in Ebalsan but nearby with the army. And I am a scion of the family, and I don't know if you know this, but every noble family has a bloodline spell that's only usable by members of the family, so it's not hard to prove who I am. So you know, it wasn't hard to get it set up to bill to the family account."

"Won't that tell them where you are though?" Nym asked.

"Maybe? But like I said, my father is here too, so hopefully when the bill makes it back to Abilanth, they'll just assume they're his expenses. Though there is a small, or maybe not so small, chance that the bills will go directly to him and he'll realize I'm here."

"That sounds bad."

Analia shrugged. "I've spent a lot of time thinking about what he did. I'm not happy about it, you know? How could I be? I just kind of want to ask him why. Why do it? Why was he so willing to risk my life chasing this crazy dream of making an ascendant? What even is an ascendant?"

She was acting nonchalant about the whole thing, but Nym could hear the hurt she was trying to hide in her voice. She flopped down on the bed with a heavy sigh and waved a hand at a stack of books on the trunk. "That pile is me trying to figure out what he was doing. I couldn't get a lot on the subject. Turns out what they call human transmutation is a bit of a taboo subject. There aren't too many people willing to even admit that they know anything about it. It's no wonder his lab was hidden even from his family."

There were four books in the pile. Nym picked the top one up and flipped through it to see a lot of anatomy diagrams, including a few that illustrated the metaphysical portion of a mage. It featured the soul well in a person's chest with lines going out in every direction like veins that reached into the limbs. The next picture added small capillaries that reached out to fill in more space.

"Is this even possible?" Nym asked, showing Analia the diagram.

"Supposedly. They're like channels etched into a mage's body to handle over-flow from the soul well. The main ones, the big ones that run down to your toes and fingers, are supposed to be pretty easy to form, if painful and time-consuming. They're good for maybe an extra twenty percent increase to how much arcana your body can hold without giving yourself arcana poisoning, but you need to be able to use third-layer arcana to do it right."

"This says it's not safe to do on another person," he said.

"Nope," she agreed. "But that didn't stop my dad."

"You're able to hold more than twice as much arcana as the average mage though," Nym said. "So he didn't stop at the main lines, did he?"

"Probably not."

Nym saw her hands clutching at her skirt and belatedly realized she'd been worrying the cloth for the last few minutes while he read. He put the book down and sat in front of her on a cushion of air. "Hey, you know this doesn't make you any less of a person, right?"

"Yeah, I know," she said quietly. "It's not that. It's just . . . He's my father. How could he do that?"

Nym had precisely one memory of the people he thought might be his parents. The man who was probably his father had been arranging for his three-year-old son to start combat training and admonishing him that he couldn't rely on anything in the world but his own strength. He shuddered to think about what kind of life he'd been destined to lead and what had gone wrong for him to end up waking up on a beach without even knowing his own name.

"I understand," he said. "Lately . . . I've been wondering, am I even a real person? And if I'm not, what does that mean? I have this one memory of my family, maybe it's not even real, but I think it must be. If it is, I'm only a few years old, and a woman is teaching me elemental magic. Then a man shows up and starts talking about how I need to start combat training. I think they're my parents, but who tells a baby that he needs to learn to defend himself since no one else will?

"What kind of people even were they that they thought it was appropriate to teach someone that young magic? How does a baby learn magic? It can't be a real memory, right? It's got to be a dream or something, unless I'm not a person. There's so much stuff that no one can explain about me. Maybe that's the answer. Maybe I'm someone's experiment that got misplaced."

Analia didn't say anything, but her hands stopped moving. She looked up from them to meet Nym's eyes. "I guess what I'm trying to say is, even if no one else gets it, I do. We'll be experiments together, right? But I'm not going to let that define me. I want to know where I came from, but I don't need to be whatever those people wanted me to be. I'll live for myself."

"That sounds good. I like that. I'll live for myself too."

"Good. But, you know, if you need to punch your dad in the face, I would support that," Nym told her sagely. "Just keep in mind that the option to do that exists."

Analia laughed, but it was sad little sound. "Thanks, Nym."

Nym looked around the room at all the books. "You're welcome," he said. "So, have you read all these?"

"Oh God, no. Of course not. I've only had a couple days, and I've been working on the golem spell. I'm stocking up for later when I have more time."

"Do me a favor when you do," he said. "See if you can find out anything about something called the Creator. The magic snow wolves told me that he, or it, or whatever it is, made them, just whipped up life out of nothing but raw arcana and intent. The matriarch I talked to said she'd met him, that she was one of the original generation."

"That's impossible," Analia said. "Not even an Archmage could create life out of nothing like that. Maybe someone modified some wolves and they passed down some traits."

Nym shrugged. "I don't know. The more I learn about magic though, the more I wonder how good a handle humans have on what's really impossible. Every time I think I have a lead into what happened to me, I keep hearing things like 'no idea how they did this,' and 'shouldn't be possible.'"

"You are pretty impossible sometimes," Analia told him.

"You're one to talk."

She smiled, a real, genuine smile this time. Nym smiled back, and then gave the books an appraising glance. "So, what kind of spell books did you pick up? I'm thinking I need to learn some magic for underwater travel and self-defense."

"Why would you need something like that? I thought you were drawn to the skies, not the seas."

"Well, you see, there's a certain shark I need to have a word with . . ."

CHAPTER ELEVEN

Nym flew back to the camp an hour later with a few spell books Analia loaned him in his pack and a small basket of pastries he'd picked up from a bakery she'd recommended. No one was at the hut they'd built for themselves when he arrived, but the camp followers were already getting things started for dinner. Great big cauldrons were bubbling and boiling when Nym landed, right next to what had to be a whole cow, maybe even two, roasting over a fire.

Nym stashed the surprise dessert in his room and used terrakinesis to pile up some loose earth together, sorted it, and then slowly and laboriously transmuted it into stone flatware. Normally someone else did that chore, as any of the earth mages could do it almost instantly, but they were still working, and Nym needed the practice anyway.

Once everything was ready, he pulled out the notes he'd copied showing the final spell construct for Analia's air golem. Under her guidance, he'd managed to successfully create one before leaving Ebalsan, and he wanted to look around using a combination of the air golem, scrying, and far sight.

A minute later, the golem was in the air and following the length of the wall while Nym looked around through it. It was kind of a nauseating experience while the golem was moving, mostly because things in motion tended to blur, which wasn't too terrible to deal with when the golem was floating in place but was almost overwhelming when he commanded it to move.

Unfortunately, once the golem got far enough away, the only way he knew what was going on was to look through the scrying spell he'd linked to it. That combined with the fact that he could only realistically stretch the connection to about a quarter of a mile limited the golem's usefulness, even though that was far more reach than he got out of any other golem model he could cast. He could picture it acting more as a sentry or lookout than a scout.

There was a lot of missing functionality in the spell, but Nym wasn't sure it was possible to make it do what he wanted, at least not with his current understanding of spell structures. If he could construct a golem made of pure arcana with no elemental flavoring to it, that might change things, but then there was the massive problem of the golem not having an actual body to operate. He didn't think it would even still be a golem at that point.

His musings were interrupted by the sight of several earth mages coming into view of the spot he'd stationed the air golem at. Nomick and Monick showed up first in the procession, with Ophelia a minute or so behind them and Bildar trailing at the end. By the time the bearded earth mage came into view, the leading workers had already reached the camp.

Nym scooped up the flatware he'd constructed and went over to claim some food for himself and his friends. The cook regarded him with a raised eyebrow when he spread out five bowls in front of the stew cauldron, holding them all steady with a minor application of telekinesis.

"It's not all for me!" Nym said. "I'm just grabbing food for my whole team."

"Sure, if you say so," the cook told him. She ladled stew into each bowl, and a second cook threw chunks of meat onto the plates he'd made. Half the camp stopped what they were doing to stare at Nym as a line of food followed him back to his hut. A few people laughed, but no one stopped him.

The twins came through the door, both of them groaning and with sweat-stained clothes. They stopped upon seeing the food spread out at the table in front of them, with Nym already seated. He'd lined the interiors of the bowls and tops of the plates with just enough arcana to heat them up and keep everything steaming hot.

"You may in fact be the greatest thing that's ever happened to us," Nomick told him seriously.

"Oh sure, you say that when I have food," Nym said. "But what was it you told me two weeks ago when I was working on that spell to predict which card would be drawn next?"

"That you were a damn cheater and I was never playing cards with you again," Nomick supplied. "I should have known Monick would teach you that."

His brother cackled. "I can't believe it took you almost an hour to realize what he was doing. You lost three shields to him."

"I gave it back!" Nym protested.

"Wait, you did? Whhyyyyyyyy?"

"Because he's a better person than you are!" Nomick said.

"Oh please," Monick replied. "Like you wouldn't have done the exact same thing."

"I didn't say *I* was a better person. If anything, I'd have made sure to teach him a bit about properly fleecing a mark before I sat him down at the table with you."

Ophelia walked through the door then, interrupting the conversation. "What's all this?" she asked, a smile on her face. "I'm sure it wasn't you two that fetched the food. So it must have been Nym."

"Of course it was Nym. When would we have had time to?" Nomick asked.

"Even if you did have time, would you have done it?"

"Nope."

Ophelia rolled her eyes and turned to Nym. "Thank you," she said. "After the day we've had, this is a welcome surprise."

Other than getting beaten down repeatedly by Babkin, Nym hadn't done much work himself. Part of him felt kind of guilty switching jobs instead of going out to the wall to help, but he reminded himself that he also had made very little money today, certainly less than he would have made staying with the earth-mage crews.

"What's all this?" Bildar asked as he came in through the door. "Dinner already waiting on the table? I could get used to this kind of treatment!"

The group sat down to eat, scarfing food while they chatted about the day's work and bemoaning the new supervisor assigned to their crew. "That one yesterday, the chubby guy with the mustache and the thinning hairline, he didn't make it through the ghoul attack. I guess he managed to hold off four ghouls though, long enough that the entire group working on the outer edge of the wall managed to escape," Ophelia told Nym.

"And the new supervisor is a lot harder to work with. He's not an earth mage and doesn't understand how these things get built properly so that they last. There's been a lot of trying to explain to him why what he wants done isn't possible, or why it's better to do it a different way, and a lot of yelling that he's in charge and we all need to do what we're told," Bildar said. "You picked a good day to switch jobs."

"Why is this bowl so hot?" Nomick asked, picking it up and looking at it.

"Oh, I used a spell I made that lets me coat a solid surface with arcana and causes it to release heat for a few hours. I used to sleep on it when I was up north," Nym explained.

The twins both stared at him for a moment, then turned to Bildar. "You need to get him back on our crew," Nomick said. "Double his pay."

"I wasn't paying him to begin with."

"Triple it then," Monick said. "We need this kind of luxury in our lives."

"You're not very good at math, are you?" Bildar said, squinting at him.

"Tell us about your first day," Ophelia said to Nym, ignoring the rest of the crew's antics.

He related the paperwork and talked about the freelancer facilities and about what kind of jobs he was authorized to do. When he mentioned Babkin and their fights in the training arena, Nym kept the details deliberately vague. He didn't much care for the burly innkeeper and would rather gloss over that whole part of the story.

As they finished up, Nym levitated the basket of pastries he'd picked up for dessert out of his room and set them on the center of the table. This set off a whole new round of surprised and appreciative noises from the Earth Shapers, as well as an argument between Nomick and Ophelia over who got the last tart, followed immediately by a group condemnation of Bildar for swiping the final custard while everyone was distracted.

Later, long after the food was gone and everything was cleaned up, Bildar sat down next to Nym, who was reading the book he'd gotten from Analia on counter-undead spells. "Next time you go to town, I've got some news for you to pass on to Analia," he said.

Nym set the book down and looked over. "For Analia? About her father?"

"Surprisingly, no. I mean, he's around here somewhere, I'm sure. There's some big project that's tied up a lot of the army's mages, but I wasn't able to find out what exactly they're doing. I do know he's running that thing though, and I guess it keeps him pretty busy. It's why so much of the fortifications was contracted out to people like us and why they've got a whole division running logistics to have freelancers do work."

"She might find that interesting, but that's not what you want me to tell her?"

Bildar shook his head. "I heard from someone that the higher-ups are thinking about instituting a draft. I guess even with the king's army out in force, and even with the freelancers who came in, we're still having trouble containing the undead. If they do start drafting people, they'll look for mages. She might be safe given her age and pedigree, but she's also right near here. It might be better for her to be proactive and either sign up for something herself or relocate to somewhere less likely to see some army recruiters."

"Ah . . . That . . . could be a problem. She figured out how to spend her family's money from afar and bought a ton of books and who knows what else. We'll need a second wagon just for her now when it's time to leave."

"Then it might be better to get involved with the military now while she still has a choice about it. Maybe she'll be able to find some work that's more suited to her talents."

"Do you really think she'd get drafted?" Nym asked. "She's thirteen."

"So are you," Bildar pointed out. "Or close enough, at least. They're letting you work, aren't they? And besides, have you gotten a look at some of those soldiers out there? Some of them are as young as fifteen or sixteen. It's not too much of a stretch that they'd press a mage into service despite being younger than usual."

That was a good point. "Thanks for the warning. I think I might have to fly back into town tonight and tell her before she buys too much more stuff or at least convince her to buy a wagon or carriage or something while she still has access to the family accounts."

"It's a bit late now, don't you think? Maybe better in the morning."

Nym shook his head. "I can be there and back in under an hour if I hurry. This is kind of important."

"That fast, huh? In that case, bring back another basket of those pastries, why don't you?"

Nym rolled his eyes. "Sure, with an extra custard for you. You're paying this time though."

He held out his hand for some money and was surprised when Bildar pressed two shields into it. "It was worth every last wedge," the earth mage told him. "If you're going to make regular runs into town, you could probably make a side business just out of bringing stuff like that back out here."

Nym couldn't help but laugh at the idea. "It might even pay better than running errands for the army. Do you think they'd get upset if I stopped taking jobs from them to be a mobile pastry shop instead?"

"Who the hell cares what they think?! We want custards!"

"Heard and understood, sir. I'll be back soon."

CHAPTER TWELVE

Analia did not take the news well. "I'm just starting to get comfortable," she whined.

Nym looked around the room. There was no furniture other than the bed, and it wasn't that big. Sure, it was a nice bed, but he knew what the rooms at the Silk Box looked like. Spending the better part of a month sleeping outdoors had done wonders for her perspective.

"It's not a guarantee. They might not do the draft. If they do, they might not want you since you're so young, or because of your family. I'm just saying that maybe we should make some preparations in case you need to make a quick exit. How much are you willing to leave behind? Can you buy a cart or wagon now to haul your books?"

The longer Nym talked, the more Analia's face soured. "If that happens and I need to dodge the draft, I'll leave this all behind. You can come collect it and get it out of town. You're already working for the army, so it's not like you can be drafted anyway. Pack it up and store the trunks somewhere, and we can collect them later."

"That . . . could work," Nym allowed. "We should probably also figure out where we're going to meet if you have to make a run for it. Or you could try to find some work with the army now."

"No way. These hands were not meant for hard labor."

"Hate to break it to you, but if you're serious about getting away from your family, you won't be able to keep spending their money. Someday, you're going to have to do some work."

"I have work. I research new spells."

Nym eyed the air-golem-spell notes pinned to the wall. "I don't think it'll be that easy. Just take some time and really think about the future, okay?"

"Fine. If you think this draft could really happen, it wouldn't hurt to have a plan prepared."

"Thanks, Analia."

He wasn't sure why he was thanking her for letting him convince her to look after her own best interest, but sometimes it was easier to just play along. He knew how smart she was and that she'd take the warning seriously, but for some reason she just had to act the spoiled noble brat.

"Of course. By the way, I did find something about the Creator in a bestiary of magical beasts. I can dig the book out for you, but the short version is that around three centuries ago, all sorts of animals started showing the ability to use arcana. Most of them were intelligent, and some could communicate. There were multiple accounts of them describing a man who spun the first of them out of nothing and breathed life into them."

"So the Creator was a real person then. The wolf matriarch didn't think he was human, but . . . Could an archmage really do something like that?" Nym asked.

"I don't think so. It's not like they go around publishing lists of their most secret magics and techniques, but there's been plenty of archmages over the last few hundred years, and the book I read said all of these species of magical creatures popped up around the same time and nothing new has ever come about the same way since."

"Do you think he was an ascendant?" Nym asked.

Analia shrugged. "We don't really know what an ascendant even is, other than a mage beyond human limits. What makes them different? Why can they do magic that humans can't?"

"What makes them different?" Nym repeated. "I wonder."

Could it be as simple as being able to see arcana? The only other living being he'd ever met who'd been able to see arcana like him was the wolf matriarch, and she had a direct tie to a being that very well could have been an ascendant. That didn't even take into account his apparently monstrous soul-well size.

Analia's dad might not be the only person in the world trying to create an ascendant, and Nym's own past might contain more clues, if only he could regain his memories. Professor Langdon had told him there were seven knots, seven memories, at the beginning of his timeline before it had been sliced away. He'd pulled two of them loose and digested their contents.

It concerned him that they were memories of him learning to do magic. He didn't know if those memories had been prepared specifically, picked out of all the hours of his life being happy, playing, eating, spending time with his family, just being a normal child. Or were all his memories of him being prepared to be a living weapon? Maybe it would be better not to remember that. Maybe someone cutting away his entire life was a gift in disguise.

"Nym?"

"Huh?"

"You were just kind of lost in thought. Did you figure something out?"

Nym sighed and shook his head. "No. If we're going to look into ascendants, our best lead is probably your father."

"It probably won't be the first thing I have to say to him the next time I see him."

"That's fair. I've got to get going. I promised Bildar another batch of those custards from that pastry shop, and I'm not sure how late they're open."

"Oh, they closed an hour ago."

Nym grimaced. "Bildar isn't going to like that."

"He's a big softie," Analia said. "But go on, get out of here. I've got researching to do. And . . . Nym . . . Thanks for everything. Not just today either. I'm glad we met."

"Me too," he said.

Even though he knew the store had closed before he'd gotten to town, Nym swung by anyway to confirm. It wasn't really a surprise once he thought about it. A bakery would open early and close early. Bildar wouldn't be happy, but there was nothing to be done about it except make an early-morning run tomorrow.

He walked out of town and flew through the dark back to the construction camp. It was almost nostalgic, flying over the forest at night. The trees looked just like he remembered, but now they were almost a blur as he flew over past them, and he wasn't worried about freezing to death or something trying to eat him while he slept.

He stopped just once to kill a ghoul he spotted trudging through a tiny glade near a stream. He took a few minutes to burn the corpse, and then he was on his way back home. It was a very different experience than his first trip through the forest.

Nym was in the air again before the sun was even up and in Ebalsan with the dawn. His first and only stop was the bakery, where he spent three shields on enough pastries to stuff all four earth mages. It was so many in fact that he couldn't physically carry them and had to resort to creating a cushion of air to rest them on.

Whether because of the early hour and lack of traffic, or just because of the heavy military presence, or maybe nobody would have cared anyway, no one stopped Nym and his three separate baskets on their way out. By the time he got back, Ophelia was already up and drinking something steaming from a stone cup.

"Good morning," she said. "Is that what I think it is?"

"Yep. This basket is full of nothing but custards. The other two have a bit of variety."

Ophelia rifled through the basket for a minute and pulled out a whole pie. She fetched a knife, a fork, and a plate, then cut herself a slice. "This is delicious. I'm adopting you. You're stuck with me for life now," she said around a mouthful of it.

"And have to fetch you breakfast every morning? I don't think so."

"What's that I'm smelling?" Nomick asked, entering the room. His eyes lit up at the sight of not one, but three, baskets. "Truly you know the way to a man's heart, Nym."

"Thanks? I think."

"Why is this basket full of nothing but custards?" Nomick asked, peering into it.

"It's for Bildar. Pilfer from it at your own risk."

"Which basket is for me then?"

Nym shrugged. "You guys can figure that out. I've got to get going before all the good assignments get handed out."

"Good luck," Ophelia said. "Be careful."

"Will do!"

Waving goodbye, Nym took to the air and skimmed over the tree line to the forward command post and landed in front of the freelancer administration office. Judging by the crowd already gathered there, it looked like showing up an hour after dawn was not going to be early enough to get first pick of anything.

Nym got in line to talk to the clerk, only to have the woman in front of him turn around and look down her nose at him. "What's a kid doing here?" she asked. "You get lost or something?"

"No. I'm just looking for work, same as you."

She was young, maybe twenty years old, skinny with long blonde hair that hung loose down her back. She was dressed in threadbare mage robes that looked suspiciously like the ones worn at the Academy, if they'd been burned and sliced and poorly mended.

"Oh, sure. No doubt you'll be heading right into the thick of things, blasting ghouls left and right with that second-circle earth-shot spell you just learned yesterday. I bet you can cast it a whole six times before you need a break."

"Maybe even seven times on a good day," Nym agreed.

There was a smattering of snickers from the line, and the woman's face started reddening. "Listen here you little—"

A hand came down on the woman's shoulder, and she cut herself off. "Take it easy," the man standing next to her said. Unlike his companion, he was well-dressed with tanned skin and a short beard cropped close to his jawline. An axe hung from his belt, and he wore a breastplate complete with greaves and gaunt-lets. He turned to Nym and added, "Sorry about that. We're just a little tense today. It's been a rough week."

"It's fine," Nym told him, even though the woman's glare made it clear that nothing was fine with her. He wasn't sure what exactly he'd done to offend her, other than having the misfortune of being next to her in line. At least it was moving quickly, and in a few minutes, he would be far away from the unpleasant woman.

The line inched forward, and Nym caught the woman giving him nasty looks every time they moved. He just kept telling himself that whatever her problem was, it didn't affect him. Eventually, the couple in front of him made it to the front of the line.

"Morning, Roly," the man said to the clerk. "What do you have for us today?"

"Well," Roly said slowly, dragging the word out. "That entirely depends on whether it'll be just the two of you again."

"You know it is," the woman snapped at him.

"Then I'm sorry to say the guidelines still haven't changed, and you need a third for any sweeper jobs."

"Oh, come on! You know we don't actually need a third. We could kill a hundred ghouls by ourselves. A hundred each!" the woman said.

"Be that as it may, you still need a third before I can sign you up for a job. I'm sorry. I don't make the rules."

"Calm down," the man told his companion. Instantly, arcana flared up around her, and she looked ready to tear his face off. The man ignored her and asked the clerk, "If not a sweeper job, what do you have for two people?"

"You could run a supply train through the wall camps. There's one leaving in an hour that's got two slots left."

Nym thought the woman was angry before, but she was livid now. "A supply train? Are you serious? That's an all-day job for what, four shields between the two of us?"

"I'm sorry, that's all that's available at the moment. If you'd like to wait, I'll let you know when something else comes up."

The pair moved off to the side, the man speaking softly to his companion the whole time and trying to calm her down. Nym moved up to the front of the line. "Wow, she's intense, huh?" he asked.

"Every single day," Roly said with a sigh. "What are you looking for today? I should warn you that you've picked the worst possible time to come in for work."

"Courier jobs if you've got them. What's so bad about right now?"

"The morning rush just came through and grabbed everything they could. More jobs will trickle in throughout the day, but right now we're almost com-pletely tapped out. I don't have any courier jobs right now unless you want to be attached to an outpost captain and relay whatever orders you're given throughout the day? It's an all-day job, pays two shields, and you'll spend most of your time standing around waiting for work."

Two shields wasn't a terrible wage for the day, but he could do better back at the wall doing earthwork. Nym had switched to freelancer jobs on the promise that he'd make good money. Something must have shown on his face because the clerk nodded and said, "Most people don't want to do them either. That's why it's still here. Look, there is one sweeper job on the books, but it's got to be a team of at least three, and at least one person in the group has to have combat authorization."

Nym groaned. "So what you're telling me is if I went over to those two and offered to round out their group, we could take this job? What's it pay?"

"One crest four. Thinning out ghouls on the northeast flank before they start pressuring the wall crews stationed there."

Nym glanced back at the two freelancers, who were now sitting a table and talking in low voices. He grimaced. "I'll go talk to them and let you know."

CHAPTER THIRTEEN

Nym approached the table the pair were sitting at. "Hi," he said, a bit awkward under the woman's glare. "Do you have a minute?"

"What do you need?" the man asked, ignoring his companion.

"Well, I'm kind of in the same spot you guys are," Nym said. "Nothing available for the kind of work I want to do, but the clerk told me we could help one another. You need a third for your sweeper job. I don't want to spend the next sixteen hours waiting for some guy to need to send a message."

"Get lost. We don't need to babysit some mageling who just learned his first second-circle spell yesterday," the woman said.

"If you don't want to work with me, that's fine. I'll find something else to do. But I can kill ghouls and have been for the last few days whenever I see them. I can fly all day long and take the both of you with me for a mile or two at least. I can incinerate remains and shape earth to put up walls or make pits. I can throw lightning bolts. I can cast far-seeing and night vision spells."

"That is an impressive skill set for someone so young," the man said. "My name is Adriarc. This is my . . . sister . . . Larian. Give us a private moment to discuss this, please."

"Sure, no problem."

Nym found an empty table nearby and claimed it. The administration office was still about half-full, though the line up to the counter had started to disperse as it became common knowledge that the morning jobs had all been claimed already. Some people hung around, waiting for work to come up, but at least half of them walked right back out the door.

The whispering coming from Adriarc and Larian's table got more heated the longer they talked, then cut off completely. Larian looked like she was about to stab someone, so much so that Nym was having fourth thoughts about this partnership. Second thoughts had happened while he was still talking to them and third thoughts about two minutes into the whispered argument.

But that money though . . . One crest four. Even if he only got four shields for it to their five each, that was still twice what he'd make running messages for a base commander all day long. If he understood sweeper jobs correctly, it would only take a few hours to do, and hopefully there'd be new courier work for him to spend the afternoon on.

Adriarc caught his eye and waved him over. "Okay, we've decided," he told Nym. "We'll bring you along. Your job will be corpse disposal and to stay out of danger. That means we'll find a place with a clearing, you sit up safe in the air, and keep the fire going to burn the bodies. You'll get three shields, and the whole thing will be done in three to four hours."

"Three? That's not an even split," Nym said.

"It's more than you're worth. We're doing all the work, plus having to babysit you to make sure you don't get into trouble," Larian said. "The only reason I even agreed to this is it's better than sitting here doing nothing. We should ask someone else, but if you can hold a flight spell that long, we're reasonably certain that you won't take too much looking after."

Nym once again reminded himself of the money. Three shields for a four-hour job was still a good rate, even if it wasn't a fair share. He didn't understand exactly how the army evaluated freelancers, but he figured tagging along on a combat mission would go further toward getting him authorized for solo jobs faster than his only alternative.

"Fine," he said. "My name's Nym, by the way."

"Nice to meet you," Adriarc said. Larian notably remained silent. "I'll go sign us up for the job, and we can be on our way."

He left Nym sitting there with Larian. She immediately got up, snapped at him, "Don't screw this up and get one of us killed trying to save you," and swept out of the office.

"You need the money," he told himself. "You don't have to like her, just work with her."

Then he got up and joined Adriarc, who was looking at a map at the counter with the clerk. "Who's working the sector west of us?" he asked.

"Nald's crew took it today," the clerk said.

"Ah, good. They're solid. We'll focus more on the north side then. I don't expect too many will get past his boys."

Roly shrugged. "However you want to do it. I know it was my suggestion, but are you sure you're fine with this? After what happened to Nodric . . ."

"We'll be fine. Oh, hey, Nym. We've got our assignment. Ready to go?"

"Yes. Larian is outside," Nym said.

"Great. Let's go catch up then," Adriarc said. "See you around, Roly."

"You too," the clerk said. "Stay safe."

Nym followed Adriarc outside, where Larian was waiting. "Which sector did we get?" she asked Adriac, completely ignoring Nym.

"Ninth outpost's. Nald's crew took the one just to the west, so it should be a light day."

"Ugh. That's a long hike. I'm going to be completely wiped out carrying us there."

"That's fine. I'll take point while you catch your breath."

She rounded on Nym and jabbed a finger at him. "And you. You'd better be able to keep up. If I have to haul you over there too, you're not getting a single shim."

If there was one thing Nym was confident in, it was his flying. He was sure Larian knew a hundred spells he didn't, but he'd only ever met one mage who could outfly him. Somehow, he doubted the woman was on the same level as Flight Master Brogan. "I'll do my best. Let me know if you need me to take over ferrying a passenger."

Her eye twitched, and without another word, an arcana aura sprung up around them. She lifted herself and Adriarc off the ground and started flying north. Nym couldn't help but run a clinical eye over her spell as he followed them at a leisurely pace. It was technically stable, but he could tell she was having trouble with the arcana output needed to manipulate the air around a second person.

He was tempted to form a few air cushions around Adriarc to stabilize the man's flight and take some of the weight off Larian, but he doubted she'd appreciate it. If anything, it would probably just result in her yelling at him some more. On the other hand, the better shape she was in when they got to their section of the forest to sweep, the easier the job would be to complete.

"Do you want some help?" he asked as he flew up next to her.

She sneered at him and said, "Just focus on keeping up."

"Keeping up? We're barely going at a walking speed. You don't need to go easy on me. Go all out. I'll let you know if I need you to slow down for me."

He heard Adriarc's muffled laughter behind him but focused on keeping his expression neutral. It was hard not to antagonize the woman when she took his very existence like it was a personal insult, and there was only so much he was willing to sacrifice to placate her ego. Taking five times longer to get there because she was struggling to draw in arcana fast enough to power a flight spell wasn't one of those things.

"Fine. You think you're so big and tough? Let's see you in action," Larian said. "You can take over the flight spell for Adriarc. I'll keep a backup ready so he doesn't fall when you realize you're too weak to support another person for an extended flight."

"Sounds like a solid plan."

He wove new air cushions around Adriarc, who immediately steadied in the air. Then Nym put on the speed, and the forest started blurring beneath them. The wind picked up around them, carrying away anything Larian might have said, but her expression was enough to get the message across. She was falling behind, slowly but surely.

Adriarc waved an arm to get Nym's attention, but he couldn't hear what the man was saying. He put up a half shell of hard air in front of them and said, "Sorry, what was that?"

"I said . . . Huh . . . That's weird. What is this?" Adriarc asked, pushing gently against the shell.

"It's a shell of hardened air to force the wind away from us. It's too hard to talk while flying without it, but it's too expensive to maintain all the time," Nym explained.

"Huh . . ." Adriarc said again. "That's convenient. Anyway, I was saying we need to go a bit farther west to get to our sector. We need to check in at the ninth outpost to let them know freelancers are operating in their area. Also, sorry about Larian. Our third died three weeks ago. He was my brother . . . Her husband. Some kid wandered into our sweep, and he got killed saving the kid from a geist. I know she's been rough, but please don't take it personally."

Nym took a moment to think about that. "That's an explanation, but it's not a justification," he told Adriarc. "You both lost someone, but look how she's acting compared to you. I'll follow your orders for this job, but I'm not going to let her abuse me just because she can't control herself."

"I understand. I've got no problem with you sticking up for yourself. She's not acting right, and I just wanted to let you know she doesn't hate you. You just remind her of the kid who had no business being out here that got my brother killed."

"Got it. Hey, is that the outpost over there?" Nym pointed to his left at a brown spot in the sea of green below them.

"That's the place. Just take us in and have a break while I talk to the outpost captain, and then we can start the sweep."

Nym angled them down, and they landed in the courtyard in the middle of the walled outpost. Adriarc went off into the biggest building around, and a few minutes later, Larian landed nearby. She was breathing hard, and her hair looked like a bird had tried to make a nest out of it. Nym didn't say anything, just watched the soldiers on the wall as they scanned the tree line for ghouls.

Ten minutes later, Adriarc came back out and called them over. "Good news and bad," he said. "Good news is they authorized a bonus for the sweep today.

Bad news is that geists were spotted in the area this morning, so we're going to need to be extra careful."

"What's the bonus?" Larian asked.

"Extra shield for each geist we bring back."

"Not bad pay if there really are any here," she said. She turned to Nym and added, "Of course, that means you need to stay out of trouble. Keep yourself parked up in the sky and just focus on clean up."

Nym turned to look at Adriarc, who nodded along. "That's pretty much what we agreed to in the beginning. Geists lurking in the area means we've got to be more cautious and go slower, but it won't change much of anything for you."

"Okay, if that's what you want me to do. Are we ready to go?"

"I think so. We're responsible for a three-mile square with this outpost in the center. Nobody's expecting us to get all of them, but the more ghouls we find, the better."

They flew back up into the air and, under Adriarc's direction, landed half a mile north of the outpost. Nym flew a slow circle, gathering deadwood to use on the bonfire they'd be throwing dismembered ghouls onto while the other two started sweeping the area. Once he was done with piling the wood up, he sat in the air, bored, and conjured up a pair of earth golems. They'd do all the corpse handling once there were dead ghouls to burn.

Now he just needed the ghouls to show up.

CHAPTER FOURTEEN

A pair of earth golems worked tirelessly, chucking body parts into the bonfire while Adriarc worked to make more limbs. He'd been pushed back out of the trees in a running battle with three ghouls barely five minutes after they'd started, and Nym had thrown out a quick scry into the trees that showed him even more lurking in the boughs.

Adriarc cut through the three he was fighting quickly enough, but more kept coming, and as fast as he worked, it didn't take long before there were five live ones harrying him across the clearing. The dismembered but still moving body parts also flopped after him, making his footing treacherous.

"I know you said to just stay up here and clean up the bodies," Nym called down. "But there seems to be a lot of them. Do you want some help?"

"Only if—oof—if you can do it safely," Adriarc said, wincing as a ghoul rammed into him from the side while he was cutting another one's arm off.

Another earth golem formed near Adriarc and tackled one of the ghouls, holding it down and pummeling it. With three of them and the flight spell active, Nym was approaching the limit of how much arcana he could pull in at once, but there was still enough for him to use basic telekinesis to brandish a log from the fire and swat at another ghoul.

With some of the pressure taken off, the warrior was able to take the offensive back and started hacking the ghouls apart. Soon, the clearing was empty but for the two of them, the earth golems, and a wiggling pile of body parts trying to flop away from the bonfire Nym had built up.

"I think I'm going to need more wood," he said. "I didn't expect so many of them so fast."

"It does seem like there are a lot today," Adriarc agreed. "I was expecting an easy day, but this is insane. I should probably go check on Larian. Are you good to finish cleaning this up?"

"I'm fine. Larian's that way, about two hundred feet in. She's killed two ghouls and is fighting a third right now."

Adriarc turned to face the direction Nym indicated and looked between the trees. "I can't see any of that," he said.

"Scrying spell," Nym explained.

"That's handy. Can you tell where the ghouls are?"

"The range is a bit limited. I can't sweep the whole forest, but I can look around us easily enough. There are plenty more back in the direction you came from. Things are a bit lighter on her side."

"Hmm. We might have to switch up our strategy. Do you think you could put together some walls and choke points we could funnel ghouls into?"

"Maybe," Nym said. "It would depend on how big the walls are and how long you need them to last."

"Let's say eight feet high and a foot thick. Rough earthwork is fine. Do a circle with single opening. Slap a hallway leading up to it and the ghouls will fight each other trying to get in to reach us. Larian and I can pick them off, and you'll handle clean up."

Adriarc sketched out a diagram in the dirt, and Nym started raising the walls. He made a foot-high ring with the bonfire in the center and attached a narrow hall to a gap in it. "Is this big enough for you?" he asked.

"Perfect. Just make it thicker and taller while I go get Larian."

Adriarc ran off into the woods and left Nym to his work. "Easier said than done," he muttered.

The right way to do it was time-consuming and arcana intensive. Instead, Nym decided to make a wider base that sloped up to a sheer drop on the outside of the wall. Anyone would be able to climb the slope if they were inside the circle, but it would still function as a wall to the outside. He decided to go twelve feet instead of eight, not trusting the ghouls not to climb it if they could reach. By Nym's reckoning, if they could climb trees, they could jump a low wall. He used the dirt from outside the wall as building material, which resulted in something like a dry moat another three feet deep and six feet wide circling the whole barricade.

The choke point leading into the circle was a different story. He couldn't just ramp up a lot of dirt and trust it to hold itself in shape with minimal work. Those had to be done properly, which involved the tedious work of excavating a foundation, transmuting dirt to stone, and inscribing rune sequences across the surface to help hold it together.

He was still working on it when Adriarc and Larian returned. "Wow, I was only gone a few minutes," the warrior said, looking at the wall. Nym was busy scratching runes into the stone with a metal stylus and funneling arcana into them.

"The walls were just brute-force earth moving. The choke point is going to take some extra work to make sure the ghouls can't just break through them. Give me another ten minutes or so before you start luring them in."

"What . . . There is no way you did this so quickly," Larian protested. Her eyes darted around the wall, and she flew up in the air to get a better view. "This much volume, over ten minutes, no. A crew of four or five could do it. Maybe three if they were all specialized earth mages."

Nym shook his head. "No, you're giving me too much credit. These are literally just piles of packed dirt. The only thing stopping a ghoul from digging through this is that they'll hopefully crowd around the choke point to get in. Do not be surprised if one starts scaling the wall or digs into it. Though I'm still not sure what the plan is for luring them here."

"I've got a spell to make a lot of noise. Once we're ready, I'll cast it," Adriarc said.

"That could work. How far will it carry though?" Nym asked. "I don't think I'd want to set this up again anytime soon."

"Maybe a quarter mile with all the trees dampening the sound. Normally, I'd expect twenty or maybe twenty-five ghouls, but they're so thick right now, I'm not sure how many will show up. There must have been some kind of surge overnight. If we start getting overrun, I'll be counting on the two of you to extract me."

Nym finished up the rune sequence on the second wall of the choke point and empowered it. "There, all set. These are only good for maybe an hour, and if the runes get damaged, probably not even that long. I'll set up two earth golems on either side of the choke point to help you take care of ghouls and put one on cleanup duty."

Larian jerked in surprise when the golems walked into view. "God's blood. What are you even doing out here? A golem-control geode costs better than a hundred crests. There's no way you need the money for this kind of work. And no way you're a kid. Who are you really?"

"What?" Nym asked. "I'm not sure what you're saying. I didn't buy the golems. I made them. Their cores are just dirt condensed from a spell construct. They'll recover from damage, but it's all powered by arcana from me."

"Adriarc, this is a bad idea. Whoever this guy is, he's not a kid. And whatever games he's playing at, we're better off steering clear of them."

The warrior frowned and looked back and forth between Larian and Nym. He scratched at his chin and thought for a second. "I don't know a lot about magic," he said finally. "Maybe a bit more than the average soldier, but I never could get to the second-circle spells. But I've worked with plenty of mages, and

Larian's not wrong. What you've shown off today isn't normal for someone who's too young to grow a beard."

"I'm not trying to trick you," Nym protested. "You asked me to build this!"

"Well I didn't realize exactly how much work went into it when I said that, and I trust Larian's judgment. If she says something is off, I believe her."

"What do you want me to do? I'm not sure how I'm supposed to prove to you that I'm just here to kill some ghouls."

"A moment, please. Larian, can we talk?"

The two moved off to discuss whatever it was they needed to figure out. Nym rolled his eyes and floated up into the air to sit on top of the walls, making sure he was upwind of the putrid smoke rolling out of the bonfire. No matter how many times he told himself to think of the money, this job was turning into more of a pain than it was worth.

He started scrying out into the trees, trying to get a count of how many ghouls were likely to be drawn in if Adriarc's plan worked, but couldn't find a single one. That was odd. There'd been plenty of them lurking in the forest, mostly creeping around on the ground but occasionally hidden up in the trees. Now they were gone.

Nym pushed his scrying out as far as he could, and there, near the very edge of his range, he found them. They were gathered together, clumped tightly, with more that were out of sight. Something had their attention, but they weren't attacking it. This wasn't a behavior he'd seen before, but he knew what happened when a bunch of ghouls gathered up.

"Hey, sorry to interrupt, but we've got a problem," Nym said, landing next to the two. "All the ghouls are gathering together in one big group. They're maybe four hundred feet in that direction."

Adriarc's face paled. "Damn it. This whole plan is a wash. It's time to run."

"What? Why? I thought the whole point of this thing was to make the choke point so their numbers don't matter."

"Because when you're this deep into their territory, a gathering of ghouls means a wight is commanding them," Adriarc explained. "We need to get back to the outpost now and let them know. Can you get a better scry on the group and get numbers?"

"Give me a minute," Nym said. He dismissed all three of his earth golems and created an air golem instead, then set it to flying over the trees with a mental command. Once it got in range, he used it as a new anchor for his scrying spell and sent it through the gathering to get a better look. "That is . . . a lot. A lot a lot."

It took him a minute before he came back to himself. "I counted about three hundred ghouls, but there were some moving through the trees, so maybe fifty more than that. There were also three people there, dead people still walking around. All of them were dressed in mage's uniforms."

"Three wights with a lot of unknown magic. This is going to be messy. How quick can we get back to the outpost?"

"A few minutes," Larian said. "Less if the mystery kid does it."

Adriarc grimaced. "Let's go. Do a lap over the gathering so I can say I verified it myself at the outpost."

Nym lifted himself and Adriarc up over the trees and flew him over to the where the ghouls were gathering. Then went up high to avoid notice, and Adriarc cast his own far-sight spell. "Blood of God," he swore. "That is a lot of them, and I can't even see most of the gathering through the trees."

"Back to the outpost?" Nym asked.

"As fast as you can. This is going to be a disaster, lot of dead bodies."

CHAPTER FIFTEEN

The guy in charge of the ninth outpost was a reed-thin man who was sweating entirely too much for the still-cool spring weather. His uniform seemed to hang off his shoulders instead of fitting him, and his hands shook as he listened to Adriarc speak.

"We'll be overrun," he said. "There are only fifty soldiers at this outpost. The ghouls alone would be a problem, but with three wights directing them, the only way I see any of us making it out alive is by retreating now."

"You can't retreat!" Larian objected. "Your job is to fight ghouls. This is literally what you're here for."

"We don't have an artillery squad stationed here, and I'd want twice the infantry to even consider holding a defensive position long-term. Unless the three of you are hiding some skills you'd like to share, I don't see that we have much choice."

Both Adriarc and Larian turned to look at Nym at the same time. He blinked and took a step back. "What? Why are you looking at me like that?"

"You're the endless bag of mysteries and surprises," Larian said. "If there was ever a time to whip something out, it'd be now."

"I don't know any artillery spells," Nym said. "Even if I did, how would I do the ritual by myself?"

"How should I know? Every time I turn around, you're doing something else you shouldn't be able to. Why are you holding out on us now?"

"I'm not holding out on you," Nym said, getting heated. "If I had some sort of spell to kill a couple hundred ghouls at once, I'd use it!"

"No one thinks you're a secret archmage in disguise," Adriarc cut in. "We can't just abandon the outpost, but Captain Lygan is correct. Reinforcements are needed to hold if we're going to hold. Nym, if you flew as fast as possible, how quickly can you get back to forward command?"

"Ten minutes?"

The captain let out a low whistle. "Either you're lying, or you're about to be my new best friend."

He started scribbling on a scrap of paper, rolled it up, and shoved it into Nym's hands. "You get this to Mage-Commander Feldstal. We need a full squad of artillery mages. Not three or four mages. A full squad. Nothing else is going to get here fast enough to make a difference. If anyone tries to stop you, you tell them we've got a code triple white and shove past them."

Captain Lygan ripped one of the badges off his uniform, uncaring of the torn fabric left behind. "Take this with you. It should get you through most of the security. Now go, as fast as you can. Delays are going to cost lives."

"Yes, sir."

Nym didn't even bother to fly back out of the building. Instead, he scried through a wall to confirm it led to the outside, then reached out with earth shaping and tore a hole through it. Hardened air lifted him up from the ground, and he shot off into the open sky.

Nym flew faster than he ever had before. A month of constant use of his magic had honed his abilities. He'd said ten minutes, but he made it in seven.

He had some concerns about talking to a man named Mage-Commander Feldstal. The odds that he wasn't about to meet Analia's father were effectively zero. The question in Nym's mind was whether he knew what had been happening back in his home in Abilanth. As much as he'd rather sidestep the issue completely, he didn't think there was much of a choice. Maybe he'd get lucky and an underling would take the message out of his hands, sparing him a face-to-face meeting.

Nym landed in front of the first soldier he saw on the wall and gasped out, "Emergency message from the ninth outpost for Mage-Commander Feldstal. Code triple white. Where do I go?"

"Triple white?" the soldier blanched. She pointed at the tower next to the main command center. "Go to that building there."

"Thanks," Nym said. He took a deep breath and launched himself back into the air with something that looked more like an extended leap than true flying. He landed at the front door next to a startled soldier and held up the message and captain's badge. "Emergency message for Mage-Commander Feldstal. Code triple white."

The soldier recovered quickly and snapped out, "Come with me."

He was led into the tower, which was structured as a hollow central core with rooms leading off from it. There were no stairs, meaning nobody got past the ground level who couldn't fly. The outside was covered with large windows, easily big enough for an adult to jump out of. The soldier flew up into the air forty or so feet with Nym following and opened a door set into the wall. They stepped into a room dominated by a large table with five chairs on either side of it. Mages filled all of them, and as one they turned to look at Nym and the soldier.

"Emergency, sirs. Code triple white."

"Another one?" one of the mages at the table snapped. "Something has changed. That's the fourth one this week. Where at?"

"Ninth outpost," Nym supplied. He ran forward to the table and passed off Captain Lygan's message and badge. The mage read it quickly and passed it down the table to the woman sitting next to him. It made its way around in moments, and the mages started discussing.

"We could recall artillery squad four," one offered.

"They're on a rest cycle for another six hours. If we pull them back into an active combat situation, we'd be lucky to get half strength out of them. They won't be able to stop a triple white that's already in progress. Maybe if they had an hour or so to prepare."

"We don't have anything else in the area that can respond in time," the first mage countered. "Half strength is better than nothing."

Nym fell back to the soldier he'd followed and whispered, "Which one is Mage-Commander Feldstal?"

He'd been expecting someone who looked like Bardin, except older, maybe with a thinner head of hair or some wrinkles. None of the mages seated at the table really matched that expectation. Plus he kind of thought someone with a rank like mage-commander would just tell people what to do instead of arguing about the best course of action.

The soldier shook his head and whispered back, "He's not here right now. They've got him overseeing some project, and he's gone with that a lot."

"Oh," Nym said, strangely both relieved and disappointed at the same time. Once the soldier mentioned it, he thought he recalled Bildar saying something about that. "Um . . . What do I do now? Are we just waiting for them to make a decision or . . . ?"

"I would suggest getting some food and taking a break. You look dead on your feet," the soldier said. "Unless you've got somewhere you need to report back to."

"I thought I'd be going back to the outpost to help my team hold it against the outbreak. We were supposed to be doing a sweep of the area when we found the ghouls massing."

"Freelancer, huh? You're kind of young, aren't you?"

"That's what everyone says."

"Hey, you two! What are you doing still standing here? Get out already!" one of the mages yelled at them.

"I was supposed to tell you that Captain Lygan said to—"

"Out!" the mage bellowed.

"Yes, sir!" the soldier snapped a salute and stepped backward through the door into the air. Nym awkwardly saluted too and followed him out. He closed the door behind him, and the pair stood in the air outside the room.

"Like I was saying," the soldier continued like he hadn't just gotten scolded. "You look like you need to hit the mess hall before you do anything else. How much arcana have you used today?"

"I don't really keep track," Nym said. "No one ever really told me how to measure it."

"Get some food in you, take a few minutes to pull yourself together, and go help extract your team."

"I . . . Yeah. Thanks."

Nym left the tower behind and slowly made his way over to the mess hall. The soldier was correct in that he had pushed himself hard already today, but he worried that if he wasted time eating, by the time he made it back, it would be too late to help the duo he'd teamed up with.

It wasn't that he felt any sort of obligation to Adriarc or Larian specifically. The man had been a decent sort, but his sister-in-law was thoroughly unpleasant. Working with them had been a chore, and they'd barely even started the job before stumbling across the disaster. But he *had* agreed to work with them, and Larian had trouble carrying a second person in her flight. They probably did need help.

Plus, he wasn't actually sure if he was done with the job. They were supposed to sweep the area and kill ghouls. Was it that much different killing ghouls from the wall of the outpost? He really could use that payday. That wasn't even considering the soldiers manning the outpost. Captain Lygan had made it seem like they would struggle on their own. Surely an extra mage would help them hold the line until reinforcements arrived.

He decided to push the decision until he got back to the outpost. Best case, he'd help Adriarc and Larian finish up the job and get paid. Worst case, he'd help them get clear. He thought about that for a second and shook his head. He hoped the worst case was only that he was transporting some people.

The fighting had already started by the time Nym got back. The outpost walls were manned on every side, with the highest concentration repelling ghouls off the north and west walls. The soldiers were paired off, one wielding some type of spear with a crossbar to pin a ghoul, and the other holding a large axe to dismember it. There were two mages stationed with the defending soldiers, and from them Nym got his first true look at magical combat.

The one in the center of the north wall had nine blades floating around her in a circle, swordlike but with no cross guards on them. He could see an aura of arcana around her with small tendrils connected to each blade. As a new wave of ghouls swarmed the walls, scrambling and clawing at the stone to scale it, she leaned over the wall and sent the blades flashing down to hack off limbs or decapitate her enemies.

On the west wall, a man stood between six barrels, each filled with water. As ghouls attacked, he sent water out like spears, impaling the undead and funneling more and more water into their bodies until they exploded outward. Then the water returned to the barrel to wait for the next ghoul.

There were three more mages working together over a ritual circle in the central courtyard. The spell was building up power but slowly, so slowly that whatever they were attempting, Nym wasn't sure they'd finish it before the outpost was overrun. There were multiple spots where ghouls had reached the top of the walls in numbers and were starting to carve their way through soldiers.

If they needed time, Nym could help with that. He ripped up a chunk of earth from the ground and sent it hurtling toward a pack of ghouls forcing soldiers backward to the point where they were in danger of falling off the wall into the courtyard. Two of the ghouls were thrown backward out of the outpost.

The earth rose up into a Nym-sized golem, which promptly leaped to the defense of the soldiers while Nym pulled up another chunk of earth. A second golem joined in the melee with a hefty supply of dirt for them to draw on to regenerate from.

One front bolstered for the moment, Nym floated over the courtyard and looked for Adriarc or Larian. Neither were on the wall, from what he could see. He looked out into the woods, wondering if they'd continued the job without him. They hadn't wanted a third to begin with, so he wouldn't be surprised.

Below, more ghouls poured out from under the trees to join their comrades in attacking the outpost.

CHAPTER SIXTEEN

In Nym's experience, ghouls weren't actually that dangerous to a prepared mage. They won primarily through numbers and ambush tactics, and they weren't even that good at ambushes since they really only had one trick. Any mage with a decent repertoire of second-circle spells wouldn't have a problem defeating a single ghoul. A simple flight spell was enough to completely negate almost all danger from them, as they had no way to pursue and never used any sort of weapons, ranged or otherwise.

Ghouls were normally very easy to distract. As soon as they got ahold of someone, it was dinner time, regardless of whether that person was still alive. Their all-consuming hunger was so great that even attacking them wasn't always enough of a distraction from gorging themselves on meat. A macabre hunting party could set out a bait pile of dead bodies and pick ghouls off at their leisure as the undead locked in on the meat and ignored the live humans around them.

The ghouls assaulting the ninth outpost were not acting the way every other ghoul he'd encountered had. For the first time, Nym understood exactly why wights were such a big deal. He was sure they were extremely difficult opponents on their own, but the fact that they forced a semblance of military discipline on the ghouls they controlled was the real problem.

Nym saw a soldier go down, his throat ripped out, and the ghoul that did it just stepped over the body to attack the next one on the wall. Ghouls retreated when they lost limbs instead of continuing to fight. The soldiers were then distracted by other ghouls, and the still-living limbs would wiggle, crawl, or flop their way back toward their owners to be picked up and reattached.

Even the body parts that the soldiers managed to kick off the back walls into the firepits set up below them were not going down easily. There were three people in the courtyard with long sticks pushing the squirming limbs back into the fire, and all three of them were busy running laps from wall to wall to keep the limbs contained.

A ghoul managed to pull itself together despite the fire and caused a minor panic when it clawed its way out of the pit to rise up and attack the noncombat staff in charge of keeping them contained. Before the ghoul could cause any damage, Captain Lygan leaped off the balcony he'd been giving orders from and split it in two with a vicious slash from an oversize axe. The pit handlers rushed forward to hack it back apart and scatter its pieces into different fires.

Nym landed next to him, surprising the man. "God's balls! Don't do that!" he swore.

"Sorry," Nym said. "Where did you send my companions? I need to get back to them."

The captain gave him a confused look. "They left minutes after you did. No freelancer is going to stick around and volunteer for this kind of a fight without an official job paying them for it."

"What? But what about the job we had to sweep for ghouls? They're all right here. Aren't we supposed to kill them?"

"You're a green one, huh?" the captain said grimly. "Come on, give me a lift back up there, will you?"

Nym flew them up to the balcony, where the captain resumed bellowing orders to various soldiers, mostly commanding the reserves to reinforce different sections of the walls as the ghouls surged. "Are those dirt things yours?" he asked, pointing at the east wall.

"Yeah. It looked like they needed something to take some pressure off."

"Good eye. Probably saved at least two of my soldiers," Captain Lygan said. He sighed and added, "But you should get out of here. You're not getting paid for this, and you're not part of the army. We'll hold until the artillery mages show up."

"About that," Nym said. "The guys who took the message were arguing about if they were going to send anyone at all. They said there wasn't a squad close enough to arrive that was combat ready."

Captain Lygan let out a blistering string of curses, stopping only to shout down at the courtyard to tell the mages working on a ritual spell down there to hurry up. One of them looked up, gave him the finger, and continued pouring arcana into the spell the three of them were building.

Nym's eyebrows shot up, but the captain just sighed and shook his head. "My brother," he said wryly. "He knows he'll pay for it later, if there is a later. But he can't help himself."

"How can I help?" Nym asked.

"You really want to?"

At Nym's nod, the captain said, "Help move the reserves faster. Get them airborne so they can react to a push instantly. That'll save more lives than anything else."

"I can do that," Nym said. "But the golems will crumble if I don't keep them powered."

The captain nodded. "Go warn them first so they're not caught off guard."

Nym lifted into the air and flew over to the east wall. There he used one of the new spells he'd picked up from the book Analia'd secured for him and wove a construct to paralyze undead. It would only hold for a few seconds, long enough for the soldiers to hopefully chop them apart. Nym unleashed it on the closest ghoul, then another, and a third in rapid succession. "It won't last long," he called out. "Take them out now!"

The golems collapsed once he cut their arcana supply, but the soldiers had the opening they needed to dismember the ghouls and throw the body parts over the back of the wall into the firepits, or at least near enough that the handlers could kick them in the rest of the way. He supposed accuracy took a back seat to speed when new ghouls were already breaching the walls.

Nym hit those with paralysis spells too before he flew back to the captain. "Ready, sir."

For the next twenty minutes, Nym ferried the eight reserve soldiers in two groups between different walls at Captain Lygan's orders to reinforce any faltering spots in the line. He watched the other mages when he could, studying their attacks to see if he could duplicate them. The water mage wasn't doing anything special beyond basic hydrokinesis with a freezing-and-expanding twist added to it, but with a large enough volume of water, it was proving extremely effective.

It was the sword mage that really got his attention. He'd tried his hand at controlling a weapon telekinetically, and while he was sure he could lift nine swords at once, he'd struggled to pull them back out of the wooden practice panels. Somehow, she was not only controlling that many weapons, but also hacking clean through most ghouls that came close. He wanted to study the spell closer, but there was little time for diversions.

He did determine that it wasn't just telekinesis but something second circle that served to increase its power while being molded with a twist of divination that he suspected gave her some kind of proprioception that helped keep track of where the blades were. Nym resolved to revisit that spell later and maybe make a trip back to that weapons store once he'd mastered it.

However it worked, the woman mage was holding a stretch of wall twenty feet wide by herself. If she could have gotten the parts she hacked off the ghouls over the walls into the burn pits, her effectiveness would have been tripled. The wights seemed to agree with Nym's assessment because two of them teamed up to work against her. One launched constant bursts of arcana she had to defend against, and the other coordinated the ghouls using some sort of hive mind spell that kept them covering for one another and recovering any lost limbs for easy reattachment.

For all of that, the north wall was probably the most stable, followed by the west wall. The ghouls had largely abandoned any attempt to breach it as the water mage there hit far fewer targets with his spells, but the ones he did had a much harder time getting back into the battle. His range wasn't great though, and when the ghouls shifted away to mass at a different point on the wall, he couldn't chase after them without another group attacking the spot he'd abandoned.

For Nym though, most of his work involved moving the reserves back and forth between the east and the south walls. The ghouls took the most losses there but only because they pressed the hardest against the soldiers who did their best to toss any ghouls they hacked up into the burn pits. The third and final wight also alternated between the two walls, and whichever side he focused on, the ghouls grew stronger and more ferocious.

"Damn it, we're not going to last at this rate," Captain Lygan said. "If they don't get that artillery spell going in the next ten minutes, we're going to be overwhelmed."

"Why is it taking so long?" Nym asked, wiping sweat from his face.

"There's only three of them. A full squad is twenty. They said it'd take an hour to finish."

"We need more time," Nym said. "If we could take out one of the wights, that would take a lot of pressure off."

"That's what the artillery spell is for." The captain pointed to a spot on the south wall where six ghouls had clawed their way up the stone and were pushing back the defenders. "Reserves there!"

Nym flew four soldiers up to help push the ghouls back and turned his attention back to the captain. "West wall is starting to have problems too. I think the mage there is almost tapped out."

"Aren't we all," the captain said. "There's no way out of this. It might be time for you to escape."

"What if I took a wall like the other mages? You could move soldiers around then?"

"That would be incredibly foolhardy," Captain Lygan. "You're strong for your age, but those ghouls won't go easy on you just because you're young."

"I've fought them before," Nym said.

The captain hesitated, then said, "It could work. I don't like it, but it could work. Are you sure you can do it?"

"No," Nym said bluntly. "I'm more than half spent, but do we have another choice?"

The captain waivered. Nym could see his mind scrambling to find another solution, but in the end, he shook his head. "Take the south wall, right in the middle. We'll shift soldiers to the west and east to help solidify those lines. You need to hold for at least another twenty minutes."

"Got it." Nym floated up into the air, but before he could leave, the captain grabbed his arm.

"The ghouls cannot get into the courtyard, no matter what. If they breach the walls and make it to the artillery mages, we're all dead."

"I understand."

"Good luck, son. And . . . thank you for coming back."

Nym flew to the center wall and landed. He launched paralysis spells at the ghouls already on the wall so that the men could cut them apart, then yelled for them to spread out and give him some room. He'd spent some time considering his options when he was shifting the reserves around and come to the conclusion that lightning bolt was too costly to use on a single ghoul when there were still hundreds of them left.

Setting them on fire didn't actually stop them until they'd burned down to charred skeletons. It was a disposal tactic, not a combat one. He didn't need to actually kill them, just hold them back until the artillery mages could take out the wights. Once that happened, the rest of the fight would just be cleanup, he hoped. For that, he opted to play to his strengths.

Simple elemental air magic to shove ghouls back as they crested the walls would take the least amount of arcana. His only concern was that if he didn't do enough damage, their numbers would begin to build up and overwhelm him. If they got too thick though, he'd fry the whole group with lightning.

The first ghouls leaped up onto the wall, and Nym got to work.

CHAPTER SEVENTEEN

Nym was panting heavily after just a few minutes. He'd drastically under-estimated the number of ghouls coming over his section of the wall. Air blasts weren't that draining, but doing it over and over again was taking a toll. The hard air cushions he lifted people up with didn't work any better, since the ghouls had a tendency to shred them as soon as they felt the air pushing up against their undead flesh.

It didn't help that he'd been forced to create three new earth golems to help. Their primary function was to get under the ghoul and shove it off-balance so that the wind blast was as effective as it could possibly be. The tactic was working, but it seemed like more and more ghouls kept piling up on him. Nym didn't want to admit it, but he didn't think he could keep up the pace for twenty minutes.

Though he knew they were needed elsewhere, Nym kept hoping the reserves would show up to help him, just for a minute or two so he could catch his breath. A few soldiers with axes to chop up paralyzed ghouls might just be a more effec-tive use of his magic, despite the fact that the paralysis spell was ten times more expensive to cast. That didn't happen, of course. The loose wight was pressuring the east wall again, and so all the reserves were concentrated there. He was on his own, fully responsible for guarding the fifteen-foot stretch of wall.

In a suspiciously coordinated effort, four ghouls leaped the walls at the same time. Nym hated when they did that. Halfway to the ground, there were ghouls clinging to the rough stone, their fingers dug into the cracks, and other ghouls were using them as stepping stones to leap up. Nym needed to clear the wall, then push those ghouls off so that they couldn't come at him in waves.

He sucked in arcana and pulled together a lightning bolt as soon as he saw four of them popping up at once. He darted off to the right to get them lined up, then unleashed the spell, striking all four. Soldiers around him let our ragged cheers, but Nym ignored them. In his rush to build the spell, he'd used the arcana reserved for one of his golems. It crumbled to dirt, and none of the ghouls he'd struck with lightning had died.

They were smoking and stunned, but it wouldn't last long. Nym summoned gusts of air in rapid-fire spells, knocking all of them back. Then he leaned over the wall and shot another wind blast straight down to pry one of the barnacled ghouls free. Chest heaving, he moved to the second ghoul and blasted that one off too.

Before he could hit the third, a soldier off to the side screamed in agony. He went flying over the back side of the wall to land in the courtyard, a ghoul clinging to him. Nym scanned the courtyard, hoping at least one reserve was down there to take care of it. There wasn't, of course. Nym didn't have an instant-kill spell, especially not at that range. All he could do was leap the back of the wall and swoop down to hit the ghoul with a paralysis spell, then pick it up and hurl it back over the wall into the woods.

That was so much easier than his current method but also so much more taxing. Nym tried to use undead paralysis sparingly, but he'd been forced to fire it off several times in the last few minutes. He steeled himself against the fatigue the maneuver had brought on, knowing that the few seconds he'd left the wall undefended would cost him as soon as he got back.

The soldiers had tried to close on his section while he was taking care of the loose ghoul, but there were only so many of them, and they were involved in their own battle. Nym rose back into the air to find another two ghouls about to leap into the courtyard. Howling winds smashed into them, sending them stumbling backward but not far enough to throw them loose. Undaunted, Nym hit them again, this time angling the wind up to lift them off their feet.

He landed on the wall and fell to his knees. Behind him and below, he could still feel the power building for the artillery mages' spell, but not fast enough. He didn't think they could hold the south wall much longer, certainly not until the spell was ready. But if they didn't, the mages below would have to abandon it to defend themselves from the ghouls.

There was another ghoul on the wall, right in front of him. Nym didn't know it where came from. Wearily, he pulled more arcana into his already aching soul well and paralyzed it. Sometime in the last few seconds, he'd lost the second golem, and he didn't have the time to make new ones. Instead, he used air cushions to push the ghoul back off the wall.

He needed something to slow them down, even if only for a few minutes. Frantically, he went through his spells, trying to find anything that would work.

He couldn't raise the walls higher and didn't have the water to do anything with hydrokinesis. Air spells were stalling at best, and he was falling behind. Fire . . . might work. It wouldn't stop a ghoul from attacking, but they might not cross a stretch of ground that was already burning.

Nym shook his head. It wouldn't work with the wights commanding them. All it would accomplish was flaming ghouls on the wall, making it that much more dangerous to everyone defending against them. He didn't have anything to stop them permanently, or even temporarily. The wall would be overwhelmed without reinforcements.

Two new ghouls crested the walls, and Nym hit them with blasts of air before they managed to climb over completely. One lost its grip and tumbled backward, but the other fought through the surge of air and made it to its feet. More wind hit it, driving it back a step, but it braced against the lip of the wall and held on.

Then another ghoul appeared. Nym couldn't take care of it with the arcana he had available. He opened another conduit, and his soul well bucked against the sudden surge. Nym held on to it, his teeth clenched, and doubled the area of the wind blast. It fairly screamed across the walls, so loud that it drowned out everything else.

The first ghoul lost its grip and went flying back out over the wall. Before the second could join it, a third one climbed up. Then a fourth. Nym pulled on the arcana as hard as he could, channeling it through him as fast as it came in. He had to push them back, had to keep them from reaching the courtyard.

Ghouls went flying, and Nym staggered forward, buffeted by his own spell. One unwilling step turned into two, and then he was pressed up against the edge of the wall. Another ghoul was right below him, hand reached up to grab the top of the wall. When it saw Nym, it shifted targets and hooked its fingers into his shirt. Then it pulled.

Nym's feet left the stone, and he found himself tumbling through open air. Shrieking in surprise, he tried to pull together a flight spell, only to discover that the ghoul had flung itself off the wall with him. They fell together, Nym unable to disentangle himself. Desperately, he kicked the ghoul away. The shirt tore, and the undead lost its grip on him.

He hit the ground, and all he knew for a second was pain, pain in his arm, pain in his legs, and pain in his chest. Nym came back to himself, crying and huddled up on the dirt. His brain screamed at him, told him he needed to get back in the air, that the ghouls would tear him apart, but it was a small voice drowned out by the pain.

He lay there in a heap, unmoving for long seconds. Something grabbed his broken arm, and he screamed in pain. Eyes wide, he looked up to see a ghoul about to sink teeth into him. Arcana surged into his soul well, and spires of stone erupted around him. The ghoul holding him and three other ghouls nearby were skewered, which didn't kill them of course. They just turned their efforts to breaking the stone restraining them.

But it gave Nym enough time to pull more arcana through his ragged soul well and blast the ghoul holding him with a bolt of lightning. Part of Nym was pleased with himself at the increased control. A few months ago, he would have fried himself with that spell, but now it struck only the ghoul, forcing it to release him. Desperately, he wove together the magic he needed to fly. It didn't want to come, and he wobbled a few feet off the ground before sinking back down.

"No, no, no no no no no nonononono," he muttered. His magic had never failed him like this. It couldn't, not now. He grabbed it and pulled with all his might. Something tore inside him, but it came, just enough to get back into the air.

Nym lurched over the wall, clipping it with his legs, and crashed onto the stone, half hanging over it. Immediately, there were soldiers there, grabbing onto him.

"Am I . . . safe?" he mumbled when the soldiers grabbed hold of him and pulled him over onto the wall itself.

"Get a stretcher," someone said. "Take him to the barracks."

"I . . . think I need . . . healer," Nym said.

That was the last thing he remembered before the pain took him.

The air smelled like burnt ghoul when Nym woke up. He was in a building with a low ceiling, filled with the moans and groans of injured soldiers. Sunlight streamed in through a few windows, as well as wisps of acrid smoke.

The first thing he noticed when he tried to move was that his ribs were busted up. Every breath hurt, but moving was so much worse. Either there was no healer at the ninth outpost or there were too many people with more immediate concerns because the only treatment it looked like he'd received was a splint for his broken arm and a sling for it to rest in.

The real problem was he had the mother of all arcana poisonings. The only time he'd ever come close to the pain he was feeling now was the very first night, when the magister had told Ciana he was going to die. Nym had been asleep for almost all of that though, and he envied his past self that luxury. Just the thought of forging a conduit and pulling in arcana made him want to cry.

An hour or so after he woke up, someone stopped by to check on him. A man, maybe thirty years old but with hair already starting to gray, moved from bed to bed, talking softly with the soldiers for a minute or two before moving on. It wasn't until he got to the bed Nym was in that he got a good look at the man.

He was tall, with stocky shoulders and his hair shorn down to the scalp. He was dressed in a standard military uniform, blue clothes with black boots and belt, though he wasn't wearing any of the armor most of the soldiers Nym had met sported. A mustache covered his upper lip and a goatee his chin.

"You're awake," the man said. "Good. Welcome back to the world of the living. Good news is that we held the outpost. Bad news is that you need to see a real healer, and ours died in the fighting. The next few days of your life are going to be extraordinarily unpleasant."

"Because of the arcana poisoning or because of the busted ribs?" Nym asked.

"Oh, those are both bad, no doubt. I'm sure you feel like you were run over by a whole parade of horses right now. But I'm more concerned about matrix destabilization."

"I don't know what that is," Nym confessed.

"No? You've got some gaps in your education. Think of your matrix as a kind of framework for your soul well. It reinforces it, helps it hold its shape when you're brimming with arcana. When it gets damaged, say for example if you did something incredibly stupid like pulled in far, far more arcana than you can hold in a very short period, your soul well's like a barrel that's leaking. No matter how much water you pour into it, it keeps coming out the hole in the side.

"That's bad for obvious reasons. You can't hold arcana safely since it will seep into your body and give you arcana poisoning. Trying to power through that to use magic anyway can result in the leaks getting bigger. So until you've healed up a bit and we can figure out exactly how badly you've damaged your soul well, my advice would be not to use any magic."

Nym wasn't really sure what to do with that information. He couldn't just not use magic. It was who he was. If he wasn't a mage anymore, he didn't know what he was. Desperate to think about anything else, he asked, "How is the outpost doing?"

"We got the artillery spell off about three minutes after your dive off the wall and drove the wights off. Pretty sure we killed at least one. After they disappeared, the ghouls went down. We lost twelve soldiers and one mage, our healer, and two cooks. Twenty-two more injured enough to be on bed rest. We need a new healer, like I said, and also a crew of earth mages to help repair the outpost."

"I . . . Thanks," Nym said. "I think I want to go back to sleep."

"Have some water first," the mage said, producing a cup from a nearby table that Nym hadn't noticed. He sipped at it, thanked the mage again, and closed his eyes. The soft drone of the man's voice as he moved on from bed to bed slowly faded, but the pain remained constant. Tears rolled down his face, unnoticed.

CHAPTER EIGHTEEN

It was two days before the healer showed up, and other than giving Nym a once-over and healing the fractured rib, he didn't look at Nym again for another day after that. The barracks grew gradually quieter every hour as the healer got more and more soldiers back on their feet. He moved with some unseen logic, working on one soldier for a bit, then moving to another without completely healing the first.

An hour later, the healer would move back to the first patient again and heal him some more. Nym assumed it was some sort of triage system, where the healer had cataloged all the injuries and was dealing with the most severe first, but at no point in time did the healer feel the need to justify his decisions to anyone within earshot of Nym.

Finally, late into the second day of his work, he came back to Nym's bed. "Let's see how you're doing," he said. "Broken arm still, we'll fix that easily enough. Already took care of the ribs. Ligaments are torn in the knees and one shoulder, abrasions on the hand. Somehow didn't give yourself a concussion. This all happened in the battle a few days ago? Doesn't look like it."

"I—"

"Doesn't matter," the healer interrupted him. "It's all going to be gone in a bit anyway."

The healer's aura rose around him, a gentle green laced with strands of blue that pulsed slowly. The spell construct the man was using was one that was familiar to Nym: the pain-relief spell. He'd wanted to cast that a hundred times over the last few days but, mindful of his own aching soul well and the mage's warning about damaging it further, had suffered instead.

Not feeling how much he hurt anymore was an immense relief, both physically and mentally. The healer started working on his broken arm, then focused on the shoulder. An hour later, Nym was exhausted but physically whole. He tried to be positive about the experience. He'd gotten to see several healing spells up close.

"You should rest a bit longer to recover from the healing, but before that, it's time to talk about the damage to your soul well."

Nym flinched. He almost didn't want to know, but he needed to find out. "How bad?"

"Fairly severe," the healer told him bluntly. "Bad arcana poisoning, though the mage who initially examined you may have overstated it. Or maybe he didn't. You look much better now than you did when I first examined you, so maybe you're just extraordinarily good at cleansing yourself of it. The real damage is to your sixth, twelfth, and twenty-second matrix nodes. I've got some bad news and some good news there."

"Let's start with the good news," Nym said. "I could use some of that."

"The good news is that it doesn't look like you've done any permanent damage to them. They're strained, the sixth one especially, but you should be able to recover fully as long as you follow your treatment plan."

"That . . . is good news," Nym said. An immense ball of tension and stress melted away. He was still a mage. He could still do magic. He mentally chided himself though because he knew there was still a catch. "What's the bad news?"

"You can't do any magic while you're recovering. Nothing at all, not even so much as creating a spring breeze or picking an apple off a tree branch out of reach."

He'd gone days without using magic before when he was recovering from that third-layer arcana injection. The downtime from work would set him back financially, but he still had most of what he'd kept from Valgo's stash. There was enough in there to survive for a few months.

"That doesn't sound so bad."

"I'm not done yet," the healer said. "The recovery process is complicated. Depending on how much you might already know, which I'm guessing is not a lot, you're going to need to learn a few new things. That's going to cost money. Maybe that won't be a problem for you. Hopefully it won't. But you're looking at probably two weeks of sessions there with a personal trainer."

"I can handle that. Money shouldn't be an issue." Well, it might be, but that wasn't something the healer needed to know about.

"Two weeks of sessions to learn the recovery techniques you'll need to repair the matrix nodes, then more time to actually practice them and perform the repairs. For three nodes, in the condition you're in, I wouldn't be surprised if it took a year to fully recover."

"A year," Nym repeated. "Is that a joke?"

"I'm afraid not," the healer told him.

"No, really though, it's a joke, right?"

"Not even a little bit."

Nym couldn't go that long without magic! Even without this supposedly expensive personal training he needed, he didn't think his remaining funds would stretch that far. "There's got to be a faster way."

"If you've got a lot of money, sure."

Nym frowned. "What do you mean?"

The healer shrugged. "Theoretically, you could be back in action in a month or so. In reality? I doubt you've got that kind of money."

"How would money help?"

"Once you've learned the recovery techniques needed, you'll be able to start restoring the matrix nodes. Normally, the nodes are unaffected by arcana. They kind of have to be, since their whole job is to keep your soul well stable. What you're going to learn how to do is open them up so they can be manipulated. Once you can do that, a healer such as myself can come in and speed this process up, but it's still a process. How many sessions you can afford to pay for will determine how much faster it gets done."

"And if the answer is none, then I'm just holding the nodes in a malleable state so they can heal up on their own, which will take . . . a long time."

"That's about the size of it," the healer agreed. "Even if you were a healer yourself, it wouldn't help speed anything up because you can't use magic without damaging them further. Your soul well needs to be empty so the nodes can heal."

"If they're not affected by arcana, why does it matter if I have any in my soul well?" Nym asked.

"They're not normally affected by arcana, unless you put too much strain on them, which you did. Now you need to learn how to . . . to relax the node, for lack of better term, so that it can be repaired, but you can't do the repairs while relaxing the nodes since your soul well won't hold any arcana."

Nym sighed. "So there's really nothing I can do but throw money at healers to help speed it up? There's no way to relax just the nodes I need to fix while the others stay stable?"

The healer shrugged. "Probably, but I bet it'd take you longer to learn how to relax one specific node instead of all of them than it would take to just relax all of them and let it heal naturally. Now, if you'll excuse me, I do have other duties to attend to so that I can get back to my assigned outpost."

"Right, sorry. Thanks for explaining," Nym said.

The healer left him alone to his thoughts. Nym was fine now, physically speaking. He could get up and walk out the door if he wanted, but then what? He couldn't go anywhere. Without his magic, he was just a regular kid. He could still see magic, but it didn't do him any good if he couldn't use his own. Nym wouldn't be able to leave the outpost without an escort, unless he wanted to risk being eaten by a ghoul.

His only hope for speeding this up was if somehow being able to see arcana helped. He'd never looked inside his own soul well, but up until a few days ago, he'd never seen another person's conduit either. There was some hope there, and even if it didn't work, the damage wasn't permanent. It might be a long, slow process, but he would recover someday.

In the meantime, he'd figure something out. If he had to run around doing errands for somebody, that was what he'd do. Before that, he needed to get off the front line, which meant figuring out when the next rotation was so he could head back to safety with the soldiers leaving the outpost.

Nym pulled himself out of bed and looked at his clothes folded on the trunk at the foot of it. They were stained with smoke and blood and who knew what else and had collected quite a few new rips and tears. Almost without thinking, he forged a conduit to cast a mending spell. As soon as he pulled arcana through it, pain spiked him and broke his focus.

"Oh, right," he said dully.

Mechanically, he dressed himself. Somehow, for all the damage the rest of his clothes had taken, the shoes were still in decent shape. It was a minor miracle, all things considered. It wasn't enough, not even close, but it was something to focus on, one thing gone right from the whole disaster. When he felt ready, he walked out of the barracks to see what he could find out.

Three days was a lot of time for a crew of earth mages to fix things. The outpost itself looked almost exactly like he remembered, except with a lot more patches of bare earth where there used to be grass. The people were another matter. Men and women worked, grim faced and silent. Tasks were completed quietly and efficiently, with almost no conversation between soldiers when they passed one another by.

That could be mistaken for a professional military atmosphere if that was all there was to it. They were after all holding an outpost deep in what was essentially enemy territory, but even the soldiers that weren't working were quiet and withdrawn. There were no games being played, no gambling, no boisterous stories or roughhousing. What Nym did see was a lot of the off-duty soldiers drinking by themselves with a sort of quiet determination, even when they were surrounded by their fellows.

"Oh, good," a voice said. "Tann said you were up. I was just coming to get you."

Nym looked over to see a familiar woman walking up to him. It took him a moment to place where he'd seen her before, and it didn't click until he saw the two swords strapped across her back. She was an average height with a slender build, shoulder-length dark-red hair framing the youthful face of a woman in her early twenties. "You were the mage on the north wall with the sword magic," he said.

"That's me," she confirmed. "You can call me Yura. Come with me?"

"Okay," Nym said, falling into step with her. "Where are we going?"

"To talk to Captain Lygan first, then I'm supposed to get you started on fixing your matrix destabilization."

She turned back to look at Nym, who'd stopped in his tracks. "You're going to help me get my magic back?" he asked.

"I'm going to show you some of the exercises. You'll still need a professional to help once you get back to town."

"Why are you helping me? How do you know how to do this?" Nym asked as he caught back up to her. They walked between a pair of soldiers guarding the door into the central building of the outpost.

"Mostly because the captain told me to. Also because I'm probably the only one here who has firsthand experience with matrix destabilization. It's . . . not uncommon with people who have larger-than-average soul wells. We all get used to being able to just do more than the other mages around us, pushing harder and ignoring warnings because we've always been fine before. And then, one day we're not."

She paused to think about it. "Not that I'm saying you were wrong to do what you did. You didn't even need to be here, and chances are we would all be dead without your help. So . . . you know . . . thank you for that."

"I didn't . . . I mean . . . Uh, you're welcome?"

"Just to warn you, Cap's not happy. It's nothing you did wrong, just the lack of reinforcements he requested has him in a bad mood. For now, you just focus on getting through these next few months and getting yourself put back together, yeah?"

"Yeah."

"Good. We're here." Yura came to a stop in front of a door that Nym vaguely recognized as where the sweeper team he'd joined had spoken to the captain when they'd reported the ghoul swarm. She reached up and knocked, waited a beat for the captain's somewhat muffled permission to enter, and then swept through, dragging Nym along in her wake.

CHAPTER NINETEEN

Captain Lygan didn't look up from his paperwork. He had bags under his eyes and several days of stubble on his face. Somehow, he seemed even thinner than he had the first time Nym had seen him. The sweat spots were still dotting his brow, but they'd multiplied and started to run down his face. Absently, he rubbed a hand across his forehead and wiped it on his pants.

"Captain," Yura said again, clearing her throat.

"Hmm? Oh, sorry." The captain looked up finally, and his face softened when he saw Nym. "How are you feeling, young man?"

"Physically? Much better after the healer got to me. But in other ways . . ." Nym trailed off.

"I understand. You sacrificed a lot for this outpost, to help keep my men alive. Thank you for that." Captain Lygan wiped fresh sweat off his face. "Unfortunately, the beast of bureaucracy strikes again. Technically, you're not a soldier. Technically, you're not entitled to receive medical care from army healers for injuries suffered."

"Oh," Nym said. "That's . . . I don't know what to say."

"It's not fair, but I don't get to change the rules. I petitioned for your recovery, but the best I was able to secure was a healer to fix up the physical wounds you suffered without cost to you. Your long-term recovery will be left to you to secure. I'm sorry. All I can do for you now is give you a head start with what little time you have.

"Mage Yura will get you started on the path of recovery. A new squad of soldiers will be here in six days to relieve our active-duty roster. You will remain here until then and return with the relieved soldiers. Hopefully, this whole undead outbreak will be taken care of by the time you're ready to fight again."

"I understand," Nym said. "Thank you."

The captain studied Nym for a moment. He gave a soft sigh and shook his head. "Dismissed."

"Sir." Yura saluted and turned on her heel. She beckoned Nym to follow her and led him to a hallway with eight doors.

"This is what we call the mage barracks. It's really just officers' rooms, which means it's tiny and cramped and the beds suck, but at least you don't have to share the room with thirty or forty other people," she explained. "This one is empty right now. Lucky you. You'll be staying here for the rest of the week and practicing what I'm going to teach you."

Yura opened the door and gestured for Nym to walk in. She hadn't been joking about the size, but considering Nym had nothing but the clothes on his back, it wasn't like he needed something grand and luxurious. There was a bed in one corner and a small, one-person table with a chair pushed in on the other wall. A single sheet and a thin blanket were folded on the bed. There was no pillow.

Yura followed him in and claimed the chair for herself. "Alright, time for your first lesson."

"Already? Don't you have things you need to do?" Nym asked.

"This is the thing I need to do. Did you have something better to do? I would have thought this was important to you."

"No. No, you're right. This is the best use of my time." Nym sat down on the bed and faced the older mage. "What do I need to do?"

Nym had a headache. It was not that he thought Yura was a bad teacher or anything; it was just that what she was trying to explain to him was a really weird concept to wrap his head around. He was very tempted to ask her to demonstrate, but without revealing what he could see, he couldn't find an excuse.

The technique was kind of like making a conduit in reverse, except it wasn't really like that at all. The way she'd explained it, he needed the same mindset he had when reaching out to a different layer of reality to harvest arcana from it, only flipped inside out to reach into his own soul well. That wasn't particularly descriptive; thus, Nym had a headache.

"Can you explain it a different way?" he asked. "I'm sorry, but I don't understand."

"That's natural. There's a reason it takes weeks to master this. I don't expect you to get it on your first attempt," she assured him. "I'm just trying to help you set up a foundation so when you get back to civilization, whoever is helping you won't have as much work to do. That'll save you some money and time."

"Okay, so then, I just . . . make a conduit, but not to anywhere?"

"You make a conduit to your soul well."

"All of my conduits go to my soul well," Nym told her. "What do I do with the other end?"

"There is no other end," she told him.

The headache got worse.

They went on like that for another half an hour, with her giving explanations that made no sense and him getting more frustrated. Finally, he struck on an idea. "You've gone through this, right? You've been on my side of this, trying to wrap your head around the concept?"

"I have," Yura said. "Why?"

"Can you do it and kind of break it down into the smallest steps possible and explain what you're doing with each step so I can follow along?"

Of course, he was banking on his recently discovered knowledge that he could in fact see a conduit behind an arcana aura if he looked right and hoping that Yura's statement that he was making a type of conduit was correct. If so, he could watch her form it in real time and hopefully increase his own understanding of the technique.

"If you think it will help," she said. "Give me a minute. I haven't had to do this in a few years."

Yura closed her eyes and took a few deep breaths. Nym watched closely, hoping to see something forming even without a cloud of arcana hugging her form. And then, with no warning at all, he did. It was like a small hole in the world, overlaid on her chest. On the other side of that hole was an endless expanse somehow confined to her body, and in the center was a glittering sphere of light made out of what appeared to be marbles with gossamer threads tying them all in place. The conduit was what bridged that gulf between Yura and the soul well inside of her.

"I have reached into my soul well and created a pathway to open it to the world," she said calmly, her eyes still closed. "It is a conduit to myself, starting at my soul well and having no other end."

Nym understood now why he was having such a hard time. That hole wasn't a conduit at all. Instead, it more closely resembled what would happen when he pulled arcana from his soul well to cast a spell. He needed to open his soul well to the reality he was in, not the realities beyond. Since he was already in this reality, the conduit didn't need any dimensions. It was literally just a hole in the vessel they called a soul well that granted access to it.

Then she flexed . . . something, he wasn't sure exactly what. It almost looked like she was pulling in arcana, only without actually having a conduit to do so. The nodes were quivering in place while the threads that connected them started fading. Instead of a wall studded with nodes, it became a shimmering net, each line connecting the nodes to the ones around it.

"The matrix is a single entity. What happens to one, happens to all. The nodes are resistant to arcana by their very nature. When one becomes damaged, all must become vulnerable so that it may be repaired. This is done by gaining control of the matrix."

Yura's voice droned on as she explained each step of what she was doing, but Nym was hardly listening. There before his eyes were depths he'd never even thought to wonder if they existed. So much of what he thought he understood about magic was called into question in those moments. Tons of stuff he had read but hadn't understood in Jaspar Feldstal's journals suddenly made sense to him.

A soul well's wall held arcana by default, but it was permeable. This was what the books had meant when they talked about adding to it. It was possible to graft onto the soul well and hold more arcana without it poisoning the body, and learning how to selectively alter specific nodes in the matrix was the crucial first step.

This was no longer an exercise to regain lost ground. If Nym was right, what he learned here would set him up to become far stronger than he was a week ago. He might even be able to hold arcana indefinitely outside his soul well, depending on exactly what made the framework for the extra vessels holding it.

Nym forced his mind back to the present. He was getting what was probably a once-in-a-lifetime live demonstration of the technique he needed to master in order to heal the damaged nodes in his own matrix. Having ideas for how to further enhance his abilities down the road wouldn't do him any good if he couldn't get back to baseline.

Yura demonstrated the technique from front to finish, and even though her descriptions of what she was doing were as confusing as ever, watching it happen gave him plenty of insights into how to replicate it. "Thank you," he said after she opened her eyes. "I feel like that helped."

"It's more uncomfortable than I remembered. I do not envy you having to hold your matrix in that state so that it can heal." She shook her head while she talked, then clapped her hands. "But we're getting ahead of ourselves. Let's start again."

This time, Nym had a much better idea of what to do. Expelling arcana from his soul well to power a spell wasn't something he'd ever consciously thought about before, but it wasn't hard to do. It felt kind of like the metaphysical equivalent of dry heaving since there was no arcana, except it was one long, continuous heave. To say it was uncomfortable was a gross understatement.

He was pretty sure he'd managed it, but just in case he was wrong, it didn't hurt to ask for clarification. "I did it," Nym said. "I think. How do I tell?"

"You'll know when you've managed it," Yura told him dryly. "It's the weirdest sensation, like there's a gaping wound in you, and all your blood should be pouring out, but nothing is there."

"Oh. Uh, maybe I didn't do it then. To me if feels more like I'm throwing up, but there's nothing there. And I just keep throwing up. At least there's no nausea."

Yura thought about it while Nym continued to hold the hole open. He didn't want to call it a conduit, but he didn't have a name for it. It was no wonder people got so confused trying to learn to do this. Conduits were superficially the same but for a fundamentally different purpose. He shuddered to think how long it would have taken him to figure out what Yura was trying to explain if he didn't have the ability to watch her demonstrate.

He wondered if he could develop some sort of divination that allowed others to see what he saw. He already knew a spell to show auras that allowed mages to see when another mage was leaking arcana from their soul well. He'd seen all sorts of diagnostic spells that helped mages determine the extent of physical injuries. The spells that Professor Langdon had used went beyond that and looked at his timeline and memories. There had to be a way to replicate what he did naturally.

"I don't really know how to confirm if you've done it right, other than to start working on the next step and see if you can do it," Yura said finally. "I didn't really expect to get past this point. Your description of what you feel is similar to mine but not exactly the same."

"And the next step is learning to feel the matrix itself so I can . . . turn it off, I guess?"

"More like suppress it so that it can be changed. In this case, changed means repaired. You'll need to be able to open a conduit into the soul well and also suppress the essential function of your matrix and hold it that way for as long as possible so it can start to heal naturally or so that a healer with the ability to cast third-circle spells can help speed it up."

Nym winced. "I didn't know I needed a master healer."

"That's why this takes so long to recover from. Unless your family is filthy rich, good luck even finding a master healer, let alone one who's willing to work on you for months until you're fully recovered.

It sounded like Nym had saved himself at most a few weeks with his shortcut. Then again, he'd need to see the rest of the process before he knew for sure. Everyone told him it was impossible to work on this himself, but he could actually see what he was doing. He might be able to use that to recover in some other way.

Or maybe he was just grasping at straws, hoping for an easy solution that didn't result in a year spent with his magic crippled. He didn't have enough money to afford treatments back when he'd thought any old healer could help. Now that he knew he needed a rare and powerful healer to fix him, there was no chance of getting back on his feet quickly using the standard treatment.

For now though, he was getting help for free. If he was lucky, he'd get to the point where he could naturally regenerate over the next few days and skip the expensive lessons. If he was frugal with his remaining funds, he could last quite a while. Perhaps he'd use the times to study runes more seriously. That was a skill that didn't require arcana to craft, only to empower.

Yura started speaking again, drawing his attention back to the present. "Now, nodes really only have two states. There's the default one, where they repel arcana and keep it contained to your soul well, and there's the one you're trying to achieve, where they are soft and malleable so that the damaged ones can be reformed properly. Switching between them is like flexing a muscle you don't have, so it's going to be a challenge to learn to do that."

The headache hadn't gone away. If anything, it was worse.

CHAPTER TWENTY

The week went by slowly, with Nym spending most of his time hidden away in his room. Yura would stop by twice a day to check on his progress, and occasionally he'd need a break and just walk around the outpost. Otherwise he barely showed his face except to get food.

His efforts weren't without fruit, but he did not progress as much as he wanted. Opening a hole in his soul well was unpleasant, a feeling he never got used to. He did manage to flip the state of his matrix so that the damaged nodes could heal, but no one had told him how absolutely exhausting it would be. He could only hold it for a few minutes at a time before the nodes reverted back to their normal state.

Despite all assurances to the contrary, he was making progress on flexing part of the matrix. It was nowhere near accurate enough for what he wanted, but he could narrow it down so that only half of it switched. That made it easier to hold it longer, and he felt just a little bit smug that he'd so quickly managed something they'd said was basically impossible.

He squashed that smug feeling immediately. Right now, he had no magic whatsoever. He was entirely dependent on the goodwill of the soldiers around him. If Captain Lygan gave the order to throw him out of the outpost, it would be good fortune and nothing else that kept him alive. He had *nothing* to be smug about, and looking back on it, he was grateful he hadn't hurt himself like this fighting the hive queen. He'd have just died out there with no one to save him.

Feeling a bit humbler, Nym got back to work. By the time the new soldiers arrived at the outpost, he'd practiced enough to work on a small portion of the matrix but still not enough to isolate the damaged nodes. It was so much easier to learn when he could see what was working and what wasn't. Nym was confident he could continue to refine his ability, given enough time.

What he'd already learned would have to be enough for now. With Yura's final reminder that the damaged nodes would only heal when he held them in a malleable state, and to do that as often as he could, Nym left with the convoy of soldiers to return to the forward base.

The mood in the outpost hadn't much improved over the last week, and it was a somber procession that marched home. They moved single file, marching through the trees with heads on a swivel and weapons in hand. Nym was near the back, nervous with each step and watching the boughs overhead for ambushes. Without his night vision spell, it was much scarier. He couldn't tell if those shadowy patches were empty or not.

They did all make it back without incident. Nym would have liked to retrieve his pack, but it was with the Earth Shapers in the hut they'd built at the third outpost. There wasn't much in that pack, but it did contain all his money and a few books, which he needed for obvious reasons.

It only took a few quick questions to determine that he was completely cut off from the outpost. There was no way anyone was letting him tag along with them to go there, no one was going to carry a letter he might draft if he managed to beg the supplies to do so, and despite his at times questionable judgment, Nym was not stupid enough to try the trek on his own.

That left the slower but much safer option: returning to Ebalsan and asking Analia for help. There wasn't anyone who'd escort him to the third outpost, but wagons full of supplies and people came and went from forward command every day. Nym hitched a ride with one, thankful that he wouldn't have to walk.

"What's a kid like you doing out here anyway?" the soldier who'd agreed to give him a ride asked once Nym had climbed up onto the bench at the front of the wagon.

"I'm a mage. I was working as a freelancer, but I got involved in that ghoul raid on the ninth outpost and hurt myself."

"Ah, and you're short on cash to see the healer, huh?"

"Something like that," Nym said. "I've got a friend in town I'm going to see."

"Well, you're looking alright, so it must not be too bad."

"It's internal. I can't use magic anymore."

The soldier gave him a sideways look. "That's rough, buddy."

"Yeah. They told me it would take a long time to heal. I've got to see what my options are."

The soldier was chattier than Nym wanted, but since he was giving Nym a ride, it was only polite to engage with him. Eventually, the soldier seemed to run out of steam, and they lapsed into what was for Nym a very welcome and comfortable silence. He watched the trees go by somewhat apprehensively, but they were behind the wall now, and the chances of running into a ghoul were significantly slimmer.

Hours and miles rolled by, and Nym passed the time trying to further master control of his matrix. Being able to see what worked and what didn't was an incalculable advantage, and even with that, he was still frustrated by his overall lack of progress. He reminded himself repeatedly that he was progressing quite quickly by normal standards, but he didn't intend to spend a year unable to use magic.

It was evening by the time he made it to the Silver Gilder and knocked on Analia's door. There was no answer. "Of course she's out," he muttered, scrubbing his face with his hands. "That's bad timing."

"What's bad timing?" Analia asked from behind him.

Nym jumped and spun in place to see her standing there, a book in one hand and a plate balanced on the other. She regarded him quizzically. "You look . . . off. What's going on?"

"Let's talk in private," Nym said.

"So I'm pretty much screwed unless we come into a lot of cash and find a master mage who's specialized in healing," Nym finished up.

"It's kind of impressive that you managed to damage three different nodes at once," Analia said. "Incredibly stupid of you but weirdly impressive. That must have hurt quite a bit."

Nym just stared at her. It wasn't like he'd done it on purpose.

"Alright, well, the good news is that I can let Ophelia know you're not dead. The crew's all been worried about you for days. I'll craft a message spell to send to her and let her know we need the money from your pack. It might be a week or two until you get it, but I've still got plenty of shields."

"Any ideas on how I'm going to survive for the next however many months?" he asked. Hopefully it was just months and not a full year.

"You're really asking the wrong girl if you think I know how to earn money without using magic."

"Oh. Right. Damn it. What do we do then?"

"Do your rehabilitation exercises for now. Maybe Ophelia will know what to do. I'll ask if she has any advice. If not, we'll count up what we've got for funds and figure it out."

Nym paced around while he thought, or rather, he tried to. Analia's room was somehow even more packed with books than the last time he'd seen it, though they did seem to be mostly new titles. In fact, quite a few of the ones he remembered looking at were missing. "Did you sell off some of your books?" he asked.

"I didn't have much choice. There just wasn't enough room, and I was already done with them."

There were a few books Nym was interested in looking through that appeared to be gone now, but he supposed that was his own fault for not asking her to set them aside for him. The idea that she'd sell them when she was done with them had never crossed his mind. He eyed up the new stacks, looking to see if there was anything he needed.

"I don't suppose you've got anything left in here about healing?" he asked. "I might as well have something to study while I'm recovering, and I was told there's a lot of nonmagical stuff to learn about anatomy."

"There's still a few. Let me look . . ."

Analia dug through the piles for a bit, eventually coming up with four thin books for him. "Thanks," he said, skimming through them. Two were on anatomy, one was on various illnesses, and one on diagnostic spells. That last one would have to remain hypothetical for him until he actually regained the ability to use magic.

"I'll send the message to Ophelia right away. You need some money to get a room, and we'll talk in the morning?"

"That sounds good. I hate to ask, but maybe some extra for a meal? I haven't eaten all day."

Analia dug into a satchel sitting on her bed and pulled out a handful of shields. "This should be enough for a night."

"Analia, this is enough for close to a month."

"Well good," she said. "Plenty of time for you to get your own money back. Though where you're going to find an inn that'll take you on for less than two shields a week . . . I just assumed you'd stay here."

"How . . . How much are you paying for this? This room is not that nice."

Nym was almost afraid to hear the answer. Even knowing that she'd managed to tap into her family's coffers to cover her expenses again, the frugal part of his soul cringed every time he saw her spending way too much money.

"Three shields a week. It comes with access to their bathhouse and two meals a day."

"That . . . is not bad actually. Maybe I will get a room here."

It was a little pricier than usual, but Nym could definitely use a bath. Analia had been polite about it, but he knew he stank, and he'd caught her crinkling her nose a few times while they talked. It was one of the reasons he'd remaining standing instead of claiming bed space to sit on. No need to have the stink linger in her furniture.

A quick trip downstairs and an exchange of coins for a key was all it took for Nym to get a room across the hall. He deposited several books he was interested in on his bed, and Analia also loaded him down with about thirty more books she was interested in but didn't have room for to be piled up in the corner. Then he got a meal, hit the baths, and retired for the night.

It got too dark to read before he could really get started, which was frustrating because a light spell was so easy, but he just couldn't do it now. Instead, he went back to work on his matrix. It was an unpleasant task, but it didn't require a light source to perform, so it was work on that or sleep. It needed to be done, and he wasn't tired yet.

There was a knock on the door, and he heard Analia say, "Nym? Are you still awake?"

He got up and opened the door to find her holding a book. "I found another book on med—wait, why are you sitting in the dark?"

"No magic," he told her.

"Oh, right. Uh . . . I can empower some light runes for you."

"That . . . would be very helpful. Thank you."

They set about writing the rune sequences on sheets of paper, which wouldn't last very long, but it was a cheap enough way to get a few hours of light when he needed it. Analia left him with the new book, and with a source of light to read by, Nym started diving into the world of human anatomy.

An hour later, he put the book down with a sigh and closed his eyes. That damn headache was back again.

CHAPTER TWENTY-ONE

Nym's personal library grew faster than his ability to read it. Just about every single book was a hand-me-down from Analia, but he wasn't going to complain about that. He focused heavily on books he could learn from without actually doing magic, and so the majority of his time was spent reading about medical anatomy and diagnostics interpretation, rune magic sequences, ritual magic, and conduit theory.

Healing and rune magic had a lot of prerequisite knowledge to be mastered before ever casting a spell, so Nym felt like he was building a good foundation for once he was able to cast magic again. Ritual magic also had a lot of ground to cover in terms of generally accepted standards when combining magic with others. There were practical portions he couldn't work on at the moment, but there was still a wealth of knowledge waiting there.

Finally, conduit theory was an unexpected gem. It turned out that while he wasn't able to pull arcana into his soul well, he could make a conduit just fine. Analia had somehow procured a rare and likely ruinously expensive book that provided philosophies and exercises regarding the creation of better, stronger, faster conduits, as well as a fair bit of musing about reaching the third layer.

It was the closest Nym could get to casting actual magic, even if it was a pale substitute. Without the ability to practice conduits, he would have gone crazy within days. In a society where a significant minority had access to at least first-circle magic, it was impossible to go anywhere without being reminded of it.

They had no luck finding a healer capable of casting third-circle spells. Nym was not surprised by that, especially not considering how many of the regular healers were currently working military contracts to keep soldiers on the front lines in fighting shape. That did unfortunately mean that Nym had no real choice but to keep fixing his matrix the slow way.

He did find a passage in one of the books Analia gave him that detailed the condition. Unfortunately, it confirmed everything he'd already been told, including that the only way for it to heal naturally was to hold the matrix nodes in a malleable state so that they could slowly revert back to their default condition. He did find that the year average assumed about two to three hours a day of treatment time, and since he was able to do almost double that, he figured he could cut his estimate down to six months instead.

The book told him it was best to do it in cycles of twenty minutes malleable, twenty minutes static, as there was only so much reshaping the node could retain as it switched back and forth. There were some complicated charts he could follow to optimize his time even further, but they required him to see a healer for some diagnostic spells to confirm which path worked best for him personally. Nym didn't understand half of what they were saying, but he hoped to figure it out as he studied more.

There were only so many hours in a row he could stuff his brain with new information. Between that and working on repairing his matrix, Nym used up probably half of his day. The rest was spent looking for work. Without his magic, options were severely limited, but he found a job at a bakery helping stock stands for the day's goods. It required him to be awake well before the sun came up, but since he lacked the ability to create his own light, he'd been going to sleep earlier and earlier anyway.

The work didn't pay much, but it helped to offset the cost to stay at the inn by six shims a week. Any little bit helped, considering he was living on Analia's charity. She'd gotten a response from Ophelia saying they'd be in town soon, and he was eagerly awaiting the visit, both because he wanted to see the rest of his friends and because he wanted to recover the funds stowed away in his pack.

It was late afternoon when the anticipated knock at his door finally came. Nym scrambled to open it, nearly tripping over a small stack of books on the floor. On the other side, Ophelia was looking at him with amusement. She opened her mouth, but before she could say anything, Nomick shoulder checked her out of the way. He and his brother shoved their way into the room and grabbed hold of Nym's shoulders.

"You're alive!" they said in unison.

"Don't ever do that again," Monick added in a high-pitched tone.

"Had us worried half to death," Nomick said with the same pitch.

Ophelia reached out from behind and grabbed both of them by their ears. She dragged them back and pitched them out into the hall. "Don't mind those two idiots. They've been making fun of me ever since Analia's message reached us."

She leveled a glare at them, which they ignored as they pushed their way back in. "It's been so terrible," one of them said, still in his Ophelia-impression voice. "Just awful!"

"Shut it, you idiots," Ophelia snapped. "Come on, let's go get lunch."

"Where's Bildar?" Nym asked.

"Waiting for us downstairs."

"Let's get going then?" Nym asked.

"In a minute. First, I think you've been missing this," Ophelia said. She pulled out Nym's pack form behind her back.

His eyes lit up when he saw it. "Yes! It has literally everything I own in it."

Monick made a show of looking around the room. "Seems to be a lot of stuff here," he said.

Nym waved him off. "This stuff isn't mine. All the books are Analia's. She's been raiding every bookstore she can find and doesn't have enough room for her library."

He pulled the money pouch out of the bag, separated three shields from it, and put the rest away. The pack was slid under his bed and hidden behind another pile of books.

"Maybe you should consider opening a bank account," Ophelia suggested.

Nym just laughed and replied, "I don't think I've got quite that much money. Come on, let's go."

They found the last two members of their group down by the door, waiting for them. Bildar gave Nym a once-over when he saw him and nodded. "How are you feeling?" he asked once they were all together.

"I'm trying to make the best of it," Nym told him. "I've been doing a lot of reading on stuff that doesn't require magic to learn, trying to set myself up with a good foundation."

"Very motivated, huh? You've got time now, I guess," Bildar told him. He blew out a frustrated sigh. "The army really screwed you over there. From what I heard, that outpost would have been wiped out without your help. The least they could do is get a healer to help speed up your recovery."

"They did have a mage there teach me how to manipulate my matrix," Nym said. "That saved me a lot of money not having to pay for lessons."

"Did they? I don't think that made it into the official reports."

"I guess maybe it wasn't something official? The captain just said he was assigning a mage to help me who'd had the same thing happen to her once. She was really helpful. I never would have even thought to try some of the stuff she told me about."

Analia guided them to a restaurant that probably cost more than Nym wanted to spend, but just once as a special treat to himself, he went with it. He hadn't seen his friends in close to three weeks. Lucky for the group, they were between the lunch and dinner rushes, and the place was mostly empty. They got two tables pushed together and started putting in orders.

"How bad is it, really?" Ophelia asked after the waiter walked away.

"Pretty bad," Nym admitted. "They said a year to fix it, but I think I can do it in under six months. I guess if you can learn to manipulate individual nodes instead of having to shift the entire matrix, it makes it a lot quicker. I'm working on it, but it's a process, you know?"

"I don't, actually," she said. "This is a problem most mages never have to worry about. You have to have a significantly larger-than-average-sized soul well for this to happen. Normal mages like me just get arcana poisoning and stop using magic long before we hit the point of matrix destabilization."

"Okay, well . . . Pretend like you know anyway and feel bad for me," Nym said severely.

She laughed. "I do feel bad for you. I just don't know the process. Still, six months is a lot better than a year, if you're right. And you're smart . . . most of the time . . . You'll figure out how to shave more time off that. By the time you're ready to go again, summer will barely be over. We can finally take the time to teach you earth magic right."

That estimate seemed overly optimistic to Nym, but he hoped she was right. "I'll do my best to meet that deadline," he told her. "I kind of want to learn healing magic too. There's a lot to learn, but it's so useful."

"Oh? Healing is a very profitable calling for any mage. What sparked the interest?" she asked.

"Mostly searching for a way to fix myself," he admitted. "It can be overwhelming, but I have the time right now to learn the base knowledge before I get into the spell work."

"What's this?" Bildar said. "You're betraying the Earth Shapers and becoming a healer instead? For shame! Shame, I say. But, uh, we'd get a discount if we needed to get patched up, right?"

Nym snorted. "I'd charge you double."

Jokes flew around the table while they ate. Nomick caught Nym up on their progress constructing the wall, which they were expecting to last another month just to meet up with the other segments and fully encircle the center of the forest. After that, the plan was to start cutting it in a grid pattern and clear out the undead one section at a time.

"But what about the thing in the middle that caused all of it?" Nym asked.

"I guess that's Analia's father's special project. It's all still pretty secret, but it's supposed to be the thing that ends all of this. Everything the army is doing now is containment and cleanup. They're just trying to keep the whole thing from escalating out of control. Either way, lots of walls and new outposts means lots of work for us."

"Guess I should have stayed with the crew instead of going for those high-risk jobs," Nym said.

"You're young. You'll recover, and you have lots of time," Bildar told him. It probably would have sounded a lot wiser if he didn't immediately start choking on his wine. "Ack! That went down wrong."

The Earth Shapers did their best to cheer him up, so Nym smiled and played along. They eagerly predicted his swift return to action, decried the army for abandoning him, and promised to lavish him with training in the field of elemental earth magic to entice him away from becoming a healer instead. He honestly wasn't sure how much they were joking about that last one, but everyone laughed, so he went along.

As the afternoon wore on, they had to part ways. The Earth Shapers had supplies to pick up, and then they had a long, flightless trip back to the sixteenth outpost, where they were now stationed. Analia decided that she had more shopping to do, but Nym was ready to head back to the Silver Gilder. He walked back alone, and once he was back in his room, he locked his door and slid down to sit on the floor with a sigh.

It had been a fun visit in a lot of ways. He'd truly missed his friends. It also served to remind him that, for the time being, he was no longer a mage. He spent a few minutes sitting with his back to the door feeling sorry for himself, then he climbed to his feet and got back to work.

CHAPTER TWENTY-TWO

Weeks went by, and Nym's money slowly dwindled. He worked most mornings at the bakery, gradually gaining more responsibilities and with them a very slight increase to his pay. It still wasn't enough to balance out the cost of the inn, and he was strongly considering switching to somewhere cheaper or even seeing if he could find a place to just rent long-term. The only thing stopping him was that every time he brought the topic up, Analia told him in no uncertain terms that he wasn't allowed to leave.

With his spare time, he continued studying, though he was steadily growing more and more frustrated by the fact that he couldn't actually cast any of the spells he found. He theoretically knew dozens of new spells thanks to his enforced downtime, but since he couldn't practice casting any of them, he wasn't confident that he could use them.

The only thing keeping him sane at this point was his work with conduits. Thanks in large part to his ability to see what was supposed to be invisible, he was actually making good progress with that. The second layer was littered with hard points to go around, but all the practice allowed him to deftly weave the conduit where it needed to go. The only problem was that he couldn't find the far end of the second layer.

Nym revisited his own understanding on conduits over and over again as he read through the philosophies espoused in the guidebook Analia had found. Each time he iterated on his conduit, it got a little stronger. Hours were spent forging it into something truly formidable. Nym was sure he was close, ready to break through to the third layer any day.

A knock at his door brought him back to reality. "Nym?" Analia said. "Are you ready?"

As a surprise, she'd found a healer to examine him and let him know his progress. Nym had spent a month and was optimistically predicting another five, but he wanted to know what an expert thought. It seemed like a frivolous expense to him, but she'd insisted once he'd confessed the desire to her and declared in no uncertain terms that she would be paying for it.

He opened his eyes and sat up on his bed, knocking over two books that were sitting open near his legs. His room was now every bit as overrun with books as Analia's, so many that he hadn't even read some of the titles. Considering he spent most of his days reading now, it was truly impressive how many books she'd gotten her hands on in the last month. It was like she was trying to rebuild her father's library from scratch.

He stepped over a few precarious piles and made his way to the door. "I'm good. Let's go," he said to her after opening it.

The walk wasn't a long one, but it was hot out in the street. Summer was in full swing now, and Nym wished he could still cast a thermal barrier just to keep the heat out. He would have doused himself with water to cool off, then just maintained that temperature while he walked around. It would have been glorious.

Walking next to him, Analia asked, "Are you daydreaming about that heat-ward spell you invented again?"

"Thermal barrier."

"Sure, that. So are you?"

". . . Yes. It's sooo hot out here."

"If I have to suffer, you have to suffer."

"I could put it on both of us," he told her.

"Wait, really?" she asked. "I didn't know that. Teach me the spell and I'll keep us both nice and cool."

"That's a good idea," he said. "I'll start sketching out how to put together the construct when we get back."

They had a brief discussion about some of his other spells, but other than the lightning-bolt spell he'd already tried to teach her, she wasn't particularly interested in anything in his repertoire. Lightning bolt was powerful, but it required air and fire to work, and it was difficult to aim. She'd managed a spark or two but nothing that would actually be useful in a fight.

"Where is this healer at again?" Nym asked. "The neighborhood is starting to look a little rough."

"It shouldn't be too much farther," she said, doubt in her voice. "I'm not lost, I don't think."

"How very reassuring," he quipped.

"No, see, it's right there," she said, pointing down the street and grabbing onto him. "That's the clinic."

"Alright, alright! I see it. Stop grabbing my arm!"

Nym jerked himself free of Analia's clutches and followed along behind her. He'd grown taller than her at some point and looked older by at least two or three years now. Not for the first time, he wondered if he'd age right into the ground in the next twenty years. He silently vowed to himself, again, to learn enough magic to figure out what had been done to him and how to fix it.

In some ways, it was nice though. When he'd looked ten, nobody took him seriously. Now he looked like a teenager, which came with its own set of drawbacks, like a patchy and itchy beard just starting to grow in. But adults gave him a lot less grief over being independent. The downside was that they were also a lot less likely to go out of their way to help him.

The inside of the clinic was just as shabby as the outside. There was a threadbare couch near the entrance, complete with bloodstains. Next to it was a wooden table with a missing leg. A tree branch had been wedged under it to keep it steady, but it wasn't trimmed to the right length, so the two other legs no longer touched the floor. Two chairs were set up against the far wall, both sturdy and clean.

"Why are we here?" Nym whispered at Analia.

"I was told the healer worked cheap," she said. "I'm . . . I'm not very liquid anymore. I put as much on the family line of credit as I could, but some things I needed to use actual shields for."

Nym immediately felt like a jerk. Of course he knew that she could get more money by pawning things she'd charged on the family name, but she'd lose half or more of the value that way. It hadn't occurred to him that she might be struggling in some ways simply because she always had a few new books every day.

"I'm sorry," he said. "I didn't realize . . . Why don't we just go?"

"No! This is important. You need to know how bad the damage is."

"Just . . . If money is this tight, we don't really need to do this. I'll get better eventually."

Their conversation was cut off by an old man shuffling into the room. "Hello there. My name is Faro," he said. "Are you in need of some help?"

He was at least seventy years old, or possibly older considering his specialty was healing magic and he probably took very good care of himself. He was no taller than Nym and moved with that slow deliberation of people who were very weak or very sick. The healer had an easy smile as he peered curiously at the two kids.

"Uh, no, I think—" Nym started to say.

"Yes," Analia cut him off. "My stubborn friend here is recovering from a matrix destabilization, and we want to check on his progress."

"I see," Faro said. "I can do that for you. Just grab one of those chairs and have a seat right here. This will take about five minutes and cost you four shims."

"That's it? That's really cheap," Nym said.

The healer laughed. "When I was a young man, I was all afire to dazzle the world with my skills and be paid handsomely for it. As you get older, you tend to mellow out. I got married, had kids, then grandkids, and great grandkids. Now I just try to keep this neighborhood in as good a shape as I can. What use is a healer who charges so much no one can afford to visit?"

"That's true, I guess." Nym looked around at the shabby furnishings. "Maybe you could charge a bit more though."

Faro's eyes twinkled. "Are you offering to pay more?"

"If I could, I would," Nym told him seriously. "Since I can't use magic now, I'm out of work. I've been helping out at a bakery to slow down the drain on my savings. But this, what you're doing here, that's a good thing."

"Well, thank you, but the price is still four shims, no matter how much of a smooth talker you are." The healer winked at Nym. "Now, let's get a look at you and see how you're doing."

Nym dragged a chair over and sat down in front of the healer, who'd pulled a small book out of his pocket and was flipping through it. "Haven't had a matrix-destabilization case in twenty years," he muttered to himself, making a mark on the page with a pencil. "Six months of this craziness and I'm up to a dozen."

The healer started channeling arcana, still muttering while he did so, and peered at Nym. "I think you're my youngest patient yet for this particular issue. Do you want to talk about it?"

"No," Nym said quietly. "It was a bad day. I almost died."

"Ah. Quite understandable. I'll just get on with it then so as not to take up your day. I'm sure a lovely young couple like yourselves has better things to do than listen to an old man natter on."

Nym blinked, then glanced back at Analia. She just shrugged in response. "Uh . . . Thanks," Nym said.

Faro didn't appear to have heard him. He was standing there, swaying slightly on his heels, and staring off into nothing while arcana swirled around him. His mouth worked, but no sounds came out. Long seconds stretched on and on, with no change. Just when Nym was about to say something, the old man snapped out of it.

"Are you alright?" Analia asked.

"Hmm? Me?" the healer asked.

"Yes, you. You were just standing there."

"Oh, yes, sorry. I should have warned you. Diagnostic spells dump a lot of information into your brain, and I'm getting up there in years. Sometimes it takes me a bit to sort through it. Though, in your case, it took me a bit longer to figure out what I was looking at."

"What? Is something wrong?"

Faro hesitated for a second, then shook his head. "Easier to just show you, I think."

More arcana flowed into the aura around him, and an illusion appeared over the table. It depicted a sphere about the size of Nym's head made up of a hundred little glowing balls connected by wires. "This is a textbook illustration of the matrix that surrounds a soul well. Each of these nodes repels arcana that gets too close to it, and even though it's more empty space than not, the light around each one creates a solid wall that keeps arcana inside the soul well."

The illusion disappeared, and a new one replaced it. "This is matrix destabilization," he said. This time, a few of the balls had cracks running through them, and the lights around them flickered or disappeared completely. "It's like having a leaky bucket. You'll give yourself arcana poisoning much faster, maybe even immediately if the damage is bad enough, and it hurts like hell to channel arcana in this state."

A third illusion appeared in its place. This was kind of a sphere, except distorted out of shape, and the balls were all different sizes. Some had hairline cracks running through them, but none of them were as damaged as the ones from the second illusion. There was still wire connecting them, but that too had been twisted and stretched to accommodate the uneven spacing and size. "This is your matrix," the healer said. "And I have no clue how you got it in this shape."

CHAPTER TWENTY-THREE

Nym just stared at the illusion blankly for a good twenty seconds. It looked nothing like what he saw when he looked into his own soul well, but he wasn't going to tell the healer that. Finally, he asked, "What does this mean? Am I not healing right?"

"I'm not really sure what exactly you're supposed to be healing from," Faro told him. "There are some small cracks on a few of these. Look here. This whole section has some. Then there are these large ones here that are completely out of proportion with the rest. If this is matrix destabilization, it's the strangest case of it I've ever seen."

"Are you . . . Are you saying I was misdiagnosed?" Nym asked. Part of him hoped the answer was yes, but another part was afraid that if it was, then whatever the real condition was would somehow be worse.

Faro just shrugged and shook his head. "I'm sorry. I don't know what's wrong with your matrix. It looks like it should still hold arcana, so I'd recommend testing that with a very small amount before you leave. But otherwise, I'm going to have to refer you to a healer I know who specializes in soul-well abnormalities. You're actually in luck there. He works with the army and isn't too far away right now, though he is also very busy for obvious reasons, so it may be a few weeks before you can see him."

Nym heard, but he wasn't really listening to anything after the healer said his soul well would hold arcana. Immediately, he forged a conduit to the first layer, then paused. He hadn't cast a single spell in weeks now because he was afraid of damaging his matrix further. The healer said he should test it, but what if he was wrong? There was only one easy way to find out. Nym hardened his resolve, pulled on the arcana, and let it start to fill him.

It felt . . . weird, hard to describe, but definitely not normal. It didn't hurt at least. That was an improvement over the last time he'd touched arcana. Hesitantly, Nym reached out to the other chair and wrapped it in telekinesis. It floated in the air, straining his arms somewhat with its heavy, solid weight.

He couldn't stop himself from grinning. After weeks of holding himself back, he was casting spells again. "It works! It doesn't hurt," he said.

Second-layer arcana flooded into him, and he floated up into the air. He frowned in concentration, pulled in more arcana, and started weaving it into something complex. Thirty seconds later, snow started to fill the air inside the clinic.

"Hey now!" the old healer protested. "I know the place is a bit shabby, but let's not make it any worse."

"Oh, this feels wrong now," Nym said, ignoring the healer. The spell went off, but he was having problems pulling enough arcana through his soul well to keep it powered. He barely had time to realize it before his flight spell cut off and he fell to the floor, only to stumble and land on his butt.

"Oooowwww," he groaned. "Something isn't working right still."

"No, I imagine not. But I must insist that you dispel this snow-creating spell immediately."

"Oh! Right, sorry."

Nym basked in the coolness for just a moment longer, then stopped feeding the construct arcana. He immediately cast a thermal barrier to keep himself nice and cool. Grudgingly, he extended it to Analia. The strain that generated surprised him, but it was within his limits.

"Okay, so it looks like I *can* still use arcana, including my biggest, most complicated spells. But I'm struggling to keep things empowered now? I can't use it as fast as I can pull it in."

Simple hydrokinesis pushed his ability to pull arcana out of his soul well to its limits. He swept up all the snow, compacted it into a tight ball, and sent it out the window. Not two months ago, what he was doing wouldn't have been enough for him to really even take notice. He shook his head. It was still better than nothing. And it didn't hurt anymore.

"Hey!" Analia said. "Pay attention!"

"What? Oh! I'm sorry."

The healer was talking, but Nym had stopped listening. He was so busy testing his new limits, comparing them to his old ones, and trying to figure out what had changed, that he'd ignored everything else.

Faro sighed. "It's fine. You've just been given good news, of a sort. I understand that you're excited. But understand that this does not mean you are healthy or that you should continue to use magic. There is something very off with your matrix, and I don't know what it is. I've sent a message spell to my friend, a healer named Doliar Kents. If he agrees to meet with you, he'll no doubt be able to tell you a bit more than I could. I am afraid he'll be rather more expensive as well."

"This has been a good day," Nym said, still smiling.

The healer just sighed and shook his head. Then he turned to talk to Analia: "When he comes back to us, please let him know what I said. And please write down the best way to contact you so I can let you know when Master Healer Kents is available."

Analia took care of those details while Nym poked around at his soul well. It didn't look anything like the illusion Faro had crafted of it, but he supposed that that was just how the divination had organized the information it had given to the healer. He could finally see what the inside of his soul well looked like when he was connecting a conduit to it, filling it with arcana, and expelling it to form spells. Maybe he could figure out why he was having such a hard time releasing arcana at high speeds.

The pair stepped back out onto the hot street a few minutes later, Analia carefully stepping around the small puddle of melted snow near the door as they headed back to the Silver Gilder. "You did the thermal-barrier thing?" she asked, looking down at her hand.

"Yep. It's so much nicer."

"It is," she agreed. With a sigh, she added, "You should probably stop now. No license."

"No one's going to see this," he protested.

"Probably not, but money's tight. We can't afford the fine just in case someone's got an aura-reading spell going and notices."

"I guess," Nym said. He let the spell fail and immediately regretted it when the heat hit him. From the look on Analia's face, he knew she was feeling the same way. He smirked at her and said, "You asked for this."

"Hush. Maybe we should look into getting licenses soon. I think I could probably pass now."

"Ehhhhh, maybe. I want to figure out what's up with this weird matrix thing and get that fixed first. I need to see that other guy, um . . . Dal . . . Dar . . . *D* something."

"Doliar," Analia supplied.

"Yeah, him."

"You're so scatterbrained today," she said. She grabbed his arm and hugged it as they walked. "But I'm glad you're in a good mood."

Nym blinked and looked down at her. "Uh . . . Yeah . . . What's . . . um . . ."

She looked over at him, her face the picture of innocence. "Is there something wrong?"

"No?"

"Good, come on. I'm hungry."

And she dragged him to a restaurant for lunch that thankfully was much cheaper than the places she preferred to frequent. It still set them back one shield two for the meal, but Nym didn't complain about the price. It was, after all, a fantastic day.

Analia wanted to talk when they got back to the Silver Gilder, but Nym begged off, saying he was tired and needed to make sure everything was alright with his soul well. They said their goodbyes, and each went to their own rooms.

"What was with her?" he muttered to himself.

He didn't want to offend her, but she'd been weirdly in his space all afternoon. All he'd really wanted was to get back so he could go over the list of spells he'd jotted down to practice. There were more than fifty of them on there, everything from a scent-tracking spell to a wide-range scry to a few more offensive options. His time on the ninth outpost's walls had taught him the need for that.

He'd focused heavily on spells to combat undead, expanding greatly on that thin primer volume Analia had found for him, but there'd been enough run-ins with human opponents that he'd picked up nonlethal subjugation spells like paralysis, blindness, and smothering aura, and then he'd rounded his arsenal out with a few elemental attacks like hailstones and crushing earth, though those had been much harder to find. Apparently, that kind of magic was heavily restricted.

But it was all academic with no practical experience, and Nym resolved to fix that immediately. A lot of his new spells couldn't be practiced from his bed, but there were a few that he could work on. Additionally, he wanted a chance to really get in there and study what was going on in his soul well when he used magic.

And none of that was even considering his growing knowledge base in anatomy and medicine. He wasn't deluding himself into thinking he could rightfully be called a healer, but there were another three or four spells in that category he was eager to try. He was looking forward to refining his pain-blocker spell now that he had some official materials to guide him, and he'd picked up two first-circle spells as well: quick regeneration and purge. The first sped up natural healing time, and the second was used to expel ingested toxins, which was a fancy way of saying it made people throw up.

Nym wasn't actually that eager to try that last one out, though it did work on *other* people. He wished he'd known how to do it back in Palmara when he'd been dealing with that stuck-up rich kid, Amos.

Nym used telekinesis to start pulling specific books out of the stacks, the ones that contained the spells he most wanted to practice. He flipped the first one open to the page he'd marked down on his list and started reading. He wanted the directions to be fresh in his mind before he actually tried to cast it.

* * *

Analia didn't slam the door behind her. That would be unladylike and unbecoming of her. But she wanted to. "Boys are dumb," she huffed out.

It could have been a nice afternoon, but no, Nym had had his head in the clouds the whole time. He didn't notice any of her hints. She'd had to literally grab onto his arm to get him to pay any real attention to her. That's what she got for listening to Ophelia's advice, at least when it was about Nym.

Ophelia also had plenty to say on the subject of magic, and there, Analia was an eager student. While she didn't see herself ever going heavily into the field of earth magic, it never hurt to round out her skill set, and the older woman knew a remarkable number of spells unrelated to her specialty. The amount of practical knowledge she'd gained about rune sequences in a mere month of casual conversation easily bested a year of book learning.

Sure, Ophelia was heavily specialized, but the foundation was the same no matter what kind of rune sequence she wanted to write. Some of the things Analia had learned, her books had never even hinted at. Some of those things were flat-out wrong, according to the books, but they worked anyway.

She sat down and started mentally composing a message to the older woman about the healer's news. The Earth Shapers would definitely want to know, and it wasn't like the idiot boy was going to have the presence of mind to tell them. Sometimes she wondered why she bothered trying with him.

She should take some time to teach him the message spell though. It only had a range of a few miles before it started getting expensive and cumbersome to cast, but it was useful in a pinch. For a range of the room across the hall, it would be easy and instantaneous and, thus, perfect. And he wouldn't be able to ignore her when she wanted to talk to him either or make the excuse that he couldn't message her back.

Analia flopped onto her bed and smiled.

CHAPTER TWENTY-FOUR

Nym stood in the shabby little clinic. A few hours earlier, Faro had sent a message to the Silver Gilder asking him to come by at his earliest convenience, and since Nym had made little progress on figuring out what he'd done wrong with fixing his matrix on his own, he was eager to see if the healer could provide him with some new clues. Unfortunately, it wasn't that kind of visit.

"Wow, this other healer must be really busy," Nym said. "Five weeks? Will the army even still be here by then?"

"If they're not," Faro said mildly, "I'm sure that means Healer Doliar is not so busy anymore and will be able to move the appointment up."

"I suppose that's fair."

"In the meantime, he sent me the diagram for another diagnostic spell he asked me to run on you. I'm not completely certain what it checks for, as it's far more complicated than anything I normally use, but it seems straightforward enough to cast, albeit quite expensive. As long as you're willing, it should give us a clearer picture of what's going on."

"Are you charging me for it?" Nym asked.

Even if he was, as long as it was something he could afford, Nym would happily pay it. His research into the subject was completely stalled. He didn't have access to the right books, didn't even know what he was even looking for, nor did he have endless finances to spend on the search.

"No, no. If anything, it'll be part of Healer Doliar's services. I'm just administering it on his behalf. If you don't want to do it now, that's fine. He'll want to do it himself when he sees you."

"Might as well get it over with then," Nym said, secretly hoping it would give him a new lead to look into.

The old healer started up the spell, which took significantly longer and also easily ten times as much arcana as the last diagnostic spell Nym had witnessed, then fell into a trance while he studied the information. Nym tried to remember if any other healer he'd seen had done that. He was pretty sure they hadn't.

Eventually, the man snapped out of it. "Huh," he said. "I don't get it, but I suppose you'd like to see?"

"If you don't mind," Nym said.

The illusion was different than the one he'd seen a week ago. This time, the nodes had different colors in addition to the odd sizes and spacing, and each one had a line of light shooting off several inches. Sometimes the lights were thicker, sometimes they were longer, and Nym couldn't really discern any pattern to that.

"What does it mean?"

"I don't know. That's just what Doliar asked me to run on you and send him the results. He outshone me a long time ago. The man's a healing genius, knows more than I ever will, and he's barely a third my age. I didn't even know this spell existed before today."

That was frustrating. He'd see if Analia had any ideas later, but between the two of them, he was far more knowledgeable about healing magic. That wasn't to say he knew a lot, just that she knew almost nothing.

"Alright, well . . . Five weeks then. I'll meet him here at your clinic?"

"Unless he tells me differently," Faro said.

"Thanks then. I guess I'll see you next month."

"So it seems. Good luck, young man. Be safe out there."

"I'll do my best," Nym promised. He had a whole new set of spells he was busy practicing now anyway. He was as safe as he could be.

It was the soft glow of arcana that woke Nym up. At first, he was confused about what he was seeing, but then he realized there were two people standing over his bed in the dark. They were using some sort of concealment spells that made them effectively invisible to his eyes but didn't extend to the auras around them.

He held very still, hoping they didn't realize he was awake until he had time to decide how he was going to respond. Double paralysis was the first option that came to mind, but that didn't actually stop someone from using magic, which these two clearly could. He had learned a sleep spell recently, but it took a few minutes to progress from alert to drowsy to passed out. Nym doubted he had that much time before they made their move.

No, it was better to flee now and put some distance between him and the intruders. He swiftly cast his scrying spell to get a look at the room, hoping the intruders had come in through the window and left it open for him. If not, he was going to need simultaneous telekinesis and flight spells. He didn't even have time to finish it and get a picture of his surroundings before they caught him.

"Target is awake and casting," one of the intruders said, lunging for Nym. He must have been using an aura-reading spell to monitor Nym or something. Nym had a split second to wonder how long they'd been looming over his bed that they'd need something like that.

The other one lunged at almost the exact same time, and both managed to catch hold of the blanket and pin Nym down under it. There was no time for subtlety after that. He summoned a gust of wind to pick up both intruders, along with a few dozen books, and slam them all into the wall. While they were distracted, he leaped for the thankfully open window and flew through it. He was free from pursuit for all of three seconds before an arcana injection lanced up from the roof of the business across the street from the inn.

Nym dipped under it while casting a night vision spell. Even with that active, it was hard to see who was shooting at him. Like the two in this room, this one also had an active concealment spell. He was so busy scanning below and behind him for attacks that he ran straight into another arcana injection coming from the front. Nym saw the flash of arcana just in time to realize what it was before it struck him.

He'd been drawing in arcana slower since he still couldn't spend it as fast as it came in. When the extra arcana hit him, it just bumped up his reserves a bit and caused a bit of a stir in his soul well since it had a foreign intent, but there was so much free space, it was easy to partition it off without it actually disrupting him. If he wasn't still half-crippled with his casting, that arcana disruption probably would have grounded him.

His forward momentum was completely arrested by a band of force slamming into his chest. Nym grunted in pain and struggled to break free, but it was like iron circling around him. Once it caught hold of him, it didn't want to move, and his flight spell couldn't force it. So Nym attacked the spell itself, but the casting mage was actively pumping arcana into it.

"Hurry up," a strained voice said below. "I don't know what he's doing, but this is way harder to hold than normal."

It wasn't a spell Nym was familiar with it, but he could see it, and he could shoot his own arcana into the gaps in the construct to start trying to pry it apart. He thought he could crack it, given enough time, but his assailants weren't going to just sit back and wait for him to figure it out. He got hit by three more arcana injections in the span of a few seconds, though only the first one stuck. The second and third ones washed over him without entering his soul well as he cut off his own magic to eliminate the vulnerability.

He fought back with targeted blindness spells, hoping that if they lost track of him, he could escape. The spells took hold, but rather than it stopping his assailants, they started using scrying magic to keep track of him instead. Nym didn't recognize the exact spell, but even from a distance he could see more than enough similarities in the construct to his own magic to know what it was.

More spells came at him from at least five mages, and Nym felt himself being overwhelmed. The threat of a barrage of arcana injections any time he tried to use his magic pinned him down and cut him off from his options. He thought he could take a few, maybe as many as four, before they started causing arcana poisoning, but his assailants were throwing that many at him every few seconds. He could only work in short bursts, and it gave the mage holding the iron-band capture spell time to reinforce it against whatever damage Nym could do.

Then they started hitting him with other spells, spells that blinded and deafened him, spells that made him feel nauseous and feverish at the same time. By the time they'd physically closed in on him up in the night sky over Ebalsan, Nym was so disoriented that he couldn't tell up from down anymore. Then the whole world pinched down on him, a feeling he hadn't felt in months.

Someone had teleported him.

Nym woke up unharmed in a small, dark room with metal walls. A single panel on one wall looked to be a door, but it had no handle. He could see the glow of arcana through a series of slits in the ceiling, but when he tried to open a conduit, he found himself blocked. It was like there was a new, incredibly dense membrane between him and the first layer, and he wasn't strong enough to push through it.

He was trapped in a mage cell.

Nym told himself to be calm, that panicking wouldn't help him. He fought to push back the fear that flooded him from finding himself squarely in the middle of a nightmare scenario. He was trapped, cut off from his magic, and it was somehow even worse than he'd expected. He had no idea who the people were who'd captured him or why they'd done it.

Every fear he'd ever had about being arrested and thrown in jail came crashing down on him all at once. He'd thought he'd escaped that fate, left the people who would be interested in him far behind. It had to be someone following him from Abilanth. His crimes were far more serious there than anything he'd done in Zoskan or Palmara. The worst he was guilty of in Thrakus was using magic without a license, and he couldn't see a squad of shadow operatives hunting him down across hundreds of miles to capture him just for that.

Whoever it was, they'd have to open the door eventually, and then he'd find out. The antimagic properties only worked as long as the door remained closed, and as soon as he could reach through the layers of reality again, he was going to set the first person he saw on fire. Then blast them with a lightning bolt. Then set them on fire some more.

Being angry helped for a little while, but hours went by, and it wasn't possible to hold on to the anger when there was nothing to do but stare at an empty wall. It drained away, along with fear, curiosity, and every other emotion that wasn't boredom. Nym was starting to wonder if that was the plan, to just leave him locked in a mage cell until he started going insane.

And then, finally, a line of light appeared on the wall with the panel. The door swung open, and the glow of arcana surrounding the mage cell went out. Nym forged his conduit immediately, only to have it rebound against the same membrane somehow. He was caught so off guard that in that moment as the door opened, he merely fumbled around.

Then there was a man standing there. He was tall, well over six feet, dressed in a combination of mage's robes and military uniform. The light coming from behind him hid his features, but Nym caught a hint of blond hair around the outline. The man looked in at him, studying him.

"I suppose I should start with an apology," the man said.

CHAPTER TWENTY-FIVE

Nym was determined to free himself while he had a chance, but when he tried to forge a conduit, he found himself once again blocked. It didn't take long to realize why. The mage cell he was in was itself inside another larger mage cell.

His escape plans destroyed before he'd even gotten started, Nym brought his attention back to the man standing in front of him, his mind catching up to the conversation. Had the man apologized?

"Who are you?" Nym asked.

"One of my overeager assistants thought you were an operational security threat and sent out a team to deal with you with rather more zeal than was necessary," the man continued, completely ignoring Nym's question. "We've since learned otherwise, of course. By then it was too late. Your own condition is completely coincidental. For that I am sorry."

"Does that mean you're letting me go?" Nym asked.

The man made it sound like this was all a big misunderstanding, but Nym wasn't so naive as to believe they'd send him on his way with a simple apology. Whatever these people were doing, they wanted it kept quiet and were serious about making sure it stayed that way. He could end up being murdered for someone else's mistake, but Nym was hoping the fact that he was still alive and talking to someone now meant they weren't going to be that extreme.

"Oh God, no. No, of course not. This actually works out rather well for me. I've been meaning to have a conversation with you anyway," the man said. He stepped back from the doorway and gestured for Nym to follow him.

"Who are you?" Nym asked again. He stepped out of the small cell he'd been trapped in to a much larger one that had been furnished to look like a sitting room. Unlike his cell, it had windows that let in light from outside. As soon as Nym got a good look at the man, he knew the answer.

They had the same shade of hair, though the man in front of him wore it longer and tied back. The nose was the same too, and though the man had the same eyes, his gaze was piercing. His lips curled up into a smirk as he studied Nym. "Yes, you know already, don't you? But it would be rude not to introduce myself. I am Lord Jaspar Feldstal, Mage-commander of the king's army at Ebalsan."

It was like looking at an older version of Bardin and not even all that much older. Despite the fact that he had to be at least fifty from what Nym understood, the man appeared to be no older than his late twenties. That wasn't unusual though. Most mages were older than they looked, although in this case it was a bit more jarring since Nym knew his son. Going just on looks, he would have said Lord Feldstal was Bardin's older brother.

Nym let himself be led to a pair of comfortably padded chairs with a small circular table between them. Lord Feldstal gestured for Nym to sit at one and took the other for himself. After situating his robes, he leaned forward and said, "I must know, young man, what are your intentions toward my daughter?"

Nym stared at him in confused shock. He didn't have intentions toward anyone. He wasn't even entirely sure what Lord Feldstal meant.

"I'm . . . sorry? My what toward your daughter?"

The man started laughing as he sat back in his chair, apparently satisfied with Nym's confusion. "I see. You have no idea then. I can see why she likes you though. She's very headstrong. That's my fault, I suppose. She was kept at home to protect her while I'm away, bored with her lessons perhaps, and here comes a boy who's adventurous, strong, smart. Well, not usually stupid perhaps. From what I've been able to gather you've made your fair share of mistakes, but then, what's the point of being young if you don't get to screw things up every now and then?"

"I . . . I guess."

"Now I'll admit I was a bit cross when I found out you were working for that rat, Valgo. God, that's a name I haven't heard in more than a decade. We went to the Academy together, you know? But then he got expelled for doing, well, much the same thing he was doing when you met him, I assume. Still, he was a useful contact when I needed materials not readily available."

"You worked with Valgo? Why did he want to steal from you then?"

"The same reason he did anything, I assume. Valgo was a man who loved money and never understood the difference between a large bank account and real, actual power. That's not to say he wasn't effective at what he did, but take a petty thief from a fallen merchant house and dress him in noble finery, and what do you get? A thief who blackmails children with manufactured evidence."

"So you're not mad about the whole breaking into your house thing?" Nym asked. At this point, he was assuming Lord Feldstal knew everything Bardin did and probably other things besides since it looked like Nym had been the subject of some sort of investigation unrelated to his dealings with the Feldstals.

"I wouldn't say I'm happy about it," he said dryly. "But the one truly responsible was Valgo, and he is quite thoroughly dead. I'm making some assumptions that it was you who did it, but the manner was consistent with the magic you used to execute several members of his gang, and he did seem quite obsessed with you.

"That having been said, there's a reason that research room was hidden. You've strained my relationship with my daughter, and I would appreciate some help repairing it. She holds you in high regard, you know? It's very unusual for her."

Nym wasn't really sure what he'd expected, but it wasn't this. He wasn't surprised that the people who finally caught him did so on the Feldstal payroll, but this man in front of him was not the Jaspar Feldstal his journals had painted him as. Nym had expected a cold, ruthless man with calculating eyes that saw the world through a dispassionate lens of gain and loss, opportunity and cost, that saw people as a resource.

Lord Feldstal was a charming, handsome man. He laughed easily and worked to set Nym at ease, at least as much as he could be in the situation he'd found himself in. Despite the fact that he'd been abducted in the middle of the night and held in an exorbitantly expensive cell, it felt more like he was being interrogated by Jaspar, father of Analia, who wanted to know all about the boy who'd been hanging out with his little girl, not Mage-Commander Feldstal who was deciding whether or not Nym would be allowed to live.

But that was exactly what was happening. He just had to keep reminding himself not to be lured in by the charming facade. Despite the smiles and easy manner being sent his way, Nym was still a prisoner. And despite his casual conversation about his daughter, Lord Feldstal was still a man who had mercilessly experimented on her in an attempt to create something . . . else, something stronger than a human was supposed to be. The costs for that weren't entirely clear to Nym.

"That's all personal business between you and me, though I would appreciate it if she'd slow down a bit on all the books she's buying or at least keep them to be shipped back home to the family library when she's done," Lord Feldstal continued.

Nym groaned and slouched down in his chair. Of course her father knew about that. He knew about everything else, so why not that she was just a few miles away? Nym didn't actually know if he was anywhere near Ebalsan at this point. Figuring out where exactly he was could wait until he was out of this cage. It didn't matter how far he needed to travel if he couldn't get away from his abductors.

"So if that's got nothing to do with why you had people kidnap me, why am I here?" Nym asked.

"Because of your scan," Lord Feldstal leaned forward again, appearing excited now. "It's quite fascinating, really. When Doliar saw it, he thought . . . Well . . . I'm not honestly sure what exactly he was thinking. Maybe he thought someone was trying to replicate our research or that someone was selling information. Like I said, someone got a little overeager and started trying to do damage control before we could properly figure out what the damage was.

"But anyway, you're here now, and that's the important part. You appear to be doing naturally, all by yourself, what we've been trying to do for years now. Based on the results of your scan, I'd say you're ahead of us in some areas, behind in others, and I would love to be able to merge whatever technique you're using to modify your matrix with the techniques we've developed."

"Wait a minute. Are you telling me the army kidnapped me because I damaged my soul well helping fight off a wight-led ghoul attack that I personally reported to the mage tower at forward command? An attack that no one bothered to respond to."

"No, no. Of course not. We kidnapped you because whatever you're doing to fix your soul well is weird, and we want to know if we can repeat it."

"That damn discount-store healer," Nym swore. "I knew I shouldn't have gone to him."

"In all fairness, Doliar Kents would be the perfect healer to help you, and it's not like we advertise who's a member of a secret government-funded military project. That guy who sent him the message with your scan results was probably trying to do his best by you."

That didn't make Nym feel that much better about the situation, but any annoyance he felt at the old healer was brushed aside as he considered Lord Feldstal's words. Other than the heavy-handed acquisition methods they'd used on him, this was exactly what he'd wanted. Here was a group that claimed to be studying the very thing he was struggling with, who was interested in duplicating what he'd done and teaching him what they'd done so they could try to merge it together into something wholly beneficial.

Nym had no doubt they'd try to extract some price from him. He was, after all, a prisoner at their mercy, and while he was sure getting his cooperation was the goal, he doubted they'd balk at forcing him to assist if they needed to. His best strategy at this point was to get as much as he could for that cooperation. Maybe, if he didn't do anything too stupid, he'd make it out with his life. If he was smart, he might even come out better than when he went in.

"So you know about how my matrix is . . . uh . . . lopsided, I guess is how I would describe it," Nym said. "And you think you can fix it because you've been working on something similar but with different results."

"That is essentially accurate."

"I can agree to that," Nym said. "I have some conditions of my own."

"Oh?" Lord Feldstal raised an eyebrow. "Do tell."

"I think it goes without saying that I don't want to be your experiment to be shoved back in that box whenever I'm not in use. I'd rather be a willing collaborator. This benefits me too, but I want to be free to go about my business just like anyone else."

"I think that could be arranged with a few stipulations. We'd want to move you to somewhere more secure than that third-rate inn. You'd probably need a bodyguard assigned to you to keep you safe and to make sure you're not revealing any sensitive information."

"Since you know so much about me, I'm sure you're aware of my current finances," Nym said.

"Down to the loose wedge bouncing around in the bottom of your pack," Lord Feldstal agreed. "That's easily remedied. In addition to seeing to your housing, we can provide you with a modest stipend to use as you see fit."

"And the other thing I want is simple. When this project is all over, I don't want to be drafted into the military, or attached to your family, or anything like that. If I decide I want to fly off to another country, I expect to be able to do so without being hounded."

"Ah, that might be a bit more of a problem. This is a sensitive project. The information you'd walk away with is not something we would want shared with our neighbors. As long as your loyalties are assured though, there's no reason you couldn't pick a nice town anywhere in Delvros to live. You would of course be added to the list, along with everyone else who completes the project."

That wasn't as bad as Nym had expected. He would need more information before he agreed to anything though. "What list?"

"The list of mages capable of casting third-circle spells. That's what this project is about: we're trying to find a way to artificially boost a mage to master status."

CHAPTER TWENTY-SIX

Nym had once read a book that said less than 5 percent of all mages made it to the third circle. It postulated some theories as to why so few people were able to reach that threshold, everything from "humans just weren't meant for it" to "those in power have deliberately held back the true methods in order to remain solely in power." Nym didn't necessarily think that was true, considering how many second-circle mages were actively trying to grow their power, but he wasn't foolish enough to think that third-circle mages were sharing every secret they knew in an attempt to expand their numbers.

If Lord Feldstal was to be believed though, there was some bottleneck that accounted for the low ratios. More than that, the nobleman implied he knew what it was and that his team was actively working on a solution for it. That seemed like it could connect nicely with some of his earlier experiments on his own daughter, so Nym was inclined to believe the man.

"What exactly are you trying to do?" he asked.

"I'm sure you've done some research on how to reach the third layer. Every mage does at some point in time. You know about how the second layer is shaped and the accepted methods for circumventing those obstacles? Well, here's the big secret, the reason so few mages are able to make it."

Lord Feldstal leaned forward and looked directly into Nym's eyes. "It's not the conduit that's the problem. Sure, it stops some mages, but almost all of them? No. The real block is biological. The fact is many, many mages do manage to reach the third layer. And then when they get there, they find out that they can't hold enough arcana in their soul well to cast the simplest third-circle spell."

Nym blinked. "What?"

"Ha! I love watching new mages learn that. Yes, it seems unfair, doesn't it? The sad truth is no matter how skilled you are, if you have an average-sized soul well, you will never cast a third-circle spell. An adult in his prime with a Helingar-Bistal score below seventeen cannot hold enough arcana from the Astral Sea to ever cast even the very simplest third-circle spell.

"Plenty of mages can and do strengthen their wills enough to pierce the third layer, and then . . . nothing. They discover they can't pull in enough arcana to do anything with it. And it's not possible to add soul channels to your body so that you can hold more arcana without already being able to cast a third-circle spell. So they stall out."

"No, this makes no sense," Nym protested. "If that's the real reason, why isn't it common knowledge? If so many mages hit this wall, surely the knowledge must have gotten around."

"Ah, you'd think so, right? I'm inclined to agree myself. It certainly seems like it's something that should be taught. Why let future mages waste their time striving for that next level when it's physically impossible to do anything with it once they get there?

"There are a couple reasons. The easiest one is that probably something like half of all second-circle mages truly can't make that conduit to get to the third layer. Then, of the ones that do, there are a few who don't understand what's happening because third-layer arcana feels *weird*. They think they've made a mistake. Of the ones who do eventually get some help or figure it out on their own, there's the few who can hold enough arcana to never run into this problem.

"And then there's that demographic you're thinking of, the ones who successfully forge a conduit, understand that they've reached the third layer, and figure out that no matter which spell they try, they aren't physically equipped to hold enough arcana or expel it fast enough to support a third-circle spell.

"The real answer is simple: It's a tradition. It's been going on for hundreds of years. Everyone in that situation hopes that someone will figure out the answer. They work on it, their friends work on it, their children work on it. There's a whole subculture of second-circle mages actively working to figure out how to expand their soul wells so they can ascend to the third circle. Reaching that point and finding yourself able to draw in the arcana but not use it is a rite of passage, a hazing ritual almost."

"That is the stupidest thing I have ever heard," Nym said immediately.

"Consider for a moment how many classically trained mages there are compared to how many are like you. Almost every mage goes through the Academy, and the real conspiracy there is the price. It's deliberately expensive so that mages need financial help to get through. That's how the army gets its mage corps. It's how noble families force indentured servitude on upcoming mages. We want to train you, yes, and we want you beholden to us. Without that training, precious few mages ever come close to approaching true power.

"So the government has a chokehold on where fresh-faced new mages learn. The faculty is measuring everybody when they come in and regularly updating those measurements throughout the years. We know who has the physical capability to become a master mage. We keep track. We're the ones new mages come to for help when they do break that barrier. And do you know what we do?"

"What's that?" Nym asked.

"We send them to me! I am the grand coordinator, the man who gathers up those mages who could cast third-circle spells but for a quirk of their biology. And I organize them into research teams, I provide the funding, I collaborate between them. Believe me, this is not a new project. King Maleotrak has been funding this for decades, and his father before him. We are *very* interested in having an army of third-circle mages ten times bigger than any other country's, and we don't want those countries to know about it until we've pulled it off."

That was disturbingly more plausible to Nym than the initial explanation. The nobles and the military controlled education and the mages; the educators knew which mages would be most likely to meet their specific criteria, and then they were recruited into the big conspiracy to figure out how to turn themselves into third-circle mages. Everything was kept quiet because the king wanted to launch a surprise invasion using his hidden military might once he actually had it.

Nym wasn't sure he bought it. That was still a lot of people keeping their mouths shut. It could be true, he guessed, but in the end, it didn't really matter much to him. Whether or not there was a conspiracy didn't change the fact that he was still in a mage cell, and even if they let him out, his matrix was still screwed up in some way that was limiting his arcana flow.

"Okay, let's pretend I trust you implicitly and believe every single word you've said to me. What are you doing here in the middle of this undead invasion? Wouldn't it be easier to do your research somewhere else?"

"Normally, yes. But here, we have research specimens. We've captured a number of wights to experiment on with some of our more dangerous theories that are too risky for an actual mage to try out. Also, the third-circle mages we do have are working rotating twelve-hour shifts to keep this whole outbreak contained."

Nym's eyebrows shot up. He considered the walls, the soldiers, the ghouls roaming the woods. "It doesn't seem very contained," he said.

Lord Feldstal waved away his comment. "Those ghouls that are getting out are nothing. That damn reaper is the real problem. We've got that ritual site locked down hard to keep it from escaping through the veil. The problem is we can't repair it yet. We need more third-circle-capable mages. And so, our little project got a lot of extra funding and was attached directly to the military in an effort to accelerate our progress."

"But the ritual site was sealed decades ago," Nym pointed out.

"It was," Lord Feldstal agreed. "And back then it was significantly smaller. One single third-circle mage and his group of ragtag adventurers was all it took. We really should have been keeping a closer eye on this place. The reaper . . . What was its name . . . ? Ul something . . . It slips my mind right now, but regardless, it's had years to pick at it, and it's widened the breach in the veil significantly. We even had an archmage in here working on it, and *he* couldn't close the damn thing either."

Nym slumped back into his chair. "This is . . . kind of a lot to take in," he said. "Give me a minute please, just to process everything."

"Certainly, take some time. When you're ready, we'll get the geas taken care of, and then we can start working on replicating what you've been doing and teaching you the techniques we've come up with."

"I'm sorry, the what?"

"The geas. Of course a conspiracy of this magnitude doesn't maintain secrecy without it being magically enforced. You'll be bound not to reveal the existence or purpose of this research to anyone who doesn't have the same geas on them. You physically won't be able to talk about it."

Nym felt the visceral rejection of that idea in his soul. No part of him wanted to bound by some sort of magical contract that guaranteed his silence and cooperation. The gears in his mind immediately started spinning, trying to find some way out that didn't involve agreeing to a geas.

"It's really not that big of a deal," Lord Feldstal said after a moment of studying Nym's face. "As these things go, it's quite straightforward. Even if you decided not to join us, which would be a mistake for you and a loss of valuable information for us but still your choice, even then, you would have to be bound to a geas before you were allowed to leave."

What Nym understood from that explanation was that there was no way they were voluntarily letting him go without getting their hooks into him. He could play along, agree to join up, then try to blast his way free once he was outside the mage cell, but he wasn't confident in his ability to fight just Lord Feldstal by himself, not crippled as he still was, maybe not even at his full strength.

And he doubted it would be just one third-circle mage between him and freedom. This group was smart, organized, and well funded. If their conspiracy was as deep and long running as he'd been told, they prioritized keeping their secrets. There would be an immediate manhunt for him, probably executed with extreme prejudice and orders to kill on sight.

As much as he hated the idea of being bound by a geas, he wasn't seeing a way out of it. The most likely path to true freedom was allowing himself to be bound, then to immediately start researching how to break a geas. Or he supposed if the project was a success and the king got his strike force of third-circle mages, the geas would possibly dissolve on its own after they made their first attack on some enemy nation.

Nym took a couple deep breaths to calm himself down. "Okay," he said. "Tell me more about this geas. What exactly am I supposed to be agreeing to here?"

Lord Feldstal studied him for a moment. "Yes, my son was right. You really don't like the idea of anybody having any sort of claim on you. I understand. I'm much the same way. It is a privilege of power not to be subjected to such things, and you, unfortunately, are the powerless one here.

"But come, my new friend, let me explain the ways of the world to you. Trust me when I say you won't find it too odious."

CHAPTER TWENTY-SEVEN

The mage cell deactivated, and Nym followed Lord Feldstal out of it. The outer outer room was just as plain and unadorned as the cell itself, with the exception of several large arcana batteries set up to power the cell and the hundreds of rune sequences drawn on the outside wall. Two men waited for them, one holding open the door to the cell they were in and the other holding the door that led out of the room.

"Sir," both men said in unison. Lord Feldstal ignored them and strode out of the room with Nym in tow.

"First things first: the geas. Then we'll want to do a few more scans on you. Master Healer Doliar will be in charge of that. Then there's going to be a discussion that'll probably be far longer than you want. That will involve your future plans. Last step, you'll be teleported somewhere and given more secure lodgings. We'll talk about where exactly somewhere is once we get there."

"Back to Ebalsan," Nym said immediately. That was where all his friends were.

"Really? Not the safest place in the world, but that's fine. We've got a lot of staff stationed out there anyway, so you'll fit right in."

Lord Feldstal talked while he moved, not stopping to make sure Nym was keeping up, and he kept up a pace fast enough that Nym didn't have any time to look around. His overall impression of wherever he was was that it was big and confusing. Everything was made of stone, and not the quick earthwork version he'd gotten used to seeing all the outposts and bases the army using, but real quarried stone. They didn't run into many people as they walked either.

The two men from the mage cell were following behind at a discreet distance.

Both looked military, which was to say big, muscled, rigid postured, and far too serious and grim. They kept eyes on everything, especially Nym. That was probably a good idea on their part. If Nym thought he could have escaped by attacking Lord Feldstal, he would have. But since he didn't expect he could overpower the older mage by himself, let alone with his two bodyguards, he followed along quietly.

They stopped at a door, which unlocked with a distinctive click when Lord Feldstal channeled some arcana into a ring on one hand and pressed it against a seal carved into the wood. He pushed it open and revealed an office that was far warmer than the stone halls they'd been traveling. It was carpeted, with wooden panels on the walls. Bookshelves flanked a writing desk. There were four chairs, one behind the desk and three in front, and a couch pushed up against the wall near the door.

"This is my office," Lord Feldstal said. "Sometimes it feels like I live here though. Come have a seat."

The guards took up positions just outside the office, both of them looking distinctly annoyed by the fact that they weren't invited in, but neither voiced an objection. Once the door was closed, Lord Feldstal rolled his eyes and sat down behind the desk. "The affectations of nobility. Sure, either of them could arm wrestle me into submission, but if this lab ever came under attack, I am the one whose magic would be defending us. And actually, if we're bringing magic into it, neither of them could beat me at arm wrestling either."

He rifled through a few drawers and finally brought out a single sheet of paper. It had rune sequences inscribed around its border, and the text in the center was written in flowing script. "This is the geas," he explained. "Think of it as a magically enforced legal document. Once you've agreed to this, the runes will lift the commands off the paper and brand them to your . . . Well . . . *Soul* isn't the right term, but it's close enough. Your very being, perhaps, but it's not physical. It's complicated. Regardless, we'll both be signing one today.

"This details your agreement to keep silent regarding the source of the information you learn as part of this Collective, to keep silent on the information itself, to keep silent on the existence of the Collective, to not risk capture and interrogation in foreign lands, to report back to the Collective in three years for renewal, and to not reveal that you are under a geas regarding any of the above. Once activated, the magic will last for five years, so you'll have some time between that three-year mark and when the geas really starts to compel you to return."

A second sheet of paper joined the first, but this one was mostly blank. "This is the geas I will agree to in return. We'll list out your conditions, and as long as I am in charge of the Collective, they will be met. Well, for five years, at least. When you come to renew your geas, we will renew mine as well. Go ahead and read this over while I pen your terms onto this blank one."

Thankfully, it was written plainly. Nym had seen a few contract examples when he'd been staying with Bardin and Analia, and nobles sometimes deliberately made the writing as obtuse as possible in an attempt to screw one another over. He wasn't sure if that wasn't the case because the geas didn't allow for it or if Lord Feldstal just didn't want to go through the trouble. If he needed capable and willing mages to do research and experiments, it was probably in the Collective's best interest not to go out of their way to take advantage of their members.

Nym did not want to sign it, even though it was far less restrictive than any other contract he'd been offered. It didn't even bind him to work for the Collective, and he couldn't find a genuine reason to refuse it based on the contents alone, but he found the source highly suspect.

It didn't take Lord Feldstal long to pen his own geas, which he slid over to Nym to review. It stated more or less exactly what Nym had asked for. He would become a member of the Collective and work to create a technique that allowed mages to artificially expand their soul wells so that they could cast third-circle spells. In return for sharing his own techniques and his continued work on the project, he would be given a modest home in Ebalsan, a monthly stipend of ten crests, and a bodyguard not of his choice to ensure his safety until such a time as Lord Feldstal agreed that he was safe and was otherwise free to do as he liked.

It was . . . extremely generous, and that made Nym even more wary about the whole thing. It was all too good to be true, even if he was giving up a measure of his freedom. There was even a clause that said he *could* still travel to another country as long as he notified the Collective and they agreed to it. It was a good deal. He knew he should take it, not in the least because he wasn't getting out without agreeing to it.

"Ready?" Lord Feldstal asked him.

Nym nodded, trying not to let the dread roiling in his mind show on his face. "Let's do it."

Simultaneously, they scrawled signatures across their geasa. Everything washed out for a second, and all he could see was the rune sequences on the paper he'd signed glowing gold. Reality clamped down on his heart like a vise as the geas wrote itself onto his . . . wherever they went.

Nym gasped what felt like his first bit of air in forever, and his eyes started working again. Lord Feldstal was sitting across from him, grimacing and rubbing at his chest. "Those never do get any easier," he told Nym.

They both took a minute to recover from the strain of accepting a geas, then Lord Feldstal stood up. "Let's get to work. I'll escort you to the lab so that Master Healer Doliar can scan you. I'd like to go over the results with him, then while you get brought up to speed, I'll make arrangements for your compensation. Do you have any preferences on your home?"

"I . . . don't know? What are my options?"

"Ah, don't worry about it. I'll find something suitable for you." Lord Feldstal hesitated for a second, then added, "A personal favor, if you don't mind. I'll find a home with an extra bedroom. Keep my daughter safe. She's headstrong and thinks she's invincible, but I'm sure she won't be too difficult a roommate."

"I think she might have some questions about how I acquired the funds for a house, even just to rent one."

"Tell her you've joined a government research team but that the subject of the research is classified. It's basically the truth anyway. Your geas won't allow you to answer any specific questions, so if she gets as insistent as she normally does about knowing everything, you're going to be in for an argument there."

Nym sighed. That sounded depressingly accurate. Once Analia got interested in something, she didn't just give up until her curiosity was satisfied. That was why he had an air-golem spell floating around in his head. She'd probably obsessed over it for days to have completed it that quickly. "What happens if she finds out?"

"Nothing. You just can't confirm anything. It'd be like asking the furniture questions. She can ask as many as she wants, but you physically will not be able to even acknowledge them."

They arrived at a room while they were talking, one that was filled with specialty magical tools like nothing Nym had ever seen. He didn't recognize even one in ten, but he did understand their purpose. They were all divination tools, used in rituals to help strengthen them in some way.

"Right, here we are. Nym, this is Master Healer Doliar Kents. Doliar, this is the newest member of the Collective. I'm sure you'll remember him."

"Ah, yes! Of course," Doliar said, clearly excited to meet Nym. "I do want to apologize for that rough start you got with us. When I showed the scans my colleague sent me to Undercommander Cremont, well . . . He was a bit overzealous."

"Doliar," Lord Feldstal cut in, "let's just get the scan started so we can go over the results."

"Yes, yes, right away," the healer agreed. "If you'll just move over to this spot here. Perfect, now we're going to do the first scan with an empty soul well."

Nym allowed himself to be steered through the room and scanned several times by various devices. They did it with his soul well empty, with it full, while he actively channeled a spell, and with his matrix flexed into the off state. Once they found out he was able to selectively flex certain node clusters, they redid all the scans a dozen different ways with those patterns.

"That should just about do it for tonight. I do have one request," Doliar said. "Feel free to refuse this one because it's a little bit dangerous. I would like to see what happens if you have arcana in your soul well while some nodes are active and others are not. Will you get arcana poisoning? If so, will it be as fast as a normal mage who's shifted their entire matrix? Or could this technique be used to draw in arcana and form healing spells to deal with it?"

"A little bit of arcana poisoning won't kill me," Nym said. "Should I draw it in first and then shift the nodes or the other way around?"

"Hmm . . . That is an excellent question. What do you think, sir?" Doliar looked over at Lord Feldstal.

"It would be ideal to get scans of both, but . . . let's start with the nodes shifted and then arcana added, that way Nym can cut off the flow if he has a bad reaction rather than flooding himself with whatever's already stored."

"I'll start with just a few nodes open and open more every few seconds," Nym said. "Ready?"

"One moment. And . . . go."

Nym flexed a small cluster, forged a conduit, and fed arcana into his soul well. He'd always thought of it as a liquid. It felt like his soul well was a barrel and arcana was water pouring in. He knew he wasn't alone in that visual. It had been described in similar terms by many other mages. When that arcana entered his soul well, he knew he was wrong.

Even though it was just a little bit, it instantly pushed against every open node he had and flowed out past it. It was more like a fine mist escaping. Arcana instantly spread through his body, causing Nym to cry out in pain. He cut the conduit and collapsed to the floor.

CHAPTER TWENTY-EIGHT

S o that was a bad idea," Lord Feldstal said a few minutes later after Nym had recovered. "It's a good thing he didn't gather enough arcana to actually cast a spell."

"It's like the arcana was alive and knew exactly where to attack him at to push through the hole in his matrix," Doliar said. "I don't think we're going to find many answers there."

"No . . . Well, it's not why our new friend was added to the Collective anyway. I've got to go take care of some business. Nym, please show Master Healer Doliar your full meditation technique for flexing small node clusters and answer any questions he has," Lord Feldstal said.

Before Nym could answer, the nobleman was gone. Nym scratched the back of his head and said, "I guess I'm just here with you until he comes back."

Doliar nodded. "Or until he sends someone to fetch you. Oh, let me just swap out this sensor before you get started."

The healer was an excitable young man, maybe in his midtwenties. He was quite handsome, slightly below average height and with a friendly smile. He worked eagerly and swiftly, then stepped back and said, "Okay, all ready. Just start at the beginning."

So Nym did. He talked about the injury and the advice he'd received at the start. He explained how he flexed different parts of his matrix and the different ways he did that. The healer listened while watching various sensors as Nym demonstrated what he was talking about. He didn't feel like he was doing a very good job, and he felt a pang of empathy for Yura, who'd tried to explain something that humans didn't really have a lot of words to describe.

If that was a problem for Doliar, he didn't show it. He just kept jotting down more notes, occasionally asking for clarification or a follow-up question when he wanted to know something Nym had skipped over. A few times, he had Nym repeat a step when he wasn't happy with the information he got from the sensors. Once they were done, he set aside the notes and started putting away the equipment.

"I have a theory," he said as he worked. "And it's just a theory, but I think that the reason you're having troubles channeling arcana at the speeds you're used to is because your soul well is distorted. Think of it like a water skin that you can squeeze to shoot water out. Except, now you've got stripes of different material in there, and it's harder to put uniform pressure because some parts need to be squeezed harder than others. Does that make sense?"

"Not really, no," Nym told him honestly.

The healer sighed and shook his head. "I could be wrong, and we'll keep researching, but based on what my scans are showing me, you've got . . . three, I'd say, different types of nodes. It's almost like they're not just growing bigger, they're getting stronger too. And as they get bigger, they're pulling themselves out of place in your matrix. Once you get everything evened out, the problem might disappear completely."

"That'll be great if it does, but how long would that take? What's the count on all these new node types?"

"Every matrix has one hundred nodes. In your case, you've got seventy-seven of what I'd describe as a typical node. Eighteen are advanced, stronger. Arcana is repelled harder from them. And the remaining five are completely different. They're more than three times bigger, and the netting connected to them is starting to thicken to compensate for the extra dimensions."

"So if I have to get every node to this stage-three style to even things out, it'll take me twenty times as long as it's already been, which is about six weeks. That'll take years!"

"Well . . . Not to worry, I'm sure we'll find a way to streamline the process. In fact, let me talk to you about the techniques we've been working on. Maybe it'll help."

Doliar proceeded to spend the next hour going over the fruits of several decades of research, which was a way to elongate the threads between the nodes that formed the net of the matrix. They had pretty well mastered that part. The problem they'd run into was that the threads just weren't strong enough to force the nodes themselves to move to accommodate the new length.

Instead of having a fine net, the matrix looked more like a pot of noodle broth with evenly spaced chunks of meat floating in it. Eventually, after a week or two of inactivity, the net would shrink down and resume its former shape.

"But I'm thinking if we can combine these two things, your nodes should be able to grow faster. There's some shredding in the net that makes up your matrix as the nodes grow. It's repairing itself, but it's not keeping up with the growth. If you elongate the net portion, I think it'll let your nodes grow faster because they won't have to fight against it. The slack will already be there," Doliar said.

"That's . . . Maybe? I guess it's worth a try, right?" Nym asked.

And so another two hours were spent on that. Doliar was a decent teacher, or maybe just well-practiced. Nym supposed every new member of the Collective learned this method, and someone had to show them how to do it. Either way, it wasn't that hard to pick up, and Nym didn't even have to cheat to do it.

Most of the time was spent stretching the net, then focusing on specific groups of nodes. Nym alternated back and forth between the two exercises, stopping occasionally for Doliar to do new scans. Once they were done, he started comparing the data.

"We might be onto something here!" he said. "Look, see, here's your original scan when you first got here. And the one I just took looks like this."

Nym stared at the two illusions the healer had crafted. "They look the same to me," he said.

"What? No. In this one, the nodes are four percent bigger. That's after ninety minutes of exercises. A little over five hours a day means you could double the size of your nodes in a week. If it scales like I'm hoping, we could call it two weeks per grouping. Twenty-five groups . . . Let me think for a second."

The healer's face screwed up in concentration as he did the mental math. "One year," he announced. "If this training regime works like I hope, in one year, a mage could triple the size of his nodes, and my best estimates are showing a fifty percent increase in the size of the soul well. That's almost enough by itself to meet our goal. And this is day one! Who knows what we'll figure out in the coming weeks?"

Nym wasn't as excited as Doliar was, but then again, he'd only been working on the problem for a few hours. The healer had probably been trying to solve it for years, and if he was understanding what little he'd learned about the Collective properly, the organization had existed for decades prior to Doliar's involvement, originally headed up by Lord Feldstal's father. The more he learned, the more he understood the motivation behind the experiments performed on Analia.

That wasn't to say that he agreed with them or condoned them, just that he understood what the goal was. The spells that let a mage work on his own body to increase his abilities weren't something that could be done to someone else, not normally at least. If Analia hadn't been born with a large enough soul well to begin with, there would have been no way to ever progress to the third circle and be able to start augmenting herself.

So her father had done it for her. It was extremely unethical, but it made sense. He'd had a brief window, and he'd wanted it for her, so he'd made the decision to risk her life. Still, the way he'd written about the experiments in his journals did not match the personality he'd displayed when he talked to Nym. It was enough to make Nym wonder which was the true Jaspar Feldstal, if either. It would not surprise him to learn that the man had no true personality and instead was a social chameleon, donning whatever mask he felt was most useful. Even in his own personal writings, knowing they'd be handed down to one of his children, he could be carefully crafting a persona to achieve some effect.

The experiments were interrupted by a knock on the lab's door. "Safe to enter?" a voice called out from the hall. Nym frowned. He knew that voice from somewhere.

"One moment," Doliar said while scrambling to remove some of the sensors he'd set up on a stand in front of the door. After he slid them out of the way, he grabbed the doorknob and twisted. "Come on in now but be careful not to bump into anything.

A young man entered the room and locked eyes with Nym. "Well, well, well. Good to see you again. Damn, you got tall!"

"Navarim? What are you doing here?" Nym asked. The mage from Zoskan's guildhall looked just like he remembered, but this was the last place Nym expected to see him.

"I would think that's obvious. I'm a member of the Collective. I managed to make a conduit to the third layer. That's partially thanks to you. You were a real kick in the butt, you know? Some little kid was a stronger mage than me! But wouldn't you know it, just an average-sized soul well. A bit under average actually. I'm ranked nine. That was a bitter pill to swallow, but then one of my mentors introduced me to this group, and here I am."

"Oh, that's a good thing to study!" Doliar said. "I can't believe we forgot to do a Helingar-Bistal Test on you. Here, go stand right here. Let me get the rest of these sensors out of the way and we'll get that taken care of before you leave."

Nym wasn't sure he liked the idea of that. He already knew the number was abnormally high, and the Collective knew enough weird things about him as it was. Then again, he did have their leader under a geas that guaranteed his relative freedom. If there was ever a group that might be able to help him solve some mysteries, it was this one.

The question was if he trusted them to know the truth. It would be easier to make that decision if *he* knew the truth first. It was probably too late on the soul-well-size test either way. Doliar didn't seem like the kind of person to give up on it, so Nym decided to go with the truth.

"I did kind of have an unofficial one done once already, but we're not sure the results are accurate," Nym said.

"That's fine. I'll do another one right now and make sure you've got the right number. You can tell me how far off the old one was after."

"If you're sure," Nym said. "You might need some more people. It took four mages to do it last time."

Doliar laughed. "Ha, funny. I didn't know you were an ascendant."

Navarim wasn't laughing though. He just looked at Nym thoughtfully, no doubt remembering Nym's flight training. All he said was "Should I go get a few more people?"

Doliar waved him off. "No offense to whoever performed Nym's last test, but I think the two of us can handle it."

"I really wouldn't recommend it," Nym warned him. The Earth Shapers had grumbled about the feedback for days.

"It's fine. Just give me a second to set up and we'll get it taken care of."

Nym just sighed.

An hour later, four mages groaned and muttered to one another while Doliar cast pain-blocker spells on them. After cautioning them to keep the incident quiet until any official announcements were made, he dismissed all of them except Navarim. "I'll know better than to doubt you next time," the healer told Nym.

It took Doliar far less time to do the calculations, even with him stopping several times to recheck things. Once he was done, he gave Nym a searching stare before redoing them a second time. "So," he said, "before I tell you the results, what did the last test say?"

"Seventy-four," Nym said.

Doliar nodded to himself as if that were the most normal and boring thing in the world. "Yep, I can see that. And that was before the matrix destabilization. Well, I did not get seventy-four," he told Nym. "I got ninety-two."

Nym's eyebrows shot up. "Are you sure? That's a lot different."

"I've got a more accurate measure on your true age thanks to all the scans. I'm sure. I think we're going to have to go talk to Lord Feldstal again before you leave."

CHAPTER TWENTY-NINE

Lord Feldstal reviewed the calculations silently while Nym, Doliar, and Navarim waited in his office. He sighed and handed the paper back to Doliar. "I'm going to assign two guards instead of one," he said. "Maintain the gag order for now until I figure out what this means. Navarim, please escort our little prodigy to his new home and keep him safe. I'll send the second guard out to you as soon as I know who it will be."

"Of course, sir."

"Doliar, you stay. The rest of you can go. Have a nice night, Nym. Best of luck dealing with my daughter."

Nym sighed and shook his head. "She's going to make this difficult."

Lord Feldstal shrugged and pointed at the paper still held in Doliar's hands. "Difficulties do tend to arise just when it seems that things are going well."

"Basically the story of my life," Nym muttered to himself.

They left Lord Feldstal's office and walked across the Collective's headquarters to the teleportation platforms. Navarim led the way, occasionally pointing out some interesting room or person that they passed by. The Collective had a lot of labs for different experiments and supposedly an archive of thousands of upon thousands of books detailing the results of their research.

"We're not the first incarnation of the Collective," Navarim explained. "Reaching for more power isn't anything new, and while the primary goal is the advancement of humanity's magic in general to make third-circle spells commonplace, there are plenty of other topics we do research on. We're not even really that secret of a society, to be fair. You just don't find out about us until you reach a certain threshold."

"Why hide at all?" Nym asked.

"Between you and me, I think the people in charge just like the grandeur and the mystique. Seems like having the members all swear geasa is overkill to me, but . . . I'm twenty-three. I am not ready to stop growing for the rest of my life, so I'll play along as long as I get to keep collaborating on finding a way to push to the third circle."

That was fair. Nym knew he wouldn't face the same problems most of the people in the Collective had, but there would probably come a day when he couldn't push his own magic any further either, and if that was due to his body not being able to keep up with his mind, he wasn't sure what would look like reasonable actions to correct that.

"Here's the teleport platform," Navarim said. "I'm sure you remember these."

"I do," Nym said. "I think you were there for almost every single one I've ever used."

"Ha. But did you ever learn how to power them yourself?"

"I did not, no. Teleportation is a third-circle spell. Wait, in that case . . ."

"Right, you need to be able to cast third-circle magic in order to make new platforms. They can be powered with second-circle arcana though. It's complicated, probably a lot more so than just casting the actual spell, and it requires a ton of maintenance. But since you're part of the Collective now, you should probably know how to activate one and pick a destination from it.

"Each platform can only contain five or so destinations. Some of the bigger ones have a few more, and there are some small ones that only link directly to one other place, but on average, five is the magic number here. It's just cheaper to build two platforms next to each other than to build one bigger one that can hold ten links."

Navarim went on for a bit about localization effects, long-distance synergies, and the cycle warp-up speed for powering the platform, none of which Nym understood. Then he moved on to the part that Nym actually needed to know about, powering the arcana battery that the platform drew on to generate the teleportation effect, which was actually five separate batteries. Destination was selected by choosing where to pour arcana in.

"Wouldn't there be some conversion loss from using the battery and then having the platform power it instead of just powering the platform directly?" he asked.

"Yes and no. There is, but it's not very much, and it's much, much simpler to have the attendant just dump arcana into one of five boxes than it is to have them trying to access the platform's rune sequences directly. In the end, it costs less arcana to keep people who don't know how to manually operate the platform away from the delicate parts than it would to repair those parts every time they break something."

There were symbols etched onto each section of the battery stack that denoted the destination. Navarim pointed out the one for Ebalsan and said, "Why don't you try empowering it? I'll keep an eye on the battery and let you know when it's got enough."

Pushing arcana into the battery was a lot like empowering rune sequences, though it was hungry for far more arcana than he'd ever used to power runes. Teleportation was not a cheap spell, apparently, and doubly so when he was using the wrong layer of arcana. He would have loved to see how the platform managed to spin that around.

"Has the Collective ever tried using this type of magic to create enchanted objects that would allow them to do the necessary changes to their soul wells?" Nym asked.

"I believe the principles used in the teleportation platform were first discovered in an attempt to do just that," Navarim told him. "As it turns out, it's much easier to use arcana in this manner on a nonliving object. Living test subjects who tried it turned . . . uh . . . also nonliving."

Nym winced. "Okay then. I won't be trying that. I think the battery is full now."

"Good eye," Navarim said. "That should be enough but give it a little bit more just to be safe. You will absolutely regret it if you ever get caught at the end of a teleportation spell that ran out of arcana. It's not fatal or anything, but you'll be so sick you'll wish it was."

After he was done, they both stepped onto the platform and Navarim pointed out where to channel a bit of arcana into the battery to connect it to the platform. The teleportation spell took hold immediately and deposited them onto a new platform in Ebalsan. The attendant started forward, but Navarim waved him off.

From there, it was a short trip to their destination, which was in a decidedly middle-class neighborhood. It was still early in the morning, barely past dawn, and the streets were largely empty, which made it easier to navigate them. Many of the homes were two stories, with businesses being run from the ground floors. They weren't cramped together and often had small gardens visible behind them. "Where are we going?" Nym asked. "This looks a little too rich for my budget."

"I didn't pick it," Navarim told him. "It should be near here somewhere. They said to look for a little decorative fence around the property and blue shutters and that it was right next to . . . Ah! Here it is."

Nym looked at the house, then back to Navarim. Then he looked at the house again. "You're kidding, right? This is a joke?"

"Well, I didn't pick it," the other mage said again, defensively this time.

The house was large, far larger than Nym had expected. It was two stories and, just judging by the number of windows he saw on the outside, had to have four or five bedrooms. It was in good shape too, though the yard hadn't been tended to in some time. There was a paved stone path leading from the streets to the front door, and a wooden fence that came up just past Nym's waist circled the whole thing. The gate was missing, but otherwise it was whole and sturdy.

Right next to it was an exotic-pet store. Nym could hear various squawks, rumblings, and barks from the street, and there was a kind of smell that he couldn't really identify in the air. He wasn't sure that he'd necessarily call it foul, but it wasn't pleasant. It was just kind of an animal smell, not as bad as being at the stockyards in Thrakus but not something he wanted to get used to.

"Do you think I can argue for a different place?" Nym asked.

"I doubt it."

He let out a defeated sigh. "Let's just get inside."

The house proved to be three bedrooms, with a sitting room, a washroom, and a kitchen all separated out. Nym had never been inside a house this big that didn't belong to a noble, but then he supposed this one might very well belong to Analia's father as well. Awful location aside, it was a very nice house that was already furnished.

"Alright, let's talk about how this whole bodyguard thing is going to work," Navarim said after they finished touring the place. They were sitting at the kitchen table while waiting for a pot of tea the mage had started using supplies from the pantry.

"Probably a good idea," Nym agreed.

"What do you know already?" Navarim asked.

"Not much. You follow me around, protect me from stuff."

The older mage sighed. "Yeah, I was kind of hoping you knew more than that. This isn't really something I ever saw myself doing, so I'm just about as lost as you are. I think they only picked me because your file indicated we knew each other. I guess we'll figure it out together."

"Did they give you any time frames? Like . . . Are you staying here with me? Are you with me indefinitely, or will someone else come relieve you in a few hours?"

"I'm with you for the time being," Navarim said. "And I guess someone else will be assigned as well, so maybe we'll . . . uh . . . take shifts? I'm not sure. I guess this is your house, so pick out which bedroom you want and I'll grab one of the spares. Whoever your other guard is can take the other."

"Hmm . . . I don't think that will work. I'm planning on having a roommate. I should actually send a message spell. I disappeared in the middle of the night, and I'm not sure how long I've been missing."

"Roommate, huh? Alright, I'll give you a minute for that. Let me know when you're done."

Nym didn't have a firm grasp on the message spell. It seemed extremely useful, but Analia was a bit annoying with it, and it turned out the more he used it, the easier it was for other people to send him messages. Nym suspected there was a matching spell that blocked messages in some fashion, but Analia claimed she didn't know if such a thing existed.

Nym was suspicious, to say the least.

He hadn't received any messages from her since he'd teleported back to Ebalsan, but it was very early in the morning. It was possible Analia was asleep still. She might be cranky if he woke her up, but he had been kidnapped in the middle of the night and assumed he'd been gone for at least one full day, considering how much time he'd spent talking to both Lord Feldstal and Doliar. All those tests had taken hours too, plus the time he'd been locked up.

She could be mad at him if she wanted. He spun the message spell out of arcana and infused it with his thoughts, then sent it on its way toward her. *[It's Nym. I got attacked in the middle of the night. Fine now. We got a house out of it. I'll come meet you at the Silver Gilder, and we can pack up the books.]*

Part of the spell required at least a rough knowledge of where the recipient was, which probably accounted for why he hadn't received any messages from her earlier. Between that and being locked in a mage cell for an unknown length of time, he'd been unreachable. The spell unfortunately did not have enough feedback to let the caster know if the recipient had actually received it.

What did let him know the message had gone through was the return message Analia sent him. *[You what?! Are you okay? Get over here right now. I'm going to let Ophelia and the rest know so we can meet up and figure out what's going on.]*

"That went about as well as can be expected," he told Navarim with a sigh.

CHAPTER THIRTY

The walk to the Silver Gilder was about half an hour, which wasn't bad by itself, but considering how many books Analia had, it was going to take all day to haul her stuff to the new house. Nym wondered if he could talk her into renting a cart or something. He could probably use air magic to lighten the load enough that it wouldn't be too difficult to haul.

Navarim followed closely, a slight glow of arcana around him the whole way. He was taking his bodyguard job seriously, even though neither of them knew much about what he was supposed to do. He walked far too close to Nym's back for about ten minutes before Nym got annoyed and told him to stop.

"Just walk next to me like a normal person," he instructed Navarim.

Things were much more natural then, and they both relaxed. When they got to the inn, Navarim went in first, and they went upstairs together. Nym started to knock on Analia's door but hesitated. He took a deep breath, hesitated again, and then steeled his will. Before he could actually knock, she jerked the door open and said, "What are you doing lurking in the hall?"

"I was just about to knock," Nym protested.

"Oh yeah? How long have you been standing in front of my door?"

"I don't know, a few seconds?"

"More than a few."

"How would you even know?" Nym asked.

"When you got kidnapped, I decided maybe it would be a good idea to keep a better eye on what was going on around me. There's an air golem floating down at the end of the hall watching us. There's another one on the roof too."

"You're up to two golems now?" Nym asked, surprised. "Congratulations!"

"It is completely exhausting. I don't understand how you can keep three or four of these running at the same time," she said. "No way I could do it with anything but air."

"Still though, nice job."

"Thanks, but don't try to change the subject! What happened? Also, who is this guy?"

"This is Navarim. He's going to be helping keep us safe at the new house?"

Analia gave Navarim a scrutinizing look, to which the mage just looked back at her, boredom evident in his posture. "Okay, you get in here," she told Nym. Then she pointed at Navarim and added, "You can wait out here."

"Up to Nym," the mage said.

"It's fine. I'm just going to help pack up some books."

"Sure, take your time. Lot of books in there," Navarim said, peering over Analia's shoulder into her room. She bristled, but Nym hurried her back through the door. He tripped over a stack of books in the process and swore quietly while clutching at his knee where it had smacked against the bed frame.

"Okay, the quick and dirty version of this for now," he said. "Some people thought I knew some stuff I didn't, we got that all cleared up, I'm working on a government contract now, but it's classified, and I can't give you any details. I got us new housing out of the deal, so we can stop being cramped in these rooms and save a bit of money."

Analia stared at him for a moment, then said, "How much of that is true?"

"Technically? All of it. Kind of."

She squinted at him and said, "Yeah, we're not done with this conversation, but we can hold off on it until later. Tell me about the new bodyguard."

"Friend from before I came to Abilanth. I think they assigned him to guard me because I already knew him and they figured I would trust him."

"Do you trust him?" she asked.

"Not particularly," Nym replied. "I mean . . . I trust him to not let me get kidnapped without a fight, but I don't trust that he'd be more loyal to me than to the—to our employer."

He had been about to say "the Collective" when something had physically forced his mouth to reshape the words. The power of the geas he'd agreed to was a bit scary. It had interfered so smoothly that he hadn't even had a chance to think about resisting when it took control of him. Nym instantly decided that he hated it.

"And who is this employer?" she asked.

"Military project," Nym said. This time he managed it on his own.

"Who's in charge?" Analia asked.

Nym didn't say anything. He wasn't even sure if he could.

Analia regarded him silently for a few seconds, then slowly, she said, "Nym, have you been geased?"

Once again, the answer was silence. She waited for him to answer, and when he didn't, she started swearing. "Okay, we're going to have to tease the information out of you. The geas isn't going to let you just tell me, but that's pretty standard procedure."

"How do you know about geasa?" Nym asked.

"I'm a member of a noble family. This is standard training. Let's see. First question: Are you still in danger?"

"No."

"Are you compelled to lie?"

"Uh . . . no?"

"Are you under a geas?"

Nym didn't say anything.

"So you can't lie, but you also can't answer on topics you're not allowed to talk about. That sounds like a standard confidentiality geas we use on servants and employees that are given access to sensitive information, and not a particularly binding one. Those force you to lie to cover them up."

"Analia, can we please drop this?"

"Not a chance," she told him bluntly. "I cannot picture a scenario where you'd willingly agree to be geased, which means you were coerced into it. This is going to be a long, frustrating conversation, but I need to know all the details so we can figure out how to break it."

"You can break a geas?" Nym asked, surprised.

"Theoretically? I'm not sure exactly how, but I know it's not easy. I might have to actually reach out to my father for help. Damn, I don't want to do that."

Now Nym could practically feel the geas compelling him to keep his mouth shut. Analia didn't seem to notice this time, probably because she was so caught up in thinking about her family that she'd stopped paying attention to him.

"Analia, can we talk about this later? I promise that this isn't a trap, I'm not in any immediate danger from my new employer, and that I will do my best to cooperate with all your questions once we get settled."

She gave him a long, hard stare, then said, "I paid for your room last night when you disappeared. Your stuff should all be untouched in there. Let's get everything packed up."

Nym had significantly underestimated the number of books they could take in one trip. Her trunk was full of mostly personal stuff, but he hoped that once it was emptied out, it would hold most of her collection. He supposed they'd find out soon enough. He ended up hauling it because of course he did, but at least with Navarim around, nobody stopped to question the blatant use of magic.

They made their way through town to the house, which took almost twice as long now that the sun was fully up and people were about their business. Eventually though, they did make it to the new house, Analia's trunk in tow. She paused when they got there and looked curiously at the business right next door.

"Is this a menagerie? How fun!"

"Really? You like that?" Nym asked. "I thought for sure you'd complain about the smell and the noises."

"Of all the cute animals? Of course not. I'll have to make some time to go browse their collection and see what's for sale soon."

"Huh," Nym said. "Well, okay then. One less problem."

While Analia was unpacking her stuff into the room she'd picked out, Nym got a message from Ophelia. *[Nym, Analia told us you were under a geas but that you're back home safe. We'll be there this afternoon to try to figure out how to break you out of it. Don't worry, you're not alone in this.]*

Even in his own thoughts, Nym couldn't speak of the geas. As much as he wanted to respond to the heartfelt message, all he could say was *[Thank you. I'll be here, and I'll make sure to get the pastries.]*

Three trips later, they'd finally cleared out both rooms and returned the keys to the innkeeper. The Silver Gilder was officially no longer their home. Nym sat at the table, sweat dripping down his forehead and exhausted from the heat. "It's so hot out," he moaned. "Can we do just a little blizzard? Just for a bit?"

"What do you mean?" Navarim asked.

In response, Nym wove together the snow-making spell in the middle of the sitting room and let it start filling the interior of the house with cold air and snow. Almost immediately, it started cooling down. Nym relaxed into his chair and said, "That's so much better."

"Do you think you could modify it to not generate snow?" Analia asked, annoyed as she brushed some off the book she was reading. Nym got a look at the cover as she waved it around: *Bound by Geas*. It looked like she had no plans to drop that line of questioning.

"Probably," he said. "I'll work on it, I guess. Not right now though. I'm tired."

"Didn't you promise pastries?" she reminded him.

"Yes . . . Yes, I did. Damn."

The trip to the bakery was uncomfortably warm, and by the time he got back to the house with Navarim, it was just as hot as it had been before the miniature blizzard. Navarim was left to lounge in the sitting room while Analia dragged Nym off to continue working on puzzling out the shape of the geas via the technique of asking a thousand questions.

The Earth Shapers showed up in the late afternoon. Everyone gathered in the sitting room for a meeting, where Analia announced the results of her questioning. "From what I can tell, Nym is currently geased with prohibitions against talking about the geas, talking about his new employer, and talking about any sort of details about the job. He was coerced into it, and it has some standard refresher clauses in it. I believe the new employer is the same organization that kidnapped him two nights ago. The job isn't really a military contract, but it is somehow involved with the military. The bodyguard is under a similar geas."

"Is it dangerous to him?" Ophelia asked.

"Not unless he tries to break it. Then the geas will try to stop him. They can be very aggressive if Nym tries to put himself in a situation where his only option is to violate it, up to the point of killing him before letting him betray the terms of the geas."

"That does not sound good," Bildar said. "And Nym can't say anything at all?"

Nym sat there, mute, and watched them all talk.

Analia shook her head. "He can't even acknowledge that it exists. Fortunately, the geas isn't compelling him to lie to cover it up, otherwise it would be much more difficult to tease out the truth of it. If we can think of the right questions to ask, we can puzzle out the whole thing."

"Wow, you got a raw deal," Nomick told Nym.

Nym thought for a second, and then carefully and deliberately said, "I am trying to fix my matrix."

Navarim, who'd been mostly amused by the conversation and hadn't said much other than introducing himself, whipped around from where he'd been standing in the kitchen to stare at Nym. Slowly, eyes wide, he shook his head ever so slightly. No one else was facing toward the kitchen, so Nym was the only one who saw.

The other mage must have thought the comment was too close to relating to the Collective, and he seemed kind of scared now, so Nym just settled back into his extremely comfortable chair and didn't say anything else while the rest of the group discussed the geas. It wasn't like there was much to add to the conversation anyway. His friends continued to debate how best to break the geas while Navarim just shook his head in the background.

CHAPTER THIRTY-ONE

Once everyone who wasn't going to be living in the house had left, Nym retired to his new bedroom to rest. His sleep schedule was all sorts of wrong thanks to the abduction and time spent in the mage cell. Even though there were still plenty of hours of daylight left, he just couldn't keep his eyes open any longer.

When he got back up, he found Navarim sitting on a couch idly flipping through a book while Analia had claimed the entire kitchen table. She had seven different books spread out around her and was furiously scribbling notes down on a loose sheet of paper.

"What are you doing?" he asked through a yawn.

"Working on breaking your geas," she said.

Nym tried to thank her, only to find his mouth refused to move. She saw him frowning to himself and nodded. "It's fine. I know what you want to say," she told him.

"Do you two want to get dinner?" Navarim asked. "I got a message an hour ago saying they want us back on-site soon, so this'll probably be your only chance to eat tonight."

"I guess we should eat then. What are we having?"

"There's a restaurant a few blocks over from here," Analia said absently, not looking up from her notes. "I had an air golem look around a bit ago. It seems decently popular, perhaps a bit on the pricey side, but since we're not renting two rooms at the Silver Gilder anymore, I think we can afford a single meal out."

"Since when do you pay attention to how pricey something is?" Nym asked.

"Since I'm down to my last three crests," she told him. "Though I suppose it doesn't matter at this point how much I use the family line of credit. I might as well just go to the bank and refill my purse with as much gold as it'll hold."

"Why's that?" Nym asked.

"Because my dad got to you, which obviously means he knows I'm here. It doesn't seem like there's much reason to hide anymore."

"Oh. Um, what makes you believe that?" he asked.

"Mostly the exotic-pet store next door," she said. "He knows how much I love menageries, which means he knows I'm here with you, probably both because they are spying on us and because of my foolish hopes about spending his money going unnoticed."

"You . . . Uh . . . You don't seem too upset about this," Nym said.

"I'll worry about it more after I figure out how to break this geas. When you go back on-site tonight, please let him know to stay away from me. I'm not ready to talk to him yet."

There was nothing the geas would let Nym say to that. After seeing what Analia's father was working on, he thought he had a little better understanding of the man's motivations for doing what he'd done to his daughter, which wasn't the same as condoning it. Jaspar Feldstal had still performed extremely dangerous experiments on his own infant daughter, experiments that could have easily killed her. Previous versions of those experiments probably had killed quite a few people working in the Collective.

"Someone's approaching the house," Analia said suddenly.

Nym noted Navarim's aura flaring up while he cast a scrying spell to see. A young man, perhaps eighteen or nineteen, was standing in front of the house. He peered around, seeming uncertain, but then shrugged and finished walking up the path to knock on the door.

"I'll get it," Navarim said. He crossed the room while casting a quick spell that Nym couldn't quite catch, then jerked the door open.

"Oh, hello," the teenager said. "Uh . . . Navarim, right? You're the other bodyguard?"

"I am. Are you with . . . ?" Navarim trailed off, his own geas preventing him saying anything else.

"Yeah, that," the teenager agreed. His mouth worked for a second like he wanted to say more, but nothing came out. Finally, he said, "God, that's annoying."

"Agreed. Worth it though."

"Oh, absolutely. Would you mind if I came in and introduced myself? Hard to do the job from the front door, you know?"

Navarim shot a glance back over his shoulder to Nym, who just shrugged in response. If ever there was a time for an assassin to attack, it was right there while Navarim wasn't looking, but nothing of the sort happened. The teenager stepped through the door and gave a slight bow to them.

"Allow me to introduce myself. My name is Jharn. I am dual specialized in fire and air magic, with a standard array of utility spells that skews slightly toward first-circle enhancement spells."

"That's impressive," Navarim said. "I'm more of a generalist myself, got a little bit of everything to keep me flexible."

"We should make a good pair then," Jharn said. He looked over toward the kitchen. "You must be Nym."

"That's me."

"Great. Good to meet you. We'll be working closely for a little while. Anything I should know?"

"Uh, I'm an air mage, I guess? Maybe air and water. I have a lot of general elementalism."

There was more, but Nym wasn't about to reveal his full kit any more than he expected Navarim and Jharn had told him everything they had. He could make some claim to having a divination utility set of spells and a small variety of short-duration curses, if he wanted to be honest.

"Air mage, huh? That's good. It means you'll be able to get away from trouble much easier while we hold off whatever's attacking."

Nym thought about how easily the abduction squad had piled on him and locked him down with a barrage of arcana injections. Five against one wasn't exactly a fair fight, and hopefully in a similar situation in the future, having a pair of bodyguards would help. Also having a fully repaired matrix would help.

"Well anyway, they sent me over to get you so we can go to work," Jharn said. "So, let me know when you're ready and we'll head over to the teleportation platform. Navarim, you can do the spell to get us back, right?"

"I can," he said slowly. "Can you not?"

"Not yet. I can only do outbound teleports. Quite annoying, so don't be surprised if I pester you to teach me."

"I'll have to get clearance first," the mage said.

Jharn shrugged, unconcerned. "I guess we'll be relying on you for the time being."

"I guess so."

Nym's two new bodyguards weren't exactly unfriendly toward each other, but Jharn had come on kind of strong, in Nym's opinion. Maybe he'd mellow out in the coming days and settle into a routine. For the time being, Nym decided to just take things as they came and not rush to judging the teenager.

"Shall we go?" Jharn asked. "Unless you need to do something else first? We've got a bit of time still I think."

"We were going to have dinner," Navarim told him.

"I can get behind that," Jharn said. "As long as it doesn't take too long."

"Bring me back something," Analia said, still not looking up from her books.

Jharn flinched and spun to face her. "Damn, I didn't even see her there. Some bodyguard I am, huh?"

"You should probably work on that," Nym said. "Come on, let's go get some food before we go to work."

Going to work made for a thoroughly boring evening. In much the same way his first night had gone, a bunch of mages ran a variety of tests and scans on him, commented on various techniques they wanted him to use, and observed his own matrix-repairing technique in real time using a complex and expensive-looking magical scanner.

They were stuck there until late into the night, but thanks to a stimulant spell Jharn taught him, Nym was still wide-awake. It was a bad idea to rely on it too much, but just one all-nighter to get his sleep schedule fixed wouldn't cause any problems. It was either that or resign himself to going to sleep around the same time the sun started rising.

Nym expected to spend a long, boring night working some of the new techniques the Collective wanted him to try. Failing that, he planned to find something quiet that wouldn't disturb anyone. That was why he was surprised when they got back and Jharn said, "You were a freelancer, right?"

"Yeah. I'm not sure if I can still take on jobs though."

"It's the army. They're big on paperwork. If you didn't receive any forms revoking your position, you probably still can. Want to go do some overnight jobs?"

"Really?" Nym asked. "That doesn't seem very safe."

"It's good money, and I don't know how much they're paying you, but I need to supplement my income. A few night shifts every week help. You just have to prove you can maintain a spell to see in the dark, and they'll let you take night missions."

"Are . . . you know . . . the people in charge of our day job . . . Are they fine with this?" Nym asked.

Jharn shrugged. "What they don't know won't hurt me."

Ten crests a month was a decent rate, especially since he wasn't going to be spending any of it on housing. He still had some money in reserve, but the longer he was a mage, the more he realized that it was expensive. It was no wonder the Academy's tuition was so high. Books were expensive, instructors even more so. Then there were supplies of various types needed to enchant anything or do alchemy or write new rune sequences, everything from equipment to raw materials to expensive catalysts and reagents. Finally, practicing magic meant not having time to work while still needing a place to eat and sleep.

He had a full library now, thanks to Analia. It was a small one, but it was theirs. There were probably a hundred spell books available to him. All he had to do was pull one off the shelf and start reading, but there were things that were far easier to learn with an instructor to teach him. And even if he didn't find an immediate use for it, he hadn't yet encountered a scenario where having more money in reserve was a bad thing.

Besides, he'd spent the last six hours poking at his matrix. He wanted to do something else. "Let's do it," he said. "Uh . . . Navarim? I know you're also doing bodyguard stuff, so are you coming?"

"No thanks. I'm off duty according to the schedule Jharn and I worked out. We overlap during the day and alternate who's staying up at night. Tonight's my night to sleep. Also, I am not a freelancer, so I couldn't participate without registering first."

"Alright. We'll be back before . . . dawn?" Nym looked over at Jharn, who nodded.

The pair left together, quickly exiting the town and flying northwest to forward command. They arrived at the freelancer's administration office in under twenty minutes, with Jharn easily keeping up with Nym's pace. Nym was somewhat frustrated with his slow speed. He knew he could do better, but it was hard to give the spell the arcana it needed to really get him moving.

He reminded himself that they'd made good time regardlesss, and that the flight was stable even if it wasn't as fast as he wanted. He would recover eventually; he just needed some patience. He could be working on that right now, but he'd wanted a break, so he really had no one to blame but himself.

Nym didn't recognize the clerk, but considering how few jobs he'd gone out on before his involuntary retirement from the field, that didn't surprise him. Jharn leaned on the counter and chatted with the guy like they were old friends and quickly got a job lined up. "Easy work. Wall patrol for the first half of the night, then a sector sweep. What's your range on undead-detection spells?"

"Depends on which spell I use," Nym said. "The one I've got that specifically finds undead is only good for maybe five hundred feet. I've got a wide-range general scry that can see farther, but it won't help me spot undead specifically. If I use a combination of spells, I could do maybe . . . maybe half a mile?"

Jharn nodded. "Sounds expensive though. How long can you keep it up?"

Nym wanted to say he could do it as long as needed, but with how much harder it was to keep channeled spells going anymore, he wasn't sure he'd be able to do a whole night straight. "I could do an area a few times an hour, I suppose."

"Alright, let's get going. I'll show you the patrol route, and we'll plan on alternating scans while we travel."

Before they could leave, the clerk took Nym into a pitch-black room and had him describe the decorations, which were several paintings. There was a range of styles that tested his ability to see shapes, colors, and fine details. It only took a few minutes to satisfy the clerk, and then they were on their way.

CHAPTER THIRTY-TWO

Nym sat on the wall and watched the forest nightlife move around him. Wide-range scrying combined with night vision gave him the most coverage but unfortunately did very little to actually find anything hiding in the foliage. He switched back to his old targeted scry with a mobile anchor, though he'd made a few tweaks to get it up to about twenty feet in diameter now.

There were a lot of small animals hidden away, going about their lives uncaring of the upheaval in the forest. If anything, things seemed to be going better than usual for them, since many of the larger animals that would have preyed on them had been hunted by the army or killed by roaming undead. Nym hadn't seen anything larger than a raccoon since he'd started really looking, and even those were rare.

Jharn landed next to him and yawned. "See anything?" he asked.

"Nothing we'd care about. You?"

"Couple of ghouls a quarter mile down the wall on the wrong side. I took care of them."

"Burned the bodies?" Nym asked.

"Of course," Jharn said, sounding mildly offended. "What kind of an amateur do you take me for?"

"I didn't mean it like that," Nym told him. "I just didn't see any light from the fire."

"Ah, I see. Sorry. I should explain, I guess. I burned them from the inside out, so it's mostly heat coming out of them as they start to fall apart."

That was a spell Nym was interested in learning. His own fire magics barely qualified as functional, and he kept meaning to do something about that. There were always so many other topics to spend his time on though and no strong reason to work on elemental fire spells over healing magic or learning runes.

"That's an interesting take on fire magic. Does it help destroy them while they're still whole, or is it just for cleanup after they're down?" Nym asked.

"It doesn't hurt, I guess, but you know nothing really slows them down except chopping them up. I think it more speeds up the aftermath if I'm already burning them from the inside out while I cut them apart," Jharn explained. He paused for a second, then added, "Plus I really like setting stuff on fire."

"How are you cutting them apart though? I don't see a weapon."

"Mage blades," Jharn said.

"Oh, that makes sense. I saw a mage once with ten or twelve swords floating around her. She chopped apart anything that got near her."

"I'm not as good with it as the mage you're describing, but I do know how to do it. I only use two small blades though," Jharn said, pulling open the side of his coat to reveal a short, thick blade sheathed in a pocket stitched into the lining. A second one was opposite it, and with a brief surge of arcana, both rose into the air. They were each about eight inches long and maybe three inches thick, sharpened all the way up and down both sides and coming to a tapered point.

The blades started spinning in place until they were going so fast that they were just blurry metal circles. Jharn sent them off into the woods to slice through a few tree limbs before they zipped back. "They get dull fast," he said. "I've got a couple spare sets at home, and it seems like at least once a week I'm sharpening the whole lot of them. There's a spell to use arcana to cut things directly, but I don't know it, so this is what I make do with."

"Oh, I know that one!" Nym said. "It's useless though. Good for making paper cuts and not much else. It might cut through a shirt, if it was thin enough."

"I don't think we're thinking of the same spell," Jharn told him.

"Here, I'll show you." Nym snagged one of the severed branches with telekinesis and brought it over to hold in his hand. Then he cast the kinetic cutting spell he'd learned months ago from that spell book in the Feldstal library and watched it slice right through the branch cleanly.

Nym stared at the severed limb for a second. "Huh. It doesn't normally do that."

Jharn started laughing. "The spell you're using, does it have one part of the construct that looks kind of like a face? And right next to it is a spot that looks like skeletal hand that's missing a finger?"

"Now that you mention it, yeah, it does."

"That's a craftsman spell, Nym. It's designed to work primarily on inanimate objects. You could carve through stone with it if you're patient enough, but it's not something you'd use against another person."

"What?!" Nym was outraged. "The book never said that!"

Jharn kept laughing while Nym gave him a sour glare. Now that he thought about it, he remembered it had worked just fine on some rope once. He should have made the connection instead of just writing it off as a useless spell. Nym couldn't think of any immediate use for it now, as he didn't have any crafting projects in mind, but it would definitely come in handy sooner or later.

"Remind me to get a couple mage weapons tomorrow," Nym said. "I went shopping for them once, but I didn't know there were special spells to use them, and I had a lot of trouble using just straight telekinesis to do any damage."

"Will do. If you don't mind me asking, how exactly were you killing ghouls as an air mage?"

"Earth magic," Nym said honestly. "It was slow and messy but also relatively safe, at least as long as there were only a few ghouls."

As he was speaking, his scrying spell picked up two ghouls moving toward the wall about a hundred feet away. "Speaking of a few ghouls, there's two of them right over there. Want to go take care of them with me?"

"Sure," Jharn said. "I'm curious about how you slowly and messily dismember a ghoul with earth magic."

The pair flew down the wall and settled into place. Nym pointed out where the ghouls were so that Jharn could watch them with his own magic, then spent the time to carefully create two earth golems. That was about as much as he could manage at the moment. His conduit could manage another set easily, if only he could get his arcana output back up to where it used to be. Nym examined it critically, trying to tell if it was any better after the last two days of exercises.

"What the hell are those?" Jharn asked.

"Earth golems," Nym said. The two golems advanced on the ghouls, which promptly attacked them. The ghouls did far more damage than the golems did, but the golems just pulled up more earth and kept regenerating from the attacks. Eventually, both ghouls were battered down and had their limbs ripped off, though it was really more like the limbs were punched repeatedly until they tore.

"Okay, I can see why you would say that's both messy and slow," Jharn said. "Let's get these torched and do another lap. I'll show you how I do a ghoul next time we find one."

Nym let the earth golems collapse back into piles of dirt and reshaped the ground into a small pit while Jharn ignited the wiggling body parts. It was somewhat gratifying to see that he also used arcana as fuel for his fire spells, but he was far more efficient than Nym, and the arcana didn't need to be aimed. His just popped into being right where he wanted it to be and ignited immediately. The ghouls blacked and started falling apart within a minute, far quicker than they would have on a natural fire.

Jharn kept the fire completely under control the whole time. Anything that tried to spread got infused with raw arcana and pulled back under his control.

There were barely even scorch marks on the grass when he finished. Nym swept the remains into the pit with telekinesis, then pushed all the dirt back on it. An effort of will packed it down smooth.

"Nicely done," Jharn said. "I can't even tell anything is buried there. That . . . uh . . . kind of has some disturbing implications."

Nym rolled his eyes. "I'm not burying bodies in the woods," he said.

"Right, right. I believe you. I just need to send a quick message spell . . . And . . . done. Don't worry, it's nothing related to anything we're doing out here."

"Let's just go find the next set of ghouls," Nym told him.

They flew a few hundred feet down the wall and started scouting again. Jharn's scrying spell didn't have Nym's range, but it worked better for finding undead in that he was able to sweep for any ghouls within a few hundred feet around him. It meant he had to fly back and forth over the canopy and then cast a few extra spells to get a visual on a ghoul when he found it, but he was still quick to spot new targets.

"Got one," he said, landing back on the wall.

"North of here, in that weird tree that's missing half its branches and is growing kind of sideways?"

"That's the one. You want to watch from here or head over?"

"I'll come with you," Nym said. He was interested in seeing the arcana being constructed into the spell, which wasn't something he could do through scrying.

The pair flew over, and Jharn unleashed his two blades. They whipped through the air on currents of his arcana, flashing through both of the ghoul's arms in one swift motion. Nym studied the spell as it cut its target apart in a matter of twenty or so seconds.

It wasn't quite the same as Yura's, but it accomplished similar effects. Hers had strands of arcana linking her to the weapons so that she could move them around, even if she couldn't see them. Jharn's version created lines of arcana that the weapons flowed across. If someone could see that arcana, it would be trivially easy to predict their paths.

While Jharn was slicing it up, he was also casting a second spell that infused the ghoul's body with arcana. It built up inside the limbs especially, and Nym found himself casting the nose-blindness spell he'd learned to keep the stink away from him. He flew back about ten feet farther to avoid the smoke that was starting to come out of the cooking limbs and waited for Jharn to finish burning the ghoul.

The pair went on like that all night, flying back and forth over three miles of wall and killing any ghouls that got close to it. They got five shields for their trouble, which wasn't really enough in Nym's mind, but the job was supposed to be performed by a single person, so he found it hard to complain about having to split the pay.

The sun was just coming up when they returned to Ebalsan. A second jolt of stimulant got his eyes open again. Nym was peppy enough that he decided to make a quick run to the bakery and spent his new two shields five on some pastries while Jharn watched, amused.

"Come on," Nym told him. "I want to go see some friends of mine. You should probably get to know them too if you're going to be my bodyguard."

"Sure," Jharn said. "I've got another four hours left before I'm off for the day. Where do they live?"

"They were near the third outpost. I'm not exactly sure where they're at right now, but I'll send a message and double-check."

"Why did we come back to town if we were just going back out to the forest?" Jharn asked, annoyance plain in his voice.

"To get the pastries, of course! You can't just go visiting people unexpectedly and not bring breakfast."

CHAPTER THIRTY-THREE

It didn't take long to find the new hut with Ophelia's help. Thankfully, she was, as always, an early riser. Nobody else was up yet, so the three of them sat at the stone table in the middle of their hut and talked quietly while the rest of the Earth Shapers slept in.

"Seems like there's a new change every day," she said, gesturing toward Jharn.

"I don't know how long we'll be working together," Jharn said. "So far, it's been an easy assignment, and he's been good to work with. I've got a little brother around his age who's a damn menace, so it was nice to not have those expectations met coming into this. I will admit I was worried."

"Sorry to disappoint. I could be more of a jerk if you like."

"I would prefer if you didn't," Jharn said dryly.

Monick shuffled out of his room and yawned. "Thought I smelled Nym visiting," he said. After sitting down and rooting through the basket of pastries, he looked around and added, "You are all way too perky."

"I blame a stimulant spell I'm using to adjust my sleep schedule," Nym said. "I don't know what Ophelia's excuse is."

"Tormenting Bildar is all the reason I need."

"There's only one custard in here," Monick said. "If he doesn't get up soon, I'm just going to eat it myself."

"Don't even think about it," Bildar said from across the room, having emerged from his own bedroom. He scooped up the basket and claimed the custard, then sat down and relinquished the rest of the spoils. "Nym, have I told you lately that you're my favorite person?"

"Only every time I bring food," Nym said with a smile.

"That's when it's most true."

"What are you guys doing today?" Nym asked.

"Same thing we do every day: grind out a few thousand new feet of wall. Sometimes I wish they'd just burn the whole forest down instead," Bildar grumbled.

"That would destabilize the whole region," Ophelia pointed out. "It would be a huge loss of lumber for the entire country, not to mention a couple dozen towns that depend on the forest collapsing. They're already struggling with this whole undead thing dragging on all summer."

"I know that, but it would sure make this whole thing easier to do. Trees grow back."

"If they did that, we'd be out of work again," Monick said.

"Oh, yeah. That's a good point. This whole wall would have been done months ago if the trees weren't in the way."

Nym wasn't willing to fight his geas to participate in a discussion about what the military was planning on what was going on in the center of the forest. He didn't think he was exactly forbidden from talking about it, but it would hit uncomfortably close to things he knew the geas would block, so he just kept quiet.

"Whatever they decide is all the same to us," Bildar said. "We'll keep building walls where they say to until the job's done or they come up with something else to build. Sure does seem like a roundabout way to go about things though. I wonder what they know that they're not telling us."

Jharn's jaw worked as his mouth opened and closed without any sound coming out. With a silent sigh, he gave up. No one remarked on it, though everyone knew what was happening. It wasn't the first time the conversation had been derailed that way. By unspoken agreement, they shifted from speculating on what the military was planning to a more benign topic.

Half an hour later, Bildar shooed them all out the door. "It was nice to see you and to meet your new friend, but we've got work to do. I'm sure you have something constructive to do with your time," he told Nym. "We'll come visit next time we're in town. Should be . . . four days? Ophelia, when's our next day off?"

"Six days," she said.

Bildar started swearing. "Six days, then," he said, a furious scowl painted on his face.

"Goodbye," the twins said, leaving with Bildar.

Ophelia made to follow them but hesitated for a second. "It was nice to see you again. Have you given any thought to the apprenticeship yet?" she asked.

"Not yet. Things have been kind of hectic," Nym told her.

"Understandable. Take your time. Have a good day and tell Analia I said not to give up. Sometimes people don't know they want something until it hits them in the face."

"I . . . What?" Nym shook his head. "Never mind. I'll tell her, I guess?"

"Thanks. Bye now. It was nice meeting you, Jharn."

"You too," the bodyguard said.

The Earth Shapers left to start their day, and Nym flew back to town. As they took off, he looked over at Jharn and asked, "What do you think that means?"

The other mage just started laughing.

Nym and Jharn stood inside a weapons shop, his coat's inner pocket heavy with fifteen shields. The bodyguard's display of magically chopping ghouls to pieces would have convinced Nym to revisit mage weapons if Yura hadn't already done it over a month ago. He just hadn't had the time or income to do so. Now that he was drawing a monthly stipend for what amounted to a few hours of work a night in addition to getting back into freelancing, a weapon seemed like a sound investment.

They hadn't gone back to the shop Nym had originally visited but, rather, one that Jharn had purchased several weapons from and that he regularly returned to when he needed replacements or maintenance. The setup was nothing like what Nym was familiar with. While there were plenty of weapons on the walls, they were there primarily for display purposes, and the actual stockpiles were kept in the back.

A huge man walked out of the back room and looked at them. He was easily over six feet tall, heavily muscled and without a single hair on his head or chin. "What do you need today, Jharn?"

"Nothing for me. My friend here is looking to get his first mage weapon. You mind if we use the firing range to try a few things out for him?"

"Sure. Take your time. Come find me once you've picked something out."

Nym hadn't needed it, but he'd still asked Jharn to write out the construct for his mage-weapon spell. Nym practiced it a few times using a loaner weapon to confirm he had the hang of it, then they'd hit the shop. He tried out a pair of spinning blades on display that looked like Jharn's and found them to be identical, which was no surprise considering the store was where the bodyguard had purchased them.

Nym also tried out some of the heavier weapons and found that, even with his new magic, they were still exhausting to swing around. He could keep three or four spinning blades going for the same amount of arcana as it took to smack the target with one heavy spiked ball. Admittedly, the spiked ball did way more damage, but against a ghoul, it was a clear choice.

Plus, when he thought about the logistics, he had no idea how he was supposed to haul around the ball. Spinning blades were the way to go, at least for undead slaying. He also picked up a pack of thin metal needles, pointed on both ends. Those were more what he considered human-defense weapons, which hopefully he wouldn't have any reason to use, but they were light and easy to store.

They paid the shopkeeper a full crest for the needles and four blades. Nym winced at the price and actually had to borrow a few shields from Jharn, but they swung by the house right after so he could restock and pay back the money. Then they hit a leatherworker's shop so Nym could get his coat modified to hold the weapons, even though he didn't tend to wear it very often anymore unless he was going flying. It was just too hot in the middle of summer.

After that, Jharn switched places with Navarim. He borrowed the spare bedroom to sleep, much to Analia's annoyance. She didn't say anything out loud, but Nym could tell by the look she gave the closed door that she wasn't impressed with the new arrangement.

"Oh, I forgot to tell you," he said. "Ophelia asked me to pass you a message. I'm not sure why she didn't just send it to you, but I said I would."

"What did she say?" Analia asked.

"Um . . . Something about not giving up and not knowing what you want until it hits you in the face?"

Analia arched an eyebrow and said, "What do you think she meant by that?"

"No idea. I'm just passing on the message."

"Let me know if you ever figure it out," she told him.

"Why would I need to . . . It's not even a message for me? Why are you laughing?" Nym demanded, spinning around to glare at Navarim. He wasn't sure what the older mage was snickering about, but he knew it was at his expense.

"You'll figure it out someday," Navarim said.

"Or you could just tell me. Is this supposed to be some kind of secret?"

"I don't know. Is it?"

"How would I know?!" Nym threw up his hands and stomped off.

Nym eyed the machine in front of him warily. "Are you sure this is safe?" he asked.

"Of course it is," Doliar said.

"It doesn't look safe. It looks . . . pointy."

"Well, yeah, but it's not like I'm going to stab you with it."

The contraption looked something like a hollow, life-size doll. It was currently cracked open down the middle, revealing a series of rune sequences carved into the interior. On the outside were about fifty spikes tacked on at various places. Nym couldn't quite figure out what the logic behind their placement was, but something about it looked familiar.

"Hey, are the spikes mapping out arcana channels?" he asked suddenly.

"Close," Doliar said. "It's actually common pain points for arcana poisoning.

The channels were designed to fill the places people most commonly bleed excess arcana into, so the positions are very close to the same, just with some slight adjustments for where it proved impossible or just too difficult to forge the channel."

"And why am I in the same room as this thing again?"

"So I can get a reading on if your pain points have changed based on the new shape of your soul well."

Nym thought about that for a second. "That sounds like you're asking me to deliberately give myself arcana poisoning again."

Doliar at least had the grace to look slightly embarrassed. "Just a little bit. You'll hardly notice it, probably have it cleared out in under an hour."

"I don't like this plan," Nym said.

"Oh, come on. Don't be a baby! I've almost got this calibrated now."

"Did you get this approved?" Nym asked.

"Approved by who? I'm the head researcher!"

"Fine, I'll do it. But in return, I want you to walk me through a few healing spells I've been trying to figure out."

Doliar frowned and said, "My time is kind of valuable. I'm sure someone else could help you with this."

"I've got the book right here." Nym patted his pack. "It'll hardly take any time at all. Plus you can monitor the arcana poisoning while I use other spells when I practice."

The healer perked up at that. "That's a good test. We should definitely do that. Okay, let me finish adjusting this. Which spells were you looking at anyway?"

Nym pulled the book out and flipped to the first page he'd bookmarked. "Here, this one. It's supposed to be a first-circle spell that speeds up natural regeneration, but every time I make the construct, it collapses. I don't see anything here saying I need to do an intent filter for the arcana, but I can't think of why else the spell keeps failing."

"That should be easy enough. There's nothing too tricky in this diagram. We'll look at it in a few minutes here. The sensors are all on. Go ahead and start pulling in arcana now."

Nym stifled a groan. The next hour or two was going to hurt.

CHAPTER THIRTY-FOUR

Nym made steady progress on fixing his matrix. The techniques the Collective knew helped him reinforce the net that connected individual nodes together while he rotated holding small pieces of his matrix in an open state. He'd found that trying to hold the whole thing at once did nothing, and it was only when he focused on a few at a time that he was able to shift them enough that they started to grow. The trick then became to rotate through each cluster and keep them all growing at an equal pace.

By Doliar's estimates, it would be another few weeks before everything stabilized, but the more Nym worked on it, the more he was able to open his soul well back up. Already he was approaching his previous levels of arcana output, and he was hopeful that he'd surpass that soon enough. Combined with the new methods he'd learned for creating conduits, he was sure he'd be able to fly faster, make more golems, and hold more ongoing spells at once.

His new conduit was a coil shape, one that allowed him to hold its structure firm while snaking around any obstructions in the second layer. It only somewhat worked, as occasionally he still got caught on a big enough knot of arcana, but it was an improvement over his previous conduit. Making them flexible enough to move through the second layer worked fine until he reached the membrane blocking the third layer. All attempts at breaking through that barrier with any conduit he'd been able to reach it with had failed.

Navarim had been extremely helpful in advising him on his conduit, having recently made one that could reach all the way to the Astral Sea himself. It was on his recommendation that Nym had started experimenting with a coiling conduit. It had taken a few attempts to get one with the right balance between strong and flexible that allowed it to curl around arcana knots without breaking but that would hopefully be strong enough to pierce the third layer.

And then, without any warning, three weeks after his talk with Jaspar Feldstal and his induction into the Collective, Nym broke through into the third layer. He was lying in his bed, testing the latest iteration of the new design, and it just . . . happened. At first, Nym wasn't even sure what he'd done. Then the arcana swept into his soul well, and he jolted upright.

First- and second-layer arcana were similar, except that first layer felt a bit denser to Nym. Third layer was nothing like that. The arcana of the Astral Sea was agitated. It battered against the walls of his soul well like it was alive. It wasn't painful, but it gave him an uncomfortable amount of feedback into the nodes that were still misaligned in his matrix.

Nym had just moments to realize what was going on, and then he was somewhere else.

"Why does every spell I try fall apart?" he asked.

"Because the arcana is different. You know this. You've felt it."

He glared at the wall they were standing in front of. It showed the instructions needed for a teleportation spell and was even enchanted to display it in four dimensions. He could watch the pattern being woven together in real time. He had watched it over and over again.

"I'm doing what the instructions say, but my arcana doesn't want to stay in place."

"Perhaps it is your will that is lacking," a new voice said. A man approached, his father. "If you are unable to master something as simple as the Astral Sea, how will you ever become truly powerful? I had thought you'd grow to be an exceptional man, not one who makes excuses."

He screwed up his face into a scowl and said, "I'm five! Mother says I have plenty of time to grow up."

"I do not care what excuses your mother makes for you," his father said. "You are being personally tutored in these spells to give you every advantage because you will need those advantages to keep hold of what is rightfully yours. Cease whining and prove you will be a man I can be proud of."

There was no point in arguing with his father. One way or another, he would master the spell. No matter how many times he had to repeat the lesson, the day would not end until he'd completed it. His father would not let it be any other way. Even if he had to drag time backward, there was only one acceptable outcome.

He had tried to compensate for the strange, chaotic pull of Astral Sea arcana, but there was no predicting it. There couldn't be any compromise between his will and the arcana. He would have to force it into obedience.

He opened the conduit again to pit himself against the arcana. It filled his soul well to bursting, and he closed the conduit. Once it was sealed off from the rest of the third layer, it was easier to manipulate. Thirty seconds later, he'd saturated the arcana with his will, forced it into gentle calmness, and was ready to try again.

He wove the arcana into the spell focused on his destination, a mat on the other side of the room. His training arena was sealed off, preventing anyone from teleporting through that seal and, more importantly, preventing him from accidentally teleporting outside it. He was as safe as he could possibly be to practice such a dangerous spell.

Under his father's baleful gaze, he finished constructing the magic and let it pull him through the arcana. He appeared across the room, one foot on the mat and one on the floor next to it. "Pathetic," his father said. "Again. And don't close off your conduit to make it easy on yourself."

Keeping the arcana under control was much harder when it was still connected to the Astral Sea. It took more willpower than he had, or at least it took special techniques he had no knowledge of. His father watched him struggle, silently judging him, as he tried over and over to master the spell in a manner that would satisfy the man.

Hours later, he still couldn't do it. With a snort of disgust, his father told him, "I'll be back to check on you tomorrow. You won't like the consequences if you're still failing." He turned his glare on the man who was supposed to be the instructor. "Neither of you."

Nym came back to himself with a gasp. The vision had come out of nowhere, and it had been so much more intense than the previous two. Maybe it was because he wasn't in some life-and-death situation and hadn't been expecting it to happen, or maybe it was just the amount of fear he'd felt, but it took him a long time to calm down again.

He'd thought the trigger for the memory visions was his life being in danger, but obviously that wasn't the case. The time with the shark and the time with Valgo had both been dangerous, but he hadn't gotten a vision when he was fighting the ice worms. As far as he could tell, there was no immediate danger to him while in his own bed.

So the triggers were something else. Perhaps there was no logic to them, and each was different, or there was a pattern he was missing. The memories could be predetermined, and the vision just triggered as soon as he could use the spell that it was about. He was making more assumptions, he knew. It was entirely possible he'd have another vision that didn't teach him a new spell.

The simple fact of the matter was that three data points weren't much better than two. All he'd really done was eliminate one possible answer that he was already confident was incorrect. He couldn't try to plan around forcing more visions to come when he had no real answers to what triggered them.

What he could do was test the vision. It wasn't that he had any reason to doubt the accuracy of what he'd learned, but if he truly was a third-circle mage now, a master mage, he would need to be able to control his new arcana. He forged the conduit again, pushing to reach the third layer. It took precious seconds, far too many to be useful in an instant, but he was confident he'd get better with practice.

Third-layer arcana poured into his soul well and pushed against the matrix holding it in place. Much like his memory self, Nym cut the conduit and took the time to fully infuse the arcana with his will. Already he had ideas about filtering the conduit with intent that would require some experimentation and research.

Nym was going to be very careful with his next moves. He was still tied to the Collective for years to come, and it wasn't like he had a lot of leverage in that relationship. He had one technique they wanted, and they'd more or less gotten it out of him already. If Analia's father decided to have him abducted and murdered now, it wouldn't cost the Collective much. The only thing really keeping him safe was the geas Lord Feldstal had agreed to.

A geas could be broken though, and Nym had no doubt that Lord Feldstal already knew how to do it. It wouldn't even surprise Nym to learn that the nobleman had already freed himself. There was precious little in the way of trust for the Collective as a whole, despite his friendships with a few members. Nym just hoped that when they'd wrung every last drop of useful information out of him, they didn't decide it was more expedient to dispose of him.

He wanted to say they hadn't given him any reason to think like that, but the truth was that they'd abducted him, and now he had two members of the Collective following him around. At least one of them was with him at all times, not that it mattered. They'd proven they were more than capable of investigating him without his knowledge.

Six months ago, he would have said it was time to run for it. Now he had friends. He couldn't just leave them behind, not in the least because he didn't trust the Collective not to hold them hostage against him. So Nym decided to keep this little breakthrough to himself. He teleported across his room, once, just to confirm that it worked, and then he released the rest of the arcana.

He would need to learn a strong and versatile repertoire of third-circle spells before he considered anything drastic, and since he barely got a moment to himself outside his own bedroom anymore, it would be difficult to practice. So far, he'd just grabbed at whatever was in front of him without a lot of planning. It worked alright most of the time, but every now and then he ran into a problem that he wasn't equipped to handle at all.

He wanted the Collective's project to succeed both because its success would mean the end of his obligations to them and because, on a much grander scale, it would lead to stopping an outpouring of undead and repairing a tear in the veil between this world and the afterlife. That might take some time while they built up their roster of master mages, but it would happen.

Nym briefly considered just telling them he'd reached the third circle. Surely if there was an organization equipped to train him, it would be the Collective. The problem was he wasn't sure what it would cost him, how much tighter he'd be binding himself to them, and there was no way he could think of to find out what they'd share without first telling them why he needed it. He'd keep it in mind as a backup option, but for now, he would see what he could accomplish on his own.

CHAPTER THIRTY-FIVE

Nym picked a day when Jharn was doing the overnight shift. He was younger than Navarim, not nearly as clever, and displayed considerably less institutional loyalty. Nym waited for hours in his room under the pretense of performing one of the many, many exercises Doliar had prescribed to work on his matrix. He scried every ten minutes or so until he noted Jharn sleeping, then continued to check up on him regularly for the next hour.

That was as good an opening as Nym was going to get. He crafted his teleportation spell with deliberation and care, knowing that it would have to be perfect to take him where he wanted to go. There was no platform on the other end to help guide the spell. He would be appearing somewhere else in the world, and it was completely on him to see the process through from start to finish.

He tried to picture it in his head, the sand, the waves, the smell in the air. He needed to hear the sound, to remember what it felt like standing there. That was the place he needed to be, and his magic was the bridge between what was and what could be. He shed arcana into the world, that essence of unreality so strong that it could change physical law.

And then, without any fanfare, what could be and what was merged. Nym disappeared from his bed and was standing on the beach. It really was just like he remembered it, right down to that *thing* in the water that always drew his attention. And now that he knew, now that he could see, he recognized the shark that guarded it.

It didn't have an aura of arcana around it, at least not something he could detect. Nym flew over the water, and it appeared below him, summoned up from the depths by his mere presence. The shark swam circles underneath him, never stopping, chasing him as he flew to the center of the cove. The closer he got, the more agitated it became, to the point that it actually breached the water several times to leap at him.

Nym floated about fifteen feet over the surface of the water, and magic shark or not, it couldn't come close to getting that kind of altitude. The water roiled under him as more sharks started to show up, equally agitated. He counted twelve fins cutting through the water immediately below him.

A few months ago, they would have been a problem for Nym. He wasn't recovered to full strength yet, but he'd been exposed to hundreds of new spells and had taken the time to commit thirty or forty of them to memory. Some of them he'd learned for the express purpose of getting to the bottom of the cove.

Nym started with the simplest solution. He didn't expect it to work in this case because there were obviously some sort of magical shenanigans going on, but it only cost him a few seconds to try. He cast a spell to hide himself from animals. If it worked, they would lose interest in him and proceed about their business as if he wasn't even there. He'd tried it on a few squirrels back in the forest and been able to walk right up to them while they were foraging.

The sharks did not ignore him, not that he'd expected them to. He let the spell fade away and started on the next one: scare animals. He didn't think it would work any better, but it cost nothing to try. If it worked, the sharks would scatter. He finished it and peered down into the water. There were . . . maybe a few less? It was hard to tell.

He switched from trying to bypass the sharks to attempting to stay out of the water completely. Hydrokinesis bore down from the surface of the cove, splitting the water and pushing it away. It went down ten feet, then twenty, and then Nym couldn't hold it anymore. The water came swirling back into place, and with it the sharks.

Nym switched to trying to magically grab the underwater thing and drag it up from the depths. It hadn't worked before, but he was stronger now. He didn't expect it to work again, but he was going to exhaust his safe options before he went into the water himself. But whatever it was down there, he still couldn't grab it with telekinesis.

A scrying spell he'd learned specifically to look into water was his next attempt. It had a component in it to increase his visual range underwater, and he'd modified it with his own mobile-anchor adjustments that allowed the scry to move independent of him. His mind was filled with a vision of the water, deep and dark. Even with the spell, he still couldn't see very far.

The scry dove straight down to the bottom of the cove and swept around in circles, looking for the mysterious thing. It was there; he knew it was. He could feel it in his head, dragging at his attention. It was even stronger now than it had been almost a year ago. He was looking at right where it was, but as far as he could tell, there was nothing there.

All this meant to Nym was that he would need to go down himself. He had a number of spells he'd sought out specifically for that task as well. First, he needed the ability to breathe and see. Fortunately, mages had long ago created spells for that, and they'd recognized the need for multiple spells without having to feed them to keep them active.

Nym's own attempts at creating new spells weren't nearly as sophisticated. It was easier to make a spell that he continuously provided arcana to than to make one that invested an amount up front and then persisted for a set period of time without any further action on his part. The only one he'd ever really done that wasn't like that was the spell he'd crafted to heat a solid surface for an extended period of time, and he'd been driven to that by the necessity of finding a warm place to sleep.

Fortunately, the ones he'd learned didn't require he keep an open line of arcana feeding them. He cast the spells in quick succession, then considered his next course of action. If he went into the water without doing anything else, the sharks would attack him. He needed to either defend himself somehow or kill or otherwise immobilize the sharks. Or he needed to move so fast that they couldn't catch him, but he didn't know how long he'd be down at the bottom even if he could pull that off, so Nym dismissed that idea out of hand.

He hadn't found an easy solution to this problem. There were plenty of ways to kill sharks, but the more he killed, the more the blood in the water would attract new sharks. Nym could end up spending hours slaughtering them only to be forced to leave when he ran out of time without ever actually accomplishing his goal.

So he wasn't going to do that. Instead, he'd found instructions for what some mage had deemed a metaspell buried deep in one of Analia's books. It was a way to take a spell he already knew, tear it apart, and modify it to function in a different method. There was a whole set of knowledge in this category that Nym had never known existed but that he was completely fascinated by.

In this case, he would be taking the daze spell he'd learned months ago, modifying it to work on animals, and then turning it into an aura that automatically smacked anything that got too close to him with it. It was going to cost him roughly four times as much arcana as normal each time he dazed a shark, but he was still fresh and expected he could last through a solid fifty dazes, more if he got some recovery time.

It would be more than long enough to swim straight down through a hundred feet of water, grab the thing, and come back up. The only sticking point Nym saw in his plan was that he wasn't exactly sure what it was that was down there or how long it would take to extract it. He just had a chronic, incessant need to go to that one particular place. It had faded somewhat as he'd traveled farther and farther away, but now that he was back at Bloodfin Cove, it was near overwhelming.

He could feel it like an itch in his teeth, under his scalp, behind his eyes. It made him twitchy coming back to it suddenly after being away for so long. One way or another, he was getting down to that spot tonight. He was just going to be smart about it so he didn't kill himself in the attempt.

Nym cast his aura daze spell and lowered himself to the water without actually going into it. The first shark swung around toward him, then suddenly veered off course. It cruised in a straight line past him, going on momentum alone. Three more sharks hit the aura in quick succession. Nym observed their reactions to it and frowned.

It was very possible he might end up getting hit by a shark just because it was coming straight at him when it got hit with the daze effect. He had a deflection spell he'd picked up that was designed to stop physical matter from passing through it, but the area of effect was barely bigger than his head and didn't last long. It could be tricky using it if he had multiple sharks coming at him at once.

He'd been hoping they'd just stop dead in the water when they got too close, but that didn't appear to be in the cards. On the bright side, the daze aura worked, and it looked like it was taking upward of a minute for them to regain their wits. He didn't see any degradation in effectiveness when they came back in and took a second hit. If anything, it seemed to work better with repeated attacks.

He was as prepared as he could reasonably be. He had three different spells going and was planning on using hydrokinesis to speed up his trip down. If for some reason everything else stopped working, he could freeze an approaching shark into a block of ice to buy time and give himself some cover. It would cost way more arcana than he wanted to spend, but it was a last resort option.

Nym released his flying spell and dropped into the water. His hydrokinetic magic grabbed him and pulled him deeper, fortunately fast enough that the sharks who entered his daze aura shot by overhead instead of crashing into him. In the first few seconds, he must have been hit twenty times, but he'd filled his soul well to its maximum before he went in and that had been enough to keep the aura going.

If they continued to attack him at that speed, he would have to retreat, but the number of sharks on him dropped dramatically as they drifted off, unaware of their surroundings. A new shark came by every second or two, but he could easily handle the strain of just one at a time.

His water-breathing and underwater-vision spells were working, and with hydrokinesis pulling him straight down, it took less than twenty seconds to reach the bottom of the cove. Confused, he looked around for the thing. He could still feel it, knew exactly where it should be, but saw nothing. Nym bent down and ran his hands over the spot, trying to find something that all his magic told him didn't exist.

His fingers closed on something hard and square. It was like a little metal box, except completely invisible. This then was it, the object of his fascination that had called out to him to come to it. Nym clutched it tightly to his chest and shot straight up until he breached the surface, then called new magic to wrap him in air and lift him free from the water.

Moments later, he was standing on the sand again. Hydrokinesis pulled the water away from him, and he dismissed the remaining magic. Finally, with no spells modifying his senses, Nym could see what he was holding. It was a small thing, maybe six inches to a side, a perfect cube made of some sort of delicate white crystal shaped like a lattice. Despite the apparent gaps in its surface, he found it to be completely smooth, his fingers tracing over the air like it was solid.

Now he just needed to figure out what it was.

CHAPTER THIRTY-SIX

Viewed through any type of magical sense, the cube did not exist. Scrying didn't reveal it. Using night vision or far sight to enhance his senses made it disappear. Even groping around blindly with telekinesis did nothing. The magic simply passed through it. If he tried to form a cushion of air to lift it up, nothing happened.

To every single test Nym could come up with except looking at it with his own eyes and holding it with his own hands, the cube did not exist. He had no idea what it was, but it was somehow immune to any and all forms of magic that he knew of.

He'd have to do some more research. Whatever it was, it was definitely important. He was half tempted to dump it back in the water rather than take it home with him, but now that he finally had his hands on it, he didn't think he could handle letting it go again. It went into his pack.

It was almost time to go home, but he had one last thing to do before he left. Nym floated up to the top of the bluffs and flew over to Ciana's home. It looked much like he remembered it, and a quick scry spell revealed her asleep inside of it. Nym floated at the door and hesitated. He wanted to see her again, but he didn't want to wake her up. He could always come back tomorrow during the day, but if he did, he'd have to explain to his bodyguards why he'd disappeared.

Hopefully, Ciana wanted to see him and wouldn't be too upset about being woken up after midnight. He knocked on the door and waited for her to answer. That gave him plenty of time to second-guess himself, slightly panic, consider flying away, remind himself that he hadn't seen her in close to a year, remember why he'd left, panic again, and there was the door opening right now and he was not ready for this!

"Who're you?" Ciana asked, her tone grumpy.

"Uh . . . It's . . . It's me," Nym said.

She peered out into the dark at him. Nym peered back at her. He pulled in a bit of arcana and created a small ball of light, barely more than a candle's worth, in the air overhead. Ciana gasped and took a step back. "Who are you?" she repeated, this time more surprised and a bit suspicious.

"Wow. I didn't think you'd forget me completely."

"I know someone who looks like you, maybe a family member," she said. "But I don't know you."

"Oh! I get it," Nym said. "No, it's me. I kind of had a growth spurt. There was some magic involved."

"A magical growth spurt? Nym?"

"Hi," he said, grinning.

She threw her arms around him and dragged him into a hug. "You're alive!" she said into his hair. Then she pushed him back out to arm's length and scowled down at him. "Do you have any idea how worried I was about you?"

"I'm sorry," he said. "But . . . I mean . . . I couldn't stay here. I still can't. I'm leaving after this visit."

"I understand," she said. "I was being dumb. It was for the best that you didn't listen to me. The captain of the guard would have had to lock you up for your own safety. Senman had a few friends who went on a rampage when everything came out. I'm glad you weren't here for them to target."

"Are you alright?" Nym asked.

"I'm good, actually. Really good. But come in, sit down. Tell me what you've been doing and why you look like you're five years older than you should be."

Nym smiled at the sight of the driftwood log he'd shared his first meals on with her. She'd done alright for herself since he'd left, probably because she wasn't trying to feed a second mouth. A table with a single chair had been added to the room, and she had a cupboard full of food. New clay jugs lined the wall near it, each one full of fresh water.

He sat down on his side of the log and gave the cauldron hanging over the fire an affectionate pat. Ciana dragged her chair over from the table so she could sit across from him. "Do you want me to put something on?" she said.

"No, thank you. Let's just talk."

"Sure. Let's start with why you look like you're almost as old as me."

Nym scratched the back of his head. "I'm not really sure. I guess there's some spell on me that makes me age faster. I'm actually kind of worried I'll be an old man in a decade. On the bright side, it does give me an advantage at magic."

"An aging spell? I didn't know that was possible," she said. "I've never heard anything like that. How did you even find this out?"

"That's a bit of a story," Nym said. "So when I left here, I flew straight into the forest . . ."

Nym spent an hour or two telling Ciana about his adventures, and his misadventures, slightly edited to leave out some of the more dangerous parts, right up until he'd been kidnapped by the Collective. That part he skipped over completely since his geas wouldn't even let him paint it in broad strokes for her.

"And then a few days ago, I figured out how to use third-circle magic, learned how to teleport, and decided to pop over for a visit," he finished.

"Any reason you couldn't do that while the sun's still up?" she asked.

"Well, it's more like I snuck out of the house for a visit," he admitted. "I'll be back in my bed before morning, and no one will ever know I was gone."

"You're not telling me something," she said. "Still hiding things, huh?"

"I wish I could say more," he told her truthfully. "Suffice it to say that I don't want certain people in Ebalsan to know that I am now capable of casting a teleportation spell. I won't be able to visit again for a while until I'm done with everything there and have more freedom to do what I want."

Ciana snorted and said, "I can't imagine you giving up any amount of freedom. You're a very independent person."

He tried to respond, but his geas blocked him. Apparently even talking about anyone from the Collective was enough to set it off. Annoyed, he changed the subject. "Tell me about Senman's friends and what happened."

"You know how he had those three flunkies he was always strutting around with? Well, when they learned that he was dead, they tried to come out here and cause problems for me, only I wasn't home. So they trashed the place, and then when I reported it, the guards went to go question them. They tried to beat up the guards."

She started laughing while she talked, and soon Nym was laughing with her. "How did that go for them?"

"One of them ended up getting stabbed, and the other two decided to go in quietly. Last I knew, all three of them sat in the jailhouse for a few months before they were let go. I haven't seen any of them around since spring started. I think they went up the road to be someone else's problem."

"Good riddance," Nym said. He looked around again and said, "I guess it's been a good summer for you."

"Like you wouldn't believe," Ciana agreed. "I had no idea how much Senman was doing to sabotage me until he wasn't around to do it anymore. I'm not scrounging for food now. I've got enough to trade in town. I barely even have to go out on the water now to pull up crabs. I mean, I still do because they're tasty, but it's still dangerous, you know?"

"I'm sure it's not as bad now that I'm not in the boat with you," Nym said.

"Well, that's true. Your shark is still in the cove though. I see it all the time. It leaves me alone now that you're not here."

"I saw," he told her. "I teleported in on the beach. It showed up almost instantly."

"It must have missed you," she told him.

"I didn't miss it," he groused.

"But did you miss me?" she teased.

"I did."

"Awww, well I missed you too. I'm glad that you're safe, even if you did go off and become an adult while I wasn't looking."

"It was bound to happen eventually," he said. "I couldn't have stayed here forever. Even with everything I've done and everywhere I've been, I've barely started to figure out what's going on with me. And honestly, I'm running out of ideas. It's hard to trust people, and I don't know where to look for answers."

"Is there anything I can do?" Ciana asked.

Nym smiled and shook his head. "Just the fact that you would if you could helps. I'm glad things are going better for you now."

He dug around in his pack for a second and pulled out his money pouch. "Could you spend crests around here without people finding it suspicious?" he asked.

"I don't need your money, Nym."

"I know you don't. But I have more than I need, and I'd like to make sure my big sister is taken care of."

He pulled out every shim and wedge he could find and piled them on the log next to him. Then he added a handful of shields to the pile. "Maybe . . . only spend the shields one at a time? Maybe space it out a few weeks? I would appreciate if no one knew I came to visit you."

"Maybe just take it all with you," Ciana told him.

"Nah, I'm going to leave it here. I guess if you don't want it, just throw it to the sharks."

"Damn it, Nym!"

She lunged for him, but he just floated backward into the air out of her reach. When she scrambled after him, he went higher and flattened himself out against the ceiling. "Oh, that reminds me. I learned some elemental earth magic too. Do you need anything built? Cellar? Secondary buildings? New, bigger main building?"

"Oh for . . . Really? Actually . . . I could kind of use a cellar. Some of the meat doesn't store well, and it'd be nice to have a cool place for it. But that's too much. You don't need to do this!"

"I know, but I want to. Going to do it anyway. Do you want stairs or just a ladder? Maybe a ladder inside and stairs outside? You'd need to do the cellar doors yourself unless you think you can use stone doors."

"Outside is good. I will get the doors taken care of," she told him.

"Want to watch?" he asked, grinning.

"Don't be a show-off."

They went outside, and Ciana picked out a spot for the entrance. Then Nym started excavating under the shack. In no time at all, he'd cleared most of the dirt out, reinforced the foundation by transmuting the square room to stone, and added a set of pillars spaced in the middle to further hold everything up. With Ciana's direction, stone storage shelves were added to the foundation so that they ringed the entire cellar. It wasn't Earth Shaper–quality work, but it'd do the job.

They walked back up the stairs together, and Nym was startled to see the light of predawn on the water. "Oh damn," he said. "I need to get back before someone notices I'm gone. I'll try to come visit you again soon, hopefully in a month or two."

He rushed over to give her a hug, then started the laborious process of opening a conduit to the third layer. It still took far too long to be useful in combat, but he didn't know any third-circle combat spells yet, and there was plenty of time to refine it.

The conduit connected, and chaotic Astral Sea arcana poured into his soul well. Before he had a chance to shape it, the whole world pulsed around him, and everything went white.

CHAPTER THIRTY-SEVEN

Aman stood in front of Nym in an endless white void. His entire outfit reminded Nym of some of the more ridiculously expensive ensembles nobles wore, just layer after layer of lavish fabrics with gold and silver threaded through them and gemstones woven into the designs. The metals were stitched into runes all across the clothing, with gemstone buttons that had their own runes carved into them.

He had long hair the same color as Nym's and was clean-shaven. The man's face was eerily familiar, but Nym couldn't quite place it. At first, he thought it was his father from the visions, but it didn't quite look right.

"If you're seeing this, that means you've regained enough magic to access the Astral Sea. It has likely been three months since I recorded this for you. I'm sure you've figured out most of what's happened already, but I will take a moment to review the situation.

"We are Exarch Niramyn. Our rival, Exarch Myzalik, has done something everyone thought to be impossible and weaponized the immortality spell that forms the basis of our eternal civilization here in the core reality. If ever there was an ascendant to do it, it would be an exarch who specializes in time manipulation, but I was arrogant and was a fool to think we were so untouchable.

"I was left with no choice but to flee the attack, and to prevent being discovered, I had to splinter my mind and sequester it away into this trinket. I've layered it with the most powerful spells I could in the limited amount of time I had left to render it undetectable to everyone but myself. It would be much easier if I could simply give you, give myself really, back my memories and abilities, but you are not ready for that yet.

"Once you become Niramyn again, they will be able to find you. The spells I was able to cast to shield you from their sight won't hide me, and right now your body isn't strong enough to withstand the spells we must utilize in order to regain our power. I have plotted a course from the fifth layer back to full strength that will take us a little over a month.

"Fortunately, there is nothing truly dangerous in the mortal realms, and I've set up a few contingencies for the most likely scenarios. I'm sure it has been a thoroughly annoying and frustrating few months living with them and dealing with them, but by now you should have acquired the magic you need to reach the fifth layer. Place the memory cube back in its hiding place until you've completed your rehabilitation. Once you've touched the fifth layer, return and I will begin imparting our memories to you so that you will understand the process of ascending."

Nym stared, slack-jawed, at the apparition that droned on. Any attempts to get in a question were ignored. It just kept talking, so pompous and arrogant and full of incorrect assumptions. The vision thought it would only take him a few months to reach the third layer, but it had taken close to a year. The only reason people had stopped commenting on his abilities was that he had physically aged up to a point where it wasn't uncommon for a person to know some second-circle magic.

Looking back on the few memories he did have, he supposed he understood why this past-life version of himself thought it would go much quicker. He'd had luxuries Nym could only dream of. The training was no doubt harsh, but in every memory, someone was there to guide and teach Exarch Niramyn. There was no sign that he struggled for food or shelter, no sign that he'd been forced to scrounge through whatever random books he could get his hands on.

"You're kind of a prick," Nym told the vision, which of course ignored him.

The vision of Exarch Niramyn kept speaking, now detailing the many spells it had cast before splitting its memories from Nym. The seed memories were of course Niramyn's doing, as was the aging spell designed to force him to physically mature faster so that his soul well would expand. The visage made no mention of how to stop that spell, which Nym took to mean that it would end when he regained his lost memories and chose to end it.

It detailed a number of obfuscation methods it had used to hide, reciting the spells one after another in a bored tone, simply regurgitating information for the sake of being thorough. Nym recognized none of the spells.

To cap it off, there was a timeline wipe that essentially removed Niramyn from the past for a period of about two minutes while he became Nym. The spell was something of his own design, crafted specifically to counter Exarch Myzalik's abilities to snoop through history and alter it to suit his needs.

"About our rival, some things must be said. He will know that we survived, but if my emergency measures have been successful, his magic will not help him find you. The mere fact that you are seeing this, months later, is all the confirmation you need. Had he been able to find you, you would never have survived. I imagine he'll be getting quite desperate to figure out where I am and what I'm doing.

"Do not think to challenge him as you currently are. Even the least ascendant could crush any human mage. One who stood at the pinnacle of our society could annihilate the entire species. Be discreet whenever possible. Avoid standing out or getting entangled in any large-scale human problems. Your disguise won't stand up to direct scrutiny against an ascendant.

"Prioritize staying hidden and staying well-fed. The growth spell is dependent on an ample food supply to run at maximum strength. By now you probably look to be a human in his early twenties, unless something has gone horribly wrong."

Once again Niramyn had underestimated the difficulties Nym had faced. The longer the vision kept talking, the more annoyed Nym got with it. His previous self had a colossal ego and had apparently literally lived in another world. He'd had no clue what kind of life he'd set Nym up for. Who knew what kind of damage Niramyn had unwittingly done to himself when he'd split off his personality and memories to create Nym.

"Finally, begin work immediately on creating the soul channels needed to increase your maximum arcana capacity. You'll need it in order to breach the fourth layer. I'm sure you'll figure this out on your own easily enough, but humans have so little understanding of how magic works that it would be unwise to trade this technique to others.

"The fourth layer is like the second layer's crystallized arcana, except instead of it randomly floating in that reality, the fourth layer is known as the Bulwark because it is made entirely of crystallized arcana. It's possible to refine it for use, but it's less effort to bore directly through it to the fifth layer. To do so, you must push arcana from the Astral Sea into the tip of your conduit and enhance it with your own magic so that it's strong enough to breach the Bulwark.

"Once you've gained access to the fifth layer, touch the cube again and merge our memories and personalities back together. We will know how to navigate Transcendence and return to our former power."

The visage faded away, and Nym felt like his whole body was being flung through space. He came to a stop without actually ever having moved, and a wave of vertigo passed through him. Ciana stood there in the predawn light, watching him. Everything was the same as when he'd first seen the vision. Not a second had passed.

Nym frowned to himself and pulled the cube out of the bag. It no longer obsessively called out to him. "I should hide this here," he told her. "Do you mind if I bury it under your cellar?"

"What is it?" Ciana asked, peering at it curiously. Her eyes kept sliding off to the side, then refocusing on it. Furrows appeared on her forehead as she concentrated. "Something magic?"

"I'm not exactly sure," Nym told her. "But it would be best if no one else knew about it until I learn more."

"Go ahead. I won't tell anyone it's there."

"Thanks."

Nym ran back down the stairs, broke open the stone floor in the middle, and deposited the cube into the hole. His magic smoothed the dirt back down and, with a small surge of effort, transmuted it back to whole, unblemished stone again. No one would suspect a thing just from a visual examination.

Then he began the process of collecting third-layer arcana again, said his goodbyes, and teleported back to Ebalsan.

"Got something on your mind?" Jharn asked over breakfast.

"Hmm? Oh, just working through some spells," Nym lied. He hadn't gotten a minute of sleep and was only conscious thanks to liberal use of the stimulant spell Jharn had taught him. He ate the food in front of him mechanically, ignoring it while he tried to sort through the implications of what he'd just learned.

If he assumed it was all true, he would be incredibly valuable to Analia's father. He was a living research specimen, an ascendant, and one who was too weak to defend himself. Nym would spend the rest of his life locked in a mage cell while they performed every experiment and test they could think of on him.

They already knew something was weird about him. His soul well was way too big to be normal. Combined with his unique history, there was obviously something there they might consider being worth investigating. Maybe they even already suspected he was an ascendant. He'd certainly figured it might be the case once he'd started to learn more about them. It sounded far-fetched, of course, but it did provide a possible explanation for a lot of the questions he'd built up.

In truth, being detained indefinitely was already a risk. Admitting he wasn't human just magnified the chances of that happening. There was no reason to tell the Collective either. Admitting that he'd reached the third layer might help in some way, but he didn't see any positive outcome to telling them he was an ascendant.

There were people he did trust, Analia and the Earth Shapers, but he wasn't sure they'd be able to help. He would tell them he had reached the third layer, but he didn't know if he wanted to tell anyone that he had finally learned the truth about his past. It didn't seem like something anyone could help him with beyond speeding up the course his past self had laid out for him: become an archmage and then retrieve the memory cube.

Nobody needed to know he was an ascendant to do that. For now at least, that was a secret he'd keep to himself. He did need to find a way to get help with learning third-circle spells though. A tutor would be ideal, but that would be an extravagant expense, and there was no way he could hide it from the Collective.

While they were eating, Nym formed a message and sent it across the house to Analia, who was taking a bath. *[I broke through to the third layer. I do not want anybody to find out. I can't explain why. Can you see about discreetly getting spell books with third-circle spells?]*

A minute later, he got a response. *[I'll set up antiscrying and privacy wards while you're out. We'll talk later.]*

Nym finished his meal and stood up. "Let me grab some stuff and we can get going," he told Jharn. They had a freelance job they'd reserved yesterday thanks to his connections with the clerks to spend their morning on.

Once he got back, he'd have his strategy meeting. That gave him plenty of time to figure out exactly how much he was willing to reveal and how he wanted to go about saying it. No doubt the geas would complicate things, but Analia was smart enough to pick up on what he wasn't saying.

He just hoped he wasn't dragging her into this mess with him.

CHAPTER THIRTY-EIGHT

Nym stood in the middle of Analia's room. She had thoroughly redecorated her space, unlike him. His room looked almost exactly as it had when they'd first moved in, save his closet had some spare clothes in it and he'd filled the empty shelves with books. Hers had new curtains over the window, three different light orbs made out of what appeared to be quartz, bedding that was considerably more vibrant than the dull coloring his room enjoyed, a new work-table that was filled odd little bits of metal.

"What are those?" he asked, nodding his head at the table.

"It's a mechanical representation of a rune sequence. The pieces only fit together certain ways that mimic how actual runes slot into one another. You use it to help figure out how runes go together without having to write the whole sequence out first."

"That sounds useful. I might have to get a set too," Nym said.

"They do make things easier, but I don't think that's what you wanted to talk about. Out with it. These privacy wards are expensive to maintain," she said.

"Right, sorry. I hit third-layer arcana like I said, and I don't want people knowing. I need to start learning spells with a focus on combat against other mages, how to avoid detection, stuff like that. I have a feeling I'm going to need to defend myself against people soon, and it would be better if those people don't know what I'm capable of doing."

"People like Jharn and Navarim?" she asked.

Nym couldn't answer, but he didn't need to. She knew about the geas, and his silence said enough. He wanted to say that neither of his bodyguards could use third-circle magic just yet, maybe not ever, but that was definitely restricted information. Besides, he was more worried about the third-circle mages the Collective had on their roster.

Somehow, he doubted Analia's father was going to be a pushover in a fight. Hopefully, it would never come to that, but he'd already been crushed in his first encounter with the Collective. They'd caught him asleep and off guard, then overwhelmed him with sheer numbers. Things had worked out well enough considering the position he was in, but it could have just as easily ended with the door of that mage cell opening and someone firing a crossbow bolt between his ribs.

"It might be better not to use your family line of credit to buy anything relating to third-circle magic," he said.

"That might not be an option. Third-circle spell books are rare and expensive. Even in the family library back home, we only had a few of them. We can probably pool our money and get one spell book with a few third-circle spells in it. Usually people who make it to this point get headhunted by someone and get access to a lot of help. There are never enough third-circle mages to meet demand, so no expense is spared training them."

"So secret training is out then."

"At least it is here," she agreed.

"Here," Nym echoed. "Where might it not be so difficult?"

Analia shrugged. "I might be able to find a place. I'm not sure. Would it matter with the two bodyguards keeping an eye on you? Would they let you go?"

"Let's just say that teleportation is a third-circle spell."

Analia's eyes sparkled. "Is that so? Well, just keep in mind that teleporting more people is supposed to be much harder than teleporting yourself. If you had access to a spell like that, it would be a good idea to practice with a friend in case a group getaway became necessary."

"That sounds like something any mage capable of casting teleport should be able to do," Nym agreed.

"It would be a shame to have to abandon all of these books though," Analia said, looking sadly around the room. "Anyway, I'll keep an eye out, but I wouldn't expect anything. You should probably keep working on a backup plan just in case I can't come up with anything to help."

"Alright. I'll keep trying to figure stuff out on my own too. The principles are the same between a lot of second- and third-circle spells. Maybe I can modify a few things and make it work."

"That's everything then?" she asked. At Nym's nod, she stopped feeding arcana into the rune sequences set up around the room and sagged down onto her bed. "That was exhausting."

"Thanks for the help," Nym told her.

"Any time, not that I did much."

"It helps just knowing that you're trying to help."

"Oh, get out of here. You've got stuff to do."

Nym felt like his soul well was as functional as it could get. He could channel arcana through his conduit at maximum speed again, and in fact his new output was actually a fair bit higher than it had been before the incident a few months ago. The techniques he'd gotten from the Collective had probably helped to expand it, though they certainly didn't help in speeding up his recovery.

That annoyed him especially because against all odds, he *did* have access to a master healer, and the man had refused to treat him on the grounds of not introducing variables to the experiment. Nym wasn't exactly mad since the end result for him personally was an increased capacity to hold arcana in his soul well. The Collective as a whole also had a few dozen mages who were slowly expanding their own soul wells.

It was a slow process, but if it continued to work, there would soon be a lot more third-circle mages in the world. Navarim had told Nym that a few of the mages who were borderline had managed to successfully cast third-circle spells. They were still working to expand their soul wells as much as possible before they began the process of creating channels, for the sake of the Collective's data.

Nym came home late. He'd been dragged through dozens of scans and then pulled into a class to answer questions about his personal technique for isolating smaller clusters of nodes so that the next batch of mages could start testing with it. The sun had long since set by the time he and Navarim appeared on the teleportation platform and started the walk home.

It was too late to get a fresh meal anywhere, though there were probably any number of taverns or inns he could duck into to get some leftovers. By shared agreement, they both skipped that and went straight to the house instead. Nym gave the exotic-pet store next door a mild glare as he walked by. They'd gotten some new type of animal the day before that would not stop howling at random times during the night. As soon as one got going, the whole pack started up.

Analia was already asleep by the time they got in, and Navarim was just as tired as Nym. They bid each other good night, trudged past Jharn, who was doing maintenance on his equipment at the table, and went to their rooms. There, Nym kicked off his shoes, hung his coat on a peg on the wall, and collapsed face down onto his bed.

He landed with a grunt as something small and hard under the blanket dug into his ribs. With a groan, Nym rolled over and pulled the bedding back to reveal a book. It wasn't one he recognized, and he definitely didn't remember leaving any books in his bed. Grudgingly, he called up a light spell and examined the book.

It definitely wasn't one of his. The book was titled *On the Efficacy of Mind-Altering Magics* and had a bookmark slipped into it close to the back. Nym flipped it open and froze in place. His lips curled up into a grin and he whispered, "Analia, you are a brilliant researcher. Where did you find this?"

The bookmark opened to a chapter all about the geas spell. It detailed exactly how it anchored itself into the brain, imprinting instructions and sinking its roots down to control actions and in some cases thoughts. The book gave examples of extreme geasa that would cause their victims to die, choking on nothing as the geas refused to let their lungs open if they violated some condition. Other cases prevented the victim from even realizing they were under a geas, with the magic itself serving to direct their thoughts away from it anytime they came close.

Nym grew more horrified as he read. He knew he hadn't been given a choice about signing the geas, but he hadn't realized the extent to which the spell could be abused. He was lucky that his geas only curbed his ability to talk about a specific range of subjects. It was also completely voluntary, which, if he was understanding what he read correctly, made it considerably less painful to be bound with than a geas that was forced on a subject.

Voluntary might be too strong of a word, since it was really more like he'd been coerced into agreeing, but in this case, the book meant one who'd agreed to the geas, even if they didn't want to. It had been an unpleasant experience; Nym was glad he didn't have to go through the involuntary version of it. He doubted he'd have gotten nearly as generous of terms.

On the other hand, by agreeing to the geas, he'd had no chance at all to fight back against it. It was firmly entrenched in him now and would be far more difficult to break than it would have been at the time it was being forced on him. Nym didn't know how to fight off something like that though, so he didn't feel like he'd missed out on anything.

The last section of the chapter was the most important, at least as far as Nym's situation went. In order to break a geas, he needed a specific spell the book called absolve. There were a couple of different versions depending on exactly what kind of geas the victim was under. The good news was that all of them were third-circle spells, so theoretically, Nym could cast them if he learned them. The bad news was that absolving himself was significantly harder than casting it on someone else.

It might actually be easier to show Analia what he'd learned so that she could cast third-circle spells too. They already knew her soul well was large enough that she wouldn't run into the same problem the mages of the Collective had, probably thanks to her father's tampering. He was pretty sure the geas wouldn't stop him from helping her advance, since the Collective's focus was on the soul well, not conduits.

That would have to be the subject of their next meeting. Nym was having problems keeping his eyes open and processing the words on the page. He'd check over it again when he was fully awake to make sure he wasn't missing any details, but it looked like they needed to find a copy of the geas-absolving spell next.

He was sure it wouldn't be easy to do, but perhaps Analia would come through for him again. There was no way the Collective was going to hand him the spell, not if it meant freedom from their control. In the absolute worst case, he could leave to hunt for it himself, but that would have to be done very carefully so that all his friends were safe from repercussions.

Those were all worries for another day. Nym hid the book on his shelf by stashing it flat against the wall with a few other books in front of it, then resumed his journey toward sleep. The bed called to him, ever so sweetly, and without hesitation, he fell into its gentle embrace.

CHAPTER THIRTY-NINE

A loud warbling screech woke Nym from a dead sleep. He flailed in place, trying to free himself from the tangle of his blanket, before falling out of the bed completely. Arcana filled his soul well, and he immediately cast several scrying spells with a focus on anything dangerous in his immediate surroundings.

His door burst open, and Jharn came through. "Get ready," he said sharply. "Undead have breached the walls and will hit us in high numbers. Every mage who can fight needs to report in."

"Um . . ." Nym stared at the mage, then past him to where Analia was standing in the kitchen with her mouth hanging open looking at him. She was wearing a purple nightgown that fell past her knees. He was wearing . . . not much of anything. He snatched up the blanket he'd been fighting against.

Red-faced, he mumbled, "I'll be out in a second."

Jharn blinked, then realized that Nym was naked. "Oh! Sorry about that."

He closed the door behind him, leaving Nym to mutter to himself while he jerked his clothes on. They hadn't been cleaned, but he expected if there was more fighting that they would end up dirtier than they already were. There was no sense in soiling another set of clothes.

Fully dressed now, he grabbed the new coat he'd had commissioned to hold his weapons. It was still leather but significantly lighter than his previous one. It was a bit hot on the ground but perfect when he was flying. The blades were already strapped in, providing a solid weight around his sides when he put the coat on.

Jharn was similarly dressed and waiting for him. Analia had disappeared, for which Nym was silently thankful, and Navarim was off that night. He had his own home back in Zoskan, which hopefully wasn't being threatened like Ebalsan was. "Where are we going?" Nym asked.

"To the keep. They're organizing the defense from there. My guess is we'll be manning the walls to repel ghouls. Hopefully it's *just* ghouls."

Nym shuddered, remembering his own encounter with a wight-controlled ghoul swarm. He didn't hear much about wights, but every now and then some horror story of a geist made its way through the soldiers. Nym had yet to see one in person, and if he was lucky, he'd keep it that way. If he did see any wights, he'd learned a few new anti-undead spells to help. It turned out that having thousands of them nearby has spurred a great many mages into sharing spells to help fend them off.

Analia came back out of her room, dressed in for perhaps the first time ever a pair of sturdy leather pants, low boots, and a pastel-blue blouse. Her hair was pulled back into a ponytail, and she had a set of palm-sized rings sharpened all the way around in a hip holster. A pair of wands were sheathed on the opposite hip.

"Are we all ready?" she asked.

"I . . . Yeah," Nym said, eyeing the outfit. He almost didn't recognize her. "You look good. Very dangerous."

Nym thought he saw her lips curl up into a smile for just a moment, but it might have been a trick of the light. "Thanks," she said. "Let's go."

Behind them, Jharn snorted and shook his head. "Kids," he muttered, making no effort to keep anyone else from hearing him.

They took off flying as soon as they were outside. Without even trying, Nym could count at least twenty other mages doing the same, all heading for the same place. The whole town was lit up, so much so that it didn't even occur to him to use night vision until he tried to look past the wall into the forest. There were already people lined up on the walls, and he heard the distant sounds of combat.

There were two tables set up next to each other in the courtyard of the keep, each manned by two soldiers. Between them, a giant map had been pinned up on a board and was covered with marks. As mages landed, they were directed into one of the two lines in front of the tables. Nym, Analia, and Jharn joined the right side, though both were moving so fast it didn't make much difference.

The soldiers at the tables asked each person or group a few quick questions, then directed them to either the east or west wall. When Nym's turn came up, the soldier asked, "How many?"

"Three," Jharn told the man.

"Fight as a group or individually?"

"As a group."

"Anyone third circle?"

"No."

Nym and Analia glanced at each other when Jharn said that, but they kept their mouths shut. The soldier directed them to the west wall with instructions to report to the sixth section, which would have two blue pennants flying from a pole. All three of them took off, leaving the whole thing behind while the soldier they were talking to started questioning the next group and his helper went and marked off another section of the map.

The wall itself was about ten feet wide with crenellations four feet high. There were thirty soldiers there, and they were responsible for a hundred-foot-long section. The lieutenant in charge was busy organizing them into units of five and spreading them out when the three mages landed.

"Oh God, civilian reinforcements," the lieutenant groaned. "Great. Just go stand in the middle and try not to get in our way."

"We can hold—" Nym started to say.

"Don't care. Ghouls are already hitting us in waves. We're down ten men already, and I don't have time to deal with you. Take your spots in the center and try not to get killed."

"But—"

"Come on," Jharn said. "We've got our orders."

They flew over the soldiers' heads, stopping in the air above the center of their section. "Right," Jharn said. "That guy is going to be no help, so our options are to stay grouped up and keep ourselves as safe as possible or spread out a bit and keep as many soldiers as we can safe. Opinions?"

"Soldiers," Analia said immediately. "We can be mobile reinforcements. We'll cut this section of the wall in thirds and help wherever the line starts to buckle."

"A good plan," Jharn agreed. "I'll take the northernmost stretch, Nym in the middle, and Analia on the south end."

"Put Analia in the middle," Nym said.

Jharn frowned. "My job is to guard you. I'm already stretching that order letting you fight so far away."

"Please, it's not like it's the first time we've fought," Nym said. "She doesn't have live combat experience with ghouls. She needs to be in the middle where either of us can help if needed."

"I'm flattered at how highly you think of me," Analia said dryly.

"It's not an insult," Nym told her. "You don't go out and fight multiple times a week. Both of us do. I'm not saying you're not a good mage. I'm saying I'd feel better if both of us were able to help if you need it."

She sighed and shook her head. There was a faint smile on her face. "Fine. I'll take the middle."

Jharn said, "I don't like it, but Nym's not wrong. You are the least experienced, and besides, if you get eaten by a ghoul, who'll restock the cookie jar?"

"Wait, you're the one who's been stealing my cookies?" she demanded, spinning fully to face him. "I've been blaming Navarim!"

"Gotta go! Looks like the ghouls are coming in," Jharn said. He flew off to take his section of the wall.

"This conversation isn't over yet!" Analia yelled after him. "There will be a reckoning!"

"Be careful," Nym told her. "Shout for help if you need it."

"I'll be fine. Go on and take your place. He wasn't wrong about the ghouls."

Nym flew over to the southernmost section of the wall. There were twelve soldiers there, spaced more or less into a single file line every few feet. All of them were looking nervously into the darkness, some surrounded by auras but not all. Nym quickly identified two night vision spells and a bunch of reflex-enhancement spells among the group.

The torches lit up the tops of the walls, but the soldiers wouldn't know the ghouls were on them until they climbed all the way up. Other sections were better illuminated by mages throwing out light spells, and Nym decided to do the same. He didn't have the time to enchant anything, but for a little while at least, he could brighten up the woods.

He pulled hard on his conduit and started channeling arcana into light constructs, then cast them out over and over again until there was a bright orb of light hanging out in the open air near the forest every ten feet or so. There were probably twenty or thirty ghouls hiding in the trees, waiting for some reason to attack. Hopefully it wasn't because a wight told them to.

The lieutenant stomped over, already screaming at Nym. "What do you think you're doing? You're ruining my men's night vision! They're going to be fighting blind as soon as you drop those lights, you worthless excuse for a mage!"

"I'm not going to drop the lights," Nym said absently. He was too busy counting ghouls to listen to the soldier's rant. "Twenty-eight, twenty-nine . . . What are they waiting for?"

"You can't hold those lights for another three hours until dawn, you idiot!" the lieutenant said.

"I can if I have to," Nym told him. "Stop bothering me."

It was a good hundred feet to the tree line. He could probably get his blades out that far, but it would be pointless. The ghouls would just collect the severed limbs and retreat farther behind cover to reattach them if they had a wight commanding them, which Nym suspected was the case. Obviously, no one was going into the woods to dig them out, so there was no point in hiding to wait for an ambush. They would attack if nothing smarter was controlling them.

The lieutenant kept ranting at him, but Nym ignored him until the man tried to grab him. Then Nym gave him a telekinetic shove backward out of his space and fixed the soldier with a frosty glare. "You weren't interested in working with us. I'm staying out of your way. Return the favor and stay out of mine."

"Get this kid off my wall," the lieutenant told his soldiers.

"I wouldn't," Nym said when one hesitantly reached out to grab him.

"This isn't a game. Get out of here before you do any more damage. People are going to die because of your stupidity, and I need to minimize the damage."

"Too late for that." Nym pointed at the forest. The number of ghouls had doubled since he'd cast the light spells, and they were all pouring out from between the trees at a dead run. "You've got a few seconds before they reach the wall."

"Goddamn their bones! Brace for the next wave!" the lieutenant bellowed. He spun to face Nym again and said, "This isn't over!"

"How are you handling the burning?" Nym asked the closest soldier as he sent all four of his spinning blades out to meet the first line. It was so much easier to chop the ghouls up than to try to push them back with air spells. If he'd known this spell months ago, his life would have been completely different.

"We're not," the soldier said. "Too risky to send someone down there."

"Of course," Nym muttered. He flew up ten feet and yelled, "Jharn! Can you start a burn pit in the middle of the field for us?"

With a surge of elemental earth magic, Nym ripped topsoil away, then started digging straight down. It wouldn't hold a ghoul for very long, and it wasn't pretty, but a four-foot hole with dirt heaped up around it might just serve to keep a pile of writhing body parts contained for long enough.

Flames rose from the pit, fed by Jharn's arcana, and Nym flew out over the open field to release his blades and hack through the closest ghouls. He launched parts into the pit telekinetically, but that didn't stop them. They simply hobbled on any way they could, even if it meant crawling through the grass. The limbs in the pits scrambled and clawed if they had the power, each one struggling to drag itself back to its owner.

Nym sighed and shook his head. It was going to be a long day.

CHAPTER FORTY

Ghouls streamed out of the forest and threw themselves at the walls. They clawed at the rough magic-shaped stone, hurling themselves upward in an unthinking frenzy while dozens of soldiers armed with spears or pikes did their best to pry them off. The tactic met with only mixed success, as the time it took and the number of ghouls assaulting the wall were more than enough to overwhelm the defenders.

Within a minute of the ghouls attacking, hundreds of them were on the wall, though thankfully spread out enough that the soldiers still managed to fight them two-on-one most of the time. Nym swept his portion of the wall regularly, not really attempting to help the soldiers on his section but instead hacking apart ghouls that were vulnerable while climbing. The parts fell to the ground, where one of the two earth golems he'd created was ferrying parts to the firepit and returning any loose limbs that escaped.

More than half of them got through the whirling mage blades, but their numbers were sufficiently blunted that the soldiers were able to force the undead back off the walls. They even did it without any casualties and were able to lend support to the units on either side of Nym's section.

Analia's tactics were similar to Nym's, except her palm-sized blades were less effective at lopping off limbs. She could still dismember a ghoul, but it took her several passes to completely cut it apart. Worse, the lack of an earth golem to take care of the severed limbs allowed more of them to get back into the fight. The soldiers in her section had to push back ghouls more often and in greater number, even with the reinforcements Nym's section of the wall provided.

Nym was considering the merits of spending the arcana to get a third golem going for her section when four ghouls jumped one of the golems he already had working. Prior to that moment, the ghouls had ignored the golems in favor of suicidally charging at the wall, but some hidden wight commander must have realized what the golems were doing and given the order to take it out.

It fought back, but the ghouls ripped it apart faster than it could regenerate. Nym couldn't afford the drain on his arcana to keep its regeneration going, so he let the golem be torn apart. There was an immediate upswing in his available arcana, which he used to chain a series of undead stunners on the ghouls at the top of the wall. The soldiers there took advantage of the few seconds it gave them to swarm the ghouls and hack them to pieces.

The tide of ghouls ebbed after about half an hour. At no point was the wall ever seriously threatened, and at least on the sections near Nym and his friends, there were no human casualties. Soldiers rushed around with torches, lighting up body parts and throwing them over the wall while mages worked to create more firepits for disposal. Nym was just one of many mages swooping through the air, collecting burning ghoul arms, legs, and trunks for disposal.

They didn't finish cleaning up before the next wave of ghouls pushed out of the forest. The line of light spells Nym had strung up were still going strong, and aided by copious amounts of fire, it was easy to see the undead streaming through the trees in the hundreds. As the wave kept coming, and coming, and coming, Nym got a sinking feeling that he might need to upgrade his best guess from hundreds to thousands.

The wall itself was a cacophony of panicked yelling and orders. People rushed past one another, running to distribute last-minute supplies or take up positions against the incoming onslaught. The number of mages in the air started increasing as the army reserves were deployed along the wall to help push back the sudden spike in ghouls. Nym had no idea there were so many mages held back, but he was glad that they were there. Without the reinforcements they provided, he was sure the wall would be overwhelmed.

The ghouls hit well before everybody was in position, and there were a few minutes of utter chaos as the living side of the battle struggled to repel the attack. More than a few ghouls pushed through the line and leaped off the back side of the wall, only to be met by roaming patrols of soldiers led by mages casting spells specifically designed to detect undead.

There was a staggering variety of spells flying through the air above the wall, though by far the highest number of attacks were ones that cut or otherwise broke apart ghouls. Most were made out of pure arcana or manipulated bladed weapons, but every now and then, Nym saw a spell that sank into a ghoul's body and detonated it from the inside. Limbs would then be blown in every direction, which of course didn't kill a ghoul any better than chopping it up did.

The important thing was that every ghoul who got ripped part, chopped up, or blown to pieces was one ghoul that was out of the fight for at least a little bit while it pulled itself back together. Some mages were liberal with their use of fire as well, and even as the burn pits were overrun, the entire stretch of land between the wall and the forest turned into one massive inferno.

Despite how badly they were outnumbered, Nym still thought they had a good chance of winning. The soldiers started to push back the tide, and as long as there wasn't yet another even bigger wave heading through the woods to crash against the wall, it looked like they'd managed to survive with only minimal losses.

That confidence was shattered when the first mage started screaming. He flailed about, flames rushing across his body as he lost concentration on his flight spell and fell toward the ground. Another mage swooped in to save him, only to be shot in the back by some sort of acid ball. The mage that did it flew off at top speed, disappearing into the chaos of battle before Nym could even think to respond.

More mages started screaming as they were attacked. Nym looked around wildly, trying to figure out what was happening. Before his brain could catch up to his eyes, a cry went up from the remaining mages, "Wight infiltration in the mage units!"

They were wearing uniforms just like the soldier mage reserves who'd come out to assist the wall guards and, from what Nym had seen, were using an almost identical set of spells. Somehow, an entire unit of army mages had been killed and raised as wights, and nobody had seen it coming. It would have been one thing for the freelancers and town mages not to know about it, but even the army reserves had been caught off guard.

Nym saw a mage in an army uniform flying toward him and quickly cast a detect-undead spell on it. The spell homed in on the mage immediately and confirmed Nym's fears. The wight, unaware that it had been spotted, continued its flight, angled as though it were merely going to fly close past Nym instead of coming in for an attack.

Nym smote the undead out of the air with a powerful lightning bolt before it could get too close. The crack of thunder echoed across the battlefield, drawing the attention of dozens of other mages. Many of them started flying in his direction, and Nym saw a dozen different mages preparing spell constructs to attack him. He realized too late that to those who'd witnessed the scene he looked like the aggressor.

"Use an undead-detection spell to find the wights!" he yelled as loud as he could. "Scan everyone around you and shoot down the undead!"

Thankfully, most of the mages immediately took his advice and started scanning the skies for wights hidden among them. Three mages kept flying toward him, two with spells readied and one without. As he got closer, Nym realized the last one was Jharn. The other two circled cautiously as they communicated with each other using some sort of instant-telepathy spell. Nym immediately resolved to make sure Analia never learned of such a spell's existence.

They reached some sort of consensus, and one of them said, "We need you to land immediately and come with us."

"Why?" Nym asked. "There are still a thousand undead out there."

"Use of an illegal spell," the mage told him.

"We're in the middle of a battlefield!" Nym protested.

"That's not relevant. Even knowing how to cast that spell is illegal."

Jharn moved in closer and said, "Can we talk about this after we stop the undead from breaking through this wall and slaughtering a few thousand people in Ebalsan?"

"This does not concern you," the mage said. "Please leave. And you, land in the courtyard now."

Nym exchanged glances with Jharn, who shrugged. "I guess let them know what happened?" Nym told Jharn. "Keep an eye on Analia for me?"

The bodyguard didn't look happy, but he nodded. "As soon as we figure out all this mess, I'll get in touch with the boss."

Jharn flew off to resume his place on the walls. The fighting around them was even worse now as the wights threw away all attempts at subtlety. Twenty or so of them duked it out in midair, trading spells with human mages and relying on their superior undead durability to take anything the mages might dish out.

"Can't believe I'm getting arrested in the middle of all of this," Nym muttered. "Bureaucracy will be the cause of the world ending someday."

They swooped low over the wall but pulled up short when a familiar voice started bellowing at them from below. "What are you morons doing?" someone demanded.

Nym looked down to see the lieutenant who'd been yelling at him half an hour ago for throwing light spells over the field. The two mages escorting him frowned at each other and flew down to speak with the officer.

"Sir, this mage used an illegal spell. We're taking him into custody."

"Right now? Did your mothers drop you on your heads when you were babies?"

"The law—"

"God shits on the law right now!" the lieutenant yelled. "All three of you get back to work! We've got thousands of enemy undead right Goddamned there!"

The mages looked at each other, shrugged, and flew back up. "Report to the keep after the battle is concluded," one of them instructed Nym before flying off.

"Thanks for the save," Nym told the lieutenant. "Do you need anything before I go back to the fight?"

"Just kill as many of the bastards as you can," the officer said. "And if you want my advice, disappear when the battle starts to wind down. Work your way closer to the forest or something and just follow the fighting out over the woods."

"Got it. I'll get back to clearing the walls for you."

Nym flew off, skimming the walls with his mage blades and hacking apart ghoulish hands and legs. He did a few passes to clear out the majority of the ghouls and hurled the loose limbs into the fires below, but it was only a delaying action. It would take far more concentrated effort to truly push those ghouls back or outright destroy them.

He did it to take the pressure off the top of the wall while he worked his way farther away from the two mages who'd tried to arrest him. Jharn watched him go by and offered him a smirk and a nod, which Nym returned with a casual wave. Then he was past the mage and moving farther up the wall toward where it went into the forest.

There were still hundreds of undead left to fight and probably dozens of wights leading them, but the army had enough manpower in that fight that Nym wouldn't make or break anything. He could be just as helpful against smaller numbers of ghouls attacking the walls elsewhere, and more than that, he was concerned about what was going on in the forest. Something had to have gone horribly wrong at the forward bases and outposts.

His friends were at one of those outposts right now.

Nym sped up, but before he got too far away, he heard a man crying out below him. "Geists! Geists on the walls!"

The shout became a shriek so filled with pain that Nym flinched at the very sound of it. He swept down lower and got his first look at the horror show that was a pack of geists.

CHAPTER FORTY-ONE

There were six of them on the wall, wrapped around a small unit of soldiers like wet blankets. The man who'd caught Nym's attention made eye contact with him for one brief moment, and Nym saw pain and desperation in that look. Then the geist enveloped him completely, and the yell was cut off.

Nym could still see his open mouth screaming beneath the geist, but the man's wild scrambling to escape slowed, then stopped. Nym flew down and immediately started throwing undead-stunning spells at the group. As far as he was aware, once a geist wrapped itself around a victim, it dissolved the skin off them and connected to their body, then piloted its unwilling host around. There was no saving the person at that point, as killing the geist killed the host.

He hoped that these men were not to that point, but he had no idea how to rescue them. He figured he had at most a minute or so before the soldiers started suffocating but didn't have a single spell that would harm only the geists. The best he could do was something precisely targeted like using his needles.

That would have to be a start. He pulled them out of his coat and shot them into the part of the geist covering the screaming man's mouth. They pierced through, probably also striking the man beneath, and Nym pulled them back to reveal holes in the undead. Hopefully that was enough for the man to breathe through.

"I don't . . . How do I . . . Someone tell me what to do!" Nym yelled.

There was no answer, of course. All over the wall, ghouls were crossing unimpeded. Every single soldier nearby was either dead or dying from ghoul claws and teeth, or worse, wrapped in a geist-skin shroud. This far out from the central keep, and with such heavy pressure behind him, there were no reinforcements and no cavalry riding in to save the day.

A geist materialized out of the darkness in front of Nym, and he got his first up-close look at the horror that was the undead monster. It looked something like a sheet or sail, its form billowing with air as it flew toward him. Pasty white skin, thin and dried out, made up the whole of the creature from the back, but as it turned and twisted through the air, Nym got a look at the inner lining of its body as well.

He was disgusted by the sight of it. There were hundreds of small rings filled with needles, like little sucking mouths with grotesque teeth. They twisted and flexed as the geist's sail-like body aligned itself to envelope Nym. Just before it reached him, he hurled a blast of lightning at it.

The geist's body arced so hard it practically rolled up on itself. Behind it, the lightning bolt struck several of the men who'd been covered by other geists. Their bodies were left blackened and smoking. In death, the geists let go of their unwilling hosts, but it was already too late for them. If the geists themselves hadn't killed the soldiers, Nym's lightning bolt had definitely finished them off.

"Oh God," Nym moaned, feeling sick.

There was no time to waste on that though. At least two of the soldiers from the unit were still alive. The geists that had been attached to them fluttered limply, no longer alive but not free to drift away in the breeze since they were partially pinned under their victims.

Nym didn't know enough about healing magic to save those soldiers. He'd learned how to fix scrapes and bruises, help a bone heal after it had been set, but the damage in front of him was far worse. Huge patches of skin had been reduced to slurry, leaving exposed muscle underneath. Even if he could knit the skin back together, he had no idea how to fix the damage beneath that.

He had to try though. Nym focused on the spells and pulled arcana through his soul well to fill the constructs. The one who looked the least wounded was closer; Nym started with him. New skin started to form where the geist's teeth had punctured it, but the man did not stop weeping and moaning. In desperation, Nym threw pain-blocking spells at them both.

"Tell me what to do," he demanded. "I don't know how to save you."

"There is no saving us," one of the soldiers rasped out. "Just end our suffering. You have no idea . . . The pain . . . It's too late."

"No, I can get you back to real healers. Maybe they'll be able to . . . to do something."

"Too late," the soldier said. "Even now, ghouls are escaping over the walls. Stop worrying about us. Just finish us off before you go."

"End it," the other soldier agreed. His mouth was busted up from Nym's needles, and blood poured out of it freely. He gurgled each wheezing breath and yet, for all that, was still somehow the soldier in the better shape of the two. "End it, before the ghouls find us. They won't kill us before they start eating."

Nym felt like his brain had stopped working. There had to be some solution, but he couldn't find it. His thoughts just kept going around and around in circles, touching on the same ideas over and over, rejecting them for the same reasons. He didn't have time to think up something clever, and he didn't know if there even was any real solution.

He'd already been lucky to get thirty seconds of uninterrupted time to begin with. His lightning bolt had killed all the geists nearby, and most of the ghouls were ignoring him in favor of jumping off the wall, but a few had noticed that there were living humans nearby and diverted their courses to attack.

Whenever the numbness tried to settle in his mind, Nym pushed it back. He didn't like it, didn't want to live on its terms. It happened less and less often as he got stronger and found more tools to deal with his problems. But in that moment, he didn't have any acceptable solutions. The soldiers knew it, and they'd told him what he needed to do. He just didn't have the stomach to do it.

Killing Senman was one thing. He'd been surprised by the new mindset, and he'd accepted it without resistance. It was only afterward that he'd reflected on the whole situation and realized how unnatural it was. There was some guilt from his actions, but the man had been trying to murder him. It was a justifiable self-defense, even if some others wouldn't see it that way.

Killing Valgo's gang of thieves was more of the same. Nym didn't really feel too bad about that, not after the kidnapping and everything else. He had felt even less guilt about killing Valgo himself. He'd been so at peace with that decision in the moment that he didn't even slip into that alternate state of mind.

Standing in front of those two dying soldiers, knowing that the only choice was to end their lives, and that he had just seconds to do it before the approaching ghouls reached him, Nym fully embraced that cold, calculating, ruthless persona. He knew what it was now, the mind of his past self trying to guide him out of some sense of self-preservation.

Mage blades flashed across both soldiers' throats, ending their lives in seconds with short, gasping wheezes that made bubbles appear in the blood. In the same motion, he sent the blades through the closest pair of ghouls while rising up into the air. There was no real reason to fight them anyway. He just needed enough time to gain some distance.

The weapons returned to him, cleaned and gore free thanks in large part to the high speed at which they spun. Nym took a moment to return them to his coat, then cast the spell he'd learned to block the scent of undead. He took a deep breath, crinkled his nose at the coppery stink of blood still filling the air, and flew away from the wall.

There was no point in trying to defend it. Even if he could plug that portion by himself, it didn't matter when ghouls were flowing over it by the hundreds elsewhere. Now that Nym really considered the matter, he didn't see much reason to stay in this region. He'd gotten what he needed from the Collective, and staying near their base and operatives would only lead to problems in the near future.

What he needed to do was extract his allies from the whole mess. The Earth Shapers were fast outgrowing their usefulness, though there was still much he could learn on the subject of elemental earth manipulation. He wanted them more for social camouflage than anything. They provided a layer of normalcy to his life that made him less suspicious, all while costing him little beyond some time and an insignificant amount of money.

Analia was far more useful to him right now. She enjoyed research and was more than willing to dig into things for him. She was a higher priority, but she was also in a location that was more dangerous to him personally. Between the idiots from the army who wanted to arrest him for illegal spell usage and the fact that there was at least one Collective member there that he was keeping secrets from, it was far riskier to go extract Analia.

At the same time, she was likely in less danger than the Earth Shapers. They were in an unknown location deep in the forest. The army had obviously failed in some large way, and the outbreak had surged with numbers. Nym suspected their entire inner line had crumbled. No doubt there were mass casualties, and it was very possible that his allies were already among them.

With a thought, he crafted a message to send to Ophelia. *[Are you alright? I'm coming to get you out of there. The army's lost control of containing the outbreak, and the undead have reached the town.]*

The response was almost immediate. *[Do not come here! We are bunkered underground right now. The outpost was completely overrun. Take Analia and get out of Ebalsan.]*

Nym considered the number of undead moving through the forest. Fighting through that would be possible with enough numbers, as long as the ghouls didn't mass up to attack like they'd done at the walls. As a desperation move, he could lift four more people and fly them maybe a mile at a slow speed. If he left them behind though and the army couldn't regain control of the forest, they'd likely die due to either discovery or starvation before they found their way out.

He could just abandon them, but they were still useful, and saving them was not going to be too hard. He just needed to know where they were, go to them, and teleport them out. It would be good practice for teleporting others, which he could do in theory, even if he hadn't tried yet. The specific destination didn't matter much.

[I have a way to get you out safely. I just need to know where you're at so I can fly over and use it.]

All the while he considered this, Nym flew west and north. He followed the curve of the wall and found almost nobody left alive near it. Several outposts had been completely abandoned or overrun, though the ghouls had left many partially mutilated bodies behind. Once again Nym wondered what had changed. It seemed like the number of wights had gone up and with that the amount of coordination they could enforce on the ghouls.

Nym did not stop to engage any ghouls he saw below. There was no point, and he'd need to save his energy. He did spot a wight or two, and while he considered attacking them to weaken the enemy's cohesion, in the end he decided it wasn't worth the risk. The forest was lost, along with all the towns bordering it. All that mattered was getting his allies out and relocated somewhere else.

Ophelia's voice sounded in his mind. *[Fine. Do you remember where the third outpost was? If you follow the wall about two miles west of that, you'll find the remains of the work camp. Look for a series of chimneys built up twenty feet out of the ground. We're in an underground bunker we carved out. Those are for our air vents. Let me know when you've arrived. Be. Careful.]*

Nym had already passed the outpost, and it took him barely a handful of minutes to find the camp. There were six stacks clustered near one another on one side of the camp, which itself had been torn apart. Several ghouls lurked in the ruins, some pawing at the ground and others roaming, sniffing the air.

Obviously, they knew there were still people nearby. That just meant they were in the way. Nym's mage blades came out, and he went to work.

CHAPTER FORTY-TWO

Nym looked down the chimney and yelled into it, "You can come out now. The undead are all, um, dead."

He'd dug a narrow pit about five feet straight down with elemental earth magic and tossed all the chopped-up ghouls into it. They weren't burning very well, and he suspected if he didn't take a more active role in their disposal, they'd eventually work themselves free one way or another, but he didn't plan on sticking around to wait for it to happen.

The earth rumbled near the chimney, and the sound of a few voices arguing came up to him. Ophelia's voice rose over the other ones and bullied them into silence. A few seconds later, the rumbling ended, and a section of the ground collapsed to reveal about twenty people in a sort of artificial cave. Nym's face went blank when he saw them.

His plan hadn't accounted for the idea that there might be other survivors, but in hindsight, it was obvious that the workers would band together. This was going to make everything much more complicated. He couldn't reveal his teleportation spell to the entire group, and he doubted he'd be able to leave the extras behind.

The not-cold voice in the back of his mind told him that those other earth mages had just as much of a right to be saved, but Nym ignored that. The goal was to extract four trustworthy earth mages, not twenty unknown mages that he needed to hide his capabilities from. Worse, as he got a better look, he realized that the underground shelter was bigger than he'd thought. It wasn't just twenty healthy mages. There were at least another seven or eight spread out on the ground nearby.

"Nym?" Ophelia called up to him. "A little help getting out?"

He wrapped her in air and lifted her up to float next to him. "This is more people than I was expecting," he said.

"Maybe a third of the camp survived, and only because we managed to combine specialties to build this bunker. Most of them don't want to leave. They're just going to wait for the army to pacify the area again."

"That's not going to happen before they starve to death," Nym said. "There are thousands of ghouls attacking right now, backed by wights. I saw a whole section of the wall overrun. Geists got the soldiers."

Ophelia paled. "God," she whispered. "How did this happen?"

The question wasn't directed at Nym, and he didn't have an answer for her anyway. "My plan was for getting the four of you out of here," he told her. "I have no idea how we're going to move almost thirty people, especially with the wounded."

"That's why we were waiting for the army to get back in. We've got enough water to last a few days. Someone tunneled to a storage building and got supplies for us before the ghouls finished tearing through here."

"Were there any plans besides waiting and hoping?"

Ophelia shook her head. "Nothing with a prayer of working. No one here can fly, and tunneling fifty or more miles to the edge of the woods is a fool's errand. It would take weeks with healthy and well-rested crews rotating every few hours. For this group . . . Months at minimum. If we abandoned the wounded, it would still take days to walk that far, assuming no undead found us."

Nym was annoyed. This was supposed to be a simple task. The presence of two dozen other earth mages messed everything up, and leaving them behind would no doubt strain his relationship with the Earth Shapers.

"What was your plan?" Ophelia asked. "There's no way you could fly four extra people out."

Nym hesitated. There was nothing to gain by telling her about his breakthrough to the third circle now, but Analia already knew, so it would come out to the Earth Shapers anyway. They'd trust him less if he lied about it now. "I learned how to teleport," he admitted. "But it needs to be kept secret, and I definitely can't do this many people."

"Telep—what? You've got to be kidding me! You're already into the third layer?"

"Keep it to yourself. Just trust me when I say I've got reasons for not advertising it. And like I said, this is too many people. So . . . New plan?"

"You're not going to convince them to leave. The bunker was the plan."

Nym shrugged. "As long as I get you four, that's what I'm here for. I guess let's talk to the whole group and see who wants to stay? We can figure out what we're going to do once we know who's willing to leave?"

Ophelia sighed but nodded in agreement. They descended into the bunker, and a trio of earth mages repaired the roof. Nym got his first good look around and spotted the twins nearby. Bildar was not in the crowd however. Instead, Nym found him lying near the back of the bunker, hidden in the darkness. He was breathing lightly, and his robes were covered with blood.

There was no need to ask what had happened. A ghoul had gotten hold of him and, from the looks of it, taken at least one bite out of the man. It was another complication to what should have been a simple plan.

"Listen up," Ophelia said, raising her voice. "We've got a potential avenue to escape. I'm not going to say it's risk free, but my friend here is a veteran at fighting undead. He's been killing ghouls for months. How many are willing to try to walk out of here with us?"

There was a lot of grumbling from a few vocal mages and a lot of hollow stares from most of the rest. A few went to sit near the wounded and whisper to them. Nym himself walked away, leaving Ophelia to argue with the other mages. He moved over to where Bildar was resting and sat down next to the man. "How are you feeling?" he asked.

Bildar groaned and said, "How's it look like I'm feeling?"

"Like a ghoul used you for a chew toy," Nym told him. "You know that I can cast a pain-blocking spell, right?"

"The only thing I would want more than that right now is one of those custards, and it's real close."

With a quiet laugh, Nym cast the spell on Bildar, who relaxed immediately. "That's good stuff right there," he said. "It's been real hard to keep my thoughts organized for the last few hours. I don't suppose your fancy new set of spells could get me back on my feet?"

"Scrapes and bruises, mostly. I could encourage a bone to heal that's been properly set, speed up natural regeneration. I don't have anything for this level of damage yet."

"Bah. What kind of a healer are you?"

"I'm a lot better at killing than healing."

"I suppose that's true."

"By the way, did you know that apparently using lightning magic gets you arrested here?"

"What are you talking about?" Bildar asked.

"Two army mages tried to take me in for hitting an enemy wight with a lightning bolt. We were in the middle of a huge battle and everything."

"Something funny was happening there," Bildar told him bluntly. "Lightning magic isn't illegal. I would have warned you about using it near the town if it was."

"Oh. That's great, just what I needed."

He'd deal with that problem later, if ever. Whoever those mages were, if they had indeed been part of the army, they were loyal to someone else as well, someone who wanted to imprison him, or at least get him off the field. He was just lucky that abrasive lieutenant had foiled that plot for him. Of course, with everything going on, there might not be a government presence by tomorrow. It was entirely possible that both those mages were already dead.

"Do you think you can walk under your own power?" Nym asked.

"I can. It's probably not good for me. It hurt to breathe before, you know. Feels fine now though, at least for an hour or two."

"You can cast a pain-blocking spell?" a new voice asked.

The woman on the other side of Nym had been sleeping when he'd first gotten there, but his conversation with Bildar had woken her up. She looked haggard and had dried blood all over her face from a scalp wound that was still oozing. "I can," Nym said slowly. He saw where this was going, and he already didn't like it. "I can't heal you though."

"Please . . . Please help me," she begged.

Nym grimaced internally, but it was his own fault. Quickly, he cast pain-blocking spells on all the wounded mages. The woman next to him let out a sigh of relief and sank back down. "Thank you," she said. "Maybe now . . . Now I can get some sleep."

He decided it wasn't worth his time to point out that she'd already been asleep when he'd first arrived. Instead, he turned back to Bilder and said, "You're going to need to see a real healer. Sooner is better. I'm going to go see what the group has decided on, but one way or another, I'm getting the four of you clear."

Even if he had to kidnap them, he'd at least accomplish that much. Anything else was a complete and total waste of his time coming out here. The whole plan should have taken less than ten minutes, and almost all of that travel time. Nym hoped that the rest of the earth mages were too stubborn to leave and that he could depart with just the people he actually wanted to save.

The not-cold voice in his head didn't like that idea, but he ruthlessly quashed it. It was survival time now. He could have empathy and morals later. Salvaging as many of his assets as he could from the situation was his sole priority, and if this wasn't resolved soon, he was on the edge of writing the Earth Shapers off completely.

"Well?" he asked Ophelia.

She shook her head. "They're all afraid to go out."

"Can't really blame them," Monick said. "I'm afraid to go out too. You're tough, Nym, but you can't fly us all. How were you planning on doing this? Ferrying us out one at a time?"

"Something like that. It's time to leave," he said. He turned to the rest of the bunker and raised his voice. "We're leaving now. Anyone who wants to come can come. The rest of you . . . I hope you survive and that the army comes to rescue you, but I have seen how bad they've been beaten back by the undead. This wasn't isolated to your camp. Ghouls are getting over the walls by the hundreds or even thousands. The army is being pushed out."

This sparked another round of arguments, but Nym didn't stop to listen to it. He just turned to Ophelia and said, "Ready?"

She glanced around once and then gave him a decisive nod. Nomick walked up to them with Bildar, helping the older mage stay upright. Even with the pain-blocking spell, his body was still so weak from blood loss that he was having trouble moving on his own.

"Open up the ceiling," Nym said. He grabbed all four of them and lifted them up into the air. A portion of the dirt overhead started to collapse and reveal the night sky overhead. The ceiling peeled back, and as it retracted, a leg fell from the ground overhead to the bunker floor.

The rest of the ghoul came tumbling in right after it, along with two more of its kin.

CHAPTER FORTY-THREE

Y ou have got to be kidding me," Nym growled. He shifted his passengers to the side and flung his mage blades out to slice through the ghouls. Fortunately, all three were still in the process of putting themselves back together and weren't all that mobile yet.

The blades hacked the ghouls back apart without any trouble beyond the fact that he was already holding five people in the air and his arcana was spread thin. He brought the Earth Shapers up to the surface and set them down, then did a lap around the destroyed camp to cut apart two more ghouls that had pulled themselves into more or less one piece.

This time he hurled the pieces in different directions. The ghouls were guaranteed to put themselves back together, but his firepit had been too hastily constructed, and he'd crammed the parts too close together. It had taken barely ten minutes for most of them to become mobile again. They'd be back in the fight eventually, but by then Nym planned on being long gone.

"Last call," he said into the bunker. "Anyone who's coming needs to speak up now before this hole gets closed over."

No one said anything, but there were a lot of apprehensive glances traded between the group. Nym looked over at the Earth Shapers, who just shrugged back. Nomick said, "If I didn't trust you so much, I wouldn't move either. On my own, I'm not going to make it out of this forest alive. At least in the bunker they're safe from the undead."

It was probably for the best. The original plan hadn't included any other mages anyway. "Alright then, good luck, guys. Feel free to close this thing back up once we're gone," he said.

"Wait, wait!" someone called out.

A thin woman shoved her way to the front of the group. She was tall and skinny, dressed in a boy's shirt and trousers with a pair of suspenders holding them up. Several metallic objects were pinned to the suspenders, each one a different shape. "I want to go too!" she called out.

Nym fought to keep his expression neutral. He'd been so close, but here at the last second was some plain-faced woman who'd mustered up enough courage to not huddle in a hole and wait for death to find her. He would be almost impressed if the situation wasn't so annoying. He couldn't just abandon her though, not with the audience.

He knew he shouldn't leave her behind anyway, that he really should be trying to save everyone. Those thoughts were given very little consideration before being brushed aside. He couldn't do that even if he wanted to. One more person wouldn't be too great a burden on his teleportation spell. Twenty-two more would. It was that simple.

He wrapped the new girl in a cushion of air and pulled her up to ground level. "Alright, let's get going," he said. "The rest of you are walking for a bit while I float the baggage here behind us."

"Hey!" Bildar said from his position in the air behind them.

"Talking baggage is still baggage," Nym told him firmly. Banter was much harder than normal, but appearances had to be kept up.

Bildar subsided into grumbling that everyone ignored. The bunker closed up behind them, which got a wistful look from the new girl. Nym didn't blame her for having second thoughts. "Probably not too late to go back," he offered, trying not to sound hopeful that she'd change her mind.

"No, I can't stay there and just wait to die while hoping someone will come along and tell me everything's fine now." She shook her head, then turned to look at Nym. "My name is Laraine."

"Nice to meet you. I'm Nym," he told her. "What were you doing out here, working with the building crew?"

"Ah. No, I'm an enchanter." She gestured toward the pins on her suspenders. "We were supposed to be installing scrying wards every few hundred feet to help feed information back about ghoul movements."

"Interesting. You work for the army then?"

She shook her head. "Freelancer."

"Me too," he told her. "I did not get paid enough for all of this."

Internally gritting his teeth, Nym started walking. He kept up a constant undead scan and, every time a ghoul got close to them, sent out his mage blades to intercept it. As long as they came in one at a time, it wasn't too hard to keep on top of them. The others didn't even usually see the ghoul.

"This would almost be a pleasant walk if not for the smell," Ophelia said.

"There's a spell to block that," Nym said absently, frowning as a knot of three ghouls moved closer to them. He got one of them, but the other two made it through the trees as the blades circled back around for another pass. A pair of stunning spells gave him enough time to cut apart another one, and he took the legs off the last one first to keep it from reaching the group. That made it harder to attack, but he could adapt to the new angles to finish the job.

This wasn't going to work. He was already starting to slow down after just a few minutes of walking. It would almost be less work to fly all six of them out if for no other reason than because they'd travel much faster. He'd probably drain himself dry in a matter of minutes, but for those few minutes, they'd get a mile or so of travel done.

"Ophelia, can we talk?" Nym asked.

The woman moved to the front of the line and asked in a low voice, "What's wrong?"

"We're not going to make it out like this," Nym explained. "What do you know about Laraine? Can we trust her?"

"I don't know. Sorry. We only met her yesterday. We can't just leave her here though. What are our options?"

"If it were just her, I could fly her out. If she wasn't here at all, I'd use teleportation. I can't fly us all, and I am reluctant to let her know I can teleport."

"Why is it a secret?" Ophelia asked.

Nym just gave her a flat stare.

"Oh, one of those geas things. That is so inconvenient. I'm sorry, I don't have a good answer for you. We can build a small bunker if you need to rest for a bit."

"Let's do that. I think I have an idea. I'll explain once we're safe."

The bunker was dug out quickly. It wasn't as well hidden, but it was designed to be short-term and didn't need to be. Once they were safe, Nym said, "Here's the new plan. Laraine, I'm going to fly you out. The Earth Shapers will wait here for me to come back. They should be safe, but if necessary, they can fortify the bunker further. I'll have to fly everyone out one at a time, but that's still faster than walking the whole way, and less dangerous."

"Why didn't we just stay at the main bunker then?" Laraine asked.

"Because I didn't think the undead would be this thick out here," Nym lied. "It wasn't this bad before. Circumstances changed, so I'm going to adapt with them."

He took a twenty-minute break, and they broke the bunker open just as the sun came up. Nym lifted Laraine up into the air and, once she was overhead, said in a low voice to Ophelia, "Tell the rest the real plan about teleportation. I'll be back in an hour, I hope."

He joined Laraine up in the air. "Any preference on where you go?" he asked.

"Ebalsan, I suppose."

"Might not be the best idea. I'm not sure the town is there anymore, but alright."

They took off before Laraine could say anything else. It didn't even take half an hour for the keep to come into sight, and Nym winced when he cast far sight on himself to get a better look. The keep itself was still standing, but the walls were crumbling in places. It looked like the wights had gotten off an artillery spell of some sort and completely blasted through the wall on the east side, along with vaporizing a corner of the town.

Of the rest of Ebalsan, maybe half of it was still standing. There was plenty of movement, but it all looked like ghoul activity to Nym. He stopped flying and turned to Laraine. "Do you have a backup location?"

"What? Why?"

"Ebalsan appears to be overrun. I don't see any people left, but I do see a lot of ghouls."

"What about the army?"

"The keep is still standing, more or less. Maybe people evacuated into it. Do you want to go there?"

"Can we swing by and see if it's empty first?"

"We can," Nym said. "Do you know where you want me to drop you off if it's not full of soldiers and refugees?"

"I . . . No."

"Think on it," Nym advised her. "No offense, but I need to get back to my friends and start working on getting them safe too."

"Are you going to go back for the rest of the people in the bunker?" Laraine asked.

"Probably not, no. It would take me a week to move them all just to here. Much faster to let the army know there are survivors there so they can send out people to help. If we're lucky, the keep will not be abandoned and you can do that while I go back."

They altered direction to fly by the upper reaches of the keep. As they closed in on it, Nym saw a trio of soldiers watching from a window. "Oh good," he said, "there are still people alive."

He peered at them closely, trying to make sure they were in fact living soldiers and not a pack of wights wearing soldier uniforms. Everything seemed to check out, so he flew close to the window with Laraine and knocked. One of the soldiers helpfully opened it from the inside, though he looked a bit confused.

"Hi," Nym said. "I have a survivor from one of the camps in the woods. This is Laraine. Can you get her taken care of? She's got the location of the underground bunker the rest of the survivors are in."

"We . . . Can we do that?" the soldier asked, looking over his shoulder at someone Nym couldn't see. After a moment, he shrugged and said, "I guess we can. Here, miss, why don't you take my hand and come on in? You too, sir."

"I'm all set, thanks. I've got a lot more work to do."

Nym handed Laraine off and, before anyone else could say anything, zipped away from the window. There was a shout behind him, which he ignored as he sped off into the open sky. Finally, the distractions were taken care of. He could fly back to the new bunker, teleport his allies out of the hot zone that was the entire forest, and start the next phase of finding Analia. If he was really lucky, she wouldn't be with the army.

In fact, it would be best to get started on that now. The more he knew about her location, the better he could plan how to reach her. While he flew, he took the time to send her a message. *[I'm about to get the Earth Shapers out of the forest. Bildar is injured. Where are you at so I can come get you too?]*

He didn't get an immediate reply, which wasn't concerning. He also didn't get a reply by the time he made it back to the rest of the group, which was less ideal. Considering how serious the situation was, that could mean a number of things, but he was sure she would reply if she was able. Hopefully it just meant she was sleeping.

Nym found the bunker and settled on top of it. He dispatched the single ghoul that was sniffing around and then yelled an all clear through the chimney they'd set up to give them air. The ground fell away around it, giving him access to the bunker.

"Is it time?" Bildar asked, his face once again tight with pain.

"Soon," Nym said. "I don't know where Analia is now. We could leave, but if she tries to message me and I'm not nearby, I won't get it."

"We need to get Bildar to a healer soon," Ophelia said.

"I know. I know. I'll just . . . I'll teleport you all somewhere else, then come back for Analia."

"What about the rest of the people in the bunker?"

Nym shrugged. "I delivered that enchanter to the army. She's letting them know so they can send a rescue party."

A bit of tension went out of the earth mages when Nym said that. "Good. I think we have a solid plan," Bildar said. "We're ready."

CHAPTER FORTY-FOUR

ym took his time setting up the teleportation spell. He'd only done it twice himself and never with an extra person, let alone four. The amount of arcana it needed scaled up quite heavily with the base spell, but he thought he might be able to modify it to a version that had a static arcana cost and just grabbed everything in a set area. If he was right, that was how the teleportation platforms worked.

The spell took hold, and the world pinched around them. Everything was dark for an instant, and then they were standing near the edge of a small town that was just starting to wake up with the new day. Nym staggered to one side and would have fallen if Ophelia hadn't caught him. "That was . . . harder than I thought it would be," he said.

"Take your time," she told him. "Just catch your breath."

"Is that Geldrin?" Monick asked, pointing at the town.

"Yes," Nym said. "It was the first town I could think of that I knew had a healer and would be far enough away that the refugees hadn't reached it yet."

"Wait, refugees?" Bildar said. "What are you talking about?"

"Like I said, the ghouls overwhelmed the walls. I don't even know how many wights were commanding them. A lot of them had soldier uniforms on, so I'm thinking something bad happened near the center of the forest and a huge chunk of army mages were killed and raised. Either way, Ebalsan is half-gone, and there're no people left. I think everyone either ran for it or is huddled up in the keep."

All four earth mages looked horrified at the news, but Nym wasn't really sure why. Their own camp had been hit even worse. It had practically been flattened by the time Nym got there, and even though most of the undead had moved on, there were still ghouls roaming directly on top of their bunker, looking for the humans they presumably smelled.

If there'd been a wight there, Nym was pretty sure that the building crews would have died. It would have understood what those chimney stacks rising out of the ground meant, and ghouls had no problems with digging. It was kind of strange that they hadn't figured that out, unless the ghouls didn't actually know anyone was there and were just loitering. Perhaps they'd heard the survivors through the stacks but couldn't figure out where they were.

It didn't matter in the end. His only goals now were finding Analia and extracting as many of his personal possessions as possible from his house. At the least, he wanted the money stashed in his room. It was over twenty crests now, more than enough for him to live humbly for the rest of his life. In fact, at his current life expectancy, he wouldn't even have to be all that humble as long as he was willing to do some work occasionally.

"Do you have any money on you?" he asked.

"Couple shields," Monick said.

"Nothing," Ophelia added.

Bildar shook his head, and Nomick just shrugged. Nym fished two crests out of his pocket and handed them over. "That should be enough for a healer and a decent inn for the night. Is there anything in your personal supplies worth going back into those woods to dig up?"

"Maybe ten crests, a few trinkets and mementos," Bildar said. "Some stuff with sentimental value. I would like to go back for it if possible, but this situation being what it is . . ."

"Should have stayed in Thrakus and fought the contractors guild," Monick said. "It would have been less dangerous."

"That was a losing battle. They had bribed damn near everybody who could have done a thing," Bildar said.

"I need to get back," Nym cut into the conversation. He'd heard that argument too many times already and didn't have time to listen to them have it again. "Are you going to be able to get to the healer from here?"

"I think I can manage to hobble a few hundred feet," Bildar said. "Are you sure you're ready? You're barely upright."

"Doesn't matter. If I don't go back, we'll lose Analia."

"Right." Bildar didn't look happy. "Nym, thank you. Be careful. There's something fishy going on with the army. Whoever those two guys who tried to arrest you on false pretenses are working for is probably still out there."

"I'll try to stay away from them. Go on now. I need to focus."

The Earth Shapers started toward the town while Nym built back up the conduit he needed to pull in third-layer arcana. There had to be a faster way to do it, but the spiral method was what he had. For now it was fine since the only third-circle spell he knew was teleport, and it wasn't a time-sensitive issue to cast it, but eventually he'd be using arcana from the Astral Sea in a combat situation, and taking thirty seconds to forge the conduit, then another ten seconds to get the arcana under control would not work.

The spell came together and pulled Nym back to Ebalsan. He'd targeted the air about a thousand feet right above his house, and when he came out of the teleport, he was free-falling toward the ground. Nym regretted that decision immediately, as it took him a few seconds to get oriented. A quick application of second-layer arcana saved him with a few hundred feet to spare, but if he'd realized how bad the back-to-back teleports would take it out of him, he'd have chosen a more secure landing and flown in.

It was too late now either way, but he'd remember for next time to give himself a longer recovery period. It probably wouldn't hurt if he limited the number of people to something more reasonable in the future too.

A quick far-sight spell revealed ghouls still crawled through the ruins, but Nym didn't see anything more dangerous than those at first glance. He switched over to scrying to get a better look at the interior of his home. It was still standing, which was more than he could say for that abominable pet store next door. The ghouls had gone through and cleaned that out completely, leaving a thoroughly disgusting mess behind as they tore through walls.

His house was miraculously almost completely untouched. It was a good thing Analia had never gotten around to actually getting a pet, or no doubt the ghouls would have crashed through a wall looking to eat it. The fact that there was nobody home had probably helped the house survive too.

His pack with his money was still where he'd stashed it. The books were all there too, but Nym didn't have a good way to transport so many. Teleport didn't take anything that wasn't being carried, and he wasn't even sure how well it would work on Analia's trunkful of personal possessions even if he was holding it. She'd just have to learn to live without them.

He took a moment to send another message to the girl after he'd retrieved his pack. She didn't respond, which was going to make things difficult. She'd had that antiscrying rune sequence added to every outfit she owned, and he doubted he'd find her without help, assuming she was still alive. Unless things had gotten far worse for the wall defenders after he'd left, he didn't see any reason for her to be dead.

Then again, Ebalsan was broken and abandoned. Ghouls had flooded over the walls and no doubt killed thousands of people from various towns surrounding the forest. Things obviously *had* gotten worse. Analia could well be dead, and if not, the only people who might know where she was were Collective agents.

Since he had nothing better to do while waiting to see if he'd get a response from Analia, Nym flew over the forest back to the Earth Shaper's camp. It was a relatively slow flight for him, but it did give him a chance to catch his breath. He'd only been awake for four or five hours, but it was hard to recall a more exhausting day in the last few months.

Nym found the camp without any issues, but when he got there, the bunker had been dug up. Twenty ghouls had descended on the mages who'd decided to remain behind. It must have just recently happened because there were still ghouls in the area feasting on some of the remains. Nym stared down at the scene impassively, less concerned with the ghouls than with finding what he'd come for.

He supposed anything he found was his at this point. It wasn't like the original owners were still around to dispute his claim. Clearing out twenty ghouls would be a pain though, especially since he still wasn't back in top form.

A glint of light caught his eye, and he turned in the air just in time to see a wight looking up at him from the ground. The creature had a hand extended up at him, and a glistening line of something anchored to it was flying at Nym. The arcana-forged material struck him before he had time to process what he was seeing, splattering against his leg and sticking there.

The wight grabbed the arcana line and pulled. Nym tried to fight back, but his air cushions broke immediately, and he tumbled toward the ground. He managed to create new ones before he crashed, but the wight was already on him, having closed the distance in moments. Its hands grabbed hold of Nym and dragged him the rest of the way down to the ground.

Arcana flared around the wight, and Nym felt his mind start to falter. It was hard to concentrate on the monster, even with its hands on his shoulder. He wasn't sure what was happening, but he did know he didn't like it. So he responded with the first thing he could think of.

An immense wave of air rolled out of him in every direction, so strong that it threw back nearby ghouls and loose sticks and kicked up dirt into a small blinding storm. The wight's grip loosened but did not falter. However, its magic broke and left Nym free to focus on a counterattack.

Lightning sparked between them and threw the wight free. Electricity crackled down the monster's arms and Nym both, but he wasn't the same mage he'd been six months ago. The lightning rolled off him, leaving him unharmed but for the claw marks sliced into his shoulders when the wight convulsed and was thrown backward.

He examined the creature to make sure it was dead for real before he floated back up into the air. With the wight's expiration, the magic webbing lost its cohesion and fell apart, leaving him free. A few ghouls crept toward him, but Nym was already back out of reach. He ignored them while he scried around for other wights.

He didn't see any, and the ghouls were already reverting to their normal feral behavior. Some of them wandered off into the woods while others finished up on the scraps of human still there. There was nothing left to do but scavenge what he could from the camp, but Nym was considering skipping even that.

That wight hadn't been trying to kill him. It had a clean shot before he'd realized it was there, and it had chosen to tether him and pull him down to the ground. Then it had physically restrained Nym and tried to use some sort of mental manipulation, possibly a spell that would force him unconscious. That meant it was trying to capture him, not kill. Nym had never encountered an undead before that had done anything but try to murder anything it found that still had a pulse.

He knew the wights were clever, maybe even as intelligent as they'd been in life, but this behavior was new and had disturbing implications. If the wights were capturing people, there had to be a reason. Whatever the undead were doing in the forest might be advancing to the next stage now that they'd broken the army's siege.

Whatever they wanted live mages for, Nym doubted it boded well for the remaining humans still alive. He looked down at the bloody stains in the dirt where the earth mages had been eaten. It was impossible to tell if the ghouls had consumed all of them or maybe just a few. Did the wights want every mage or only ones with specific spells?

It might be time to cut his losses and leave. Losing Analia would be a blow, but the situation was escalating beyond his ability to handle it. The best course of action would be to recover his strength and teleport out.

[We need to talk. I know you're still in the area. I know whom you're looking for.]

Nym frowned and considered the message. The voice was familiar, not Analia's though. Then it clicked. It was her father.

CHAPTER FORTY-FIVE

Message was an undeniably useful spell, but it was also relatively difficult to cast and had a whole host of restrictions and limitations. The caster had to have at least a rough idea of where the recipient would be and had to know them well enough to form an accurate mental image of them for the spell to latch on to. There was no feedback in the spell to actually let the mage sending the message know if it had been received, and the magic couldn't just linger until it successfully found the recipient. Even if all the other conditions had been met, the spell might fail just due to the target taking a nap at an inopportune moment.

Nym would not have been surprised to get a message from Navarim, even though they weren't all that close. Jharn would have surprised him just because the spell wasn't really part of the mage's established areas of expertise. But he really hadn't interacted with Jaspar Feldstal after the first day, so it was quite a surprise to get a magical message from the man.

Apparently, the leader of the Collective had been paying more attention to him than he'd thought. That probably wasn't a good thing. More than that, he didn't think he could send a message back, and the deliberately cryptic wording didn't give him much to go on. Lord Feldstal didn't tell Nym what he wanted or give him any directions.

He had to be missing something. There was no point to a message that Nym couldn't respond to. Maybe this was the Collective's way of getting him to come in voluntarily, to just send him a vague message and hope he'd start looking for someone to teleport him back to the base. That didn't seem like a winning plan to him, and he wasn't sure what the logic would be there. It wasn't like Lord Feldstal could hold his own daughter hostage to ensure Nym's cooperation.

He sent out another message to Analia, but it remained unanswered. The only thing Nym could think to do was wait and see if they tried to contact him again. While he waited, he flew the length of the walls to the next camp, then sent down a scrying anchor to investigate the ruined buildings. There was a surprising amount of money there, but he supposed when he considered how isolated the labor camps were, it made sense that people were hoarding it when there was nothing to spend it on.

Nym added it to his stash, did a quick scan for anyone still alive, and flew off. Half an hour later, he was close to thirty crests richer, though most of it was in the form of shields and shims. His pack was getting heavy with coins now, to the point where it would clink when he walked. Nym had never had more wealth in his possession at any one time, not even when he'd looted Valgo's hideout.

[I know you're still here. Come to the table and negotiate. I realize I've grabbed a snake by the tail here, but surely we can work out something mutually beneficial.]

The message was different this time. Nym couldn't quite place why it was, just that it was more open-ended. The arcana that carried it to him lingered in the air, like it was waiting for something. Nym examined it curiously and found a hook on it, keeping it stuck to him while it stretched off into nowhere.

"Oh, that's clever," Nym said, realizing what it did. Somehow, Lord Felstal had modified it to accept a return message. It must have been hellishly expensive to cast it that way. He crafted his own message, but instead of picturing someone to send it to, he just attached it to the message lingering around him.

[What do you want?]

With a kind of mental nudge, he unhooked the message spell from himself and let it snap backward. It faded from his sight about twenty feet away, pulled back through whichever layer of reality allowed for it to travel the distance. He wasn't confident it was a second-circle spell, not without seeing it being cast.

The answer came back almost immediately. *[We need your help to stop the undead.]*

The message also had a response hook to it. Nym spent a moment considering what was going on. Lord Feldstal had obviously figured out something, but Nym wasn't sure what. He was on the back foot, probing Nym like he was expecting to be swatted down. Whatever he thought he'd learned, things would go better for Nym if he knew it too. If he somehow thought that Nym could turn this whole debacle around, well, it wasn't like Jaspar Feldstal was a stupid man.

Nym sent his answer back. *[What are you offering?]*

[Release from the geas you agreed to.]

[And Analia?]

[Safe. We extracted her from the battle when it turned against us. She's in a safe house I own, unaffiliated with the Collective. She can leave once the area is safe.]

Being released from the geas immediately sounded good to Nym, but at the same time, the Collective had gotten what it needed. By all appearances, anyone with at least a size-twelve soul well would be able to grow it to the point that they could cast third-circle spells just with the current techniques. Nym had benefited from it as well but only in terms of speeding up what he would have accomplished on his own.

There was no reason to renew the geas when it dissolved on its own, and the only thing it was preventing him from doing that really mattered was leaving the country. More to the point, he already knew that there was a spell to absolve the geas. It was just a matter of finding someone to teach it to him before the geas started pushing to be renewed in a few years. He was willing to bet there were plenty of nobles who knew how to do it.

In short, being released from the geas sounded nice, but it wasn't as valuable now as it would have been. Analia was still useful to him, and the part of his brain that liked to play nice was demanding he cooperate to rescue her. That part wasn't in control anymore, and Nym pushed it aside. Analia was a somewhat poisoned resource now, tied too closely to her father. Nym wasn't sure how trustworthy she was anymore.

It wasn't that he thought she'd betray him. It was that her father was entirely too good at keeping tabs on her. Her brother might have tried to keep her in Abilanth, but Jaspar Feldstal obviously had different plans for her. Nym couldn't even begin to guess the extent of her father's spying on his daughter and, by extension, Nym. The Collective also had weeks of data from various tests. It was possible they'd figured out he was an ascendant before he'd confirmed it himself.

That would certainly explain the change in attitude. They probably didn't know what to make of him. Ascendants were supposed to be godlike beings, and here he was, getting taken out by a late-night hit squad and being forced into a geas. He could probably use their assumptions to force a good deal just by bluffing, but he wasn't really sure what they had that was worth staying involved.

[We can meet, but you'll have to offer more than that if you want me to stay and fight undead. This looks like a pretty decisive loss for humanity to me.]

There was no reply for a minute, then with a quiet crack, Lord Feldstal himself appeared in the air next to Nym. He floated easily, though his version of the spell used the same wind-based suspension Analia had used when they'd first met. Her father's control was much finer, and even if his clothing whipped around him, the wind was sharply contained to only support him without any stray gusts.

"Hello," he said, his voice modified with magic to cut through the winds holding him aloft.

"Hi," Nym said, his arms crossed as he stood on a plane of hardened air. "Let's start with what exactly you want me to do."

Lord Feldstal gestured around at the forest. "This, all of this, is intolerable. The outbreak is no longer contained, and we will have a solution in six months when we needed one yesterday. We want you to help to cull the undead and eliminate the source."

"And why would I be able to do any of that?" Nym asked. He was sure he knew the answer, but he wanted to hear the nobleman say it.

"Because you're not human. You're beyond us."

"Am I?"

"I don't know what games you're playing," Lord Feldstal snapped. He stopped himself and took a steadying breath before continuing in a much calmer tone. "Whatever your reasons, you're obviously an ascendant. I have a thousand questions I'd love to get the chance to ask, but this is more important. You could end this with a snap of your fingers. What price do we have to pay to get you to act according to your true nature, not this disguise you're wearing?"

They'd made a lot of assumptions about Nym, most of them incorrect. That was the problem with the whole meeting. If he really could just wave a hand and make the undead disappear, he probably would have done it already. It was hard to bargain for something when he couldn't come through on his end.

"What makes you think this whole mess is more important to me than maintaining this disguise?" Nym asked, stalling for time.

"I am very sure that the affairs of mortals fall far beneath an ascendant's notice," Lord Feldstal said dryly. His voice had a bit more spine in it, but he was still dancing around cautiously. He was afraid of saying the wrong thing and being obliterated by a power he couldn't comprehend.

Nym wanted to laugh at the ridiculousness of the situation, but all he could do was hold to the bluff and hope to find a way out. He did still want Analia back, but that was barely enough to convince him to help at all, let alone reveal his true nature.

"Tell me what happened. You had this under control. What went wrong?"

Lord Feldstal hesitated before speaking. Nym could practically see the gears turning behind his eyes. He was trying to figure out what to reveal and what to hide, trying to figure out if he dared lie to the creature he thought Nym was. While he was thinking, Nym took the opportunity to cast a spell he'd rarely had a chance to use: the truth-seeking spell he'd watched Bardin use when he'd interrogated Nym back in Abilanth.

It wasn't a perfect lie detector, and he wouldn't trust it against a mage as powerful as Lord Feldstal normally, but right now, it might just give him the edge he needed. He waited with the spell running while the nobleman struggled to figure out how much he wanted to reveal.

"The third-circle mages working in shifts to keep the veil pinned closed were doing a shift change. Something must have gone wrong; we're still not sure what. The veil opened enough for the reaper to reach out. It started killing mages and raising them as wights. Things cascaded from there, and before we knew it, we'd lost thirty mages to the undead. The tear opened up completely, and thousands of ghouls passed through with plenty of new wights to command them."

"The reaper didn't pass through as well?" Nym asked.

Lord Feldstal shook his head. "The tear still isn't big enough. We called in Archmage Veran to help. He's still there, as far as I know, holding the tear closed by himself. He can't do anything else but buy us time. If he lets go, the tear will open up and start expanding again. Then everything gets worse. But he's still just a man, for all his power. He can't hold it forever."

"And you want me to go fix it all," Nym said. "Just make all your problems go away."

"Please." There was a hint of begging in the word.

There were no lies there that he could detect, but Nym couldn't do what Lord Feldstal wanted. He'd have to refuse and leave, pretend like he just wasn't interested. "That sounds like a lot of work for very little reward. Your offer is to remove a geas I could remove myself and guarantee the safety of your own daughter, who is already quite safe. In return, I have to shed my anonymity, derail my own plans, and clean up a mess I had nothing to do with."

"She would also be free to continue traveling with you, for whatever your plans are," Lord Feldstal said weakly.

"Your concern for her well-being is touching," Nym sneered. "I almost can't believe you subjected her to all your little experiments when she was a baby."

The nobleman bristled, and Nym feared he'd pressed too far. Then Lord Feldstal sighed and shrank back into himself. "Fine, if none of that is enough, what else could we offer?"

"I doubt you have anything I want that bad," Nym told him.

"If not me, perhaps Archmage Veran himself might have something to interest you. It might only be a trinket by your scale, but trinkets can still be fascinating."

Nym was about to refuse again when he felt something grab hold of him. The world pinched him, and suddenly he was standing in the air above the ritual site next to a man who looked to be in his eighties. He had his eyes closed, and an intense aura of arcana roiled around him.

"You look quite young for an ascendant," the man said.

"Archmage Veran, I assume?" Nym asked.

CHAPTER FORTY-SIX

Y ou'll forgive me if I don't bow," the archmage said.

Nym had been fighting to keep from reverting too much back to his child personality. He needed to be sharp and ruthless right now. It had been a strain though as that part of his mind kept trying to push back to the forefront. When a literal archmage, one of the strongest humans in existence, grabbed him with a teleport and pulled him to the heart of the undead scourge, everything froze back over. There were no more arguments between personalities. Nym was cold and sharp as ice now.

"Think nothing of it. You've obviously got your hands full with all of this right now."

Nym didn't think he could keep his bluff going much longer. Talking to Lord Feldstal had been bad enough, but now there was no leaving unless Archmage Veran let him. Somehow Nym doubted the old man would simply take no for an answer.

"Indeed," the archmage said. "Quite the mess. If I'd known back then what I know now, I could have fixed this properly instead of merely delaying it. It is fortunate that you survived your encounter with the frost wraiths and warned us in time to prepare for it."

"You know I was involved in that?" Nym asked. That wasn't good. He'd been even more helpless then than he was now. There was no way this guy was going to believe Nym was some all-powerful god being just slumming it for nebulous reasons.

"Of course. Leaf went and found me immediately to let me know what the two of you uncovered. I got the whole story from him and Babkin. Incidentally, I'd like to apologize for his behavior. He was never very good at social interactions, and he has a soft spot for children. You obviously aren't one, but I hope you can understand the mistake."

"It's in the past," Nym said. "Let's talk about why I'm here now."

"Well that very much depends on whether you'll admit that you actually are an ascendant like little Jaspar thinks. Sorry, Lord Feldstal. He gets touchy if I call him little Jaspar."

"What if I tell you I'm not?" Nym asked.

"I guess I would be disappointed that you felt the need to lie to me and perhaps a bit insulted that you think so little of my intelligence that this disguise would fool me."

"I wouldn't want to anger an archmage. I suppose I must be an ascendant after all."

Archmage Veran started laughing. "Ah, I wonder what happened to you, my old friend. I've never seen you look quite this young. And the stories they told me of your exploits . . . You don't seem like yourself."

Nym's eyes widened slightly. He knew Archmage Veran? Or rather, Exarch Niramyn did. He was completely screwed now. Maybe if he'd had the time to try out that new conduit and push to the fifth layer, he would stand a chance, if only because it would have allowed him to unlock his memories. But he didn't have that time. He'd barely even started working on the third layer, and he only understood about half of what his past self was talking about when it came to burrowing through the fourth layer.

"Nothing to say?" the archmage asked. "I understand why you don't want to get involved. 'Mortal problems are for mortals to solve. Why did I bother teaching you magic if I was going to have to come take care of it myself?' But I'm afraid that this time, the problem might just be beyond my abilities."

"I'm not who you think I am," Nym said.

"Yes, clearly something has happened to you. That or you're playing at a game I can't even begin to guess the purpose of."

Nym's mind went into overdrive. The archmage knew he was an ascendant and perhaps even knew his past self's true identity. He felt some sort of affection for Exarch Niramyn, perhaps enough to help Nym now. There had to be a way to use that. Having such a powerful connection could ease his rise through the third layer and help him reach the fifth. If there was anyone who could show him the way, it was an archmage.

It was time for some creative truth telling. "Let's say that I decide to help," Nym said. "But let's say that I can only help you as I appear to be, a young human mage with a decent grounding in second-circle magic. What would you want me to do?"

"Second circle?" Archmage Veran raised an eyebrow and looked at Nym. "I'm sure you must mean third. I'm not blind."

"My mistake," Nym said. "Of course I meant third."

"If we're maintaining the fiction, then I suppose I would pass off the spell I am holding to you. You're more than strong enough to maintain it, and it is only third-circle magic, after all. Then I would start working on a more permanent solution to all of this."

"If one mage with a third-circle spell can hold this closed, why did they need so many?" Nym asked.

"It took, and forgive the term, pinnacle magic to pull the tear closed by myself," the archmage explained. "I am only using an admittedly complicated third-circle spell to keep it from opening back up. It will hold for a few hours longer if I maintain it, but eventually I'll grow too weak to do so."

Pinnacle magic? Nym supposed he meant a spell that used fifth-layer arcana. "And as payment for this, I would want something appropriate for this form."

"What would that be?" Archmage Veran asked.

"I need to learn how to make a conduit to the fifth layer."

The old man barked out a laugh. "You want me to teach you what you taught me? Very well. It's a small enough favor in return for your help."

Nym worked hard to keep his expression smooth. This whole debacle could actually play out in his favor after all. He just needed to hold a spell construct steady for a few hours while an archmage cleaned up the mess below. Granted, it would be a bit more complicated in practice, but he was confident he was getting the better end of the deal.

"Explain to me what you want me to do," Nym said.

"There are two spells at work right now. The first is a pinnacle spell that is reaching into the tear and subjugating the reaper trapped on the other side. Without it putting pressure on the veil to tear it open further, much of the strain of holding the tear closed disappears. It's an expensive spell though, very complex and using a lot of irreplaceable tools that I've burned up in the process. It will hold on its own for perhaps another six hours.

"The second spell is a variation on the ritual spell planar lock that group of third-circle mages was using. It's designed to keep anything else from passing through the tear but needs to have arcana channeled into it constantly. It's easier to maintain as long as the pinnacle spell is still running, so you should be able to handle it yourself. As soon as the reaper is free again, we'll lose the spell, and the tear will split back open.

"You'll keep channeling arcana into the ritual planar lock while I work on cleaning up the influx of undead. Once everything is stabilized, the army can get back in here and resume locking everything down."

Nym looked down at the forest below them. Everything was blurry, like looking through a window that had been coated in grease. Even with that, he could still see a stone mausoleum with a roof overgrown with moss and lichen. The grounds around it were a muddy, churned-up mess from the sheer number of undead that had passed through. Wispy, fog-like tendrils hung in the air around the whole thing, shifting unnaturally in various directions and completely ignoring the breeze that moved the trees.

When he concentrated on what he was seeing, Nym could almost make out the tear in the veil inside the building, if only because of the aura of Archmage Veran's arcana surrounding it. "How do I take over powering this spell for you?"

"It will be delicate, but I'll manage that. This spell is technically a ritual spell designed to be powered by multiple mages. The number of people who could do so single-handedly is . . . low, but I don't think that will be an issue for you. I'll integrate you into the active ritual and then shift powering the components of it to you, one at a time."

They set to work. Nym started drawing in third-layer arcana with Archmage Veran's guidance and found it much easier to manipulate when using a series of filters he implemented into the conduit at the archmage's suggestion. It slowed the arcana coming in and helped break it off from the Astral Sea, which made it much more manageable without having to close the conduit completely.

Once they were sure he could manage the needed arcana flow, Nym was pulled into the ritual so that he could sync his arcana up to Archmage Veran's. Then, one at a time, he was slowly handed off the various pieces of the construct. It was rather like playing a game of cat's cradle, where he was instructed to hold or pinch various pieces of the structure while his partner manipulated other pieces.

In the end, he had the entire thing supported in his arcana, and Archmage Veran disengaged completely from the ritual. With each step back the old man took, it became harder and harder to maintain, so they went slowly. All told, they took over an hour to transfer the planar-lock spell to Nym's control.

The spell was so ridiculously complicated that Nym couldn't even begin to unravel how it worked, but he didn't need to. He just needed to hold it in shape and feed it arcana. That was a considerable strain but not so much that he was in danger of losing it anytime soon.

"How long do you think you can hold it?" Archmage Veran asked.

"Maybe an hour. Two perhaps?" Nym said.

"Truly? That is . . . considerably less than I was expecting. I had best get to work then. Do not move from this spot. The camouflage screen below us is the only thing keeping the wights from realizing we're here and attacking."

And then Nym was abruptly alone in the air. Archmage Veran's teleport spell was so smooth and so fast that there was barely even a flash of arcana around the man before he disappeared. Nym looked around, trying to spot him below and expecting to see some extremely powerful magic tearing through undead like they were nothing.

Instead, it was just him, sitting in the air, by himself, holding on to a spell and hoping he didn't mess something up. Minutes went by. Undead roamed around on the ground, doing whatever undead things they liked to do when they weren't busy hunting and eating the living. Nym was starting to wonder if this was some sort of joke where they just wanted to see how long he'd stay there, holding the spell and looking stupid, while they scried on him and laughed.

Then a column of fire exploded into the air about three miles away. It easily cleared the treetops before expanding in every direction, and it was so loud that Nym could actually feel it. The spell he was maintaining started to slip from his inattention, and Nym clutched desperately at it to keep its shape. Fortunately, it wasn't too far off from how he was supposed to be holding it, and it wasn't difficult to fix it back up.

Another column rocked the forest a mile north of the first one. Nym gritted his teeth and held tightly to his own spell construct as the shock wave washed over him. "And to think I wanted that excitement right below me," he said. "That was a stupid idea."

CHAPTER FORTY-SEVEN

The next two hours of Nym's life were extremely stressful. Archmage Veran did laps around the forest, sometimes detonating spells so close that it threatened to unravel the planar-lock spell Nym was holding on to for him. Other times he'd travel far enough away from the center that his attacks were nothing more than flashes of light and rolling booms that sent flocks of traumatized birds up into the air.

The strain of holding the spell wasn't too bad at first, but by the time the half hour mark set in, his eyeballs felt like they were going to pop out of his head. An hour after that, he was barely cognizant of the world around him and was weighing the risks of finding a place to stand so he could cancel his flight spell. He knew that was a terrible idea for a lot of reasons, but if he didn't let something go soon, he was going to lose everything.

Nym drifted in and out from there on. There was nothing left but the magic and holding on to it. It wore down on him, slow and steady, every minute just a little bit harder to keep going. And then the pressure was gone, just like that. Archmage Veran sat in the air in front of him, holding the planar-lock spell and supporting Nym's weight on an air cushion.

"You did well," the archmage said. "But it's time to rest now."

"Did you get everything done you needed to?" Nym slurred as he wobbled in place. Holding his own body upright was a struggle now.

"I suppose it will have to be enough. The army will have to move quickly to reclaim this area, and it will be that much more difficult to hold on to it, but they'll have a fighting chance."

"You won't help them?" Nym asked.

"I help them every single day, but even I can't close this tear in the veil, not with Ul'tuthik on the other side. Its very presence holds it open. With the loss of so many third-circle mages, it will be much harder for the army to keep it under control. I suspect we will see a marked increase in frost wraiths, probably too many for me to contain on my own. Those are more dangerous to the average soldier than anything else."

"I had wondered where those all went."

"Yes, dealing with them has been the primary focus of the army's mage division. They kept the frost wraiths completely contained to the center of the forest and dealt with the worst of the wights. A lot of those mages were killed though, and Jaspar's pet project is still months away from delivering new third-circle mages, if it ever does."

Archmage Veran sighed and shook his head. "It's quite the conundrum for us lowly humans. We can't kill the reaper, and we can't repair the veil as long as it's still alive. Well, *alive* might not be the right word for anything that exists on the other side of the veil, but you know what I mean. Regardless, I'll just hold on to this planar lock until the army gets everything set up, and then we can go."

It took Nym a moment to parse through all the words. Most of it was just noise washing over him as it got harder and harder to follow the conversation. It was becoming a struggle just to keep his eyes open now that he'd been relieved of the burden of holding the planar lock. A vague thought popped into his head. He wondered how Archmage Veran was still going when Nym knew for a fact that his own soul well was roughly four times the size of a human's at the archmage level.

"Where are we going?" he asked.

"My private sanctum. I have an obligation to you, and I can't let it be said that I do not meet my obligations. In fact, I might send you there now so you can rest while I finish up here."

"What about my deal with Feldstal?" Nym asked.

"Ha, you're as greedy as I remember. I'll personally take care of that geas later on tonight, and I'll make sure he lets his daughter go free. He's done enough damage to her already with his misguided attempts at creating an ascendant."

"That's . . . That's good," Nym said after thinking it over. "Thank you."

"You're welcome, my one-time master. Rest now. I'll see you soon."

Nym found himself sitting on the floor of a washroom. There was a tub of steaming water in front of him, a not-so-subtle hint that he would probably offend the nose less after a bath. Nym stripped down and climbed into the tub, then groaned when the heat hit him.

By the time Nym was ready to get out an hour later, he was feeling much better. A quick application of a few second-circle cleaning spells restored his clothes to a semipresentable state, albeit one with quite a few stains. He was sure Archmage Veran wouldn't mind. Now he just had to wait for the old man to show up so they could get started.

Jaspar had never been so scared of a perceived threat in his life. Every time another report about that damn kid came in, it felt like a hand was reaching into his chest and squeezing his heart. Every way they knew to measure a mage, Nym was at least twice as strong as he should be. In some ways, it was upward of five times as strong. And his growth was incredible.

In short, he was everything Jaspar had hoped to imbue his own progeny with, with none of the familial loyalty he also wanted to see. Nym had been easy to read and initially seemed like a gold mine. The technique he'd seemingly discovered by accident could very well turn out to be the key the Collective had been looking for since before his father's time.

And then he'd realized the truth. He wasn't in control. That naive boy who was so easy to maneuver was a walking calamity. Jaspar had grabbed onto a bolt of lightning with both hands and tied himself down to make sure he didn't fall off. He'd laughed to himself about that geas he'd signed for Nym's sake and absolved himself of it as soon as the boy had left his office. Nym was probably laughing twice as hard at Jaspar's foolishness.

He'd made sure to never be at the facility when Nym was there after the first day. He had no idea what kind of game that kid was playing, if he even really was a kid, and he had no desire to get caught in the aftermath. There was opportunity there, yes, but oh so much risk. At any moment, the bomb could go off and burn his whole world down in ascendant-backed alchemist's fire.

He'd been so busy worrying about the snake he'd invited into his den that he'd been completely blindsided by the problem that actually blew up first. The Collective itself hadn't been too badly damaged as very few of their members were actually third circle, but Jaspar Feldstal was still the mage-commander of the army, and losing so many combat-capable third-circle mages in one blow would have been devastating enough.

Having them rise back up as wights to fight for the enemy really sealed the deal for them. He'd been left with only one choice: beg the hidden demigod walking among them for help. Nym, of course, wasn't willing to work for free, but what he'd asked for made no sense. Nothing about him made sense.

Thankfully, the archmage had taken over that negotiation. Jaspar had rallied his remaining troops after Veran and Nym had done whatever it was they'd done. Jaspar had seen the aftermath and was glad he was nowhere near it while it was happening. Regardless, the military had regained tentative control of the region, and that was what was important for the moment.

Unfortunately, he was being held to his end of the bargain. Nym wanted

Analia released and returned to him, and Jaspar didn't dare disobey. So he found himself walking down the hallway of one of his many countryside manors to where his daughter was being kept safe. He hadn't talked to her since he'd left months ago to oversee the army's mage division, and he'd been content to leave her alone until she was ready to approach him once Bardin had reported the discovery of his lab to him.

Events had dictated otherwise, as they so often did. But Jaspar had people to do things for him, so he still hadn't actually seen his daughter face-to-face. That would change now though, and he found himself somewhat dreading the upcoming conversation. She was no doubt still angry with him, and trying to rationally explain to a teenage girl that what he'd done was for her own good wasn't likely to go over well.

He knocked on the door and waited for a reply. There wasn't one, which didn't much surprise him. She no doubt knew who was there already with her little magical spies. He was proud of her for that one, the air golem. Sure, she'd gotten the initial spell construct from an ascendent, but Jaspar's spies told him that she'd modified it to use air instead of earth all on her own.

He pushed open the door and found her sitting on her bed, arms crossed and a ferocious scowl on her face. He smiled slightly at that scowl; it reminded him so much of her mother. What a woman she'd been. She wouldn't have approved of the experiments if she'd known, but she hadn't been a mage and didn't understand the hurdles her children would face.

"Hello, my dear," Jaspar said.

"Father."

"Is this a bad time?"

"Would it matter if it was?" she snapped. "Since when do you care about me at all?"

"I have always cared about you. I wanted what was best for you. Someday you'll understand the why behind it all. When that day comes, don't think that it's too late to mend our relationship. I will still be your father."

"How very convenient for you."

"I suspect you'll find out sooner rather than later," he said. "Your little boyfriend has negotiated to allow you your freedom to continue roaming the world at his side, doing as you please. He'll also be released from his geas, if he hasn't been already, and I imagine once he fills you in, you'll understand everything."

"You could just tell me yourself. I might like it better to hear it from you."

"Ah, if I could," Jaspar lamented. "But not all geasa are created equal, and this one even I can't break. Believe me, I've tried. All this secrecy, my father's paranoia, it's understandable, but it's also a hindrance to the work I do."

"So it's to be more excuses and lies then, Father?" That imperious tilt of her chin reminded Jaspar again of her mother. How Analia had managed to pick up so many mannerisms from a woman who'd died before Analia was old enough to remember her was a mystery to him.

"I don't see the point in lying now. There's nothing to be gained from it. Speaking of truths to be told, has your boyfriend told you what he is?"

"He's not my boyfriend," Analia said. "And what are you going on about now?"

"Not for lack of trying on your part, as I understand it. I would advise you to put a little more distance there and harden your heart against him. The boy is no boy. He's an ascendant, and I have no idea what he's doing here."

"We thought he might be."

Jaspar was momentarily flabbergasted. She knew and stated it so casually. Worse, there were implications to that statement. They thought he might be an ascendant? They didn't know? Only an immense amount of training and practice kept his expression smooth as he thought back over his own interactions with Nym again. He'd go over things in greater detail when time allowed, but he was beginning to think he'd been hoodwinked.

"Regardless, whatever romantic intentions you have, you would be better served by giving them up. The boy is the spawn of God, graced with his benevolence and granted magic beyond any mere mortal. He is not of this world, and whatever his machinations, no mortal who gets swept up in them will come out ahead."

Analia just stared at him, unimpressed, just like her mother used to when he went on long diatribes about the latest political maneuverings among the nobility. Jaspar sighed and said, "I see. If your mind is made up then, so be it. You may stay here as long as you'd like, and I will personally teleport you wherever you'd like to go when you leave. We're still working on figuring out where Nym himself has gone, but we probably won't know for sure until he finishes his business with Archmage Veran."

"I'll make my own travel arrangements, thank you."

"If that so suits you. Please remember my advice. You might learn great things from him, but in the end, he will leave this whole world behind. His kind aren't meant for us, nor we for them."

CHAPTER FORTY-EIGHT

Nym felt off. All week, he'd felt like he couldn't make up his mind about anything. That cold, cynical part of him that belonged to his past life, that only cared about himself and saw other people for what they were worth to him instead of as friends was constantly intruding in his thoughts. Normally it was easy to shut that part away. Normally, he didn't think those kinds of thoughts in the first place.

That had changed after the day the undead had broken loose. Perhaps it was a result of relying on it too much, or perhaps it was just an inevitable merging of personalities as he learned more and more about who he used to be. Either way, having two different thought processes pulling him in different directions made it difficult to interact with other people.

Fortunately, he wasn't doing a lot of interacting at the moment. One thing both he and his past self agreed on was that he needed to continue to advance his magical capabilities. In that matter at least, it was easy to talk to Archmage Veran. His past self's personality pushed him to try to find another way to take advantage of the man, to be as greedy as possible, but Nym didn't let those thoughts control him.

His bargain with the archmage was still in full effect, and Nym felt kind of bad about it. His spiral conduit that reached the third layer worked, technically, but it wasn't efficient, and it wouldn't help him reach the fourth layer, let alone bore through it to the fifth. That didn't mean it was a total loss though, as it did allow him to start the process of enhancing himself. Under Archmage Veran's skilled guidance, Nym started carving arcana-overflow channels into his body.

That was just the first of many enhancements that could be made, and his new teacher assured him that a true ascendant knew a thousand more methods for altering a mortal body to be stronger, more efficient, and faster to react. Third-circle spells were the threshold when mages could start making permanent changes to the world, changes that would last long after the magic was spent.

Of particular interest in Nym's case were alterations he could make to his brain that made it easier to enforce his will on the world. A stronger will essentially meant a stronger conduit on a fundamental level, so strong in fact that all his complicated work-arounds to navigate the second layer became redundant.

An archmage did not need to navigate the layer with finesse. Nym could simply break through any obstacles using willpower and momentum. He learned how to shape the tip of his conduit into a sort of splitting wedge that, given enough power, could crack the chunk of crystallized arcana blocking his way in two.

Puncturing the membrane was a different matter, but there was, inevitably, a solution to that in Archmage Veran's bag of tricks. He set Nym to a series of training exercises designed to increase his mental flexibility so that he could learn to shift a conduit he'd already formed without remaking it. Those exercises were infuriating. Nym hated them so much, but he grudgingly did them.

Each one made his brain hurt, like trying to trace the lines in those impossible pictures where everything seemed right as long as he didn't look too closely or as long as he only looked at a small piece. They were impossible to connect together and difficult to envision how the lines should look while the picture was still in front of him. The training exercises were like that, and Nym never once completed one without a splitting headache accompanying it.

He was a dutiful student, but everyone needed the occasional vacation. After a week of breaking his brain, Nym took a much-needed trip out of the sanctum. Archmage Veran had many other duties to attend to anyway, so when Nym decided to leave, he simply informed the old man that he was going to check on his friends and make sure everything was fine with them. He'd seen them once on the second day when he'd dropped off what he'd salvaged of their belongings, and they were still staying in Geldrin while everyone recovered and they planned out their next move.

Nym was hoping Analia would be with them. Archmage Veran had assured him his conditions had been met and she'd been returned to her friends, but Nym had been busy acclimating to some of the new modifications he'd made. Now that he'd finished the physical adjustment period and learned how to compensate for the changes, it was time for a little fresh air.

He still needed his coil conduit for the time being, but the filters he'd learned kept it calm enough to channel continuously. Between that and the mental reinforcements, it was easy to handle the third-layer arcana now. Nym built his teleport construct with the alteration needed to bypass the sanctum wards and teleported into the air above Geldrin. There was no disorientation now, and he appeared smoothly in the sky above the town.

A quick scrying spell showed Ophelia and Bildar eating lunch together, though the twins were nowhere to be found. Analia was not visible either, but Nym wasn't surprised. Hopefully she'd be there anyway. He landed in front of the inn they'd taken rooms at and walked in.

Bildar saw him first. "Oh, there he is," the bearded mage said. "Just disappears for a whole week and then walks in like it's nothing."

Ophelia twisted in her chair to look at him. "You look older again," she said. "Maybe sixteen now? And you definitely need a razor and someone to teach you to shave. Not Bildar, of course. The whole reason he even keeps a beard is he can't shave it off without cutting his face up."

"Here now, that's not true, and you know it," Bildar protested. "You're just jealous that I can cover up the bottom half of my face and you can't."

Ophelia snatched up some kind of bread roll and pelted Bildar with it. He grinned as he snatched it out of the air after it rebounded off his face. "Don't hate me because it's true," he told her solemnly.

"Hmm . . . A shave, huh?" Nym mused aloud. He wove a quick first-circle spell and swept it across his face. The patchy stubble that was starting to come in fell free from his skin and landed on his shirt. Nym dusted it off and let it fall to the floor.

"Now that's a useful spell," Bildar said.

"Is . . . Is that . . . Where did you learn that spell?" Ophelia asked.

"Yes, it's the spell you're thinking of, just modified slightly."

"What are you two talking about?" Bildar asked, looking back and forth between them.

Ophelia ignored her brother. "Where did you learn it?"

"Found it in a book," Nym said offhandedly.

"And what, pray tell, were you doing with a book like that?"

"A book like what?" Bildar demanded. "It just looks like a basic hygiene spell to me."

"Where do you think I get most of my spells from?" Nym asked Ophelia. "I would think the source would be obvious."

"Ah . . . Hmm. I shall be having a talk with that girl. She's too young for those kinds of spell books."

"What in God's name are you two going on about?" Bildar said.

"That spell is not meant to remove hair on a person's face," Ophelia told him. "It's not meant to remove hair on a man at all."

Bildar's eyes widened, and his face reddened. He slumped back into his chair and said in a very small voice, "Oh."

"What other spells did you learn from that book, Nym?" Ophelia said sharply, turning back to Nym.

"None that I think it would be smart to admit to," Nym told her. Most of the spells were innocent enough, if not terribly applicable to him, but a few of them dealt with certain other matters that had made Nym blush far harder upon reading them than Bildar was at the table.

Nym hooked a chair from a nearby table with his foot and dragged it over to sit down. "Speaking of, where is everyone else at?"

"Oh, somewhere off in the foothills north of town." Bildar waved a hand behind him, apparently not realizing or not caring that the west wall of the inn was to his back. "Analia's been trying to rebuild her stock of alchemical supplies for days. She dragged Monick and Nomick off to 'keep her safe,' in her words, which I took to mean 'use as a pair of pack mules.'"

"I didn't know she was doing alchemy," Nym said, surprised.

"For over a month now. You've been lost in your own little world and not paying much attention to what the rest of us have been up to lately."

"Ah . . . Yes. I have. Sorry. There were . . . things that, actually, I can tell you about now. I had the geas absolved a few days ago. Once everyone gets back, I'll tell you some of the deep, dark secrets the nobles are keeping from us."

Bildar snorted. "It's going to be five or six hours before she shows up. They won't even turn around until it gets dark out."

Nym did have another visit planned for his day off. He had thought he'd do lunch in Geldrin and dinner in Palmara. He wanted to check on the cube as well. It wasn't that he expected it to be gone; it was just that it contained literally his entire life prior to a year ago, and that apparently included an unimaginable amount of magical might.

He still had only a vague notion of what exactly an ascendant was compared to someone like Archmage Veran. The old man was impressive enough on his own, and Nym couldn't imagine a mage so powerful that his magic made an archmage look like a child. He supposed he'd find out soon enough.

Then again, he might not. Nym had a lot of mixed emotions about the whole idea of resuming his former life. Exarch Niramyn was a repugnant, selfish man, judging by what Nym had learned of him. Almost universally, everything he'd learned about his former life painted the picture of a man who'd cared for nothing but his own power, and his intruding thoughts supported that picture.

The only outlier was the mysterious bit of charity he'd shown Archmage Veran about fifteen years ago when he'd taught the human mage how to reach the fifth layer. The archmage remembered Exarch Niramyn fondly, but that one single act of kindness didn't really match everything else Nym had seen. He suspected there were ulterior motives and planned on figuring out what those were as one of his first projects once he had access to his old memories.

Nym brought himself back to the present when he realized Ophelia had said something but he'd completely missed what it was. "I'm sorry?" he said.

"I asked if you wanted to order something to eat," she said.

"Oh, no. I think I might just come back for dinner so I can talk to you all at once. I've got something else I need to do today anyway. I was going to do it after spending some time here, but I think it'd be better to flip it."

"That'll be fine. You're leaving right away then?" Bildar asked.

Nym nodded. "No point in putting it off. I'll see you in five hours or so?"

"We'll be here," Bildar said. "We can tell you what we're thinking of doing next as well. Maybe you'll want to come along. I promise there will be no undead this time."

Nym laughed. "That's a good selling point. I'll see you guys for dinner."

He teleported directly out of the inn and appeared on his favorite stretch of beach. Sitting in a boat with her back turned to shore, pulling up a rope line hand over hand, was Ciana. With a small smile, Nym lifted himself into the air and flew the few hundred feet out over the water to her boat, then set himself gently down behind her so as not to alert her.

"Hi," he said.

Ciana yelped in surprise and jumped so hard she fell out of the boat. Still laughing, Nym grabbed her and lifted her out of the water with his magic. Dripping wet and wild-eyed, she glared at him. "That is not funny!"

Nym just laughed harder.

CHAPTER FORTY-NINE

You're not funny."

"I don't think anyone else would agree with you," Nym argued.

"Fine, if you're so funny, you can row the boat."

Nym considered that for a second. "I don't see the connection here," he told Ciana.

"The connection is I'm all wet now!"

"Well, I'm a big shot mage now, so I could just fix that. Like . . . this."

A twist of elemental water magic dried her clothes and hair out. She gawked a little bit as it formed into a ball between them before splashing back into the cove, but then said, "As impressive as that might be, you still get to row the boat."

Nym cast a quick scrying spell to look at all the crab traps, noted which ones were full, and used elemental water manipulation to pull them all up at once. Nine traps rose to sit on top of the water, which he used telekinesis on to remove the trapped crabs and reset the traps while he sent the crustaceans all flying over to land in the bucket between him and Ciana.

"Where exactly am I rowing to again? The shore?"

"Listen here, you! That . . . That . . . That was very helpful. Thank you, Nym."

"You are quite welcome. So, what are we having for lunch today?"

"Oh God save me, he's turned into a teenager. My pantry won't survive having him in my home."

Nym scowled. "I dug you a whole cellar last time I was here! I even left money for you to stock it!"

"Food doesn't just appear out of nowhere, Nym."

Before he could respond, something bumped into the boat. Nym looked over to see a familiar scarred shark circling. "Really?" he asked the shark. "I thought you'd given up after I beat you."

The shark swam another circle and scraped up against the boat again. Annoyed, Nym sent the water beneath him flowing toward the beach. The boat rode the wave that rose under it until it was in the shallows. A bit of fine manipulation pulled it up the rest of the way to its normal resting spot. Behind them, the shark cruised forward, only to circle away when the water got too shallow to continue.

"It's just like old times," Ciana said with a small smile. She glanced at the bucket of crabs and added, "Well, almost."

"Stupid shark. It's not even there anymore, why are you still bothering me?" Nym yelled at the water.

"Come on then, shark whisperer. Let's get these home."

Nym lifted both of them into the air and flew them back to Ciana's shack. He examined it with a critical eye and said, "Are you sure you don't want something better? I could seal this all up nicely for you."

"Ask me again when it starts getting cold. I like the breeze this time of year."

"In a month when summer ends?"

Ciana gave him a flat glare and said, "I liked you better when you were a little kid instead of a lippy teenager."

"Yeah, yeah. Love you too, Big Sis."

They went down to the cellar, where Ciana had left the bucket with a weighted lid placed on it to hold the crabs. Nym cracked open the stone floor and confirmed his cube was still safe, then smoothed the whole thing back over while she watched.

"You never really told me what that thing is," she said as they walked back up the stairs together.

"It contains all my memories," Nym explained. "I just can't access it yet. Hopefully that'll change soon."

"Oh really? Did you find out . . . you know . . . why?"

"Still working out the details. I guess someone's trying to kill me, and I'm in hiding."

"What?!"

Nym shrugged. It wasn't the first time he'd almost died, though if he understood the threat, a fully powered ascendant was far more dangerous to him than a giant ice worm or a psychotic criminal stalker. He'd just have to trust his past self's preparations to hold until he was ready to become a real ascendant again.

The threat of this other ascendant, this exarch, was nebulous and far-off. Nym knew intellectually that it was real and lethal if they ever caught up with him, but he was pretty good at getting out of trouble. He was willing to bet he could outfly just about anyone at this point, and that was without even considering teleportation.

Then he thought about someone like Archmage Veran deciding to come after him, someone who could teleport himself whenever he wanted, who could toss around literal earth-shattering magic all day without getting tired, and tried to imagine a mage who was even stronger. There existed a possibility that he was vastly underestimating the threat.

He hadn't gone out of his way to interact with the archmage too much outside of their lessons. The old man already knew too many of Nym's secrets. Even though his association with the Collective had ended in what was probably the best possible way for him, Nym didn't really feel like he'd come out ahead. He'd saved himself a few months at the expense of permanently losing his anonymity. No doubt other higher-ups in their organization had realized what he was, even if Lord Feldstal hadn't told them himself.

"So, lunch?" he asked, trying to distract himself before he started brooding over it again. "I know a great restaurant if you want."

"I . . . I don't know if you going into Palmara is the best idea. You are still wanted for questioning for Senman's murder. I don't think they'd try to arrest you, but they . . . you know. They weren't exactly as interested in the truth of the matter as I expected them to be. There were politics. People his family were friends with cared more about revenge than justice."

"Are you sure you want to keep living here?" Nym asked.

"Yes. This is my home."

Nym looked around the shack. It felt smaller than he remembered it being when he was living there. For a single person, it was enough space, but it could use better furnishings, maybe an actual cooking stove and a real bed with blankets that weren't threadbare.

"Your choice. Anyway, I wasn't talking about going to Palmara. I was thinking steak at a place I know called the Quarterhouse."

"That sounds expensive," she said hesitantly. "Are you sure that's what you want? I did save a bit of money, but . . ."

"I'm paying," he said, his voice firm. "I don't know if I told you this, but I'm a pretty talented mage."

"A pretty egotistical mage, maybe."

"It's not ego if it's true. Just think of it this way. I still owe you for your unexpected swim. I'll handle travel and meal expenses for today." He could see her wavering. She just needed a push. "Did I mention their bar has an extensive selection?"

And there it was. He had her. "Fine, you win," she said, her hands held up in surrender. "Where are we going?"

"City called Thrakus. Uh, don't mind the smell."

He pulled in third-layer arcana, a feat that only took a few seconds now instead of close to half a minute, and wove together a teleportation spell. They disappeared from the coast and reappeared just off the road outside of Thrakus. That pungent livestock smell hit him immediately, just like he remembered.

"You get used to that," he continued. "But if you go away for a while, it comes back."

"It's certainly . . . strong."

"Come on, the sooner we get away from the stockyards, the better the air will smell."

They walked down the streets of Thrakus until they reached the Quarterhouse, where Nym treated Ciana to a delicious lunch and plied her with several glasses of various beverages. She was a bit tipsy when they left and, as it turned out, very giggly in that state.

Then he sprung the second part of his surprise on her. Nym knew she wouldn't accept it sober, so he'd deliberately chosen a good restaurant that he knew served a wide variety of alcohol she'd be open to trying. And then, with her still tipsy, he took her shopping.

She tried to protest, but he ignored her and dragged her through a few stores. She got three new outfits, with the promise from the tailor that they'd be altered to her size in the matter of an hour after Nym gave him a generous tip. She got a few packs of dried tea leaves, several pounds of jerky, a new hunting knife, and a few other practical necessities that weren't always available in a small town like Palmara.

Her new pack loaded down with the fruits of their shopping labors, they returned to the tailor and picked up her outfits. By now, the buzz had worn off, and Ciana was looking uneasy at the amount of stuff she was carrying with her. She didn't say anything while they were in the store, but once they got back outside, she stopped on the side of the street.

"This is enough," she said. "It's too much, really."

"You saved my life. I figure I owe you a lot more than this."

"I didn't do it so I could spend your money later."

"Didn't say you did," Nym said. "But you know I'll always be grateful to you. Let me spoil my big sister for a day before she goes back to live in her beachside shack and I go back to my life of opulent luxuries."

She rolled her eyes and hefted her pack. "Come on then, this was a nice afternoon, but let's get home."

"You sure?" Nym asked. "There's a café not too far away that sells chocolate. I have a friend who insists it's a delicacy."

"Why are you making that face when you say *chocolate*?" Ciana asked.

"I did not find it to my taste, but I thought you might like it."

Ciana said something, but Nym didn't hear it. He'd noticed two men staring at him from across the street, two familiar faces from his last visit to the city. They were members of the contractors guild that had attacked him and Analia during the early-morning hours when they'd been leaving. Both were scowling in his direction. Nym met their eyes and grinned.

He sent a little pulse of arcana into the dirt beneath their feet, just enough to make it shift a bit. Their arms flailed while they tried to keep upright, and they ended up grabbing onto each other for support. Nym watched them disentangle from each other and run off, then turned back to face Ciana.

"Sorry, thought I saw someone I knew. You said you were ready to go home?"

"Something like that," she said. "You've got your mischief face on."

"My what face?"

"The smirk you get when you're causing trouble."

"I do not!" he protested.

"You definitely do. What are you planning?"

"I'm not planning anything," Nym said. Technically, it was true. He hadn't planned anything; he'd just seen an opportunity and taken advantage of it.

"I don't believe you. It's probably best to get home before you get in trouble. Which way was it to the gates again?"

"We don't need to walk that far," Nym said. "It was just easier to teleport into an open space. We can teleport out much easier."

He led her off the main street to a dirt road lined with houses. Once they were away from the crowd, he cast the teleportation spell again and whisked them away to her home. She laughed a bit and shook her head. "What was it you said, a talented mage? I suppose it is true after all."

"I'm shocked and offended that you thought I was lying," he deadpanned.

"You'll be alright." She looked thoughtful for a second, then she said again a softer, more serious tone, "You will be alright. It's a lot easier to believe that now than it was a year ago. You're kind of amazing, kid, even if you are pretty weird."

"Please, I already paid for lunch. No need to keep trying to flatter me."

Ciana gave him a shove. "Still a smart-mouth though. Come on, let's go inside."

"You go on," Nym said. "I've got another appointment with some friends."

"You know multiple people who will tolerate you now? That's more impressive than the magic. You should bring them around to visit sometime."

"Maybe I will," Nym said. "Just to prove they're real."

They shared a good laugh, and then Nym teleported back to Geldrin. It had been a good day, but it was time for a more serious conversation.

CHAPTER FIFTY

They got a private room for dinner at Nym's request. Everyone made small talk until the food arrived, then Nym empowered four papers with different rune sequences designed to block scrying, keep sound from traveling outside the room, sever connections to remote sensors like Analia's air golems, and reveal invisible or transformed mages.

The others watched him silently while he worked magic after magic. He'd been preparing for this meeting for a few days in between his practice sessions and planned for it to be as private as possible. Just because he was going to share a few secrets with his friends didn't mean he wanted anyone who happened to walk by to hear.

"This seems like overkill for a catch-up meeting about everyone's plans for the near future," Monick said.

"That's not what this is about," Nym said, his back turned to the table while he affixed the last paper to the door. He didn't need to look behind him to picture the glances they were giving one another.

"I'm free of the geas," he told them once he was done. "I figured you'd like to know what that was all about, but I do want to warn you that it's probably not going to be something you'll want to share. These people protect their secrets pretty rigorously."

"Nice!" both twins exclaimed at once. "How'd you do it?"

Nym's food was cold by the time he finished explaining what the Collective was and what they'd wanted with him. The amount of outrage around the whole table when he told them that none of them except Analia would ever be able to cast a third-circle spell on their own was a sight to behold.

"But you know this technique," Ophelia said. "You could teach it to us."

"I . . . can. Yes. The Collective's early estimates put it at a fifty percent increase to your soul well's size, so Bildar would theoretically be able to do it, but no one else could."

"It doesn't matter right now anyway," Bildar said. "Congratulations on reaching the status of master mage, but none of the rest of us can do that. Sure, a bigger soul well would be nice, but that's not what's stopping us right now. We've all been mages for years, in my case close to two decades, without ever breaking through to the third layer."

"It's still not right that they're hiding this from us," Nomick argued.

"Oh no, the nobility is colluding with the government to keep secrets from us," Ophelia said dryly. She glanced over at Analia, winced, and added, "Sorry. I'm not talking about you right now."

"Nobles keep just as many secrets from one another as they do from everyone else," Analia told her. "Even when it's your own family."

"Anyway, yes . . . I can try to teach you this technique they developed off what I was doing to repair my matrix if you want," Nym said. "It's still experimental though, and we're not sure even how much the soul well will grow or what long-term effects there are."

"We'll debate that some other time," Bildar said, cutting through the chatter. "You still haven't told us how you broke the geas."

Nym had taken the opportunity to scarf down some of his now-cold food while they argued, and when Bildar put him back into the middle of the conversation, he could do nothing but chew while they all stared at him. He looked down at his plate, back up to the people staring at him, then down to the plate again. His fork inched over to grab another bite.

The entire table started shouting some variation of, "Don't you dare!"

Chuckling to himself, Nym put down his fork, swallowed his mouthful of food, and said, "I talked an archmage into absolving it for me."

"You did not," Monick said immediately. "No way."

"That's how they got the forest back under control," Ophelia realized. "An archmage showed up to fix the mess. You met him then. What did he ask for in return?"

"My help holding the planar-lock spell keeping more undead from pouring into our world," Nym said. "Turns out having a huge soul well is good for something after all."

"That's not it though, is it?" Analia asked quietly.

"No," Nym said, frowning at her. "It's not. They didn't just pick my name out of a hat. Your father figured it out, of course. All the tests, it must have been obvious. But he made some assumptions."

"Hey, stop being vaguely mysterious and just tell us already," Nomick said.

"I . . ." Nym paused for dramatic effect. Nomick chucked a bread roll at his head. "Am an ascendant."

"You have some mashed potato on your shirt," Ophelia pointed out. "Doesn't seem very godlike to me."

"No . . . Really, guys, I am," Nym said while flicking the offending lump of potato away.

"Yeah, we know," Bildar said. "Was this the big surprise?"

"What do you mean you know?" Nym demanded.

"Your Helingar-Bistal score was insane. Ophelia went through it over and over. You've been with us for a few months now and yet you look like you're three years older. Every time I turn around you've got some new spell figured out, half of which it seems like you invented yourself. You came back from a nasty matrix destabilization in a fraction of the time it should have taken. Nobody here thought you were a normal kid."

"Plus you and Analia have been researching ascendant stuff like crazy," Monick added.

"But . . . If you all knew, why didn't you say anything?"

"You didn't mention it, and then you had a pair of bodyguards following you around and the geas on you. It seemed like it would be a bad idea to talk about it openly. If you wanted people to know, you'd tell them."

"Huh. Well, I guess that all makes sense."

Ophelia snorted. "Still a kid after all."

"Wait, if you all knew, why were you giving me a hard time about meeting an archmage and everything?" Nym asked.

"Because it's funny," Nomick said.

Nym just sighed and took another bite of food. He couldn't believe he'd wasted all those hours writing rune sequences. "Anyway, turns out the whole reason I'm here is because I lost a fight with someone and had to run away. Everything is a disguise to give me time to recover. I guess once I'm able to channel fifth-layer arcana, I'll be able to get back all my memories and magic."

"That's good news, right?" Ophelia studied Nym's face. "You don't look happy."

"My other self is kind of a jerk. I don't like him. I don't think I want to be him. I want my memories and my magic back, but I don't want to act like him. He's selfish and only cares about what he can take from people around him."

"That sounds like a lonely existence."

"Yeah, but I don't know if I've got a choice. According to what I learned from the memories my past self did leave me, this enemy of mine is still looking for me. If I don't get my magic back, I'll be dead the instant he finds me. And he will, eventually. It's another ascendant, one who already beat me once."

"This is a race against this other ascendant then. You need to get back into fighting shape before he finds you," Bildar said bluntly. "But, Nym . . . You do a lot of crazy stuff, but reaching archmage levels in . . . what? A few months? A year? How much time do you have? It takes decades to manage that for us."

Nym waved his concerns away. "I know how to do it. I've just got to build up to it. I'm reworking how I do my conduits right now, and there are a bunch of enhancements that are locked behind the ability to channel third-layer arcana. It should only take a month or two to be ready for fifth layer."

"He says it like it's no big deal," Nomick said. "I guess that's what being an ascendant means."

"It took you a year to go from second to third," Ophelia pointed out. "What makes you think you'll be able to go to fourth so fast, let alone fifth?"

"My arrogant previous self didn't leave me any instructions for reaching the third layer, but he did tell me how to get to the fifth. And I have Archmage Veran personally helping me do it."

"Well don't just sit there, share the knowledge with us, man. What is the secret to catching up to you?"

Nym explained how he'd made his coil-shaped conduit to get to the third layer and how Archmage Veran had helped him with his early body and mind enhancements that allowed him to make a conduit that split the crystallized arcana instead of having to weave around it. They talked for another twenty minutes or so about various techniques and exercises, the philosophies behind some of his experiments, and what sorts of permanent enhancements could be done with third-circle spells.

The spells went down soon after that, and they finished up their meals without discussing anything else sensitive. Instead, the topic turned to the Earth Shapers' future plans.

"It's not great," Bildar confessed. "That big keep on the border was a bust, and with the army getting spanked like it did, I wouldn't be surprised if it gets delayed another year or two. Thrakus didn't work out. Too many bribes and corrupt councilmen. We're coming up into the winter season now and didn't bank anywhere near what we needed to just ride it out."

"I . . . may be able to help with that," Nym said. "I may or may not have picked up some loose change from a few camps that the ghouls had overrun."

"Battlefield looting? You know that's illegal, right?"

Nym shrugged. "There weren't any survivors to claim it, and it's only illegal because the military wants first dibs on the spoils."

"You're not wrong," Ophelia said, "But still . . ."

"How much did you take?" Bildar asked.

"About thirty crests' worth."

There was a moment of stunned silence, then Monick started laughing. "Of course you did. Your flight speed, the scrying spells, you probably tore right down the wall and cleared out camp after camp in minutes. I bet whoever was in charge of salvaging those camps was tearing their hair out over the lack of money they found."

Nym looked around the table and said, "All of you . . . I owe you a lot. Whatever you decide you want to do, wherever you decide you want to go, I'll help."

"Could go down south where it doesn't get as cold," Bildar mused. "Travel would be . . . Well, no it wouldn't. Nym could just teleport us over there. A bit of seed money to get us going again, and we could just work through the winter to stay afloat."

"I can't actually teleport to places I haven't been," Nym said. "But I fly really fast now, and I'm working on a third-circle flight spell that's used specifically for long distances."

"What are you going to do after your private tutoring sessions are done?" Analia asked.

"I don't know. I guess see what I used to know and figure it out from there?"

"I meant, where are you going to go?"

Nym just shrugged. He really hadn't thought beyond getting access to the rest of his memories. "Like I said, I'll figure it out as I go. That's what I've been doing all along."

They parted ways there, with Bildar and Ophelia putting their heads together to figure out where they could likely find work in the warmer southern reaches of the country, or even beyond the border, and Nym promising to find a way to get them there once they knew their destination.

He teleported back to Archmage Veran's sanctum, a complicated process due to the wards but one that he was able to do thanks to the knowledge his new mentor had shared with him. It was like a puzzle, and each piece had to be slotted in at the correct time, in the correct order. As long as he did that, he was able to pass through the wards without breaking them.

It had been a good day. He'd caught up with all the people he cared the most about. But now it was time to get back to work.

CHAPTER FIFTY-ONE

The problem with learning from an archmage was that he was a very, very busy man. He generally spared only twenty minutes a day to answer any questions Nym had and point him in the right direction to explore and investigate. It wasn't exactly what Nym had in mind when he'd requested help forging a fifth-layer conduit, but it was what he got.

On the other hand, Nym also got access to a rather extensive library once he'd successfully managed to reforge a conduit that reached the Astral Sea. Archmage Veran recognized the need for a balanced set of spells and specifically pointed out a few tomes that contained some of the more immediately useful third-circle spells.

Nym did learn that overland-flight spell he wanted, though it would take some practice to hold it long enough to actually make the journey. The spell would make him fly so fast that without a few supplementary spells to help him see and protect him, it was a terrible idea to even try. He could just picture himself cut and bleeding, his clothes shredded around him and hanging off his body.

It wasn't an elemental air spell either. Those were left behind with the second layer. Third-circle spells didn't much care about having materials to work with. They just used raw arcana to alter reality using whatever guidelines the spell had. That made the spells more arcana intensive and complicated, but also significantly less limited than their second-circle counterparts.

Nym picked up a few other spells to go with his new flight spell. He found kinetic barrier's older and meaner brother: hyperkinetic barrier, which could stop far more than small projectiles and would keep him from tearing himself to shreds up in the sky. He also found a spell called perfect sight that would allow him to navigate while flying, as well as let him see details much farther away than far sight did, even in the dark.

Greater telekinesis, dispel construct, and obscure self rounded out his new third-circle repertoire. Greater telekinesis functioned just like telekinesis, only without being restricted to what he could physically carry himself. Finally, he could pick enemies up and just throw them away from him, though there was still a weight limit of a few thousand pounds. Nym could think of numerous times over the past few months when being able to just pick someone up and move them around without them being able to fight back would have been helpful.

Dispel construct was exactly what Nym had already been doing manually, just automated into an admittedly complex spell that would probably take longer to cast than it would to just do it himself. For mages who couldn't see arcana though, he assumed it would be an extremely valuable spell to know. For him, it was mostly something he wanted to play with to see how it saw enemy constructs. He had some vague notions about combining that with an illusion spell to create a new spell that imitated what he saw naturally.

Obscure self was his answer toward trying to remain discreet. It allowed him to exist as no more than a hazy memory to people, quickly forgotten and with indistinct details if someone asked about him. The spell book promised the effect wouldn't be obvious at the time, and people would only realize something had happened if they tried to remember specific details about their encounter with him.

The final new spell he learned was an alter-weather spell. It wasn't relevant or practical, but it was so similar to the one the ice-worm hive queen had been using that Nym picked it just as an act of sentimentality. It only took him an hour to figure it out since he had firsthand experience with it already and knew the second-circle version. There were some slight changes, as it had an open spot in the construct for different types of weather instead of being locked in blizzard mode.

Perhaps more important to Nym were the once-a-week sessions where Archmage Veran continued to assist Nym in expanding his arcana channels, modifying his matrix, and altering his physical body to assist in making new conduits. Though Nym had never used much ritual magic himself, he knew the theory behind it. It involved investing arcana into objects, or in some cases another person, to share the load of a spell.

Nym's mind became partitioned, allowing him to work on multiple spells at once. This wasn't the same as what he'd previously done, where he built spells one at a time and then kept them powered. Instead, he could actually cast two spells at once, regardless of complexity. As Archmage Veran explained it, this would become necessary the stronger he got, and there were further levels of partitioning beyond it, but they had to be done incrementally, or he would break his brain.

Really, the whole arrangement was far beyond the letter of their agreement and even beyond the spirit of it. Nym suspected that at some point, he'd be asked for a big favor in return, and he was pretty sure he knew what it was. They wanted him to take care of that reaper so they could close the veil for good. Archmage Veran had already admitted that, at best, he could hold it back, and even that had taken a tremendous amount of resources that would take months to build back up.

Nym was nowhere near ready to attempt something like that, so he hoped the archmage wasn't planning on asking him anytime soon. He was still learning how to effectively use third-layer arcana in a combat scenario. It only took a few seconds to make the conduit now, but until he could do it instantly, he wouldn't consider himself prepared.

That wasn't to say that Nym didn't ever fight. He regularly teleported back to the forest outside Ebalsan and did laps around the area to clean up undead and conduct salvage operations. He managed to recover a few of the Earth Shapers' magical possessions he'd missed the first time, though most were damaged to the point of being unusable. Most of the camps had been picked through already by the army when they'd retaken the area, meaning it was hardly worth his time to fly around looking for them.

Since he never did figure out what was going on when two mages tried to arrest him, Nym avoided the army while he was there. Added to that was the connection between the army and the Collective, and he spent more time flying around the countryside outside of the forest hunting random undead than he did flying over the trees.

Nym was fine with that. His actions when the undead had routed the army had been incredibly self-serving, much more Niramyn than Nym, and now that he was back in control of himself, he felt like he should make up for that. Hunting down undead over vast stretches of land was something he was well equipped to do.

Usually, it was too late to save whomever the ghouls had attacked. They tended to find small villages or isolated farmhouses and swarm them, often killing anyone who couldn't flee. Nym would find great clumps of them squatting in the wreckage and annihilate them, then spend an hour or two scrying the surrounding countryside to pick up the ones roaming around by themselves.

It was tedious and somewhat heart-wrenching work. Very rarely were there any people left, and it made the work harder if there was. The ghouls would track down survivors, kill them, and be even more scattered. Once or twice, Nym would find a survivor before the ghouls did, but it rarely worked out that way.

Nym came upon something new one evening when it was just starting to get dark. Usually, farms were small and isolated. They grew enough for themselves and a little extra to trade in nearby villages and towns. This farm wasn't like that though.

It was more of a plantation, bigger than some towns he'd seen, and completely walled in. The ghouls were attacking it, and they were well enough organized that Nym suspected a wight was leading them, possibly two. The walls weren't high enough to keep them out, nor were the farmhands skilled enough to do more than delay the undead despite outnumbering them five to one.

Nym swept the outer perimeter where the ghouls had breached the walls and used a lot of greater telekinesis to rip them away from whomever they'd attacked. The undead were flung back over the walls en masse, much to the confusion of the farmhands below.

Once he was reasonably certain he'd expelled the ghouls, he started excavating a large pit in the middle of one field. "Collect any free wood you've got and get a fire going in here," he instructed the nearby farmhands. "The ghouls won't die until they're reduced to ash. Your job is going to be to keep any parts from crawling back out."

"Who are you?" one of the older farmhands asked.

"Just a mage passing by," Nym said. He had no plans to identify himself and was in fact using his obscurement spell to keep them from remembering what he looked like.

The new burn pit was near the wall, and Nym quickly started filling it with dismembered ghouls. His mage blades combined with greater telekinesis made the task almost trivial, even with the wights lurking somewhere in the background directing the ghouls. Nym put his new dual processes to work and set one part of his mind to casting various detection and scrying spells to try to locate them, but his lack of range was working against him.

The farmhands were still fighting fresh ghouls as they came over the walls, but with Nym's help, it was a lot easier to gang up on them and hack a ghoul up before it could cause real damage. The burn pit was going strong, with dozens of people surrounding it wearing cloth masks and wielding hoes and rakes to keep the ghouls burning inside from escaping.

The numbers were thinning, but Nym didn't want the wights to escape. He needed to hunt them down now, before they cut and ran. "You guys can take this from here," he said, turning to a nearby farmhand. "There's some strong undead directing them from the back. I'm going to go hunt them down before they escape and start rounding up new ghouls."

"Wait a second! What are we supposed to do without you?"

Nym looked around. Everywhere around him, farmhands were working in groups to pin ghouls down with whatever long-handled tools they had available, then hacking limbs off with woodcutting axes. "Keep doing what you're doing. You've killed enough of them that you can handle this. I'll be back in a bit."

There were more sounds of protest, but Nym ignored them. He flew over the wall and sent his mage blades to work on the ghouls approaching, but that was just a cover for his real activity: wight hunting. Once he was mobile, he was able to scan farther away from the plantation and found one of them quickly enough. It was hiding in an old windmill a quarter of a mile from the farm, organizing groups of ghouls and sending them out to run the distance in units.

That explained the weird mix of organization combined with a lack of adaptation. The wight was doing just enough to help the ghouls exercise some pack tactics without being close enough to risk itself. At least, it thought it was safe.

Nym cast his new hyperkinetic barrier and barged into the windmill. Mage blades flashed out, chopping two ghouls to pieces while the other part of his mind put together a lightning bolt to smite the wight where it stood. Mission accomplished, Nym lifted the whole heap of body parts and ferried them back to the plantation's burn pits.

"One down," he told the farmhand who was directing the defenses in his absence. "I think there's another one, but I haven't found it yet."

"Wait!" the farmhand grabbed his sleeve. "Something happened up at the house. We heard screaming a few minutes ago. A few of us went to go check, but I haven't heard back."

Nym nodded. "I'll check it out before I go."

CHAPTER FIFTY-TWO

Nym flew over to the manor house overlooking the fields and immediately saw what had happened. A pack of ghouls had broken through a window on the ground floor and further torn the wall apart around it when the window had proven insufficient access. The room they'd come into was covered in blood and had several dead bodies tossed to the side. There was a trail of bloody footprints leading deeper into the manor.

He was a bit hesitant to go inside. Nym would lose most of his mobility and range, which was fine if there were only ghouls in there. His barrier could protect against a physical attack from a ghoul long enough to teleport out if he needed to; he'd tested it thoroughly to confirm. Against the other wight that he suspected was involved in the attack, he was less confident.

If the ghouls had breached the walls and started indiscriminately killing and eating, he wouldn't be worried. But they'd targeted the manor and were ignoring meat from their own fresh kills. It was all but guaranteed that something was directing them. The weird thing was that Nym had only once ever seen any undead try to do anything but kill and eat, the night that wight in the forest had tried to capture him.

He couldn't imagine what the goal of that was, just like he couldn't figure out what they were looking for at the plantation. Before he set foot inside, he conjured up a scry anchor and sent it sweeping through the manor. It was a big building, clearly designed for dozens of people to live in, but Nym had plenty of practice doing this. The blood trail certainly helped, but he was still going to be thorough and check the entire place over.

In addition to the scrying spell, he also formed an air golem and imbued it with his new perfect-sight spell, then ordered it to follow the blood trail and try to get eyes on the undead. His own scrying revealed eight living people hiding in various rooms, all safe for the moment. It also revealed that the ghouls had rushed straight toward one particular room, killing anyone they encountered but otherwise ignoring the rest of the house.

The air golem reached the room and found some sort of hidden passage hanging wide open. The footprints were less blood and more mud at this point but still easy enough to follow considering the amount of damage to the floors and walls the ghouls did as they crowded one another in the halls. Once they went underground and the stairs became unadorned stone, the trail got harder to see.

It didn't matter though because the passage only went one way. It ended in a set of three rooms, but the ghouls were piled up in the hall outside. Past them, a wight was tossing one of the rooms, growling to itself as it dug through drawers and cupboards. Precious and fragile lab equipment was shattered in its haste, not that the wight cared.

The other two rooms were in similar states, so whatever the wight was looking for, it hadn't found it. The whole thing had Nym scratching his head. Why was the wight there? How had it known about the secret passage? What even was it looking for? Perhaps most relevant to Nym, what was the best way to kill it?

The straightforward approach was to go down, set up a hyperkinetic barrier, unleash his mage blades, and let them hack the ghouls to pieces. Then he'd lightning bolt the wight in the face, cart out all the parts, and throw them into the burn pit. There were a lot of ways that could go wrong, but now that he had third-circle spells, brute force was probably the quickest and most efficient method.

Alternatively, he could wait for them to come back out of the manor and ambush them. That had the drawbacks of potentially allowing some ghouls to escape as well, placing the manor residents in danger, and delaying him unnecessarily when he could finish the fight much quicker and then get back to the wall to make sure there were no casualties among the farmhands. It seemed like a bad plan.

He could seal off the entrance to the passage. There was probably more than enough time to create a stone wall to block the entrance, and he doubted the ghouls would dig through that before he had time to come deal with them. They would get through it eventually but not in a few minutes.

Nym shook his head. Simple was best. There was no need to overthink this with complicated plans. He flew around the outside of the house, punched out the window with a quick blast of greater telekinesis, and flew into the room with the open passage leading underground.

Nym sent the mage blades down ahead and placed his barrier across the top of the stairs. Using his air golem's sight to navigate and control the blades, he chopped the ghouls apart in short order. The only hitch came when one of the ghouls managed to catch a blade, but Nym remedied that by slicing the offending fingers off that hand with a second blade. He winced when they clanged together, knowing he'd be taking them in to be resharpened after that.

The wight noticed what was happening, of course, but there wasn't much it could do about it. At least, that's what Nym assumed since he was blocking the only way out. The damn thing didn't even seem to care though. It checked on what the disturbance was, then went right back to tearing apart the furniture.

Nym watched it cautiously. It obviously knew something that he didn't if it wasn't worried about its minions getting taken out. He unceremoniously chucked the ghouls into one of the other rooms where they immediately started putting themselves back together, then switched up his barrier from a solid, immobile wall to something that wrapped around him in a deflection aura. It was significantly more expensive, but if he was going to be playing with the wight, he wanted as much protection as possible.

Nym ghosted down the stairs and up to the wight, his lightning-bolt construct completed and waiting for him to release it. He arrived just in time to catch the tail end of a spell the wight was casting. The spell went off before Nym could do anything about it, and the wight turned to insubstantial mist or, rather, something that looked like mist.

Elemental air and water found no purchase on it, and the mist seeped up through the cracks in the stone. Nym sent his scry anchor after it but couldn't get a visual. Somehow, the wight had managed to phase through solid matter and was escaping. Worse, Nym still didn't know what its reason for attacking the plantation and raiding the basement lab was. He didn't even know if it had gotten whatever it had come for.

He flew back up to the ground floor and outside as fast as he could. His golem went with him, and they both started scanning the plantation, searching in opposite directions. The wight managed to make it over the wall or maybe went through it, Nym wasn't sure, before they spotted it. He flew off after it and managed to catch up.

Nym slowed as he got there, unsure of how to proceed. He didn't really have a capture-undead spell, and he was concerned that whatever it had taken from the manor house might be both valuable and delicate. Blasting the wight with a lightning bolt would surely destroy it, but it might also destroy whatever it was stealing. Since Nym didn't know what that was, he was reluctant to resort to something quite so damaging.

His scry anchor revealed the answer to him. The wight had stolen a book and a vial with some kind of liquid in it. Nym swooped in close and hit it with an undead stunner, pilfered the two items back with an application of basic teleki-nesis, then held them up to the fading light to look at them. The vial was maybe six inches long, stoppered with a piece of cork, and contained a murky black mixture that looked like liquid smoke splashing against itself.

The book was something else entirely. It was bound in pale leather with ribs on the spine and the title was embossed on it in a hard white material that Nym suspected was bone. The fact that it was titled *A Manuscript on the Manipulation of the Mind and Spirits* certainly didn't make it seem any less sinister. Nym didn't have time to flip through it before the wight broke out of the stunning spell.

Rather than continue to flee, it spun in place and launched itself at Nym. He was surprised by the quick turnabout, but his hyperkinetic barrier held strong against the attack. The wight snarled in anger when it was knocked back but recovered immediately and pointed a pale white finger at Nym.

Arcana built up around it as it constructed a spell, but Nym injected spikes of his own arcana into the delicate pattern. He pried key pieces apart and twisted them hard enough that the entire spell failed. It was nice to see that working, since he hadn't had much of a chance to practice dispel construct against a live opponent besides Archmage Veran, and the archmage's willpower was frankly too strong for his spells to be easily undone.

Against a wight using nothing but second-circle magic though, Nym's tech-nique worked just fine. In fact, he didn't even need to use the third-circle spell. Instead, he just shaped raw arcana to simulate the effect and manually guided it using his own sight. The spell broke apart almost instantly, stunning the wight again in the process.

Arcana backlash wouldn't stop a living mage for more than a moment or two, and against an undead one it was even less effective. The wight immediately lunged at him again, presumably thinking it would overpower the hyperkinetic barrier. Repeated blows hammered against Nym before he could fly up and back.

"Give them back!" the wight howled, launching itself through the air to chase Nym.

Nym was so surprised he almost fumbled the barrier and lost it. He'd never heard a wight talk. Nobody had ever mentioned that they could. They were obviously intelligent, and it made sense that they could speak since they were supposed to retain their skills from before their deaths, but wights didn't talk.

Except here was one who could, and did, and was happy to kill to get what it wanted. Nym had what he needed, and the smart move would be to finish the wight off and get back to the plantation to help with the cleanup. But now he was curious. Did no one know about this, or did they know but no one cared, or was this wight special?

The wight battered at Nym's hyperkinetic barrier again while he considered how best to move forward. He didn't have a good way to contain it, and in the end, it was responsible for leading an attack that had killed quite a few people. Whatever mystery there was in the potion and the book, it wasn't worth risking people's lives over. The right choice was to kill the wight.

Nym blasted it in the face with a lightning bolt and sent it tumbling backward. Surprisingly, it was still alive after taking the hit. A second lightning bolt finished it off before it could attack him again. Nym stuck around for a minute to make sure the corpse wasn't going to get back up again and made a mental note of the location he'd killed it at.

Then he turned back to the plantation and helped them finish destroying the rest of the undead. He'd talk to Archmage Veran when he returned and see what the old man had to say about the unusual turn of events.

CHAPTER FIFTY-THREE

Nym was flipping through a book on necromancy when Archmage Veran appeared in the library. The old man glanced at him casually, did a double take when he saw what was in Nym's hands, and cleared his throat meaningfully.

"So I met a wight who could talk today," Nym said without looking up. "Never saw one of those before. Seemed like it might be important. It was leading a group of ghouls in an attack so that it could steal that book over there."

Nym gestured toward the pale leather tome he'd taken from the wight. "I'm no expert in the matter, but if I'm understanding what I'm reading here, that wight was bound in service to a necromancer."

"Hrmm. Yes, they have begun to appear more frequently over the last few weeks," Archmage Veran said. He peered at the book without touching it. "Some sort of body-snatching ritual perhaps? I will assume this vile concoction came from the same source."

"That's the part that concerns me. I was doing a flyby and saw ghouls attacking a plantation, being led by a wight. The whole attack was a distraction to allow a second wight to slip in from the other side and break into the manor house. They had a secret basement full of all sorts of stuff, including that book and potion."

"A local necromancer then," Archmage Veran said thoughtfully. "Or possibly a whole family of them."

"Someone from the plantation? Or someone who used to live there maybe. They knew exactly where the hidden laboratory was but had to tear it apart to find what they were looking for in it."

The old man's brows furrowed as he thought. He stared off into the distance, obviously turning something over in his mind but not yet ready to share. Finally, he said, "I would like to see this plantation you visited."

"Really?" Nym was surprised. With all the important matters taking up the old man's attention, he hadn't expected this to rate high enough to warrant a personal visit. Nym had thought he'd ask a few questions, maybe get a better idea of what was going on, and then the whole matter would probably be turned over to the army for further investigation.

"Yes, this is . . . concerning. It brings up old memories from twenty years ago, issues I had thought long resolved."

Nym waited, but Archmage Veran did not elaborate. He just stood there in silence for another minute or so, absently flipping through the book Nym had recovered. He started in place when Nym said, "Did you want to go right now, or do you need some time?"

"Now is fine," the old man said. "Yes, the sooner, the better."

They teleported together, with Nym leading and the archmage using him as a beacon to follow. The two of them appeared in the sky near the plantation, as had become Nym's preference. There was less risk of bumping into something if he was off by a few feet here or there that way. It had only been a few hours since the attack, and the firepits were still going below. They glowed a sullen red in the night, and the shadows of farmhands moved around them, shepherding struggling limbs back into the flames.

Nym waited while his mentor went through a string of divinations and scrying. His face sagged with each spell, and he suddenly looked decades older. "This is getting more troubling by the moment," he said. "There have been some other reports . . . I'll get little Jaspar to compile them for me."

"When you're done mumbling to yourself and being mysterious, do you think you could fill me in?" Nym asked.

"Ah, yes. My apologies. Let's head home and I'll tell you all about it."

They teleported back to Archmage Veran's sanctum and took their spots in overstuffed and extremely comfortable armchairs. A book floated down from one of the shelves high overhead and landed in Archmage Veran's outstretched hand. "Let me see now," he said, flipping through the pages. "I haven't had time to do much journaling in more recent years. Running the Academy is enough to fill anyone's day, and this problem with the veil has aged me beyond my years." He paused and chuckled. "Though perhaps not as much as my training under you did."

"I have no idea what you're talking about," Nym told him honestly.

The laugh died in the archmage's throat. "Ah, yes. Quite. My mistake."

"It's fine," Nym told him. "I'm sure I'd think it was funny if I could remember."

There really hadn't been any way to hide that he wasn't Exarch Niramyn, though he hadn't shared the cause of his transformation to a childlike state or the reason he'd removed his own memories. The fewer people who knew, the better. He was already trusting Archmage Veran's discretion more than he wanted to. Circumstances hadn't left him with much choice.

"Twenty years ago, we were investigating a rash of disappearances around a town called Waring on the southern border of the Great Forest. There were some suspicions of bandits early on, but people kept going missing who had no reason to be on the roads. Unless the bandits had taken to breaking into houses at night, it seemed unlikely that they were the cause.

"In the end, we traced the disappearances back to a remote farm. The family that lived there was on bad terms with Waring due to the threat of them losing the property over taxes owed. They'd had a string of bad harvests and blamed it on a neighboring farm a few miles away for sabotaging them. The family from that second farm had all disappeared, which was how we linked it to the perpetrators.

"The oldest son had some talent as a mage but couldn't be spared to actually leave the farm for training. He had gotten his hands on a few necromancy books though and decided to slaughter and reanimate certain villagers to use as free labor. The family went along with it for the most part.

"Further evidence uncovered at the farm revealed a plan to cash in on one last profitable harvest and then abandon the land, as the taxes owed on it were far more than it was worth, and they were looking at debtor's jail once it was taken from them." Archmage Veran paused. "That's not really relevant to this discussion. My apologies for getting carried away."

He cleared his throat and continued, "We found labs hidden under the farmhouse, which were sealed up after the capture of the family. The necromancer fled into the forest and eventually managed to tear the veil in a foolish attempt to summon a powerful undead guardian. He was stopped, of course, and I personally did my best to repair the veil. I believe we are all familiar with how that turned out.

"The one point of interest that sticks out to me is that the necromancer had a brother, believed to be an accomplice who knew at least a little magic himself. Some of the rituals used in reanimation were too advanced for me to credit the necromancer with accomplishing. My theory was that the brother perished in the spell that tore the veil, claimed as a sacrifice to draw the reaper's attention.

"Waring itself claimed the farm, which had been expanded by a tremendous amount in a short time, and the town banded together to keep it running. Whatever experiments the original owners had been doing provided for a marked improvement in the soil quality. I can only speculate at what specific rituals were used and the loss of human life that made up the materials. Regardless, Waring continues to be a highly profitable farming community today, and its plantation, built on the site of the original farm, is its most valuable stretch of land."

The journal rose back into the air and floated to its place on the shelf overhead. Archmage Veran fell silent while he waited for Nym to process the new information. Eventually, Nym said, "There must still be a connection between that plantation and the tear in the veil. I'm assuming this isn't secret knowledge?" The archmage nodded, and Nym continued. "Then surely someone from the military has investigated. For that matter, why didn't you clear out the labs decades ago?"

"Oh, we did. I assure you, there was nothing related to necromancy in those rooms when I was done. Someone else has been using them since then. The real question is who? I was under the impression that the townsfolk were going to raze that farmhouse to the ground and build something new and that the labs would be destroyed in the process. It appears someone changed their minds and built onto the house until it became the manor that stands there today."

"So it could be any of a hundred people who knew about the labs years ago or any of the thousands of people who might have been told about them since," Nym said. "That's not exactly a small suspect pool. What will you do now?"

"I will be doing very little, I think. You, on the other hand, may find yourself quite busy over the next few weeks."

"Me?" Nym squawked. "Why me?"

"These are the kinds of jobs I have apprentices do, and you're already familiar with the background. Come now, where's your sense of adventure? Where's your curiosity?"

"I'm not your apprentice," Nym said sourly.

"Details! You are studying from my library, benefiting from my lessons, and staying in my home. You are an apprentice in all but name."

Technically speaking, the only thing Archmage Veran had agreed to was to help Nym craft a conduit that reached the fifth layer. Everything else was just the old man being a gracious host. Nym ground his teeth. He should have seen this coming.

The truth was that he was curious though, and as long as the investigation didn't drag him into the middle of the army's territory, there probably wasn't much harm to it. He was not the same mage he'd been a few months ago when he'd helped defend an outpost from a ghoul attack, and it would take something more powerful than anything he'd come across in the forest to hurt him now. At least, it would as long as he wasn't careless.

"Fine. I'll do it."

"Excellent. Now, come with me. We'll see what we can learn from this wight you encountered."

Nym followed the archmage out of the library, confused as to where they were going. "Why not just teleport back to the plantation?" he asked.

"I have moved the body to the sanctum to better study it," Archmage Veran said.

Nym missed a step. He hadn't noticed anything extra being teleported when they'd left. They hadn't even looked at the body when they were at the plantation! But soon enough they were in a medical bay, one that Nym had stepped foot in a few times to reference some of the medical texts stored there.

Archmage Veran gestured, and a new shelf appeared above the ones already visible. The books on it were much closer in appearance to the one Nym had brought back than anything else he'd seen in the sanctum. Several floated down and opened up as they landed on a table. Floating in the center of the room on a bed of arcana was the body of the wight Nym had killed with lightning.

"There are ways to temporarily part the veil and summon the spirits of those who have passed beyond them. It is not something done lightly, of course, and those who lack a delicate touch can cause terrible damage. I trust I need not lecture you on the results of such damage if left unattended. If you'll look at the book with the blue binding, we'll go over the spell needed to speak with the dead. It is, of course, of the third circle."

Nym spent a few minutes reading about the spell and studying the construct that was described over the next few pages. Archmage Veran was right; it would take a delicate touch to properly put it together. Some of the dangers the book outlined if the spell was cast incorrectly sent shivers down his spine.

He wondered if learning this spell made him a necromancer. "Isn't this illegal?" he asked.

The archmage just chuckled.

CHAPTER FIFTY-FOUR

The magic invaded the corpse and spread through its limbs. It was a slow, steady progression that spiraled out from the construct imbued into its chest, taking a solid minute to reach the hands and feet and then sweeping back up to the construct. Each time the arcana cycled, more of it was left behind, and the body regenerated closer to pristine condition.

Once the corpse was fully infused with arcana, Nym activated the second step. He twisted the construct, pulling on it in certain places so that it collapsed down into a new shape and feeding it more arcana. Pulled on strings of magic, the wight jerked upright. At this point, it was more or less whole again, though there were still burns across its body from the lightning bolts.

The arcana tethering Nym to the wight split apart, leaving it with nothing but the magic he'd already invested in its body. It looked around, confusion evident in its expression. "What is this?" the wight growled.

It reached out a hand toward the two living humans in the room, only to be stopped by a barrier that circled all the way around it. Experimentally, it tested the barrier, even going so far as to cast a few subtle spells, but nothing broke the magic. Nym waited patiently for it to finish.

"I have some questions for you," he said once it gave up prodding the barrier that was keeping it trapped. Nym produced the vial full of murky black liquid. "This potion, what does it do?"

He was pretty sure he already knew the answer or, rather, that Archmage Veran had known the answer and told him. Whoever imbibed it would have their soul ejected from their body, leaving it open for possession. If a clever spell caster could manage to fully transplant his consciousness into the victim, he would effectively gain a new body.

Nym wanted the wight to confirm it, to make a rational choice. If he had to invoke the contingency spell they'd woven into the body before reanimating it, then the whole exercise would be pointless. He needed the wight to choose something besides mindless hatred. It had already shown it had the capability to do so.

Some undead existed as nothing more than a bundle of impulses steering a meat suit. Ghouls were perhaps the most famous example of those. They destroyed, and they ate; that was it. Unless something capable of actually thinking came along and took over, a ghoul would never change its behavior, never learn.

Physiologically speaking, there was more to them than that. Unlike other undead, their bodies were actually made of some material from beyond the veil. That was why they regenerated from anything short of being reduced to ash and never, ever stopped. That was why an endless wave would just keep pouring out of the tear unless steps were taken to hold it shut.

Wights were different. They were the reanimated corpses of actual people, complete with their memories and abilities. But when they came back, they also got a bundle of impulses to drive them. Most wights couldn't overcome that and bent their talents and knowledge toward destruction and carnage. Every now and then though, a wight who'd been strong enough, or smart enough, or maybe just lucky enough, could control that bundle of raw, seething hate.

That was what they needed, and based on the fact that it could and was talking, Nym thought they just might get it. If so, they could bargain for its help. It could reveal who'd bound it prior to Nym slaying it. They could wrap this whole mystery up in the next half an hour, if only the wight would come to the table.

He was metaphorically holding his breath, waiting to see what the wight would do. It stared at him from the other side of the barrier, eyes unblinking, hands clenching and unclenching. Nym waited. Finally, with a grimace, the wight said, "It's a catalyst for another spell."

Nym fought to keep his expression calm, to act like he'd known the outcome all along. "What does the spell do?"

"I do not know the details. I was only given instructions to retrieve it by any means necessary."

"Who gave those instructions?"

The wight's eyes glazed over, and its mouth clamped shut. Archmage Veran had coached Nym thoroughly before they'd reanimated the wight, and one of those lessons was not to play games with it. He was to ask the questions, wait to receive the answers, and ignore its attempts to subvert or redirect the conversation.

This felt different though. The wight almost seemed to have lost that spark of unlife that animated its body. Something was wrong. He kept his eyes locked on the undead but heard movement behind him. The archmage must have sensed something had changed too. He took a step forward to stand next to Nym and peered at their captured wight through the barrier.

"Interesting," he said. "The necromancer who originally bound it built contingency spells into its very soul to ensure its loyalty. It may need a jolt of arcana to shock it out of its trance. This will be a tedious interrogation, it seems. You'll need to focus on asking questions that don't revolve around the necromancer but that indirectly hint to him."

"Got it," Nym said. "Anything else before I shock it out of whatever loop it's caught in?"

"Hmm . . . Nothing immediately important comes to mind. I'm sure you'll do fine."

Nym grumbled to himself under his breath. It would be easier if the old man would just do it himself, but he'd insisted Nym could use the practice. Reluctantly, he got back to work and conjured another pulse of arcana to sweep through the wight's body. It blinked a few times and looked around, that initial look of confusion back.

Then its brain, or whatever it was that generated thoughts for it now, caught up, and it focused on Nym again. Once he was sure he had the undead's attention back on him, he asked, "Where were you taking the potion to?"

"Cave in the woods," the wight spat out, almost unwillingly. It seemed surprised at itself that it had answered. Nym's binding was holding, but the compulsion was a delicate thing. Too much force would cause it to snap and drive the wight into a rage. They might never coax it back from that. Too little though, and it wouldn't answer their questions.

It was a fine balancing act, but if it failed, Nym hoped it would fail on the side of too little compulsion and that they could tempt it with their contingency plan. He didn't want to go that far though, since according to Archmage Veran, it would cost them quite a lot of crests, not to mention time that they might not have.

"Why this cave?" Nym asked, hoping he was skirting far enough around the question of who the wight would meet there.

"Connects to the underground network," the wight said.

Nym blinked. That was new. "The what now?"

Behind him, he heard the archmage shift in place. It looked like Nym wasn't the only one who'd never heard of an underground network.

"It's a bunch of tunnels and caves that open up to various points," the wight explained.

"Well that explains how the undead kept getting behind the army's front lines," Nym said with a frown. He shook off that thought before he got too far away from the point. There would be plenty of time to examine it later. "Does this network stretch through the entire forest?"

"I don't know," the wight said. It seemed more relaxed and willing to answer questions now. If Nym wasn't staring at a pasty white face that still had that little root-looking pattern on it from being hit with his lightning spell, he could almost think he was having a casual conversation.

"Are there a lot of undead in the caves?" he asked.

"Mostly ghouls and the wights who know earth magic."

Nym thought back to that wight who'd tried to capture him and the missing earth mages from the shelter. He'd assumed the ghouls had eaten them based on the few tattered scraps left behind. Maybe that wasn't the case though.

"They're digging their way out," he realized. "Something got smart and started converting the army's workforce over to wights."

It was perfect. The ghouls could dig and, directed and assisted by earth mages turned wight, they'd make miles of new tunnels every day. The workers wouldn't tire. The wights would use earth magic to compact and clean out the dirt, then stabilize the tunnels. If anyone found one of the exits, a tidal wave of undead would fall on them before they could escape. It might even mean a new wight to continue the work.

This was way bigger than Nym was expecting. He'd thought he'd be tracking down a necromancer holed up somewhere nearby, probably isolated except for some undead minions, and that the majority of the work would be figuring out where he needed to go. Instead, he was looking at an operation that would probably require hundreds of mages and soldiers doing some nasty, close quarters, underground fighting against swarms of undead.

He wasn't even sure how it would work. Ghouls didn't die, and it wasn't like they could burn them in the tunnels without burning up all the air they needed to survive. His imagination painted a vivid scene of screaming men being buried under thousands of grasping and clawing arms, of limbless ghouls flopping around biting at anything they could reach. It would take magic greater than Nym's to survive something like that.

Nym glanced back at Archmage Veran. "Do you want to take over?" he asked. "This is kind of getting out of hand. We're way past hunting for a lone necromancer now."

"Hrmm . . . Yes, I suppose I'd better," the archmage said with a sigh.

Almost gratefully, Nym relinquished his position. What followed was a series of rapid-fire questions that made his head spin. Apparently, his idea of delicate was far different than his mentor's. Archmage Veran shot off dozens of questions in the span of a few minutes, everything from how many wights were in the tunnels, how many were former army personnel, if there were any living humans down there, how many exits there were, what was in the middle, if any areas were off-limits, if any other wights were going on similar missions, and finally, what the wight knew about any long-term plans.

A lot of those questions went unanswered, not because the wight was unwilling or unable to talk but simply because it didn't know. A few times, Nym thought it would clam up again, but Archmage Veran must have had a good idea of the shape of the spells preventing it from talking. It reminded Nym a lot of his own interrogations when he was still geased. There was a lot of information that could be teased out, as long as he knew which questions to ask.

"That's enough," Archmage Veran said. "You may return to your rest."

The wight looked confused for a second, then terrified, and then its eyes went dead, and it fell over, just a corpse once more. Archmage Veran stood silently, staring at the wall and chewing on his beard while he thought. While he waited, Nym used greater telekinesis to put the wight's body back on the table. No doubt there'd be more questions in the future. He started on the preservation spells the book had described but cut them short when the archmage shook his head and said, "Leave it. There's no time for that now. Come. We're going to have a busy night."

Without another word, Archmage Veran swept out of the room. Nym trailed after him, wondering just what exactly they were going to be busy doing. They never had quite managed to piece together why the wight needed instructions and potions for a body-swapping ritual after stumbling across something far more urgent, but whatever wanted it almost certainly was behind the underground tunnel network.

He wondered if the tear splitting open had been a natural progression of events after all or if something had taken an effort to hasten it along, something long dead perhaps but looking for a new meat suit to walk around in.

Nym had no desire to meet such a creature, but he suspected he would be before much longer.

CHAPTER FIFTY-FIVE

The thrill of watching the land go as just a blur wore off after the first ten minutes of flight. Nym streaked through the sky about a quarter mile above the ground, going south so fast that he soon left the parts of the country he was familiar behind completely. His destination was a town called Valderbough, where supposedly it didn't get that cold even in the deep winter months.

Nym had a mental image of Cold Paw napping on the beach, snuggled up next to Analia while Monick and Nomick built elaborate sandcastles using magic. Bildar would be out swimming, and Ophelia would be sipping at a foaming mug of beer. It was a nice image, one he hoped would come true someday. Cold Paw would need a thermal barrier to protect him from the heat, but Nym could practically hold that in his sleep at this point. At least, if he could figure out how to keep channeled spells going while he was sleeping, he could.

He spent the flight daydreaming, not coming out of it until he reached the southern coast of the continent some two hours and the better part of fifteen hundred miles away. He wasn't sure exactly where his destination was, other than on the coast. That was fine because his plan was very much to just scan the coastline until he found a town and ask people to point him in the right direction.

Worst-case scenario, he didn't find Valderbough, and the Earth Shapers got set down somewhere else. They'd picked it more or less at random, so he didn't suppose it would matter to them too much. On the off chance that someone did have a reason for the specific destination of Valderbough, Nym thought he should at least attempt to get close to it.

He spotted a fishing village a few miles away and flew off toward it. One of the nice things about leaving Delvros was that he no longer needed to worry about having a license. He landed near a middle-aged woman tending a huge cauldron, the kind used to cook communal meals, who gave a start at the sight of him.

"Gaah!" she yelled, her accent thick. "Do not do such things!"

"Sorry," Nym said. "I didn't mean to scare you."

"Foolish child! At my age, the heart does not like these kinds of games! Shoo! Be gone. Go back to playing with your friends and leave me alone."

Nym waited for her to finish scolding him, then said, "I'm a little lost. I'm not sure where I am now, but I'm looking for a town called Valderbough. Can you tell me which way to go?"

She squinted at him and gave the cauldron another stir. The aroma coming up from it wafted over to Nym, prompting his stomach to gurgle. Unable to help himself, Nym gave his attention over to the food. "I might want to buy a meal from you as well," he admitted.

"Of course you do. Boys your age are stomachs on legs. Very well, I shall make a bargain with you. I will tell you which direction you need to fly off to, and I will give you a bowl of this stew. But first, you shall take lunch out onto the ocean and deliver it to my husband. His name is Revaro, and he works on a fishing boat. It is very large and should not be hard to find."

"I'd rather just pay a bit of copper for it," Nym said.

"I do not want copper. I want my husband to enjoy a warm meal on his lunch."

It was revenge for scaring her, he knew. He could just fly off and find someone else to ask for help, but that stew did smell delicious. "Fine," he grumbled. "Where is this boat at, and what does it look like? And what does your husband look like?"

Nym got his directions, then wrapped the bowl in a layer of hardened air to keep the stew from spilling and a thermal barrier to keep it hot. He took off out over the water, looking for the large boat painted white with two sails on it. It did not take all that long to find it, as most of the boats stayed within a mile of the coast, and judicious use of the perfect-sight spell let him observe them from a ways away.

Five minutes later, he touched down on the deck of the two-master next to a bearded man, thick across the chest, and whose hands were knotted with scars. "Are you Revaro?" Nym asked.

"It depends on who wants to know," the sailor said, eyeing him warily.

Nym presented the stew. "One stew, to be delivered to Revaro, per his wife's instructions."

The beard split open to reveal a grin, and the sailor started laughing. "That old devil woman. This is why I married her. Here, hand it over."

Nym relinquished the stew and released the magic he'd cast over the bowl. The pent-up steam billowed out for a moment before it was carried away on the sea breeze. Revaro didn't bother with a spoon or anything like that; instead, he just tipped the bowl back and took great swallows from it, pausing to chew for a second or two and then repeating.

Nym just shook his head, bemused at the sailor's actions, and flew off. He was ready for his own lunch and had other things to do with his evening. Hopefully Revaro's wife wouldn't be upset that he didn't stick around to collect the bowl and return it.

A few minutes later, he was eating his own bowl of stew, and it was every bit as good as it smelled. The woman, whose name was Resari, was giving him directions, none of which were all that helpful. They involved a long list of towns and which direction of the road he should follow when he reached each one.

The problem was that she gave him directions to walk on foot, which included going around a lot of impassable landscape and avoiding certain areas that she deemed unsafe. When Nym tried to interject and tell her that he was going to fly the whole way, she just scoffed and told him he'd never even get close.

In her defense, most people didn't do overland flight. She'd likely assumed he'd come from somewhere nearby and would be on the road for weeks or months making the trip. Nym asked if she had a map he could follow along with, but there was no such luck.

Finally he hit on an idea. "Let's say I got on a boat and just followed it up the coast. I'd go northwest, right? And how many miles would I have to go in order to reach Valderbough?"

Resari snorted. "There is no boat here that would be so foolish as to attempt that voyage, no matter how many shiny coins you tossed around."

"Look, please just tell me where I am right now in relation to Valderbough. That's all I need to know."

His stew was over halfway gone. Once he finished, he was leaving one way or another. He could not for the life of him understand what was wrong with the woman. It was a simple question. He wouldn't blame her if she didn't know the exact number of miles, but surely a guess wasn't out of the question.

Nym finished his stew, thanked Resari, and flew up into the air. "Wait!" she called out. "I have not finished giving you your directions."

"Yeah, thanks for the meal. Your directions aren't really helpful. Have a good day."

An hour later, and several hundred miles northwest of the fishing village, Nym tried again. It resulted in the same kind of dickering where random people wanted to trade favors for information. Nym could only assume it was a cultural thing and declined to help. He had other stuff to do. Eventually, he found a small coastal city and approached a foreign sailor on the docks, hoping for better luck.

"Excuse me," Nym said. "Could you tell me which port this is?"

"Karu," the sailor said shortly. He waved Nym away and kept walking.

That was rude but also better than he'd gotten from talking to the natives. More importantly, he recognized the name from the maps he'd studied back home. He wasn't quite sure how to get to Valderbough from Karu, but he knew the general direction he needed to travel.

He gave himself another hour to travel, and that was as close as he was getting. He needed to get back up north soon. Archmage Veran was taking steps to disseminate information about the underground tunnel network they'd uncovered, and there were plans for a strike force to start cleaning them out once soldiers with mage support units had gotten into position to block off as many exits as possible. He'd told Nym he was putting the strike force together personally and wanted Nym on it.

By the time his hour was up, Nym was pretty sure he'd overshot where he needed to be, so he picked a nice little town called Dohr that was about fifty miles up the coast with roads leading away in three different directions as his teleportation point, then headed back to Geldrin to get the Earth Shapers.

A quick scry showed Monick building some sort of chicken coop for a farm nearby. Nym flew over and landed next to him while he was hunched over, etching runes into the base of the wall. "What's this for?" he asked.

"Ahh! Damn it, Nym, don't do that!" The earth mage spun in place to glare at him. "Everyone hates when you sneak up on them."

"Yeah, I know."

"You don't even have the decency to bring pastries with you anymore."

"The bakery doesn't exist anymore," Nym countered.

"There are other bakeries," Monick muttered. "Did you need something?"

"Wanted to know where everyone is. I found a town that's . . . close to Valderbough, I think."

"How close?"

Nym shrugged. "It's someplace warmer than this town is going to be in a month. I also have some news for you, so . . . We should gather everyone up?"

"Uh, my brother is a few farms that way. Ophelia and Bildar are discussing putting up a new town hall with the village council. I'm not sure where Analia's at."

"I'll send her a message. Think we can get the whole crew together in an hour? I've got some work to do this evening."

"Maybe. I'll let Nomick know. You go talk to the rest and tell us, huh?"

Plans made, Nym sent off messages to Analia and Ophelia, then walked down the road with Monick. They chatted about what was new in Geldrin, and Nym regaled Monick with tales of difficult southlanders and their endless requests in response to simple questions.

Soon enough, they had everyone gathered up for lunch, though Analia was somewhat annoyed at being called in. She'd been out hunting for herbs again and had to fly back. After Nym promised to take her back out when they were done, she mellowed out. Everyone got their food, and then Nym asked, "Are you guys ready for your teleport down south?"

"What, right now?" Bildar asked.

"In the next hour or so, yes."

"What's the rush?"

"Well," Nym said. "We kind of found out that there's a bunch of undead in some secret tunnel network under the forest and that a lot of the earth mages who didn't make it out weren't eaten by ghouls. They're wights now, helping dig the tunnels faster and farther. And we're going to be taking a run at them this evening, so . . ."

Everyone stopped eating to stare at him.

"What?"

Five different voices started talking at once.

CHAPTER FIFTY-SIX

There was some argument about Nym's participation, particularly from Ophelia. She got into a heated debate with Bildar off to one side of the room while the other four sat at the table and discussed what was going on.

"Wait," Monick said at one point in the story. "You're a necromancer now?"

"Uh, in that I know three spells that involve dead bodies, I guess. I don't plan on making it an area of focus."

"That's gross," Nomick said. "You should have just become an earth mage, like us. That's the best kind of mage."

"I . . . think I would probably go with air magic, if I had to pick any single element."

"Bah. You have no taste."

"I'm happy with the current direction of my growth," Nym deadpanned. "Though I should probably spend some more time working on healing magic."

He'd spent all those hours studying anatomy, after all. He needed to round that knowledge out with some practical experience parsing the information he could gain from diagnostic spells, and then acquire what was truly a prodigious number of spells designed to fix very specific problems. The more he learned, the more he realized he'd barely begun to acquire the knowledge an expert healer needed.

It was much, much easier to break things.

"Do you think you'll go to Dohr?" Nym asked.

The twins glanced at each other and shrugged. "The boss'll figure that out. I'm not keen on trying to survive the winter up here with how little we managed to save up, so I guess we'll probably be heading south. We might go for Karu instead of Dohr though. It doesn't much matter to me."

"And do you think you'll go with them?" Nym asked Analia.

"I'm not entirely sure where I'll go next. Money is . . . limited. I need to cut all ties with my family now. Leaving Delvros does sound like a good idea, and it would be nice to have friends nearby, but I'm not convinced I want to go to Karu or Dohr. That entire area's culture has a well-deserved reputation for being stubborn and unreasonable. The people you talked to were by no means unique. I'm told it can be quite frustrating to immigrate into their communities."

"I . . . Yeah, there were a few people I talked to who made it harder than it needed to be to ask for simple directions."

Ophelia and Bildar returned to the table, neither looking happy. Without any sort of preamble, Bildar said, "We would like to go to Karu. We would like you to come with us, but we recognize that you can make your own choices and that you are far more powerful than any other mage in this room. Situations that may seem unreasonably dangerous to us are not necessarily dangerous to you."

He kept his eyes locked on Ophelia while he spoke, and she glared right back. This had been the gist of their harshly whispered argument, and while everyone else had done their best to ignore it, it wasn't really possible to block out what they were saying.

"I'm going to stay, but it means a lot to me that you guys care." Nym paused and frowned. "I know you've got stuff going on here in town, but leaving today would be better. We're going to be throwing rocks at a hornet's nest, and if the army screws up on the containment, there could be thousands of ghouls spilling out in every direction. I don't know when I'll be able to get back here. I don't know if this town will be safe."

"We've got obligations here we've agreed to," Ophelia said. "We won't be ready to leave for at least a week. And besides, once we leave, how will you ever find us again?"

"Well, I do have an archmage tutoring me. I'm sure I could pick up some extremely long-range scrying spells."

"That . . . is a good point."

"See," Bildar said. "It's fine. We'll still see him again. He's going to be fine, and the little prodigy over there will find us once it's all over."

"What about you, Analia?" Ophelia asked.

"I don't know. I'll take the week to consider what I want to do." She seemed troubled as she spoke. "Right now, I have a lot more ideas about what I don't want than what I do."

"Guys, I want to stress again that I can't promise Geldrin will be safe. If the ghouls make it this far, you might have to flee."

"We're days out from Ebalsan," Bildar said. "It may be relying on you too much, but if everything goes sideways, I expect we'll find out directly from you long before the first ghoul is spotted around here."

"That's . . . maybe true," Nym admitted. "Still, if I'm not going to teleport you today, we should figure out where you'll retreat to if needed."

That plan ended up being simple. If for some reason Geldrin was overrun before Nym got back, the Earth Shapers and Analia would simply keep moving east to the next town, and the one after that, all the way back to Thrakus if they had to. None of them were expecting to need to, not in the least because if ghouls started to show up, the first thing they'd likely do was start building a wall around Geldrin.

Plans settled and lunch demolished, everyone went their separate ways. Nym and Analia flew back out to the countryside so she could continue hunting for various herbs and plants to experiment with. It was a casual flight, especially after the overland-flight spell he'd been using throughout the morning. They barely even needed the shield of hardened air Nym put up out of consideration for her.

"Are you sure you want to do this?" Analia asked while they were flying.

"I guess," he said. "It's kind of a huge problem, and I do have the power to help, so I probably should. Also how often do you get the chance to use an archmage's library? There are so many third-circle spells in those books. It would take me months just to catalog everything I could learn there."

"He would still help you make your fifth-layer conduit though, even if you didn't help," Analia pointed out. "That was the deal you made for helping him last time."

"That's true," Nym said.

"Plus," she continued on, "won't you just get your old magic back once you regain all your memories?"

"Theoretically. It's just . . ."

"Just what?"

Nym took a minute to gather his thoughts. "I'm not sure I want them back now," he said finally. "My old life, the ascendant life . . . I don't think I was a very good person. The memories I do have are not pleasant ones. The enemies I have are terrifying to even think about. It might just be better to keep being Nym."

"If that's how you feel, then why are you pushing to get to the fifth layer?"

That was a good question, one Nym wasn't sure of himself. Part of it was just a simple desire to keep advancing. There were still years of learning in regard to second- and third-circle spells, but he had an opportunity now to push past those and access what Archmage Veran called pinnacle spells. Even once he was able to cast them, the archmage confided that very rarely did he use them. Forging a conduit to the fifth layer wasn't something done on a whim, at least not for humans.

That wasn't the only reason though. Part of him did want to know what was behind that door, what secrets were locked away in that little metal cube. Even if he ultimately chose not to pursue it after that, he would at least have the key he needed to give him that option. And if it came down to it and someone from his past did find him, Nym might just be able to save himself by having the option to access those memories instantly.

"I guess I just feel like I need to," he told Analia. "That's probably not a very good explanation. It's like . . . I can, so I should. I should have that option available, just in case I need to take it later."

"I think I understand," Analia said. She changed the subject. "Will you be working with my father again?"

"I don't think so, but I'm not entirely sure. I should know by tonight. I think our exploratory force that will be going into the tunnels is something Archmage Veran put together himself, but there's going to be a lot of coordination with the army, so I guess we'll see."

"You're going to leave us all behind eventually, you know that?"

"I wasn't planning on it," Nym said.

She shook her head. "No, you will. Look at you. You started over from nothing. It's barely been a year, and you broke through to the third layer. Most mages never accomplish that, though I guess the number is higher than I thought. Still, in a year you've done what some people can't manage in a lifetime, and mages live longer than regular people anyway. Where will you be next year or the year after that?"

"Just because we're not still studying together doesn't mean I'm just going to forget that we're friends."

"It's not even just that, Nym. Look at yourself. When we met, I would have said I was a year older than you. Now you look three or four years older than me. That's a good reason to keep advancing if nothing else. You need to figure out how to break that spell."

Nym grimaced and nodded. Archmage Veran hadn't known how to break the aging curse either. It might force Nym to return to his previous life if for no other reason than his current life span was probably measured in less than two decades. He still had time for now, and he honestly was happy to age up a little bit more first. His soul well would keep growing up to as late as his early twenties, and it was much easier to get things done without being second-guessed all the time now that he didn't look quite so young.

"One way or another, you'll leave us behind. None of us can keep up with you. You're aging five times faster than me. What's the future going to look like for us in a year? Two years?"

"I don't know," Nym said. "I'm not going to stop being your friend just because we don't look the same age anymore."

They landed on a little glade halfway up the side of a nearby mountain.

Analia gave him a long, searching look, but whatever she hoped to see, she must have been disappointed. She just sighed and said, "You don't get it. I don't think you ever did."

"Don't get what?" Nym asked, confused now.

"It doesn't matter. I don't want to talk about it anymore."

"Talk about what?"

She sighed again and said, "Thanks for bringing me back out. Don't get yourself killed doing stupid things. I'll see you in a few days, okay?"

"Yeah . . . Be careful out here too. Ghouls aren't the only dangerous thing in the world."

Nym teleported back to Archmage Veran's sanctum a few minutes later. The old man was already there, along with a few others. He recognized the uniforms of two people from the army but not the faces. Standing next to the archmage, or really more looming over him, was Babkin. A woman who looked to be in her midthirties and was draped in layers of brightly colored clothes stood on the other side of the berserker.

"Who's this?" a familiar voice asked behind Nym. He turned around to see Leaf standing there, though he looked much different now. Gone were the casual clothes, and instead he wore a lot of armor and had a pair of swords strapped to his belt. Leaf looked him over and said, "You look familiar."

"It's Nym."

"Impossible. You're at least five years older than Nym."

Babkin looked over his shoulder at Nym and nodded. "It is him," the berserker said simply before turning back to the map he was examining with the rest of what Nym assumed was the strike force the archmage had assembled. Now that he'd been down to the southern coast, Nym realized he knew the source of Babkin's accent. Somehow, it was not surprising.

"Huh," Leaf said, scratching at his beard. "Well, that's something new then. It's been a day for new things. So you're working for Veran, huh?"

"Something like that," Nym said. "I got dragooned into coming along to flush these tunnels out."

Leaf's eyebrows shot up. "That seems like a bad idea."

"Tell him that." Nym pointed to the archmage.

"Well, don't you worry. I'll keep an eye on you," Leaf assured him.

Nym just rolled his eyes.

CHAPTER FIFTY-SEVEN

The only thing they were waiting for was the army to finish getting soldiers in place. They'd lost a lot of their earth mages, their combat mages, and just all-around soldiers in general, so there wouldn't be any fortifications set up. It was going to be nasty up on the surface if the push into the tunnels was successful. Nym did not envy them that job.

Of course, it was going to be just as bad underground, if not worse. For one, Archmage Veran was not going with them. There'd been a round of objections when he'd announced that, followed by a second round once he'd informed the group that Nym would be taking his place. The archmage had ignored all of that and simply informed them that he had no choice but to personally attend to the tear and ensure that no reinforcements came through.

Nym wasn't surprised. With so many third-circle mages killed and reanimated as wights, there simply weren't enough people to rotate through the ritual spell needed to hold the tear closed. The archmage had been personally picking up that slack to keep things from getting worse. Every day he looked a bit more exhausted, but he never complained about it.

He'd missed the introductions, but Nym was able to pick up who the two military people and the woman in the brightly layered clothes were through context. One was a communications specialist whose primary job would be coordinating with the aboveground forces, and the other was on disposal. He would be ashing ghoul parts with powerful heat spells that didn't actually generate fire. The other woman was one of the original members of the team from twenty years ago who'd been called in to help by targeting wights.

Nym did not catch her name, but he did get the impression that both army specialists were a bit afraid of her. She rarely spoke or added anything to the conversation, and it was easy to forget she was there despite her bright clothing. If not for the occasional spark of arcana around her refreshing whatever magic she was using, he might have forgotten about her completely.

The army specialists, on the other hand, were quite formal and kept addressing each other as Major Stelton and Sergeant Grom. Stelton was the army mage in charge of communications, and Grom did cleanup. They were both in their thirties, both looked haggard, and their uniforms were covered in patches and stitched-up tears. They looked nothing like the personnel Nym remembered from his time working directly with the army.

The plan was simple, at least for their team. They would go in through a predetermined entrance, Babkin leading, and start carving their way through undead. Leaf would be on dismemberment and protection duty since Babkin would not be slowing down to make sure each ghoul was thoroughly chopped up. The sneaky woman would spearhead their primary objective: killing as many wights as possible.

Nym's main job was live scouting and crowd control for Leaf. Babkin would be left to his own devices, per his request. Nym would also be backing Leaf up on the limb-removal front as well and possibly helping Grom with cleanup if he got too far behind, though he didn't know the army mage's heat-disintegration spell yet. It wouldn't take him long to figure it out, he was sure. As far as the rest of his team knew though, he'd be using regular fire and copious amounts of air magic to direct the smoke away from them.

They had a giant map of the forest pinned up on the wall with the results of Archmage Veran's scrying on it. A huge, tangled web of lines sprawled across the forest and out into the surrounding countryside. It would take weeks or even months to walk them all, but fortunately they had a clear goal in mind.

In the center, underneath the mausoleum where the tear was, there was a spot that even the archmage himself couldn't get through the wards to scry. That was their secondary goal, one no one expected to get close to just by pushing into the tunnels. After they'd thinned the number of earth-mage wights out, they had plans to tunnel down from the surface as close as they could to it to attack That had been the initial goal of the excursion, but there were too many concerns about ghouls scattering in every direction, and army manpower had been devoted toward containment and sweeping instead.

It reminded Nym uncomfortably of his time under the snow, except that this time he wouldn't be invisible to the enemy. Of course, he also wouldn't be alone, and ghouls wouldn't just pop out of the walls like the ice worms had. On the other hand, ice worms were much easier to kill. If ghouls would burn up from lightning bolts, Nym would be a lot less worried about the whole thing.

Since that wasn't the case, he was glad to have Babkin standing in front of him. A hyperkinetic barrier was all well and good, right up until he was buried under a literal pile of squirming, writhing ghouls. Even then, he was sure he could teleport out, but the whole mission would be kind of pointless if they only made it a hundred feet in before they had to abandon it.

Eventually, Stelton piped up to let them know everything was ready. Archmage Veran gave them one last call to gather their supplies, and then teleported them into the forest. It was time to begin.

"This doesn't look like much," the sneaky woman said. All six of them were standing in front of a shallow cave, maybe thirty feet deep, plus another three army mages working under Grom as part of the fire team. Another twenty soldiers were waiting nearby to advance into the cave and hold it against any ghoul spillage once things got hot.

The sneaky woman glanced back at Nym. "Scrying tell you anything?"

"Cave wall is only about two feet thick at the back end, and most of that's hard-packed dirt instead of stone," he reported. "I can have it open in a minute or less."

"Good. Babkin, you're in front. Leaf, keep an eye on these guys for me. Last thing I need is Veran whining about getting his apprentice killed."

"I'm not—"

But the woman was already gone. Even watching arcana twist around her, Nym was still surprised to lose sight of her. "Huh, well then . . . Should I open this up now?"

"Do it," Babkin said. He pulled a pair of small axes off his belt and took a deep breath, then strode into the cave.

Nym didn't need to be all that close to work with the earth. He reached out past Babkin with his magic and broke through the thin stone shell easily. Then it was just a matter of shifting the dirt out to finish forming a doorway into the underground. It wasn't quite big enough for the towering berserker to walk through, but Babkin didn't even slow down. He just hunched a bit and walked into the darkness.

Nym could see a sullen red glow forming around the man already. It brought back memories of Nym's own duel with Babkin, memories still vivid enough that his nose hurt just thinking about it. He could almost pity the first ghoul to encounter Babkin. Almost, but not quite.

The others flowed in behind the berserker, with Leaf in the lead and Nym clumped up with the two army mages in the back. He sent a scrying anchor out to scout down the tunnels and quickly found the first ghouls lurking in it, but there were no surprises he could spot.

[Communication link is up,] Stelton's voice echoed in his mind.

[Keep chatter to a minimum,] the sneaky woman said. *[Advancing two hundred feet down the tunnels. Nothing but ghouls.]*

[No sign of wights so far,] Nym added.

Rather than words, a tangled snarl of emotion burst through the link. It wasn't hard to guess the source. Up ahead, Babkin's aura flared up, and the sounds of metal slashing through flesh filled the tunnel. The rest of the group moved up behind him, with Nym casting perfect sight on himself to make sure he didn't miss anything. Stelton was providing lights for Leaf, and presumably the other mages, to see by, but they weren't bright enough to see that far ahead.

Babkin was already a hundred feet down the tunnel, and dozens of ghouls were twitching on the ground in his wake. They were starting to pull themselves together, and Leaf snapped out through the link, *[Keep those parts separated and ash them.]*

It wasn't an order that needed to be said, in Nym's opinion. He was already using greater telekinesis to gather them up while keeping them from reconnecting, and Grom had started pouring arcana into a construct that made a miniature furnace in the air in front of him. His assistants worked on either side of him to feed more power to the spell, while Nym chucked the parts in as quickly as he could.

A roar echoed down the tunnel from up ahead. Nym exchanged a glance with Leaf, who nodded back. "Not much point in being quiet then," he said. "Alright, let's pick up the speed on this. Even Babkin won't survive a hundred ghouls at once without backup. Probably. Maybe."

"Working as fast as I can," Grom said. It was actually quite impressive how fast the ghouls were disintegrating inside their magic, but Nym was gathering parts to feed him faster than they could keep up. The weak link in their plan had become obvious almost immediately, but no one was really surprised. It was common knowledge that cleaning up after the ghouls was the most time-consuming part of the job. Even with three of them, they weren't fast enough.

Nym's mastery of elemental fire was still the weakest of the four elements, but he'd learned a lot from Jharn and had plenty of time to practice while he was out hunting ghouls solo. He started cooking them from the inside out, which was almost as fast as the army's new method, though it did create far more smoke.

A bit of elemental air control took care of that, and soon the group was moving again. They made it about a hundred feet before they had to stop for another cleanup. Babkin himself was even farther away. Leaf groaned and shook his head. "We need at least four more mages on cleanup to keep up with him."

It wouldn't have been a problem if they could get Babkin to slow down, but all attempts to communicate with the berserker were ignored. Eventually, Nym switched from wight spotting to tracking Babkin down with a scrying spell. He was so shocked at what he saw that he almost lost the spell.

Babkin was standing in the first big underground cave on the route, maybe two hundred feet ahead. There had to be thirty or forty ghouls attacking him, and the crazed berserker was laughing as he mowed them down. He was a whirlwind of death, axes flashing around him in a blur. Any ghoul that got within five feet of him started losing limbs, and half of them couldn't even keep up with him as he darted around the cavern.

There were dead wights there too, though none of them bore the kind of wounds Babkin was dealing. They'd been killed before Nym had even scried them out. He mentally upgraded the sneaky woman to scary sneaky woman. There were no signs that even a single spell had gone off from the wights.

"Why are we even here?" Nym asked Leaf seriously. "Those two are tearing through everything without our help."

"Mostly to clean up after them," Leaf said. "So not much has changed. They have . . . specific skill sets. Neither is good at much besides extreme violence, though Tira's is more directed. It was always like this whenever it came to a fight. Just keep cleaning up the ghouls. Uh, Stelton, maybe you could help with that too?"

"Me, sir?" she asked. "I'll try, but it's not really my area of expertise."

"Just go as fast as you can. I'll keep you guys safe."

They got to burning, while Nym swept his scry spell around the cave Babkin was fighting in. He kept expecting the berserker to be overwhelmed, to retreat, to call for help, or even to just slow down a little bit. None of those things happened, of course. Every now and then a new wight would enter the cave, but Nym was quick to spot them and call them out for Tira to kill.

The real problem with Babkin's rampage was that he was so far ahead that ghouls he'd already gone through were putting themselves completely back together before the fire team could get to working on them.

"How do we get him to slow down?" Nym asked.

Leaf just shook his head.

CHAPTER FIFTY-EIGHT

Originally, they'd planned for Nym to help with ghoul disposal only if needed, but Babkin was showing no signs of slowing down, and they already couldn't keep up with him. Nym was spending all his time scrying to find wights and relaying locations as best he could through the communication link. That assassin woman, whose full name was Tiramaya, was working overtime to take out wights as fast as he could locate them.

"Babkin could slow down a bit and make this easier on everyone else," he muttered to Leaf again.

"He could, but he won't. That's just not how berserker magic works. He'll go at full speed until there's nothing left to fight or he drops dead on the spot. I've seen him bedridden for weeks after a particularly hard fight, but the magic won't let him slow down, not when he's this deep in it."

"Who built a spell like that?" Nym said. "Why would anyone want that?"

"Ask Veran later. Maybe he knows." Leaf turned to Stelton. "Can we get a few more army mages in here to help clean up these ghouls?"

"I can put in the request, sir."

"Good. Do it. At least . . . I don't know? Three more? Four? How many do we need?"

"As many as we can get," Grom huffed. "We're not going to last another ten minutes at the rate we're going."

Behind him, his burn team groaned in agreement. All of them were putting out . . . Well, to Nym it didn't seem like very much arcana, and he was stealthily adding a bit of heat to the same spot as their spell, but he was sure it was full power to them. The spell wasn't too complicated, but it was draining, and he didn't think he had his intent filter exactly right.

Probably half of the ghouls Babkin cut apart managed a full recovery without ever being touched by the fire team, which honestly wasn't that far off the normal ratios in a combat scenario with ghouls. The problem was this wasn't a normal scenario. The ghouls weren't retreating to patch themselves up at a wight's command. They were just climbing back to their feet, after having reattached those same feet completely uncontested.

Babkin was surrounded on all sides by ghouls, with more coming at him every second. He probably should have retreated to at least a tunnel where they'd only come at him from one direction, assuming the rest of the group could incinerate everything behind him. He wasn't doing that, of course. He wasn't even making an attempt.

But Nym couldn't honestly say the berserker was losing. Eventually he'd fall over dead, but right up until that moment, he was killing ghouls faster than they could overwhelm him, and if he'd taken any wounds, they weren't slowing him down in the slightest. Tiramaya was assassinating wights fast enough that none of them made it to the fight, though it was debatable if any were even trying. If they were smart, they'd be retreating somewhere more defensible. Ghouls were far more replaceable and far less useful than wights, after all.

Babkin was deep enough into the tunnels now that as ghouls picked themselves back up, they started targeting the rest of the group instead of chasing after the berserker. Leaf kept in front of them, and Nym started splitting his attention between scrying and helping out with his mage blades. Both spells demanded too much of his attention to continue subtly buffing Grom's incinerator or keep perfect sight going, and since he wasn't keen on sharing how he'd managed to copy the mage, disposal got a bit slower, and his vision was limited to what Stelton's light spells could reveal.

Fortunately for their backup, the tunnel was still a straight shot, and there were no ghouls behind them. Two more army mages showed up, conferred quietly with Grom, and went to work. All three of his original assistants bowed out, and Grom himself wasn't looking too good. He doggedly kept the spell going, though very little of the arcana was coming from him now. The efficiency of their ghoul incinerator took another hit.

[Three wights coming in from the tunnel north of Babkin. I don't think they're earth mages,] Nym sent through the link.

He took a moment to reflect on the communication spell Stelton was powering. It was a handy little spell, though of limited use in his everyday life. As always, Nym saw something new and wanted to learn it, even if he didn't see himself using it all that often. It would probably make those group meetings with the sensitive information easier to organize, plus they wouldn't all have to gather in one room. On the other hand, it was nice to get all his friends together in one place and have a meal while they talked.

Refocusing on the matter at hand, Nym discovered he'd been lax in providing new ghoul limbs for the incinerator spell. He scooped up a few dozen more with greater telekinesis and started feeding them in again while the army mages gave him dirty looks. A few minutes later, one of the original trio came in to replace Grom, who was panting and sweating.

After that, the spell lost so much efficiency that Nym was confident he could do it better by himself than the army mages were managing together. "This isn't going to cut it," he said. "We're still falling farther behind."

Stelton shook her head. "They won't send anyone else in. Ghouls have started coming out of the side tunnels behind us. I'm actually kind of surprised we're not getting hit from both sides now."

"Shouldn't have said that," Leaf said with a grunt as he decapitated a ghoul coming at him. "You good to hold the back, Nym? Should be a bit lighter than the front."

"Might lose the scry if it gets too busy," he warned. "But I'll keep an eye behind us."

It actually took a few minutes for the first of the ghouls to show up, despite Leaf's dire prediction. The soldiers stationed in the cave must have been doing something to attract their attention, but Nym couldn't spare the time to scry behind them and find out what. Whatever it was, at least it was keeping the numbers down.

Stelton put up another light behind them so that Nym had a bit more lead time to cut down incoming ghouls. He didn't necessarily need that time, but it was nice to have the buffer just in case anything went wrong. No one in the group had the healing skills to patch someone up if a ghoul got through and tore into one of the fire team.

The added pressure of ghouls coming in from the back slowed them down even more, of course. It was already slow progress, and now it was becoming untenable. They'd killed more than thirty wights—well, Tiramaya had at least—but even with the reinforcements, they couldn't dispose of the bodies fast enough to keep them from getting back up. Leaf was probably good to go for a while, and Nym suspected he could keep the back clear as long as the numbers didn't pick up.

But they would pick up. He had no doubt about that. When more than one or two ghouls started coming in at once, there'd be problems. He'd have to pull out stronger magic, and he would get tired faster. Then he'd need to teleport the team out, except now there were nine of them, not even counting Babkin and Tiramaya.

Bringing Babkin in had been a mistake. He was undeniably effective, quite impressive, really. But he was causing problems now by pushing forward by himself, and they had no way to bring him back. Eventually he was going to die if they couldn't get him to retreat. There had to be thousands upon thousands of ghouls packed into the tunnels, and no matter how many Babkin put down, they'd just get back up once the burn team was fully exhausted.

"What was the plan to extract Babkin?" Nym asked. At the same time, he sent through to Tiramaya, *[A wight just came onto the killing floor from that eastbound tunnel high up on the wall.]*

"Let him keep hacking through them until he comes back out another tunnel into the forest," Leaf said.

"That's a bad plan."

Nym couldn't believe he'd gotten in the ring with the berserker. He'd trusted Babkin's self-control, thought the man could deactivate the magic. Maybe he could back then, or maybe he could if he only used it in short bursts, but they'd been underground for half an hour, and Babkin had been running at full strength the entire time.

"Tira will make sure Babkin gets out alive," Leaf said. He sounded confident, but Nym noticed he didn't mention any specifics about how that was supposed to happen. Maybe this wasn't an unusual strategy for the group.

"How do we get out?" Nym asked. "This is too many people for me to teleport."

"Walk back to the entrance and kill any ghouls between here and there."

Nym slashed about another ghoul coming up from behind. "At least it's simple. When do we retreat?"

"We need you down here calling out wights for Tira for as long as possible. That's the whole point of this mission."

"I don't have to be down here for that!" Nym protested.

Leaf actually paused for a second and looked back at him. "You don't?"

Nym shut down a ghoul coming at the man with an undead stunner. "Pay attention!"

"Right, whoops." Leaf got back to work. "But you can scry through the ground? I didn't think that was possible."

"It's not," Stelton said.

"I'm pretty sure I know how my own scrying spell works. I'd lose a bit of range, but we're only"—Nym paused and sent his scry anchor straight up—"fifty feet below the surface."

Suddenly he was wondering if he should have admitted that. Every now and then, something like this tripped him up, where he realized he had built a unique spell that no one else had ever seen. Analia had told him months ago that his thermal barrier was unique too. Other spells heated a person up or cooled them off, but Nym's actually prevented a change in temperature instead.

"We'll stay until we can't dispose of ghouls anymore," Leaf decided. "As long as Nym can keep scouting for Tira from aboveground, our usefulness down here ends as soon as the fire team is exhausted."

"Won't be long now," Grom said. He'd rotated back in a minute or two ago when Nym wasn't paying attention. At this point, between guarding the back of the tunnel, scrying for more wights, and feeding limbs to the incinerator, he didn't have a ton of attention left to spare for which mage had shuffled in or out of their little ritual.

Three ghouls came in at once, leaving Nym scrambling to hold them back. Stelton gave a surprised and undignified squeal as she jumped away from the ghouls, and four of the burn team echoed her sentiments. Grimly, Nym cut down the first one while he blasted the other two with stunners.

A wave of dizziness hit him, but he shook it away and cut up the remaining two. "We should probably go now," Nym said. "They're starting to come in groups of two or three regularly on this side."

"Is that all you can handle?" Leaf said, teasing him. "I'm doing three or four over here."

"Are you also scrying and cleaning up severed limbs at the same time?"

"That's a good point," Leaf acknowledged. "Alright, everybody, let's back it up."

[Tira, we're retreating now. Nym says he can continue to support you from above.]

[Understood. I'll flank Babkin for now and keep him alive. I'm going to try to steer him out of here in a few minutes.]

The group fought their way back to the cave entrance, leaving Babkin behind. It would be more accurate to say that Nym and Leaf fought their way back while the army mages huddled up between them. The fire team wasn't even trying anymore. Every single one of them was wavering on their feet, which Nym couldn't logically blame them for, but he still found it annoying.

Then they were through the unit holding the cave mouth and out into the fresh air. They'd spent less than an hour underground, torched probably two hundred or so ghouls, and killed at most forty wights. Hopefully the other probing teams who'd gone in had done better, else it was going to be a long, long campaign fighting to the center of the tunnel network.

CHAPTER FIFTY-NINE

Nym and Stelton stood in the air above the treetops while he continued to scour the tunnels below for wights. Tiramaya still wasn't showing to his scry, which was annoying, but he'd gotten used to it. Babkin was their reference point, and she seemed to be able to compensate easily enough for directions that were based off his location instead of hers.

The easiest way he had to track her was to watch things die. It appeared that there was a sphere maybe six or seven feet wide that his scrying just didn't notice. He himself couldn't even tell he was skipping a section of the tunnel until she moved and he realized what was there. What he could see was a line of bodies scattered in her wake.

It wasn't every ghoul, of course. She only attacked the ones that got in her way, or got too close, or some other criteria he couldn't divine. But he was able to track her progress and make a guess where she was based on when he stopped finding chopped-up ghouls squirming around. He had to give it to her, she knew how to control Babkin.

She would still kill wights when Nym reported one in hiding somewhere or coming in, but otherwise she spent her time running interference on tunnels she didn't want Babkin going down. The berserker naturally followed the flow of ghouls, meeting everything attacking him and moving on to new enemies when he'd downed those. By depriving him of ghouls in specific directions, she steered him toward an exit tunnel.

"Nym," Stelton said.

It looked like she'd run into a problem though where Babkin had hit a junction with five tunnels that met up at one intersection. There were ghouls coming from multiple angles, and it was tight enough that he assumed she couldn't skirt around the melee without getting tangled up on it.

"Nym."

He didn't have a spell to attack remotely, but he thought he could possibly construct an earth golem at range. There was plenty of material at least, and a pair of them could hold incoming ghouls off long enough for Babkin to head down another tunnel.

"Nym!" Stelton shouted.

"What?" he asked, coming out of his scry.

"Geists incoming!"

"What? Oh." Four of them were coming more or less directly at them, at least as much as the wind currents would allow them to fly in a straight line. Nym waited for them to bunch up tightly enough, then loosed a lightning bolt that fried all of them at once.

"Thanks. Good spotting," he told the army mage.

"I . . . You're welcome," she said, staring past him at the tattered remains of the geists fluttering down to the forest floor.

"Let me know if you see anything else trying to sneak up on us," he told her.

"Sir!"

Nym shook his head. "No need for that."

Stelton just looked down at the dead geists again and muttered, "Whatever you say, sir."

Nym rolled his eyes and got back to work. *[I'm going to set up a pair of golems to hold the south tunnel. We should be able to get Babkin into one of the two west ones. Either is fine. They'll link up in a few hundred feet.]*

[Understood.]

It was an immense strain to create them from a hundred feet away, especially since he couldn't see the spell construct through his scrying. Fortunately, the ground itself wasn't an impediment to his arcana. It was akin to closing his eyes and drawing blind. He knew where everything went, but it was hard to line it up right with no frame of reference.

But human mages did exactly that for every spell they cast. It was no wonder it took them so much practice to master a new one, and if they could do it, so could he. It just took him a few attempts to get it right, no more than six or seven. After about two minutes of trying, the first golem formed out of earth and leaped to stop the ghouls coming down the tunnel.

The second one came easier, though it was still three attempts to get it properly built. Nym resolved to practice blind casting more in the future when he had time. Killing the ice-worm hive queen would have been much easier if he could remotely assemble golems out of sight back then. For now, he directed the two golems using scrying magic. They mostly fought to hold back the ghouls, which was made easier by the fact that the tunnels weren't all that wide.

The amount of arcana they were draining from him to keep up with regenerating from the attacks they took was exhausting. Between that, the flight, and the scrying, he was starting to hit his limit. It wasn't so bad that he was struggling to keep arcana in his soul well, but if he had to suddenly cast a third-circle spell on top of the ones he was holding, he was going to be in for a rough time.

[There's another wight behind that knot of ghouls in the north tunnel. It's using them to screen its own movements, but if you kill it now, the ghouls will probably go straight to Babkin and lure him in the wrong direction,] Nym reported.

A few seconds later, he noticed that the wight and the ghouls were all dead. Well, the wight was. The ghouls had been de-legged but otherwise left where they were. Nym had to admit it was a smart tactic. There was no point in wasting time and energy hacking them up so they'd stay down longer when they really only needed a minute or so for Babkin to fight his way farther down the tunnel.

Nym ordered the golems to make a fighting retreat of it and follow Babkin into the tunnel he'd taken with the goal that no ghouls coming from behind would keep the berserker moving forward. He was only about a thousand feet from open air, and the unit holding the exit had already been informed to expect him.

Ghouls all around and behind Babkin were cut down when Nym wasn't looking, and between Tiramaya's work and the golems blocking the ghouls from chasing Babkin down, they were able to steer the berserker into open air. Soldiers parted around him, and he rushed through, eyes locked onto a ghoul in the trees a few hundred feet back from the cave.

Tiramaya appeared amid the soldiers, causing a few of them to shout in surprise and flinch back. She snorted in amusement and walked through them, but Nym thought there was a lot of weariness in her steps that hadn't been there before.

"I think we're done," he told Stelton. "Where should I drop you off at?"

"Back with my unit, where we first entered?" she asked as much as said.

Nym took a few seconds to reorient which way they needed to go. He'd been flying around, mostly following the tunnels as they twisted on one another and trying to keep close enough to maintain the utility of his scrying spell. It only took him a few moments to find his destination though, and they accelerated smoothly for about thirty seconds before coming to an abrupt stop.

"Oh God," Stelton groaned. "I think I'm going to be sick."

Nym brought her down to the ground and asked, "Any of you guys know which direction the bald guy with the swords went? No one? Of course not. He's probably at the other cave or something."

Nym flew over there, but there was no sign of Leaf or Tiramaya. For that matter, Babkin was gone too. Without Stelton to provide the communication link, he didn't have any way to get in touch with them. He might be able to get a message to Babkin, assuming the berserker had calmed down and was still conscious, but none of them were mages. They wouldn't be able to respond.

He added duplicating Lord Feldstal's two-way message spell to his list of things to learn, or rather, added it again. It was already on there, but other spells had taken priority, and working out a new conduit to reach the fifth layer had trumped learning third-circle spells. There was too much to do and not nearly enough time to do it.

Nym threw out a wide-area scry, which honestly didn't work all that well in a forest setting, but he was hoping to spot someone. When that came up empty, he gave up and teleported back to Archmage Veran's sanctum. Wherever they were, they'd figure things out, and the mission was technically over anyway.

After being down in those caves hacking up ghouls, he wanted a bath and clean clothes.

Nym had a pile of twenty books on the table next to him with another seven open in front of him when Archmage Veran appeared. The old man looked even more worn out than normal, but he took in Nym's workstation at a glance and laughed. "Looking for something in particular?" he asked.

"That two-way message spell Lord Feldstal has," Nym told him.

A fat book easily thicker than Babkin's arm floated down from one of the upper shelves. "I believe you'll find it in there."

Nym blanched. The book was three times thicker than average. Even skimming it, it could take him hours to find what he was looking for depending on how badly organized the writer had been. At least he had the right book now. "Thanks," he said, trying not to sigh as he eyeballed the book.

Archmage Veran's eyes twinkled. "There are plenty of other useful spells in there too," he added.

"I'm sure there are," Nym said with a sour frown. He decided to change the subject. "Where did the rest of your team get off to once we were out of those caves?"

"They took a recall gate to our hidden base," the archmage said. "You'll forgive me, I hope, if I don't share the location with you. Maybe someday, if you're going to continue to be Nym for a while longer still."

"No, it's fine. I understand. I just wasted some arcana scrying around the forest. No one said anything to me before they left."

"Ah, yes . . . Leaf is sometimes forgetful, and Tira was exhausted. Babkin . . . Well, he wasn't talking to anybody. I doubt we'll see him again for at least a few days."

"Yeah. How'd your end go?"

The archmage sighed and pulled out a chair. "It's getting harder to keep the tear from splitting further. We're reaching a tipping point, where we'll need to decisively end this or we're going to lose. There's talk of giving up and burning the whole forest down. It would cripple the entire country's economy for practically an entire generation while the forest regrows, but the alternative . . ."

"I'm sure a concentrated effort could harvest a considerable supply of lumber, enough to last for years, before they burned the rest."

Archmage Veran chuckled and shook his head. "Ah, my young-again friend. You truly do not understand the scale of what you're proposing. Hundreds of trees are felled every week to be turned into lumber for the rest of the country. We would need to clear a few square miles of forest just to meet the country's demand for the next few years. It would take months of dedicated effort.

"And just between us, the government has been stocking up on wood. I have it on good authority that we've taken almost five times as much lumber from the forest as normal over the last four months."

"So if they don't want to burn it down, what are they going to do? The army's holding on by its fingernails at this point," Nym said. "Most of the freelancers bailed after the breakout. Their ability to build new outposts and forts was almost completely destroyed when the wights started concentrating on hunting down earth mages to convert for their tunnel project."

"It may very well come down to burning the forest to the ground, but that's an absolute last resort, and it honestly won't stop the undead problem alone. Let me ask you though. Do you have any plans over the next few days?"

"Why? What do you need?" Nym asked.

"How would you feel about getting a look at what's going on under that mausoleum?"

CHAPTER SIXTY

Nym stood in the air above the archmage's camouflage screen. Below them, the mausoleum was crawling with undead, far more than there'd been the first time. Now, however, there were thirty other mages up there with him, all of them working jointly to hold the ritual spell that was keeping the tear held closed and thousands of new ghouls from spilling out into the world.

Archmage Veran was among them, was in fact sitting on a cushion of air right next to Nym. His presence alone was the sole reason they were maintaining the ritual with so few people. It was many, many times stronger than the one he'd fed by himself, and yet it was still barely enough to hold against the pressure pushing from the other side of the veil.

A part of Nym was curious about this creature, this reaper, that he could sense but not see. He wanted to send his scrying anchors through the tear and view what was on the other side of the veil, but he'd been warned in no uncertain terms that it would be the height of idiocy to attempt such a thing. It was almost certain to result in his death, which might be the best-case scenario for everyone involved. Another strong possibility was that the reaper would seize the spell and use it as leverage to work the tear open further, possibly enough to fully emerge through to the living world.

With that warning firmly in mind, Nym was instead spending his scrying efforts looking at the mausoleum and trying to determine what was underneath it. He'd picked up a few new third-circle scrying spells just for the occasion, ones that could theoretically pierce scrying wards or would at least let him know that there was something there instead of just glossing over them.

They'd worked when he was practicing the spells in Archmage Veran's sanctum, but out in the real world, there was a lot more interference. All the mages and their ritual were only the first layer. There was magic coming off the mausoleum itself and off every single undead below them. Normally he wouldn't see it passively like that; it turned out his ability to see arcana was mostly limited to active workings of magic and occasional enchanted items, also usually only when they were active.

The scrying spell was different. It didn't so much see arcana as it was sensitive enough that arcana could interfere with it, at least in the quantities currently on display. It was kind of like trying to feel out what something looked like when it was sitting in a bucket of mud, where the arcana was the mud.

He was mucking around, trying to get a feel for what the spell was showing him, but the sensations he got were so distorted that they were practically useless. What he could easily see with his eyes, the scrying spell had scrambled completely. It physically couldn't go deeper either. He'd tinkered with it, trying to find a way to give the new scrying spell that component of seeing through solid objects his old spell had.

The results were . . . not great but not so terrible that he didn't feel it was worth the effort to try. Neither Nym nor Archmage Veran were expecting to get much information from the exercise, especially since the archmage's own scrying spells had also failed to penetrate whatever scrying wards were present inside and underneath the mausoleum. Nym wasn't really sure why he was trying when Archmage Veran himself had failed, but he guessed his mentor was hoping he'd come up with another of those unique ascendant spells.

That hadn't happened. He knew there was something down there and that it was heavily warded. They'd already been able to guess that info long before Nym had started poking at it with scrying spells, and in fact the warded area was so large that he couldn't miss it. He reported his findings back to Archmage Veran, who took the news calmly.

"This is exactly what I was expecting," the old man explained. "We never had much hope that our first plan would work, but it cost so little time and effort to try it that it would be criminally negligent to ignore the opportunity to gain free intelligence. Our next plan of attack will be to send a team down into the caves to physically survey the area."

"That seems . . . dangerous," Nym pointed out. "Going through the tunnels will be a long fight. Digging straight down from here will involve holding back a thousand or more ghouls, not to mention the geists, wights, and frost wraiths still floating around."

"I believe we will simply be teleporting straight down into a nearby tunnel that we can scry."

"Risky," Nym said. "You'd have to be very accurate to teleport into a tunnel that size, not to mention the risk of there being undead on top of where you're trying to go."

"Well I am an archmage, after all, and I'll have you to help," Archmage Veran said.

"Me? What am I doing in this plan of yours?"

"Assisting me, of course. You'll primarily be scrying, but your kit is versatile enough to help break wards, fend off ghoul attacks, drop tunnels behind us to cut off pursuit, or place barriers to protect us. I am certain we'll find a good use for your talents."

Nym was not keen on the idea of going back underground. It had been extremely stressful the first time, especially with Babkin driving the pace and nobody else able to keep up with him. This was more of a targeted precision strike though. He couldn't see a place for the burly innkeeper in this mission.

"Who all will be going?" Nym asked.

The old man chuckled. "Not Babkin, if that's what you're wondering. He's not recovered from his last rampage yet, even if this were not a delicate matter."

"That's a relief. I'm not sure how feasible this plan is though. If something goes wrong and we lose the ability to teleport out, we're going to die down there. It would take hours of uninterrupted work to dig our way free."

"It's a risk, to be sure, but I think you might be underestimating my prowess slightly. Even if they've managed to set up trap wards that block teleportation, I am sure that we can break through them. None of the mages who were killed and raised as wights were all that powerful."

Nym was less confident. They'd lost quite a few third-circle mages, and he was just starting to realize how big the gulf between second- and third-layer arcana was. There were a lot of things that simply weren't possible to do with second-circle spells, effects that were so far removed from reality that even as group rituals, they just failed. Third-circle spells could handle them easily, however.

With an archmage on their team, they'd have access to pinnacle spells, but those took time to set up. They took time just to properly forge the conduit! Even the simplest pinnacle spell would take several minutes of prep work, and while Nym was confident he could hold a tunnel against an unlimited number of ghouls for five minutes, he was far more concerned about holding it against an assault team of wights casting third-circle spells.

Individual wights were far easier to destroy than ghouls but also far more dangerous. Nym had assumed that their first trip into the tunnels was to trim the number of earth-mage wights and stop them from expanding, but now he wondered if it hadn't all been a setup for the next stage of their master plan.

"Just how many wights did we kill the other day?" he asked. "And how many do we estimate are left?"

"One hundred and fourteen," the archmage rattled off immediately. "Possibly as many as half of the total wights."

"And what happens when the ones that are left drop the ceiling on us and bury this group of ours alive?"

"Why do you think I want you along, Nym?"

Nym shook his head. "I can't stop a dozen wights from doing that."

"No," the archmage said. "What you can do is see the arcana from their magic and warn us ahead of time. There is no shortage of third-circle mages powerful enough to cast the spells we need. What we don't have is someone like you who can see the attacks coming."

It had been a bit of a shock to discover Archmage Veran had known about his ability to see arcana, but in hindsight, it made sense. "Look, it's not that I mind helping, but this is asking for a lot. I appreciate you letting me look through your library, but that doesn't do me a lot of good if I'm dead. I kind of have other priorities."

He was still devoting the majority of his free time to forging a conduit capable of even reaching the fourth layer, let alone boring through it. Navigating the Astral Sea was a completely different experience. His conduit would be questing forth, then suddenly it was somewhere else, going in a different direction. Just intuiting which way was deeper into the third layer was a challenge by itself.

Archmage Veran had explained it as a mess of two-way gates. They were scattered randomly all over the Astral Sea, but thankfully they didn't tend to move. Learning a pathway through, from gate to gate, was the key to reaching the fourth layer. He would never have a conduit long enough to just stretch the distance, but he didn't have to. He just had to finish learning how to navigate the path laid out for him.

"I understand, Nym," the old man said. "But perhaps it would help to think of this as a way to help yourself. After all, how much of my life is spent here right now? How much more help could I give you if I didn't have to spend any time or energy on this mess? By assisting us in ending this threat once and for all, you're freeing me up to focus on teaching you everything you want to know."

Nym just gave him a flat stare.

"And I'll devote some time and effort to figuring out how to break the aging curse you're stuck under," the archmage added.

That was tempting. Right now, the only sure way he had to break it was to become Exarch Niramyn again, and Nym still didn't know if he wanted to do that. He wanted the knowledge and the spells, sure, but he didn't like the kind of person he used to be. It wasn't entirely clear how much of a package deal that was, but Nym didn't like his chances of remaining himself if he chose to unseal that part of his personality from the cube.

There was every possibility that the aging curse was some ascendant-level magic and that there truly was no other possible way to break it. In that case, it didn't matter how much he railed against the inevitable. He'd become Niramyn again, or he'd die after a short life. If he was lucky, that short life would be twenty or so years ending in death by old age.

If it wasn't ascendant magic though, he wasn't likely to get someone better suited than an archmage working on his behalf. This was quite possibly the best chance he'd ever get to rid himself of the curse without following his past life's plan. It just meant he needed to teleport into an underground tunnel, already a task with a very slender margin for error, hold back assaults from the undead roaming the tunnel for an indeterminate length of time, and deal with whatever was hiding behind some powerful antiscrying wards.

That was simple enough, in theory. It might actually be suicidal, but it sounded simple.

"I can't believe I'm agreeing to this," he muttered to himself. "Fine. I'll help. When is this happening, and who all is going?"

CHAPTER SIXTY-ONE

Their team of eight was standing together on the roof of the keep near where Ebalsan used to be. There wasn't much left of the town at this point, unfortunately, but the keep itself had held against the undead. There were a few familiar faces in their little group. Leaf and Tiramaya were there. Archmage Veran, of course, was at their head. Nym himself rounded out the half he was familiar with. The other four were new to him.

One thing he knew for sure was that none of them were military. They were all in their forties or fifties, though most looked younger. Nym was getting better at judging the ages of various mages, though the archmage himself was . . . weird. He was fifty or sixty at the oldest and should have looked like he was in his midthirties but instead looked at least eighty.

Nym hadn't asked him what happened, but from context he'd picked up during their conversations, he was pretty sure he, or rather Exarch Niramyn, had something to do with the archmage's apparent advanced age. It seemed like it might have been a sensitive topic since the old man never brought it up, so Nym had left it alone.

Regardless, he was guessing based on the average age of everyone involved besides him that the old team had called in some favors to round out their numbers. Of the four he didn't know, two of them were mages, and the other two probably had some unique skills like Tiramaya. Leaf might actually be the least dangerous person standing on the roof, though to be fair, Nym hadn't exactly seen him cut loose down in the tunnels.

It was unusual to see people who weren't mages tap into the second layer of arcana, but it did happen on occasion. He still wasn't sure entirely how Tiramaya's stealth magic worked, but it definitely wasn't a first-circle spell. Whatever tricks the other nonmages had up their sleeves, Nym did not doubt they would be potent. They'd been handpicked by an archmage, after all.

To be honest, he was a little intimidated. Intellectually, he knew he was an ascendant and could theoretically end this whole thing with a wave of his hand. In reality, he was just one mage who could go a lot longer and a lot harder than the average mage but who didn't really have any world-changing magic of his own. Someday he would, maybe even someday soon, but not today.

"Are there any last questions?" Archmage Veran asked. When no one raised a hand or voiced any concerns, he nodded sharply and said, "Let us begin then. We will be teleporting in shortly."

The magic took hold of the entire group all at once and pulled them through space. Nym honestly wasn't sure if he could manage an eight-person group teleport, considering how badly five had wiped him out. He supposed the archmage had both a great deal more practice and access to spells specifically designed for nonstandard teleports that would reduce the strain, but it was still an impressive feat of translocation.

Contrary to Nym's expectations, they did not land in a tunnel. Instead, they were floating in the air of a cavern about twenty feet off the ground. Almost immediately, a wight spotted them and sent a swarm of rocks flying their way. Nym caught about half of them with greater telekinesis and hurled them back, while one of the other mages—Nym thought he'd heard someone call her Sakaro—got the rest with an application of counter-elemental earth magic and crushed them into dust.

Tiramaya disappeared from the group and reappeared behind the wight. A short sword fell into her waiting hand out of nowhere, and she rammed it through the wight's skull. The movement and attack took less than a second. She vanished again, and Nym lost track of her.

Third-layer arcana flared up around the other mage, a man named Ogric, and he unleashed a wave of fire into the ghouls below. Strangely, the heat didn't reach up to them, and no smoke rolled off the bodies as they burned. Ghouls being ghouls, none of them tried to flee. Nym was forced to knock them back down a few times as they climbed over top one another trying to reach the hovering group, but within a minute or two, they were all reduced to ash on the ground.

That was a spell Nym would not have minded knowing about during his first tunnel run. The construct itself looked simple enough, but there was something weird in the conduit fueling it. His best guess was that the spell required some very specific intent filters that he didn't quite have enough time to tease out. It seemed that all the best spells did.

Leaf had told him privately that Ogric was a fire specialist, so it made sense to him that he had some unique insight into the discipline and that his skills included intent filters that could do things like turn an entire ghoul swarm to ash without even singing the eyebrows of innocent bystanders.

Leaf had also told him that Ogric had a temper and to make sure to stay out of the man's way. Nym was under no illusions that he could take the older mage in a fight, so that sounded like good advice to him. The last thing he needed was a pyromaniac setting him on fire while he was supposed to be holding a tunnel against a bunch of incoming ghouls.

"Clear," Ogric rumbled, his accent thick. Arcana flared out around him, and all the ash swept away to one side like a giant wave of black crashing up against the wall. Even that wight Tiramaya had killed was burned away. Hopefully she wasn't a pile of ash herself now. He doubted she'd die that easily, but the fire mage hadn't even checked to make sure it was safe before he'd incinerated the whole cavern.

He scried up and down the tunnels connecting to the cavern, hoping to see some sign of her work, but there was nothing. He frowned at the fire mage, who didn't notice and was waiting for the archmage to make the next move.

"We proceed north from here. It should not take long to begin running into the first wards. Zerek, please alert me when we run into them," the archmage announced.

One of the two nonmages gave a grunt and said, "You got it, boss man."

Out of time to look for Tiramaya, Nym refocused his scrying on the tunnels closest to them. "Ghouls coming up in that tunnel," he said, pointing behind them and to the left. "Maybe . . . thirty. No wights that I can see."

Ogric sent another wave of fire down the tunnel. It lit up the interior even as it passed out of sight, and Nym's scrying spell caught it washing over the ghouls. They crisped and blackened, but without the continuous pressure of more fire being poured on them, it wasn't enough to char them completely.

"All of them are still up," he reported.

The big fire mage glowered at the tunnel, took a deep breath, and sent another wave of fire into it. This one was easily three times denser than the first, and when it struck the ghouls, it clung to their flesh instead of passing over them. The first of them started to crumble away as they rushed into the cavern.

"Makes a man feel a bit self-conscious about his own choice of weaponry," Leaf muttered to Nym, gesturing to the twin swords strapped to his belt.

The last member of their team, a woman named Blanchet, patted him on the shoulder. "You'll be okay," she said. "You just wait until he runs into a monster that's immune to heat."

"That is when I leave and let someone else handle it," Ogric responded. "It is an important part of being so specialized, knowing when your skills are not the right ones for the job in front of you. But this, ghoul control, this I can do."

"Where were you last time we were down here?" Nym asked.

"Plague-wasp infestation in Byramin," the fire mage told him seriously. "Fire is the best way to destroy the hives so that they do not come back next season."

"Oh. Uh, right. That sounds important too."

He had no idea what a plague wasp was, and he didn't think he wanted to know. They sounded nasty. Wherever Nym decided to go once this whole undead crisis thing was over with, he was going to make sure it was a place where they'd never even heard of something called a plague wasp.

The drawback to Ogric's flaming attacks was that they were not subtle. Nym's scrying anchor flitted from tunnel to tunnel, often going through solid earth to do so. "They're pretty much coming at us from every direction now," he said. "Also, I have no idea where Tiramaya is, and I'm a little bit concerned we might kill her on accident."

Leaf started laughing. "Don't worry about that. Tira won't be hit by attacks like this."

Ogric bristled, seeming insulted by Leaf's statement, but all he said was "Very well. I will not hold back for her sake then."

Her job was arguably more important than Ogric's anyway. He was there to destroy a lot of ghouls, but she was hunting wights again. Of the two, a single wight could be far more dangerous than a hundred ghouls. He'd much rather collapse some tunnels and start transmuting earth to stone to slow down the ghouls' digging than deal with a squad of wights armed with unknown magics.

The group advanced into the north tunnel, with Ogric in the back and Leaf walking next to Zerek in the front. Ogric regularly shot great gouts of flame down the tunnel behind them whenever Nym noted the approach of more ghouls. He was already starting to miss Stelton's communication spell, if only because the fire blasts were surprisingly loud, and their roars echoed down the tunnels. It was difficult to talk over the noise sometimes.

"Hold up," Zerek told the group. "We're hitting the first line of wards now. Looks like some sort of marker to draw the attention of any nearby ghouls to us. It might be scent based, or maybe some analogous sense that only undead have."

Blanchet looked over and said, "Ghouls have a kind of life sense that points them at anything with a pulse. It's how they find people trying to hide from them, though the range is short."

Nym hadn't read anything like that when he was studying up on ghouls. It made sense; he was just surprised at the source. He would have assumed something like that would be common knowledge, but he supposed it didn't much matter to the army when they were in the business of actively fighting the undead. There was little use in hiding from them.

"Could be," Zerek agreed with the woman. "Either way, I can break it if you give me a minute. Might keep ghouls from coming at us quite so fast."

"Could they come at us any faster than they are already?" Leaf asked.

"They definitely can. Just ask Babkin," Nym told him. "You should have seen how bad it got once we stopped burning his leftovers."

"I'm sure the elimination of all the nearby wights didn't help to keep them from swarming," Leaf said. "Still, for as many as we've killed . . ."

"Their numbers have been replenished and then some," Archmage Veran said firmly. "The spell being used to hold the tear in the veil closed is not a perfect seal. New ghouls are still clawing their way out. The count swells by several hundred a day, at the minimum."

It was no wonder the army never made any significant progress. It was all they could do to hold the undead back from spilling out of the forest, and they'd failed at doing even that once the undead forces had gotten an influx of wight commanders.

"Got it," Zerek announced. "We're clear to advance, but it's going to be slow going. That was only the first ward."

Nym wondered how long it would take to reach the center of the network, and he was worried about what they'd find when they finally got there.

CHAPTER SIXTY-TWO

Ghouls were more industrious than Nym had given them credit for. Three times now, he'd dropped tunnels behind them to slow them down, and each time they dug through them in under a minute. It wasn't until Sakaro started working with him that they got defense under control.

She put up some barriers and obfuscation to give Nym time to work, and he built a shell of stone a foot thick around them. It had a hole in the back where the tunnel went, but it did force the ghouls to come around and attack from one direction. Ogric handled those though while Zerek worked on breaking down the next set of wards.

Other than the scrying wards, none of what they encountered was active, though Zerek assured the group everything was primed and just waiting for its triggering condition to be filled. Every single ward had the same trigger: something alive passing over the threshold. They'd barely advanced a few hundred feet down the tunnel, and he'd already disabled wards that marked them for the undead to find, wards that would cause dizziness and fatigue, and wards that would just straight-up explode.

Most annoyingly, there were trap wards mixed in with the regular ones that would attack Zerek directly when he tried to disable them. Those ranged from arcana injections to brain scramblers. The really serious ones, Archmage Veran stepped up to assist Zerek with some counterwards to help protect him in case anything accidently got triggered.

Meanwhile, the rest of the group bought them time. They mostly worked in overlapping shifts, each one spending a few minutes fighting before rotating out to rest. No one was sure what they were going to find past all the wards, but everyone wanted to be fresh to face it.

"Got it," Zerek announced. "Please let this be the last one."

He moved up another few steps, stopped, looked down at his feet, and started swearing. "Okay, this is ridiculous. Who puts this many wards in one spot?! How would they even power them all at once?"

"They couldn't, I hope. Perhaps it would be better to trigger a few of the less lethal ones and let them drain the source of arcana so that the others fail naturally," Archmage Veran suggested.

"Eeeeehhhhhh. If we weren't down in this tunnel, I'd agree with you. We're at the end of a blast cap right now though. If something blows up on us, then the best-case scenario is we get blown through that stone barrier into the arms of the ghouls on the other side."

Blanchet shook her head. "This isn't a winning strategy. In any battle against the undead, time is against you. You will get tired long before them. You will start to make mistakes. Even if you are many times stronger, eventually they will wear you down. And that is only considering things like the ghouls behind us. We have an intelligent enemy here, who undoubtedly knows we are coming and is preparing for us while we waste time on these wards."

"I can't do this any faster," Zerek told her. "We can try to teleport past them, I suppose, but if we were going to do that, there was no need for me to come along to begin with."

"We can't teleport," Nym said. "I already looked into it. The place is warded against that too. It'll probably be the very last ward we find, right next to the scrying ward."

The others regarded him for a second, then as one turned to look at the archmage. He nodded in agreement. "Nym is correct."

Considering his main job was keeping an eye on the battlefield, Nym was a bit insulted that no one trusted his knowledge of what was going on. He felt like he'd proven himself competent already, but apparently he was the only one who'd thought that. The nasty, mean voice in the back of his head had a few things to say about the disrespect they'd shown there, but Nym shoved it aside.

"How confident are you that all of the inactive wards' triggers are the presence of something alive?" Nym asked Zerek.

"Every single one has been so far. Why?"

"Do you think an elemental golem would trigger them?"

Zerek shook his head. "Not any of the ones I've seen so far. I can only speculate over what's still ahead, but unless they're devious enough to switch the ward triggers deeper in, no, I don't think a golem would trigger them."

"What are you thinking?" Archmage Veran asked.

"Air golem with a sensory link," Nym explained. "Maybe we can get a look in there through the antiscrying wards. They're basically invisible too, so any lurking undead might not notice."

A quick round of discussion and refining saw all of them safely behind one of Sakaro's shields, which was being reinforced by the archmage's own magic. Nym put together an air golem, gave everyone a warning notice, and sent it down the tunnel.

"Fifty feet away. Sixty. Seventy. It's going around that bend now. I'm going to activate the sensory link."

The air golem continued its journey, drifting over various wards without ever triggering them. Nym got a good look at what was coming up, including a lot of undead that were steadily trickling in and holding position. "They're definitely preparing for us on the other end of this tunnel. I'm seeing geists clinging to the ceiling, probably two hundred ghouls lurking in various tunnels, and an occasional wight in army uniforms mixed in."

Nym conjured an illusion based on what the air golem was showing him and pointed out where each danger was. The others crowded around it and started discussing plans for who would take care of what. While they did that, Nym took the air golem up and down a few side tunnels so that he could provide more information and accurate head counts.

"I'm at the scry ward now," he announced. "We're about to find out whether or not it'll block the sensory link."

Nym held his breath, took one last look around the tunnel, and willed the golem to move forward. It went over the ward like it wasn't there, and he was treated to a view of a dark, dingy cavern littered with rotting corpses. There were a lot of bones scattered around too, enough to make up a hundred skeletons at least.

"Good news is the link held. I can see past the scrying ward. Bad news is . . . there's nothing really here? There's a lot of bodies on the ground, most still rotting, some just skeletons. Four tunnel exits that I can see. Nothing moving."

"Show us," Archmage Veran said. "This cavern wasn't so well protected for no reason."

Nym switched his illusion up to show what he was seeing himself through his air golem. This time he projected it onto the wall so that there wouldn't be six other people crowding around him.

"What are we looking at?" Leaf asked. "Why aren't any of them moving?"

Blanchet pointed to a spot. "See this here? This is a disassembled bone behemoth. A tiny one, but that is what it is. As soon as something triggers it, it's going to start pulling in meat and bones to form its shell. And here's another here, and one over here. There might be enough material in the room for maybe one more, but I do not see a core for it."

"Then what's the point of guarding it if all it is is more monsters?" Leaf asked.

"That cavern is not the goal," the archmage said. "It is merely another defense to be bypassed or overcome."

"It's underneath the mausoleum," Nym said. "That's the real goal. This is just our way in. We're going to dig up through the ceiling."

"There probably won't be any digging," Archmage Veran said. "The wards surrounding the mausoleum are spherical. This was the easiest way to access them. If we can remove the antiscrying ward and the teleportation ward, I will relocate us directly into the mausoleum."

Nym tried to send the air golem up through the ceiling of the cavern, but it couldn't pass through solid objects, and even though there were plenty of tiny cracks, none of them led to where he wanted to go. Eventually he gave up and sent it out exploring again to see if he could find any obvious arcana batteries connected to the wards.

"Blanchet," Zerek said suddenly. "Could a bunch of wights be powering the wards?"

"Yes," she said slowly. "For this many though . . . Thirty or forty just to keep the ones that are already active going. Hundreds more to power the rest."

"What about something . . . bigger? Something reapier?"

"Reapier?" Leaf echoed.

"I don't think that would work. These wards are human magic. Whatever undead was fueling them would need to be able to use arcana the same way we do."

"I didn't see any signs of dozens of wights standing around," Nym pointed out. "Unless they're in the mausoleum itself, I don't think that's what's doing it."

"The physical dimensions of the mausoleum would preclude that," Archmage Veran said. "No, this is something else."

The stone cracked behind them, and a ghoul's hand broke through. More rubble fell out of the hole, and soon the ghoul was halfway through. Sakaro put up a barrier to hold it in place while Ogric started sending fire over and around the ghoul. "That is good. Hold it right there as a plug, and I will cook everything behind it."

"Ha! I think I found the teleportation ward!" Zerek announced suddenly.

"Keep the ghouls occupied," Archmage Veran ordered. "Once we break this, we'll switch strategies."

"You'll need to bring down the antiscrying ward too," Nym said.

"Yes, but we'll teleport into the room you discovered and attack it from the other side. My belief is that it will be the final and smallest ward."

That meant fighting those bone behemoths, but they had more than enough fire power that Nym had no doubt they'd make short work of them. At least, they would as long as all the undead lurking between their current position and that room didn't swarm them all at once. There were four open entrances into the room, with the possibility of new ones being dug. That would be way more difficult to hold than their current position.

"We need to figure out how we're going to split up defense while they work on cracking the last ward," Nym said. "What do bone behemoths even do? I've never heard of them."

"They're generally made out of entire battlefields, so these ones will be tiny. They're sort of undead siege engines. Not smart, but strong and very, very durable," Blanchet explained. "Burning them doesn't really work that well due to the sheer size. It might work in this case, but Ogric would be better at protecting us from incoming reinforcements in the tunnels."

"How do you normally take one down?" Leaf asked.

"Break them into pieces until you dig down to the core. That's vulnerable to physical attacks. We'll want to break them as quickly as possible once we teleport in."

"Right. I'll take one, you take one, Tira gets the last."

"Where even is she?" Nym asked.

"I'm here," she said from right behind him.

"Gah!" He jumped in the air and spun to face her. If Ciana could have seen him, she'd have laughed herself silly.

"Another twenty wights destroyed," she reported. "Several ghoul outbreaks have occurred up on the surface when the packs the wights were controlling went wild. The army is containing it for the time being."

"We're through," Zerek said. "Get ready for the teleportation."

The mages quickly divided up the tunnels between them, with Nym and Ogric each taking two while Sakaro supported them. Leaf, Blanchet, and Tira each knew where their target was. Everyone was ready to go.

Arcana poured out of Archmage Veran, and the teleportation spell took hold. A moment later, they were standing on top of mounds of rotting corpses, ones that were shifting underfoot as they were dragged toward the pulsing cores.

CHAPTER SIXTY-THREE

The next few minutes of Nym's life were pure chaos. Leaf, Blanchet, and Tiramaya all went for their assigned cores as quickly as possible. Tiramaya even managed to crack hers open before a bunch of meat and bones piled onto it, but none of them were able to actually break the core prior to the bone behemoths animating.

His first impression was that the names were a bit of a misnomer. They were actually made of a lot of stinking, rotting meat slapped together and strung through with a wire skeleton made of arcana. All the bones were on the outside, glued to the meat in random spots, often piled on top of one another to form a full coating of armor. There were a lot of spikes and jagged edges in that coat, enough that Nym couldn't imagine it going well for anybody who tried to jump onto one of them.

They had four limbs, though Nym was hesitant to decide whether they were all legs or not. Each was thicker around than he was, like a set of tree trunks stuck onto an enormous barrel. There was no head or tail, and it seemed able to walk upright as easily as it did on all fours. The only upside that he could see from the whole thing was that they'd sucked up so many corpses that the floor was relatively clear now.

As soon as the bone behemoths started forming, the undead lurking in the outer tunnels surrounding the cavern attacked. They poured into the cavern in a steady stream, or at least they would have if the team had let them. Sakaro's barriers flashed into existence about twenty feet down two of the tunnels. Her face was tight with concentration holding them up as the first of the ghouls hit them.

Nym took a different approach and started dual casting greater telekinesis to shove them back while simultaneously ripping down great chunks of the ceiling after transmuting seams of rock to sand. It was a controlled cave in, and not one he thought would hold for long. He was lucky to have found the patch of rock there at all; most of the terrain had been hard packed earth so far. The earth mage wights had gone around or removed the stone buried underground.

Flames roared through the room, swirling around the humans and scorching the bone armor of the behemoths black. They also torched three geists that had managed to sneak into the room unnoticed and were descending on Leaf. He was so preoccupied trying to carve chunks off the behemoth he was fighting that Nym doubted he even noticed the geists.

Nym threw up a hyperkinetic barrier against the back side of his impromptu rock wall to support it and turned his attention to the second cave entrance he was responsible for. "I've got this one," he called out to Sakaro. His mage blades came out and flashed down the tunnel. That combined with a few strategic stunners was enough to keep the ghouls pushed back.

A pair of wights appeared in the middle of the ghoul pack, some working of ritual magic filling the air between them. Before they could release it into the cavern, Nym fired lances of his own arcana into the spell and twisted it. It shattered between the wights and dissipated into nothingness. A well-placed lightning bolt arced through the ghouls and struck both wights, hurling them from their feet and back into the tunnel.

Hopefully they were dead, but Nym didn't have the time to follow up. "Ogric!" he yelled. "Switch with me and burn these ghoul parts down, will you?"

They made the switch smoothly with Sakaro's help. Nym threw three stunners at the closest ghouls to trip the advancing line up while Sakaro popped a fresh barrier over the tunnel Ogric was actively working on. The two traded spots, and the chopped-up ghouls in the tunnel started to disintegrate.

They traded back and forth a few times, with Nym hacking apart incoming ghouls in one spot while Ogric toasted them on the other side, but then his original blockage failed. He felt the hyperkinetic barrier snap just before ghouls started pouring into the room, only to be picked up by the dozens and slammed into the ceiling with an application of greater telekinesis.

That didn't do much beyond get them out of the way momentarily, but that was enough for Nym to gather up the arcana for a massive push of air. It howled down the tunnel, bowling over ghouls and sending geists tumbling hundreds of feet backward. More importantly, it gave Nym the time to restack the rocks and even transmute them into something slightly more solid. He left a new barrier behind them and sent his mage blades up to massacre the ghouls he was holding on to.

Things were tense, but between the three of them, they were holding the four tunnels. Nym was under no illusions that it would last forever, but it'd be more than long enough for Zerek and Arch-mage Veran to break the antiscrying ward preventing them from seeing into the mausoleum overhead.

Then a behemoth slammed into his back and sent him flying into a wall.

It wasn't even a direct attack, though it took Nym a few seconds to put that together. It had merely brushed against him while it was focused on fighting Blanchet. He'd been winged hard enough to throw him ten feet into a wall and leave him groaning in pain. The barrier he'd been maintaining had failed, and Ogric was now floating overhead in the middle of the room, shooting fire in every direction while Sakaro tried to herd the ghouls with strategically placed barrier walls.

Nym regained his feet and flew overhead to join the other mages. It was impossible to see down the tunnels from that angle, but getting hit by a behemoth once was enough for him. Zerek was safe under a barrier of some sort Archmage Veran had put up, and the two of them were busy ignoring the general chaos around them while they worked.

"We've got to drop these behemoths already," Ogric said. "Can you block all four exits?"

"Maybe for a minute if it's just ghouls. As soon as some wight comes in and starts throwing spells at the barrier, things are going to start failing," Sakaro replied.

"One minute. We can lay down some serious damage on one of those behemoths in a minute. Maybe we could even get all three."

"Do it," Nym said. Those things weren't like ghouls. They were made of real corpses; a lightning bolt would probably shut them down hard unless they had some sort of special resistance to it.

She nodded, took a deep breath, and closed her eyes. Barriers snapped up in all four locations, and Nym pulled hard on second-layer arcana. His soul well filled to the brim, and both parts of his brain started chaining lightning spells.

The cavern was filled with deafening booms that rolled around and echoed off one another as he hammered bolt after bolt after bolt into a behemoth that was missing a big chunk of its bone armor. Leaf was the one actively engaging it, but there was enough space between them as he scrambled to avoid its flailing limbs that Nym felt safe targeting it.

The behemoth shuddered when the first bolt struck it, collapsed from the second, and started smoking on the third. By the time the fifth one hit, it had superheated to the point where the bone armor cracked and blew apart, along with a thousand pounds of blackened meat. The core fell to the stone, fully exposed for the first time since they'd teleported in.

Leaf pounced on it and drove his sword clear through, shattering it into pieces.

The display blinded and deafened them momentarily, and it certainly drew the attention of everything still moving in the cavern. Nym switched to a localized scrying spell to see the room and took advantage of the moment to send his mage blades into action against a few ghouls who'd managed to slip in when one of Sakaro's barriers started to give. It looked like her ability to hold them for a full minute was perhaps a bit too optimistic.

Two people hadn't reacted to the display of lightning. Zerek ignored it completely, perhaps hadn't even noticed it behind Archmage Veran's barrier. The archmage himself certainly noticed it but had apparently dismissed it as unimportant.

Not to be outdone, Ogric laid the heat down on another behemoth. Within seconds, Nym could smell the acrid stink of it cooking from the inside out, somehow a different smell than the one he'd blown apart by slamming it with lightning bolts repeatedly. Blanchet knew exactly what was happening too, and she switched strategies from attacking it to keeping her distance.

Far away from the others, Tiramaya had her behemoth completely under control. She was slipping in and out of the shadows, disappearing completely and popping back up somewhere else. The behemoth swung around crazily, limbs flailing in every direction as it slammed itself up against the wall repeatedly in an attempt to crush her.

Normally, Nym was confident in his ability to aim his lightning. It was something he'd practiced in his off hours quite a bit, but in this case, he couldn't keep track of the scary woman in the bright clothes, and he didn't want to risk hitting her. A quick scan of the room told him he'd be most useful going back to blocking at least one tunnel so that Sakaro could focus on the other ones while Ogric finished cooking the closest behemoth.

"I've got this one," he called out, floating down to the barrier that was starting to fracture and let ghouls through.

She let the barrier fall completely, and he went back to work slicing apart ghouls. It was a mountain of effort to get caught up enough to clear the mouth of the cave, effort made worse by how drained he felt from his trick with the chained lightning bolts. Both partitions in his brain felt that one. The fight wasn't over though, so he kept his mage blades moving.

Then everything went black, and his entire body lit up with pain. In a slim sliver of a moment, he felt the sting of hundreds of needles stabbing into him, followed by a burning sensation on his skin. His mind blanked out from the pain, just long enough for him to start screaming.

He summoned more magic, and lightning burst out of him in arcs going in random directions. A skintight cocoon of air slid into place, separating him from the geist that was trying to eat him, and with an effort of will, it billowed out and ripped the undead off of him. It was already dead by the time it let go, fried from the inside by Nym's lightning and smoking as its body drifted on a current of supercharged air to smack into a wall on the far side of the cave.

Chest heaving and blood running down his body from hundreds of puncture wounds, Nym glared around the cavern. There, in a crack that had split the wall near where Tiramaya's behemoth had slammed into it, were more geists slipping in. He forced more arcana through his soul well and sent twin bolts of lightning to splash against the wall and kill the geists there.

Ogric got the ones that were already flying through the air with bursts of fire. Below him, a second behemoth lay in a pile of crispy flesh, its core shattered to pieces. With only a single behemoth left, the warriors on the ground managed to surround and overwhelm it easily. The beasts were huge and ponderous, deceptively fast for their size but ultimately too slow to keep up with the nimble humans attacking them.

They brought it down and broke it apart, carving a hole in one spot where they concentrated their attacks until the core was visible still inside the behemoth. Tiramaya took the strike, breaking it apart and prying it loose with the tip of her blade. The pile of meat and bones she was perched on collapsed on the spot.

Nym's flight spell gave out then, and he tumbled to the floor. "I think I need a break," he said to no one in particular.

The ghouls still pouring in didn't seem inclined to let him take a breather, so he pulled himself to his feet and readied his next spell.

CHAPTER SIXTY-FOUR

Agout of fire flashed down the tunnel in front of Nym, strong enough to drive him back a few steps. It was followed by a barrier sealing the mouth and blocking the ghouls from getting in. There were three more possible entrances though, and adding to that was the fact that a portion of the south wall crumbled as ghouls finished digging their way through.

A new hole opened up to the right of where Archmage Veran and Zerek were working. Nym had just enough time to notice it before arcana surged out of the archmage and the ground itself clamped down on the ghouls pouring out like a giant maw. It even had jagged stone teeth that rent the undead limb from limb.

The whole group watched in stunned silence for a second before Ogric shook his head and said, "Perhaps I chose the wrong element to study."

"You and me both," Nym replied.

He decided right then and there that he would never, ever, ever tell Bildar and the others about that spell. There would be no end to the jokes about earth magic being the best. It was better for his sanity if they just didn't find out that it existed.

There was no more time to stop and gawk. That one hole was sealed off, for the moment, but there were still ghouls coming in from others. He spotted another geist slipping across the ceiling toward Leaf and ended it with a lightning bolt.

"I'm not one to complain, but this is getting a bit overwhelming," Sakaro announced. "Are they almost done—"

Arcana surged out from Archmage Veran, flashing across the room in an instant and grabbing hold of them. Everything went dark, and when Nym could see, they were standing in a room with walls made of worked stone. There were no undead of any kind rising from their graves or coming down the stairs in front of them.

"Oh, thank God," Sakaro continued, like she hadn't been interrupted. "I am about to drop."

The rest of the group made noises of agreement while they caught their breath. Nym extended a scry anchor out and swept it around, first below him to confirm there was no connection between their current location, which he assumed to be the mausoleum, and the cavern they'd left behind.

It only took a second to set his mind at ease. Before he let the scrying spell drop so that he could rest, he needed to know there was nothing waiting for them up above. The anchor swept back up past them, halfway through the ground when it found something odd. He got a split-second glimpse of what appeared to be a black twisting tree root, as thick around as his waist, snaking through the dirt.

Then his anchor cracked down the middle, and the backlash of arcana dropped him to his knees. Nym bit down on his tongue to keep from crying out, and he felt something wet running down his face. He wiped it away, and his sleeve came back bloody. Bewildered, Nym climbed back to his feet.

None of the group was looking at him. Instead, they were staring up at the wall opposite of the stairs. There, half sunk into the stone, was a human corpse. It emerged from the wall just above the waist, revealing a stomach, chest, head, and arms. The top of the corpse's skull was tilted back so that its hair splayed out behind it, but the individual strands seemed to be carved from stone and merged into the wall. Each arm was sunk up past its wrist as well.

The corpse's skin was slate gray, and like so many other corpses Nym had seen over the last few months, it struggled against its bonds. Its back was arced out, and its mouth hung open, giving it the look of a living statue in perpetual agony as it struggled to break free. There was very little room for it to actually move other than jerking its shoulders as it tried to tear itself out of the wall.

"What in God's name is that?" someone whispered.

A terrible storm of arcana whipped up around Archmage Veran. His normally placid expression was twisted into something grim and implacable as he wove arcana into a spell far beyond what Nym had ever experienced. A pinnacle spell was forming around the archmage, something that promised absolute destruction.

"Retreat to the stairs," he ordered without turning around. "Sakaro, the strongest barrier you can form. Nym, reinforce her work."

There was a mad scramble for everyone to get clear. He and Sakaro took turns laying defenses around the group, full spherical shields built on top of one another, one after another. Nym handled kinetic damage, while Sakaro shielded them from various elements. Both of them glanced nervously at each other.

If the rest of them could have seen the amount of arcana condensing around Archmage Veran, Nym suspected they would have been far more scared. It hung off the old man, so thick it was almost a solid, physical thing. Each pulsating crystalline construct grew like it was alive until they were so intertwined that they formed a solid shell obscuring the man standing in the middle.

Then the spell detonated, and the mausoleum was filled with roaring sound and blinding lightning. Blistering heat rolled through the room in waves as fire melted stone, only to become solid again a moment later when a deathly chill swept over them. The earth itself buckled and cracked, ripping the tormented corpse free from the wall.

It hung suspended in the air for only an instant before it disintegrated to ash under the immense power of Archmage Verin's magic. Even as it fell apart, tendrils of darkness pierced the cacophony and reformed the body. It hung suspended in the air from black roots like some disgusting fruit, endlessly destroyed, endlessly regrowing.

The root itself ignored the destructive vortex centered on it. More and more stone fell away, revealing foot after foot of its length. Nym realized with a start it was the same thing he'd accidentally brushed against with his scrying anchor and shuddered to think of how much pain Archmage Veran was enduring from his own magic coming into contact with it.

The spell was directed at the wall with the corpse root on it, but the rest of the group was not safe from the collateral damage. Sakaro's shields were taking the brunt of the fire and ice, but she was quickly weakening. If they didn't support her quickly, the defenses would falter.

Ogric wove his own fire-eating shields into the mix and took a lot of pressure off her. They took a beating from the cold waves washing over them, but he poured more arcana in to reinforce them. Nym took a different approach.

Raw arcana flashed out of him as he wove an impromptu lightning catcher. It was based off his efforts to improve the aim of his own lightning bolts, though it wasn't something he'd ever designed to stand on its own. It was the only thing he could think of to reduce the impact of the archmage's magic on his shields though, so he spun it up and threw it out into the room.

It was struck three times in the first and only second of its existence, but those were three bolts that were pulled away from where his group huddled. A second lightning catcher was thrown out, then a third. And then it was over.

The walls of the mausoleum had completely melted, revealing raw dirt and stone. Liquid rock dribbled down off the ceiling, some of it still on fire. In other spots, it had frozen over like a choppy lake in winter, ripples and all. And standing in the middle of it, untouched by the devastation around him, was Archmage Veran.

He stood in front of the corpse, which had regrown again from a coil of the root. Its arms were sunk into the black surface, but its posture was now slumped forward instead of arched back. The hair that had formerly been trapped in stone hung limply off its skull, hiding the corpse's face.

The archmage stared at it, his eyes smoldering, and Nym worried he'd start up another spell. The rest of the group would need to teleport out first if he did. There was no way their barriers would hold against a second round. But the old man didn't summon up another storm of destruction. He just looked tired, tired and sad.

"What a fool I was," he said softly. "If we'd found this twenty years ago, how many lives could we have saved?"

Leaf picked his way over the shattered stones to stand next to his friend. "Is that who I think it is?" he asked.

"The brother, yes. The one we never found, that we thought was sacrificed to create the tear," the archmage replied. "Alive all this time, in a manner of speaking."

"What do we do now?" Leaf asked.

"This tether of magic is the true problem. This is what holds the tear open, what gives this necromancer the power he has. I suspect he is in terrible, unending agony. Aren't you?"

Something that could conceivably have been an attempt at words came from the corpse's mouth. It sounded more like a hiss of escaping air than anything, but that the corpse made any noise at all was more than Nym had expected.

"God's beard!" Zerek yelled. "It's still alive after all that?"

"It is not alive, but it cannot die so long as the reaper maintains the link to it."

Blanchet stepped forward to examine it. "Fascinating," she murmured. "I've never seen an undead like this. It has some similarities to a lich, except it has physically manifested a connection beyond the veil. I doubt this was done on purpose. The host body seems barely aware and is completely enslaved to the reaper."

"How would you advise destroying it?" Archmage Veran asked.

She just shook her head. "It may very well be impossible. A link like this, even a physical one, going directly back to the tear, to a reaper. Every archmage in the world working together might not be strong enough to sever something like that."

"It doesn't go back to the tear," Nym said.

"I—what?" Blanchet asked.

"I saw a piece of it underground when I was scrying. It was heading away from the mausoleum. The tear is above us, right? Why would this thing be in the stone under our feet if it was going straight back to the reaper?"

"Interesting. Perhaps redundant copies. Nym, please continue your scrying. If my guess is correct, we will find more bodies like this one connected to the link in other places."

It was delicate work following the root without actually touching it, but the antiscrying wards had all been well and truly broken. Nym stretched his range to its limits tracing them through the ground, but he canvassed the entire root network without leaving the mausoleum.

"There are three more bodies on the link," he reported. "What does it mean?"

"It means that we must destroy all of them at the same time. Any single one that survives will send a new copy of itself through the link. I believe that if we can destroy the anchor, this necromancer, on the side of the living world, it may collapse the link and finally allow us to close the tear and make the veil whole here again."

Leaf pursed his lips and looked around at the group. "So we're splitting up," he said. "That's . . . risky. None of us is really in the best of shape anymore. Maybe we need to retreat and bring back some help."

"I am afraid there's no telling what defenses this monster will think up if we give it the time to do so," the archmage told him. "I must ask you all to dig just a little bit deeper. We will destroy all four bodies, and then I will burn out this undead rot at the root."

CHAPTER SIXTY-FIVE

Nym shared illusions he crafted from what his scrying spell showed him. The first corpse root in the link was embedded in a random tunnel wall, almost completely buried except for its face. It would require some excavating to dig it out but not so much that anything other than basic terrakinesis was needed. Sakaro and Tiramaya were assigned to that one.

The second corpse root was trickier. It was in a cavern near the ceiling, with maybe a third of its body visible but heavily concealed behind stalactites that had grown around and in one case through the body. Nym wasn't sure exactly how feasible that was naturally, but he supposed with a few squads of earth mages working on expanding the tunnel network, oddities were bound to crop up. That one went to Ogric and Leaf.

Nym was partnered with the undead scholar, Blanchet, and as his elemental earth skills were the best in the group besides the archmage himself, he fittingly got the corpse root that would be the hardest to dig out. This one was fully entombed inside a patch of thick clay with a shelf of rock underneath it. They'd either have to break through a foot of stone or else dig four times as far to go around it. Nym was tempted to ask the archmage to switch with him, but he knew that the old man had kept the hardest target for himself.

The corpse in front of them was the direct link to the source. It would be stronger and harder to kill, but it would at least be possible if they could eliminate the redundant clones in the necrotic root network. The problem was less disposing of the corpse roots than it was dealing with all the ghouls still filling the tunnels.

At least, Nym hoped that the ghouls would be the harder part. He couldn't lay down the sort of punishment Archmage Veran had displayed. If that's what it took to take out a corpse root, they were going to have a problem. Nym doubted everyone else together could do half the damage the old man's pinnacle spell dished out.

"I will clear the areas and teleport you in one at a time," Archmage Veran said. "Nym, if you could shift your scrying to the first drop point?"

He did as requested, and once they had a visual on the first corpse root, the archmage cast some sort of complicated spell made up of raw force that flattened everything in the area. It probably killed the sole wight it caught but definitely didn't kill a single one of the ghouls. Still, considering the amount of space covered combined with the distance it was cast at and the fact that it was being targeted using nothing but an illusion Nym provided based on his own scrying . . . It was scary impressive.

[Group communication link is up,] Archmage Veran said in Nym's head. *[Teleporting now.]*

Ogric and Leaf appeared in the middle of the squished ghouls. They were reinflating but too slowly to save them from Ogric's flames. Nym didn't just leave the scry anchor there to watch though. He had it speeding through the ground, searching out the second corpse root. The illusion he was projecting shifted, and the archmage repeated his ghoul-squish-and-teleportation combo.

Sakaro and Tiramaya appeared in the illusion, and the former immediately laid down a barrier across the floor, one that kept the rapidly reforming ghouls firmly squished. It was a stopgap effort at best, but she must have thought she could hold for at least a few minutes. Hopefully new ghouls wouldn't appear to harass her.

"And now your turn," Archmage Veran said. He waited for Nym's illusion to shift to the final location, a small cavern with three tunnels intersecting at it. The corpse root was buried overhead, necessitating the use of multiple simultaneous magics to reach it. Surprisingly though, there were no undead in the immediate area. He supposed that the ghouls must have been drawn to the sounds of combat from the other two groups.

He wasn't about to complain about it, since it would take more than three times as long to reach his target. As soon as the teleport took hold, he pulled in arcana filtered with that solid intent he always worked earth magic through. Chunks of the ceiling started falling away, only to be flung off to the side with greater telekinesis.

"I feel like I should warn you that I'm not much of an actual fighter," Blanchet said. "I'll keep watch for you though."

Nym grunted and kept working. He'd already known that. Though his primary focus hadn't been on the bone behemoths, it was easy to see who was struggling the most to contain their opponent. Blanchet was passable with a weapon, but she was mostly there to advise on the possibly unique undead they'd expected to find.

He didn't think bone behemoths qualified as unique, but they certainly weren't anything he'd ever heard of. The corpse root though, that was something none of them were familiar with. It might not exist anywhere else in the world. Nym certainly hoped it didn't, since it seemed like it could only flourish if there was a nearby tear in the veil.

He decided to break through the stone rather than dig around it. It might take slightly longer, but it would make a more straightforward access point and allow him to retreat quickly if he needed to. Besides, stone wasn't that hard to reshape with the right spells, which he did know.

It cracked and crumbled as it turned into sand, one little chunk at a time. He didn't need to get rid of all of it either, just enough to get through. More sand fell away, and some of the dirt resting on top of the stone started to trickle through as he breached the breadth of the slab. Nym started to widen the hole.

"We've got a geist incoming," Blanchet said from below him. She pointed down at what Nym thought was the south hall.

He dipped down and spotted the geist swirling along the top of the tunnel, though he wasn't sure exactly how since there were no real air currents to carry it. "How do they fly underground?" he asked Blanchet as he summoned up a lightning bolt to fry it.

She blinked at the streak of light and said, "It's kind of weird actually. They basically just . . . punch themselves, I guess, with blasts of telekinesis and then sail along for as far as they can go. The ones down here are rubbing up against the ceiling to keep tugging themselves forward when they need to, or maybe to build up some speed."

"Weird. Well, it's dead now," he said. "Let me know if anything else shows up."

[Second point is ready to go,] Ogric said through the group telepathy link.

[Still working on securing the area,] Sakaro responded.

[I haven't finished digging yet,] Nym added.

More stone broke away, and Nym reached up with terrakinesis to rip down a chunk of dirt. Once he pulled the center through, it started pouring out of the hole to pile up on the ground beneath him, and he got his first look at the corpse root. It was only an arm sticking out of the dirt, but it told him he needed to start being very careful about brushing up against it with his magic. Once was enough, and he was not looking forward to actually attacking the damn thing.

[I've found it,] Nym reported. *[But I'm going to have to dig a little bit more to fully expose the corpse. I should be ready to go within a minute.]*

"Two ghouls wandering in. I should be able to—ah, they spotted me. I'll take care of this. Just keep digging," Blanchet said.

"You sure?" Nym asked without turning to look. He was relying on gravity to pull the dirt away from the body once he'd scooped up everything beneath it and spending more of his arcana on widening the hole he'd broken through the stone than anything else.

"I can handle this," she said, readying a sword. "Ghouls aren't that smart. It wouldn't hurt if you burned the pieces after I'm done though."

"Okay. Let me know if you change your mind."

He did his best to ignore the sounds of combat below him and carefully scooped away the rest of the dirt. "Ahhh!" he yelped, shooting backward as the corpse root tumbled forward into the open hole to dangle headfirst into the tunnel. Its legs were still up above the stone, but the rest of it flopped around in the open air.

"So that's done," Nym said. He started up the heated disintegration spell he'd copied from Sergeant Grom the other day and fed the remaining ghoul pieces into it.

[Ready to go,] Nym said.

[Second point is also ready.]

[Having some trouble with more ghouls coming in,] Sakaro said. *[I wouldn't say no to some help cleaning them up. I don't really have the fire I need, and it's getting harder to keep them pushed back.]*

Nym sent a scrying anchor out to find her. She was standing by herself, no surprise considering she was partnered with Tiramaya. There were still a dozen dismembered ghouls underneath the barrier she'd created to keep them flattened, but easily twice that many had appeared in the cavern and were circling a dome-shaped barrier she'd created.

Even as he assessed the situation, someone's magic swept through and picked all the ghouls up. They slammed into the walls and ceiling at random points, some impaled on stalactites, but most falling back to the ground a few limbs lighter. The sheer force of the telekinesis being used on them was ripping limbs off from torsos, a sure sign that Archmage Veran had interfered.

[Please destroy your corpse root on my mark,] the archmage's voice sounded in their heads.

"Hey, Blanchet. Do you think these things are made of the same stuff ghouls are?" Nym asked.

"Almost certainly. Why?"

"Because my lightning-bolt spell doesn't work very well on ghouls. I'm going to have to get more creative here."

[Begin.]

Nym directed the incineration spell up to the corpse root and then, for extra good measure, threw up a thermal barrier around the whole thing so it would heat up even faster. As soon as the magic touched the root, pain spiked through his head. Nym dropped down to his knees but held the spells steady.

"What's wrong?" Blanchet said.

"The corpse root doesn't like magic. I think it would feel like using it directly on the veil."

"Oh no. I just assumed you knew. You haven't learned to separate yourself from the touch of the veil. You can't use a channeled spell. It's got to be something with a battery of energy that's fully separated from you."

Nym had a few offensive spells like that but nothing that would be strong enough to turn a regular ghoul to ash, let alone the corpse tied directly to the reaper lurking behind the veil. "Don't have that," he said through gritted teeth. "Just need to hurry up here. I'll be fine."

The corpse was started to break down to ash, and even as it tried to reform, the new parts were disintegrating too. After about a minute, there was nothing left in there except the root. It writhed and squirmed around, but Nym didn't let up until he heard the archmage's voice in his mind.

[We've done it! Confirm no more corpses are hanging from the root.]

[Confirmed,] Sakaro said.

[Confirmed,] Ogric echoed.

Nym let the spell go and slumped down in exhaustion. He started to respond, *[Confi—ack!]*

The root lashed out at him like a living thing. It snaked out of the hole he'd created, the one he'd made so he'd have an easier time retreating, and struck down at where he was sitting on the floor.

"Look out!" Blanchet said, moving to intercept, or to shove him out of the way, or something.

It didn't matter what her intentions were. She was too late either way, and Nym was too drained to move under his own power.

The root struck him in the chest, and it didn't let go.

CHAPTER SIXTY-SIX

Nym felt something invading him, not physically, but grasping at his soul well. If he hadn't already injured himself, hadn't already spent so much time staring inward while he tried to fix it, he would never have been able to stop the root.

Thankfully, and that felt odd to think, he had destabilized his matrix. He could feel the root attacking him, and more than that, he could see it. He knew how to look at what was going on inside him. It had split into a thousand little tendrils of something that was not quite arcana but close enough for its purposes. It was trying to overshadow his nodes one by one, trying to consume them, to fill his soul well with the essence of undeath.

Nym had no intention of letting it do that, of course. He flooded his soul well with his own arcana, as much as he could possibly hold. It pushed back against the root, and maybe if his soul well had been full prior to the undead tendril's attack, the root wouldn't have found any purchase. That wasn't what had happened, unfortunately, and by the time Nym had filled his soul well to bursting, the root had already found a firm foothold.

That did not mean he was just going to let it keep worming its way in. He'd never really manipulated arcana inside his soul well before, but there was a first time for everything. Finally, the chaotic nature of arcana harvested from the Astral Sea worked in his favor. He didn't even try to leash it, just braced himself and let it lash around inside his soul well.

The arcana beat against the infection, smacking into it, breaking it apart and pushing it back. Little chunks floated into the arcana, which was probably a bad thing, but he'd start with removing the vast majority of it and move on to filtering out what little bit was left. Slowly, one grasping tendril at a time, the root was forced back.

And then, suddenly, it was severed from the source, and what remained latched on to Nym floundered. No longer reinforced by the rest of the root, it lost much of its potency, and he expelled it with a pained scream. Essence of undeath rushed out of him, filling the air with a cloud of mixed arcana and necrosis.

Blisters and sores split his skin open, but Nym could handle that. What he couldn't tolerate was the remaining slivers of darkness clinging to the nodes of his matrix. He needed to flush everything out, and he could only think of one way to do that.

He forged a new conduit and filled himself to the brim and beyond with first-layer arcana. The soul channels he'd forged in his body were stretched to their limits, ready to burst. And then he flexed his matrix, let it all flood out and with it the shards of undeath stuck inside him.

Intense pain wracked him, but it worked. The shards dislodged from his soul well and washed out into his body where healing magic could remove them. He came back to himself, lying on his back in the cavern, the root hanging overhead now charred and pitted instead of sleek and glossy. Archmage Veran stood over him, a font of fire bursting from an open palm. He lashed waves of ghouls that swarmed over them, causing them to spontaneously crumble to ash.

"Have you expelled it?" the archmage asked calmly, as though he wasn't standing there holding off fifty ghouls by himself.

"The root? Got it out of my soul well. Did you cut it off at the source?"

Archmage Veran nodded. "I thought it would be easier for you to fight it if you weren't connected directly to the reaper."

"There are still slivers of it in my body," Nym said. "I need to see a healer. A good one. Gave myself one hell of a case of arcana poisoning, but I think I can take care of that myself."

"It would be better if we removed it here. I would like to keep this contained. The root appears to be dead, and I do not want it sprouting again somewhere else."

"I'm not sure I can," Nym admitted. He didn't even think he could move, so if Archmage Veran refused to relocate him, there wasn't much he could do at this point. It was only first-layer arcana, but there was a lot of it. "Where's everybody else?

"I sent them away from danger. It is just the two of us down here. Any secrets you might need to reveal, or a . . . break of character . . . will not be witnessed by anyone else."

Nym groaned and let his head fall back to the ground. If he knew how to heal himself, he would have already. The best he could do was clean up the excess arcana. It would probably take an hour or more to remove the majority of it, and he'd be at it all night and likely into the morning to fully rid himself of the arcana poisoning his body.

"Unless you can bring a healer here, I don't think there's much more I can do."

"Nym. I am an archmage. I'm sure I could manage the healing myself if I weren't otherwise occupied. I can still advise you on how to do it."

"Oh, right. I don't know why I didn't think you'd know any healing magic."

"Your persona would do well to learn some as well," the archmage said.

"I'm trying. It's complicated. There are so many spells for so many specific use cases, and those diagnostic spells give so much confusing information."

"Hmm, yes. When you do it that way, there's a great deal of expertise required."

Nym craned his neck to give the old man a glare. "Nobody told me there was another way to do it."

"Far be it from me to disabuse you of that notion. Of course your way is the correct way to use second-layer arcana to heal. I wouldn't argue that fact."

"But third-layer arcana can do so much more," Nym said, letting out another groan. He'd spent so much time, wasted so much money and effort. "Anyway, can you get the rest of these shards out of me?"

"Hardly," Archmage Veran told him. "You may have noticed I'm a bit preoccupied at the moment."

That was true. The old man hadn't stopped channeling arcana for even a second while they spoke. It was a minor miracle they could even see each other with all the piles of burning ghoul surrounding them. Whatever disposal spell he was using, it worked quickly but left an inordinate amount of greasy smoke hanging in the air.

Nym tried not to think of what exactly he was breathing in with that smoke. It wouldn't help anything to dwell on that. He could practically see it congealing on the cavern walls and briefly wondered what kind of long-term effects it might have on anything growing in the region. In fifty years, the whole forest might be shrouded in some sort of necrotic mist due to all the ghouls burned to ashes during the conflict.

"While it's great to know the possibilities of third-circle healing magic, I don't actually know how to cast it. If you can't help right now, we're going to have to risk leaving," Nym said.

"Of course you know how to cast healing magic," Archmage Veran said. "What do you think you've been doing with every modification you make to your body?"

"That's . . . Huh. That is a good point."

Nym had made quite a few modifications to how his mind and body functioned. Without them, he would never be able to dual cast, nor would he be able to split knots of arcana in the second layer so that he could push straight through to the third. He'd even tweaked a few things involving his metabolism and muscles as well so that he wouldn't get tired as quickly.

Those were changes though, not healing. They were permanent. He could change a broken arm into an unbroken one, but without the base knowledge of how it was supposed to function, he could end up doing more harm than good. But then, he had a lot of that base knowledge already. And in this case, for the removal of a foreign substance, he even knew more or less exactly what everything was supposed to look like.

He could remove the splinters of root in his body. He'd already done the hard part by flushing them out of his soul well and pushing them back into the physical world. At this point, a determined surgeon could physically cut them out, though Nym would likely die in the process without magical aid. All he needed to do was locate them, remove them, and heal whatever damage he did to himself during the extraction.

Of course that would all be a lot easier if he wasn't trying to keep from throwing up from all the arcana built up in his body. He didn't really feel like this was the best possible time to start experimenting with this line of thought, but the man who was supposed to be teaching him had apparently decided to throw him off the pier and see if he could swim.

Nym didn't really believe Archmage Veran couldn't maintain a barrier to keep the ghouls back and extract the root slivers at the same time. He thought it was more likely that the old man was trying to push him to stop holding back. A generous interpretation might be that the archmage was trying to help by pushing him, but unless the whole scenario led to him unlocking another memory shard, the only way to make him more like a true ascendant was to reach the fifth layer.

A less generous interpretation was that the archmage was simply trying to get rid of him now that Nym had fulfilled his obligations. That didn't track though, not with what Nym knew of him personally or with the fact that he was literally standing over him, keeping the monsters at bay.

And then Nym saw the real truth. The old man was just tired. Once he really stopped to look, stopped seeing an indomitable figure, it was easy to see that Archmage Veran wasn't doing so well himself. His posture was slumped, and his hands trembled at his sides. He was in fact risking his life to give Nym a chance to rid himself of the root splinters rather than just abandoning him.

There wasn't really a lot of time to mull that over. Nym was working overtime trying to clear out as much arcana from his system as possible, and he had reached the point where he felt ready to perform some magic. First on the list was a pain-numbing spell. He wasn't skilled enough to do this in any way that wasn't going to hurt, and he didn't need to lose his concentration in the middle.

"Okay, I'm giving this a try. I'm confident I can get the splinters out, but . . . Uh . . . Maybe be ready to teleport out of here and do some real healing just in case I don't get everything patched up properly."

He located the first splinter, buried deep in his leg. A very delicate and precise application of the tip of his mage blade parted flesh down to the muscle, and a gentle telekinesis spell pried the splinter out. That set his teeth on edge, even through the pain-numbing spell. Whatever that stuff was, touching it with active magic hurt worse than just having it in him.

Nym flung it away and used third-layer arcana to pull everything back together. He was almost completely sure he didn't do it right, but for now the wound was closed, and that was the important part. It would hold for a few minutes until he was done.

There was one floating next to his ribs, fortunately on the outside and not nestled up next to his heart, and another in his shoulder. The one on his lower back was the worst to get out and, considering how close it was to his spine, probably the most nerve-racking to do. That involved a lot of work by feel and was probably far messier than the rest.

Eventually he'd pried out every last splinter. Archmage Veran burned them away into nothing, and then the two of them teleported back to his sanctum. The old man practically fell off his feet from the effort, and it was only through sheer willpower that he managed to stay upright.

"Come with me. We'll get you looked at and fixed up."

The two of them limped slowly over to the medical station down the hall, and Nym cursed the teleportation wards that made the walk necessary.

CHAPTER SIXTY-SEVEN

Nym took the next few days easy. It turned out he'd botched quite a few things trying to heal himself, and what he'd done right had been more of an accident than anything. Archmage Veran patched him up enough to keep him alive, but neither of them had the energy to do more right then. The problem was easily remedied by a visit to an accomplished healer, one who just looked at the hack job he'd done of it, shook her head, and recommended not trying to do it himself next time.

He agreed with her but didn't feel like he needed to justify his actions by explaining the circumstances leading up to his experiments in surgery. She fixed him up, he gave her a crest, and then he left. That was all he'd wanted out of visiting the clinic, and he was perfectly happy with the work she'd done.

What he wasn't happy about was the state of his soul well. He'd barely gotten the thing patched up, and now he was right back in there repairing the nodes that the corpse root had mangled. It was a small consolation that he at least knew what he needed to do to fix his matrix, and he suspected he'd be back to full strength by the end of the week unless things went sideways.

It did mean he missed the big event where they sealed up the tear once and for all. Nym heard that Archmage Veran had called in one of his colleagues to help, and then the two archmages assisted by sixty third-circle mages patched the whole thing up right this time. Nym didn't see him that day or the next, but the wards blocking access to his private chambers were fully powered for days on end.

One day, while Nym was eating breakfast and reading a book on the intricacies of reconnecting severed limbs, the archmage popped into existence across the table from him. Nym jerked so hard that the bread roll he was eating flew out of his hands and bounced off the wall. He caught it with a burst of telekinetic arcana before it could hit the floor, then shot Archmage Veran a scowl.

"You didn't even form that into a proper spell," the old man noted.

"It wasn't that heavy, and I didn't have that much time. How could you tell?"

"The way the roll flopped through the air like that. Your telekinesis spells mimic motions your own body would do, but that one didn't."

"I guess that's true. Are you feeling better?"

"As much as I can at my age. How are you doing?"

"Still cleaning up the damage, but I should be done in another day or two."

"That's good to hear. I will be hosting a small dinner for our companions from our adventures tonight here. You are welcome to attend, but I will understand if you do not want to. If you'd prefer, I can drop you off outside the sanctum so you can finish your recovery with your own friends. You would of course be welcome to return when you're ready. I have not forgotten my debts, after all."

"I'll go," Nym said. "As long as you don't expect me to do anything but eat your food, at least."

Archmage Veran laughed. "That will be fine, I think. I realize that we're a bit behind on our work together, but I should have significantly more time to assist you starting tomorrow."

"I'll look forward to it or maybe dread it. I'm not sure yet."

"I won't hold it against you if you feel the need to curse my name over the next few weeks," the archmage assured him. "God knows I cursed yours often enough when I was learning to channel fifth-layer arcana."

"That's not reassuring," Nym said dryly. He finished his roll and added, "How did sealing the tear go?"

"It'll hold for the rest of my natural life span," Archmage Veran said, his voice suddenly tired. "It's not a true fix though. I doubt anything less than an actual ascendant working on it would reverse the damage. The work itself was quite boring. I did the equivalent to holding the cart up while Teltin changed the wheel. Oh, sorry, Teltin is a Nordramese archmage I sometimes collaborate with. It was a thoroughly exhausting day in which very little of excitement occurred."

"Glad I missed it then," Nym muttered. With his luck, showing up would have caused the reaper to burst through the tear into their reality and kill everyone. He had no idea how that would have happened, but it honestly wouldn't have surprised him. It was just another reason to hurry up and make it to the fifth layer so that he could see if it was possible to regain his lost magic without the personality that came with it.

He hadn't missed the not-so-subtle hint that an ascendant could solve their problems for them. Nym wasn't even a real ascendant, not in his mind at least, and he was already starting to understand why they didn't hang around with regular humans. The last thing he wanted was to live his life solving the problems of every random jerk who found him in the streets.

Some of the big ones, like a tear between the veil of life and death, would warrant his attention, of course. He wasn't heartless. Maybe he'd come back to that and fix it properly once it was within his power to do so. That could still be years away if the whole memory-cube thing didn't work though.

"So it's done then? Nothing left but to hunt down the loose undead, which won't be repopulating anymore? Then the rebuilding?"

"Probably. It'll start getting cold soon, long before any of the towns have been rebuilt in any meaningful way. Your earth-mage friends could no doubt find a decent amount of work in the area."

Nym shook his head. "They're heading south for warmer weather. I'm not sure they'd want to come back here anyway, but I'll let them know."

The conversation meandered away from heavy topics after that, and soon enough breakfast was over. Archmage Veran left to attend to things, citing a need to catch up on Academy business, and Nym kept himself safe from boredom by browsing a few of the many, many books stored in the sanctum library.

The normal table had disappeared from the dining room, and in its place was a monstrosity easily twenty feet long and big enough to seat seven or eight to a side with plenty of elbow room. That was good because Archmage Veran's guest list was larger than Nym had expected.

Everyone from their most recent adventure was there, and so were Babkin, Grom, and Stelton. A man Nym didn't recognize sat next to the archmage, and he quickly figured out from eavesdropping on the two army mages that he was the Nordramese archmage. Nym wasn't exactly keen to meet someone so powerful, and he hoped his mentor was keeping his secrets.

Speaking of secrets, he was less than thrilled to see Lord Jaspar Feldstal at the table. The nobleman didn't go out of his way to talk to Nym, which suited him just fine. In fact, they were seated on the same side with five people between them. All the important people were up at the head near Archmage Veran. Nym was back at the far end with Grom and Stelton. Babkin sat across from him, and Leaf was next to the burly innkeeper.

Babkin did not look good. Even after a few weeks to recover, he had that sallow, wasted look of someone who'd been sick for a long, long time. Nym waited until everyone was seated and platters of food started appearing out of thin air to float down onto the table. The aura of arcana around Archmage Veran gave the trick away: he was teleporting the dishes in from another room.

Once they'd had a chance to get started, Nym said, "Are you alright? You look terrible."

Babkin rumbled out a laugh, but it was a pale echo of his former robustness. "Berserker magic is not gentle. I will recover, eventually."

"I'm keeping an eye on him," Leaf added. "I don't think we'll be participating in the cleanup though. The whole group is going on vacation."

"My inn has been destroyed anyway," Babkin grumbled. "The entire town was flattened. Cern was very nearly killed when his shop blew up."

Nym winced. He was by no means an alchemical expert, but he distinctly remembered the aftermath of one of Cern's accidents in a controlled setting. The idea of some of his reagents being randomly smashed together sent a shiver down his spine. "Is he alright now?" he asked.

"The healer's bill was quite hefty, but he will live," Babkin said.

"Hmm. I know someone who's interested in alchemy. He might be able to hire on as a tutor if he needs some work. I could ask?"

"He would likely appreciate that. He expressed strong displeasure at the thought of bunking in a refugee camp for the winter."

"I'll see if I can find him something to do for the winter," Nym promised. "Will I be able to contact you through Archmage Veran?"

Leaf started laughing. "Using an archmage as your messenger service? You've got God's own testicles hanging off you."

Nym waved him off. "He owes me a few favors now."

"He what?" Stelton said next to him. "Why would he . . . No, none of my business. I'm not even sure why I'm here."

"Because you were part of the team that helped clean up this entire mess," Leaf said. He winked at the woman, who blushed in response. Then he added, "And because I told Veran to invite you."

"Well, I see why she's here," Grom said dryly. "Why am I?"

"Because I told Veran to invite you for Babkin," Leaf shot back.

"I . . . What?"

"He is joking," Babkin told the sergeant. "You are far too scrawny for me."

"I feel like I should be offended," Grom said. "But then again, who's not too scrawny for you?"

"You should see some of the women down south," Leaf said.

The food was good and the banter entertaining. Nym had some concerns, but overall, it was a fine dinner, and he was glad he'd decided to attend. He was, until it was time to end it. Archmage Veran started teleporting guests away after speaking with each for a minute, and Nym was ready to return to his own room.

Jaspar Feldstal slid into the seat opposite him shortly after Babkin left. "Good evening," he said. "Do you have a few minutes to talk?"

Nym eyed him warily. "That depends on what you want to talk about."

"Oh, this and that," the nobleman said lightly. "We didn't get a chance to speak over dinner. I wanted to inquire after my daughter, as well as a few other things. I haven't had much of a chance to speak to her lately."

"She's doing fine," Nym said. He met Lord Feldstal's gaze and waited for him to reply. If Analia wanted her father to know how she was doing, she would tell him herself. He certainly wasn't going to elaborate.

The dining room continued to empty while they talked, and perhaps noticing a sudden rise in tension, the guests started clearing out much faster. Soon enough, it was just Nym, Lord Feldstal, and their host left.

"Jaspar," Archmage Veran said, "are you ready to depart?"

"One moment, please. I had a few topics I wanted to touch on with our young friend, but they were sensitive enough that I felt it prudent to hold off until the rest of your guests had departed."

"Nym?" the archmage asked.

Nym locked eyes with Lord Feldstal. "It's . . . fine. We can talk."

"Splendid." The nobleman's mouth curled up into a grin. "First, let me congratulate you. You've been particularly impressive this last month or so. But then, I'd expect nothing less, all things considered."

Nym just stared at him.

"Yes, fine. Down to business, I see. Very well then."

CHAPTER SIXTY-EIGHT

We've hit something of a dead end," Lord Feldstal said. "I'm not saying it's impossible to solve, and we do have more time now that this current crisis is all but dealt with. However, our funding is going to drop drastically, and we'll need to show our progress."

"What does this have to do with me?" Nym asked.

"You're our most successful case study. I'd like to get new scans to present."

Nym almost couldn't believe the audacity of the man. The Collective had kidnapped him, stuck him in a mage cell, and bound him with a magical geas to force him to maintain their anonymity. On the other hand, they had also given him a place to live and a generous stipend and hadn't really restricted his freedom in any meaningful way.

The worst they'd done was insist that he teleport to their headquarters every day, but that was just part of having a job. It would be like getting mad at the bakery he'd worked at for a few weeks for expecting him to show up every morning. He supposed from their point of view, they'd treated him pretty well.

He might have agreed except for the introduction. Nym was still sore about that one, and he didn't expect to change his mind anytime soon. The only reason he's squirmed out of that was that they'd figured out he was an ascendant and gotten spooked. There was no way he was getting involved with them again.

"Nope," he said. "Not my problem."

"I'm sure we can find a suitable compensation for you."

"I really don't think you can."

"Come now," Lord Feldstal said. "What is it you need? Money? Tutoring? Land? A title? How about I smooth things over with the law for you?"

"I will earn my own money. I'm already being tutored by an archmage. Can you top that? I don't need lands or titles There's nothing you can offer me, and you'll understand my reluctance to let you exploit me any further."

"*Exploit* seems harsh," the noble protested. "It was a mutually beneficial arrangement."

"I think you benefited from it far more than me. Look, it's fine." It wasn't really, but there wasn't any need to go into that. "I've moved past what the Collective has to offer, and you don't have anything I want."

"I'll admit, you are a hard one to tempt." Lord Feldstal leaned back in his seat and gave Nym an appraising look. "I'm not out of options yet though."

"Just stop," Nym said. He leaned forward. "You know what I am. I don't think we need to go into the hows and whys, but just ask yourself this: Is there really a single thing you can offer me that I need but can't get myself?"

Unlike the last time they'd spoken, the nobleman was much surer of himself. "I think that I let myself be blinded by some assumptions I made the first time, and that was a mistake. So yes, my young friend, ignoring the hows and whys, I think there are plenty of things you need that I am in a position to assist you with."

"I disagree," Nym said, standing up. "I have no interest in working with the Collective again. If that's all you want to talk about, this conversation is over."

"That is all of the official business," Lord Feldstal said stiffly. "When you change your mind, come find me. I'll be in the area for another month or two before I return to Abilanth."

"I'll keep that in mind," Nym told him. "Have a good night."

He walked out of the dining room without another word, though he could practically feel Lord Feldstal's eyes boring holes in his back. Somehow, Nym doubted it was the last he'd see of the man. He'd tried to give as complete and total a rejection to working any further as possible, but it seemed Analia's father wasn't going to take no for an answer.

If his only goal was to get away from Lord Feldstal, he'd teleport back down to the south coast and keep on going. The world was a big place, and he was sure he could get lost in it quite easily. Of course, by doing that, he wouldn't be able to continue his lessons with Archmage Veran, not to mention he'd have to abandon all contact with his friends in that scenario.

So no, Nym wouldn't be doing that. He would stay on guard against possible ambushes whenever he was outside the sanctum, and he expected he would be looking into spells and strategies for mage-on-mage combat now that the undead threat was taken care of. His primary goal needed to remain forging a fifth-layer conduit though.

As usual, there was too much to do and not enough time. As soon as he'd finished dealing with the matrix damage the root had inflicted, he'd go see his friends and get them set. He also needed to talk to Analia about taking on Cern as a tutor.

So much to do. It was hard to keep his ever-shifting priorities in line, but for the time being, the only two that mattered were getting back into top form and getting to the fifth layer.

His predictions were accurate, and within two days, Nym was fully recovered. Archmage Veran still needed a few more days to get caught up on all his administrative duties at the Academy, so Nym used the time to teleport back to Geldrin to see his friends.

"Good news," he told Nomick, the first one he found. The earth mage was carrying a basketful of various plants, all neatly divided into their own containers. He jumped when Nym spoke, then spun around to glare at him.

"What have we all told you about sneaking up on us like that?!"

"That it's hilarious when it happens to anyone but you?"

"Exactly," Nomick said. "Which is why you should do it to everyone else but me."

"But you all say that," Nym said. "If I listened to everyone, I wouldn't be able to surprise anyone."

"Which would also be acceptable."

Nym made a show of considering it while he floated around Nomick. "Nah, doesn't sound fun."

An aura of arcana formed around the earth mage, and a chunk of dirt flew through the air at the back of Nym's head. It wasn't the first time one of the Earth Shapers had tried that trick, and Nym already had a scrying anchor viewing them both from off to the side. He saw the dirt coming easily and dodged out of the way.

"Wow, rude! And here I was bringing you good news."

Nomick paused in the act of grabbing another clump of dirt. "Are you going to tell me the good news or make me wait hours until everyone comes in for dinner?"

"Thought I might make you wait."

Nym dodged the second dirt clump and laughed. "No, I'm just kidding. The whole undead thing is basically taken care of now, so there won't be any need to evacuate and no real pressure to go south before you're ready to."

"Ah, that is good news," Nomick said. "If you'd brought a basket of pastries with you, I might even thank you for it."

"I fear I shall never live up to those expectations I so foolishly set in the early days of summer," Nym lamented. "It will be a struggle, but I shall soldier on."

"Yeah, yeah. You tell the others yet?"

Nym shook his head. "You're the first one I found."

"Bildar and Ophelia are working on that new building for the town. We already did the foundation, and they're the ones who handle all the fine detail work, so Monick and I had to find other ways to occupy our time."

"And you chose . . . gardening?"

"These are alchemical reagents!"

"Yeah, I know. I'm just giving you a hard time. Are they for Analia?"

"No, these are mine. She gets her own herbs now."

Nym nodded, though inside he was groaning. She could be anywhere. He'd have to fly around and fire off a few message spells to see if he could get her attention unless someone knew where she was.

"Speaking of alchemy, I have an alchemist friend who lost his shop when the surge hit. I was thinking of seeing if Analia needed a tutor."

"God, yes," Nomick said. "I regret telling her that I have an alchemy certification. She asks more questions than the exams did."

"Great. It's nice to see friends helping each other. Now I just need to find her and everyone else to let them know.." Nym looked at Nomick. "You know where they are?"

After getting directions, Nym flew around and delivered the news to each person individually. Analia was last on his list since she was nowhere near town. He did eventually find her, if only by following a plume of smoke and then the sound of a long string of uninterrupted swearing. The girl was standing over what looked like a fox that was almost four feet tall at the shoulder, its fur an odd ruddy orange with black highlights.

The fox was crumpled up on its side, extremely dead and with smoke billowing off its body. Analia stood, hands curled into fists, and glared down at it while reciting a long litany of insults against the fox's heritage. All around her, other plumes of smoke rose into the air from small grass fires, and chunks of ice the size of his head littered the field.

"Am I interrupting?" Nym asked as he landed next to her.

"This stupid smolder fox burned my halthium thistle," she said, pointing toward a small blackened smear. Nym supposed that whatever that little crispy thing in the middle was could at one time have been a plant. It was definitely useless now though.

"I am guessing you didn't take that very well," he said, looking pointedly at a particularly bloody chunk of ice near the dead fox's skull.

"I . . . may have lost my temper," she admitted. "But I've been looking for one of these for a week now! I finally spot one, and before I can get it, this thing comes running out of the trees, spreading fire everywhere. It ran over the thistle immediately."

"Bad luck," Nym said. "If you can spare a moment away from cursing that fox's memory, I have something to talk to you about."

She sighed, gave one last mournful look at her burnt plant, and said, "Go ahead."

Nym took some time to explain who Cern was and what had happened to his shop in Zoskan, that the alchemist could use a job and a place to live outside the refugee camp. "And I thought if everyone was interested, I could bring him here to meet you and you guys could figure out if you'd like to hire him as a tutor."

"That . . . sounds good," she said, hesitantly. "Except I don't know if I could afford to pay him."

"Ah. Hmm. I didn't think of that. I'm not used to you having a budget."

"Oh shut up," she said, giving him a shove.

"I've got some extra crests if it comes down to it, and maybe we can work something else out besides money. We are friends with a whole building crew. Plus I'm a third-circle mage with access to an archmage's library. I can do all sorts of stuff now that's in high demand."

"That is all true, but don't you have more important things to worry about?" she asked.

Nym shrugged. "I can't spend every waking moment studying. Sometimes it feels like I've spent more hours reading books over the last year than anything else. Don't get me wrong, I like learning new magic, but I also like flying around and doing stuff."

"Alright, I guess it wouldn't hurt to meet him and see if we can work something out."

"Great," he said. "I'll see if I can get him soon. I don't think there's any rush, but we should probably check with Bildar and Ophelia about when they want to leave. Oh, and did you decide if you're going with them?"

"I think that depends largely on where you're going," she said.

"Huh. I don't really know yet. I guess we'll figure that out too."

CHAPTER SIXTY-NINE

The refugee camps were functional at best. They were made completely from earth magic, which was fine for making thick walls and large buildings, but were going to be hard to keep warm. Nym understood why they'd raise twenty long halls each capable of holding fifty or more people, but keeping that warm was going to be impossible, and the people stuck living in them would be getting little to no privacy.

Hopefully, the forest would soon be completely clear of undead. With the tear no longer open and no new ghouls pouring out, the army had finally started to take control of the area. Nym had flown over it himself and scried for undead, and he'd been pleasantly surprised at how few he'd found. He'd left the ghouls for the army to kill but had gone out of his way to execute three wights and a geist he'd spotted.

A squad of soldiers were manning the gate into the camp when Nym flew up, and one of them waved him over. He saw arcana wash out of a soldier and recognized it as an undead-detection spell. That was a reasonable precaution to him, considering the surprise attack the wights had pulled where they'd come in wearing army uniforms and no one had realized they weren't humans until they'd started killing.

"Nature of your business?" the soldier asked.

"Visiting a friend," Nym said.

The soldier looked over at the one who'd cast the undead-detection spell. She nodded back, and he said, "Go on in."

Nym flew over the wall rather than go through the tunnel, mostly because he'd scried the camp as he approached and knew there were a few traps in there. It wasn't that he expected the soldiers to activate them, but he really needed to be better about leaving himself vulnerable to ambush. His talk with Lord Feldstal had reminded him of exactly how he'd ended up getting dragged into the Collective in the first place, and it wasn't something he was eager to repeat.

So he'd scried the entire camp before entering, used perfect sight to help him see it from far away, and then took a few minutes to look at the active magic, if only to try to gauge how strong it was. It was honestly kind of exhausting, and he wasn't sure he could keep up that level of paranoia and caution for any conceivable length of time.

But for the next few weeks at least, especially after having turned down Lord Feldstal's request, he fully planned on being vigilant. He wasn't even completely sure he trusted his safety in Archmage Veran's sanctum, but if his mentor decided to bind him with a geas and hand him over to the Collective, there wasn't much Nym could do to stop him.

Nym decided that he was extremely ready to be done with the entire kingdom of Delvros. As soon as Archmage Veran fulfilled his half of the bargains they'd made, he was moving somewhere far, far, far away from all those people. He could teleport now; he could live wherever he wanted and still visit his friends regularly.

Cern was in one of the smaller workshops at the edge of the camp. It seemed that someone thought it was worth investing in Cern, since he was still doing alchemy. His equipment and supplies were pitiful compared to what he'd had in his old shop, but at least the workshop included an attached room for him to live in.

Nym landed in front of it and walked in. The alchemist glanced up from where he was grinding up some sort of moss with a mortar and pestle, a scowl already on his face. The look transformed to one of confusion when he saw Nym.

"What . . . Can I help you?" he asked, studying Nym closely.

"More like I can help you," Nym told him.

Cern had put on some weight and lost the bushy beard, though on closer inspection, it appeared to have been burned off. Well, it wasn't the first time that had happened. He studied Nym with a tilted head, his face going from confused to incredulous.

"Nym?" he asked. "They said you'd grown taller, but . . ."

When he'd first met the alchemist, Nym had barely been up to his chest. Now, Nym could look him in the eye without tilting his head. He'd grown more than a foot and a half in the last year and filled out as well. Nym had been decidedly scrawny when he'd first arrived in Zoskan. He wasn't muscular by any means, but his limbs were much thicker and his shoulders much broader.

"Bit of a growth spurt, I guess," he said. "How are you doing?"

Cern snorted. "Bit of a growth spurt," he repeated. "I'd like to know what fertilizer they're throwing on you. And how's it look like I'm doing, stuck in this stone icebox mixing up grubby little bottles of medicine? Life savings is gone, completely tied up in my shop, which is a big pile of charred logs."

"Right, that's why I'm here. Babkin told me you were looking to get out of the refugee camp before winter sets in. I thought I might be able to help."

"Hmm." Cern scratched at the remaining stubble of his beard as he thought. "I would like to, yes, but I'm lacking in coin right now, and I'm honestly not sure how far I could get before the snow starts coming down. Even if you were to plop a sack of crests on the table, there's no teleportation platforms anywhere near here now."

"I can teleport you," Nym said.

"You can do what now?"

"I can teleport. It was the first third-circle spell I learned."

The alchemist just stared at Nym, his hand still raised to scratch as his face but no longer moving. Finally, he let out an almost puzzled, "Huh."

"Yeah. Anyway. I have a friend who's taken an interest in alchemy and could use a good tutor. I thought maybe you two could meet and see if you can work something out. It'd be a chance to get some seed money to start up a new business, plus get you out of the camps over the winter months."

"I could do that," Cern said slowly. "When and where?"

"As soon as you're ready to go," Nym told him. "In a town east of here called Geldrin."

Cern just snorted and shook his head. "Teleportation," he muttered. "Give me a few minutes to finish this and get it packaged."

When he was done, Nym teleported them both into the air above Geldrin and brought them down to street level outside the inn everyone was staying at. Cern staggered when they landed and clutched at Nym's arm. "God's balls, don't do that!"

"Sorry, it's easier to teleport into the air. No chance of landing inside a wall that way."

"Is . . . Is that a common risk?"

Nym shrugged. "Hasn't happened to me yet."

Cern gave him a less than complimentary look, then took a deliberate step away and straightened his clothes. "Alright, let's meet this potential student and see where it goes from there."

One habit Analia had never fallen out of, no matter how much she'd changed in other ways, was stitching those antiscrying runes into her clothing and keeping them fully powered. It made it a pain to find her, and he once again bumped learning how to overpower them up his priority list, where it would surely be pushed back by a dozen more pressing issues.

"I'll send her a message to meet us here," Nym said. "We can get lunch while we wait."

He didn't quite understand how the message spell managed to find her through the antiscrying runes, considering that it used scrying magic itself to locate the intended recipient. One day he'd have to get a look at the rune sequences again. He suspected it was something on her side that specifically let certain types of magic through while blocking others.

Perhaps he'd just gotten lucky, or maybe she'd kept herself limited to the workshop she'd rented near the edge of town because she knew Nym would be showing up with Cern, but either way it only took a minute or so for her to come flying over. She was dressed in pants and a blouse again today, with her hair tied up and pinned back. Her hands had little pink burn marks across the backs of them, and two of her fingers were bandaged.

"What happened?" Nym asked.

"Splashed myself with an acidic solution trying to make a potion earlier. It's fine. My mistake for being clumsy."

"Do you want me to heal that?"

"Do you know how to?" she asked.

"Yeah, I've gotten surface wounds pretty much down. It's internals that I'm still having problems with. The diagnostic spells are really complicated, not just to cast but to understand what they're trying to tell you."

"Not to interrupt," Cern said, interrupting, "but perhaps you could introduce us while you work."

"Right, sorry! Cern, this is my friend Analia, a second-circle mage and budding alchemist. Analia, this is Cern, a master alchemist I used to scrounge various flowers, mosses, and herbs for when I first got to Zoskan and needed some money."

"A pleasure, miss," Cern said. His gaze moved down to her burnt hand. "You'll forgive me, but you're a little on the young side still. Not to brag, but I am a highly accomplished alchemist, and my services don't come cheap. You might be better off seeking someone less . . . experienced to teach you the fundamentals of the field."

"I am far past the fundamentals," she said, somewhat icily. "I am in need of an accomplished alchemist to teach some of the more esoteric techniques."

"Indeed? Why don't we head inside for lunch, and we can discuss your current skills and what branches you intend to develop further. Then we can discuss the compensation for my services in assisting you."

What followed was a lightning barrage of questions back and forth across the table, almost all of which went right over Nym's head. He didn't even know what most of the terms meant, what any of the technical names for the equipment were, or why it would matter that the ectoniamic regulator was kept isolated from all thaumatergic reactions, lest the runes get overcharged and ignite into a Scalinger's Cascade.

Presumably, that was bad.

Analia slowly thawed out as they talked shop, and Cern certainly warmed up to her almost instantly. As soon as it was clear that his prospective student was not someone who needed to be taught the names of basic ingredients and lectured on the best way to store them, he started getting excited.

Then they hit a snag. "I definitely think I could teach you quite a bit. There is, however, the matter of the money," Cern told her.

"Yes, of course. There is also the matter of travel. I'm not planning on remaining in Geldrin for much longer. My friends are all going to the southern coast for the winter. I'm still determining where exactly I'd like to go, but I do not intend to stay here."

"Ah. Moving an alchemy workshop is a pain. So much delicate equipment. Are you leaving soon? It might be better to wait until you've settled in at your new residence."

"That will depend on Nym, I think," she said. "I am still waiting for him to decide where he wants to go."

"You are?" Nym asked. He'd thought she was joking.

She let out an exasperated sigh. "Yes, dummy. I thought you might want to have some input on where we go next."

"It's all the same to me," Nym said with a shrug. "I can do a thousand miles in an afternoon of flying now, assuming I can't just teleport straight to my destination. Plus I'll be staying with Archmage Veran for at least a few more weeks, I think."

Though the more he thought about that arrangement, the less he liked the idea of living there. Perhaps it was time to find his own place again. He wasn't sure exactly where he wanted to go, other than that he would like no one from the Collective to know where he was, or from the army for that matter.

"Ahem. As I was saying though, we need to talk about my fee," Cern said.

"Right. Sorry. Money. That's important."

"It is, but I have . . . an alternative idea that the two of you might find acceptable."

CHAPTER SEVENTY

If you don't mind international travel, there's a city in Byramin known as the birthplace of alchemy. It's called Shu-Ain. Many alchemists still go there to train. It's an incredibly fertile region, flush with the types of materials we need. However, the prices of finished goods are correspondingly low. There's an easy supply and plenty of alchemists practicing there, so . . .

"But!" Cern said, gesturing to Nym. "But most people don't have a master mage capable of transporting the stock to better markets. The fortune we could save on shipping costs alone! We could go to Shu-Ain and rent a workshop. You can get materials needed to practice new potions and elixirs cheaply while I focus on bulk production of the moneymakers in foreign markets."

Analia considered it for a moment. "It seems like a good place for me to continue learning alchemy, but Cern's business plan relies entirely on you helping, Nym. I can't agree on your behalf."

"I was actually thinking about moving out of the country anyway," Nym said without hesitation. "I'm not interested in running a remote shop for you, but I don't mind dropping a few crates of merchandise off every month or so."

"We'll need some seed money to get started," Cern said. "I . . . uh . . . am a little light on that right now."

"How much would we need?" Analia asked.

"To rent a workshop? Maybe ten or fifteen crests a month. If we're lucky, we'll be able to rent one that's already equipped with all the tools and glassware we'll need. I expect that'll be twenty crests a month for a fully setup workshop. Otherwise I'm going to figure thirty crests for equipment to furnish an empty workshop."

"So if we're lucky, twenty crests to rent a furnished workshop," Analia said. "If we're not lucky, upward of forty. It'll save money in the long run, but it's also a lot up front. And we haven't even discussed material and manufacturing costs."

"It's a large investment, to be sure," Cern agreed.

"I don't have that much money," she said. "Not even close."

"I do," Nym said.

"Wha—you do?"

"I've been staying at the sanctum. No rent, no food expenses. Plus I did a lot of freelancing for the army."

That wasn't even counting his pay from the Collective or what he'd scavenged from the work camps after the undead had attacked. Nym wasn't rich by any means, not like a noble house or even a merchant family, but he was up to about seventy crests. If he hadn't been thinking about leaving the country, he might have finally opened a bank account.

"That's good. Money is only one hurdle though. We'll need to get there too. International teleport platforms are a lot stricter than domestic. That could be an issue for us too."

Nym waved his concern off. "I'll just fly over so I can add it to my teleportable locations. I've got a third-circle overland-flight spell that'll get me there in a few hours."

"Of course you do," Cern muttered. "Are you sure you're the same kid I was paying to collect mushrooms and moss for me last year?"

"Are we doing this then?" Analia asked.

She didn't seem concerned about living in a new city in a foreign country or about working in close proximity with a man she'd just met. Nym trusted Cern, but he was acutely aware of how helpless a person could be living somewhere new with no support and how much more likely it was that a young woman might be targeted.

Of course, Analia was nowhere near as weak as Nym had been when he'd first arrived in Abilanth. He couldn't imagine her dealing with the kind of struggles he'd faced back then. Still, she'd lived a sheltered life up until recently. He wasn't sure she really understood what kind of dangers were out there.

It wasn't his place to tell her what she could and couldn't do. If she was set, he'd support that decision. "I can fly out to Shu-Ain tomorrow afternoon."

"I guess we have a deal, Mr. Cern," Analia said.

"Good to hear. Now, some lunch I think, and then I'll see about getting a room here for tonight. Within two days, we'll be setting up in a new home."

Nym left them to discuss specifics, everything from various markets to tap into to which potions could be brewed in vast cauldrons to mass-produce them. He had to admit that most of the technical talk went over his head; he was far more interested in rune sequences than he was in alchemy. But the business ideas were pretty simple. Make stuff in a cheap area, transport it to an expensive area, profit.

"Nym, do me a favor when you go to Shu-Ain," Cern said.

"Hmm?"

"Check the exchange rates for me, will you? It's been a decade since I was there, but it was something like six dakars to one crest. I'm hoping my numbers aren't too far off, but we won't know what finances we have to work with until we know what the exchange rate is right now."

"I'll find out and let you know," Nym promised. "I've got to get going now. I'll stop by tomorrow before I set out, and you can give me any additional details or requests."

Nym sat across the table from Archmage Veran. "It is profoundly unfair that you have the ability to do this," the old man said again. He said it every time they did this exercise.

"I am aware."

He wondered what other advantages he'd had the first time he'd learned this. He'd know soon enough, he supposed. Thanks in large part to watching the archmage forge a fifth-layer conduit, Nym had successfully navigated his own path across the Astral Sea and reached the threshold of the fourth layer.

As he'd been warned, boring through it was completely different than splitting the chunks of solid arcana in the second layer. Archmage Veran demonstrated the technique of backfilling the conduit with third-layer arcana, causing the conduit to practically vibrate from the pressure. He was deliberately agitating it, and as it struck the membrane to the fourth layer and pierced through, it started to twist like a corkscrew.

Nym could follow it, but he was still having trouble keeping his conduit flexible enough to get that motion at the end. Worse, he could tell that he wasn't getting the kind of pressure the archmage easily achieved. That was the result of an imperfect intent filter. He needed the arcana to be fast and wild, and he needed a conduit strong enough to hold that and channel it to where it was needed.

"I'm confident I have the mechanics of the forging down," Nym said. "I know what I need to do. It's just a matter of refining the intent filter and hardening my will to withstand the force."

"Very well," Archmage Veran said. "We still have some time. Would you like me to supervise your practice?"

"Actually, I wanted to pick up a few new spells," Nym said. "Some variations of teleportation, long-range scrying, and communication."

"Oh? Thinking of spreading your social circle?"

"I'm considering it, yes. Even if I don't, they seem useful to know."

"I see. I'm going to guess that the long-range scrying spells you're interested in will allow you to find someone from hundreds of miles away or more, and you'd like to be able to have a two-way conversation with them?"

"Correct," Nym said.

"Very well. There are a few books in the library that can help you. Why don't you teleport us there and we'll discuss it further?"

Nym hesitated. He wasn't great at precision teleportation, even when it was just him. Archmage Veran himself didn't generally bother in his own sanctum, citing the effort not to be worth it. Worse, bringing someone else along made the spell more than twice as hard to cast. Doing it through the sanctum's antiteleportation wards would be impossible. Obviously, the archmage thought differently, or he wouldn't have asked Nym to do it.

"I'm missing something," Nym said, more to himself than to his mentor.

"Are you?" Archmage Veran leaned forward and regarded Nym over steepled fingers.

"You know I am. Are you going to tell me what?"

"What would be the fun of that?"

Nym gave him an annoyed glare. "I'm really not in the mood for a game tonight."

The smile died on Archmage Veran's lips. He studied Nym for just a moment and sighed. "Of course. I forgot myself. Please forgive an old man's jokes."

Arcana enveloped both of them, deliberately slowed so Nym could watch it build. The basic construct was as he'd been using himself, but when it extended from Archmage Veran to Nym, there was an additional component to it, one that synced caster and target, coupling them together. Nym didn't do that. He just widened the effective area of his teleport to include everyone.

Archmage Veran's spell caused the teleport effect to envelope both of them but none of the space in between. It was perfectly efficient, a skintight field of arcana, one that didn't waste a single shred of effort. Getting through the wards was more a matter of finesse and skill than a specific modification to the spell, but the archmage navigated through them like they weren't even there.

They spent the evening together in the library, going over the variations to the spell's structure to move multiple people more efficiently, to teleport others without teleporting himself as well, to teleport objects instead of people, and what kind of limitations Nym would have to work under as long as he was still limited to third-layer arcana.

It was a highly productive evening, even though they barely touched on scrying or long-range communication. By the time they were finished, Nym was quite satisfied and in a good mood. He went to bed smiling.

The next morning, Nym teleported to Geldrin and gathered the Earth Shapers together. They'd wrapped up their final projects in anticipation of the move and were, more or less, ready for him when he arrived. He teleported them and their luggage to Karu, then stuck around long enough for them to find a new place to stay.

"I promise, as soon as I get the hang of long-range communication spells, I'll let you know. Until then, just try not to leave suddenly, okay? I don't want to lose track of you guys," he said.

Ophelia pulled him into a hug and laughed. "You're not getting rid of us that easy!"

"Have a good trip," Monick said. "We'll be here when you get back."

"Bring us a souvenir, okay?" Nomick added.

"I'll see what I can find," Nym told them. "Alright, I'm off!"

Bildar grabbed his shoulder and said, "Hold on a second, Nym. Come on, walk with me for a bit."

The two walked back onto the street and started heading in a random direction. "Look," Bildar said, "I don't want to tell you how to live your life, and God knows you're strong enough to take care of yourself now. But I don't know this alchemist, and Analia is only strong for her age. How much do you know about Byramin?"

"Not a lot," Nym said. "Why, is there something I should know about it?"

"Slavery is legal in Byramin, and the slave traders there—they call them flesh carvers for reasons that I think should be obvious—like to target people who aren't native. There's a lot less of a chance that anyone will raise a fuss if they press-gang a foreigner into a slave crew."

"Are you saying we shouldn't go?" Nym asked.

Bildar just shook his head and shrugged. "I don't know. That alchemist isn't wrong about Shu-Ain being the birthplace of alchemy. It's probably one of the best places in the world to learn. I just want you to be aware of the risks."

"I understand. Thanks for looking out for me. I'll be careful. I promise."

"Alright, go on then. Come back and see us soon so we know you're still alive."

"Will do," Nym said.

Then he flew straight up into the air, wove together arcana pulled from the Astral Sea, and shot off at supersonic speeds. He followed the coast south and east until he reached his destination: a port city on the southern tip of the continent. Then he flew off over the open ocean, hundreds of miles until he spotted an island in the archipelago that made up Byramin.

From there it was a simple matter to find Shu-Ain, it being one of the largest cities in the island chain. Nym slowed down and landed on the outskirts of the city. It was time to explore someplace new.

CHAPTER SEVENTY-ONE

After a year spent wasting his time mucking around in the minds of various weak-willed humans, Abdun was desperate to be off this job. He was of the opinion that Niramyn had actually died when he'd fled, but Exarch Myzalik wasn't interested in the opinions of a lowly sixth-layer ascendant such as himself. Then again, even if he'd reached the eleventh layer, Abdun doubted it would make a difference. Exarch Myzalik listened only to Exarch Myzalik.

This lead was a bit more promising than the ones he usually followed up on. A group of humans researching some pathetically low-level soul-well-modification techniques thought they'd stumbled upon an actual ascendant to use as a test subject. The idea was laughable really. No ascendant would ever submit to the will of a bunch of humans, most of whom were barely even able to touch the third layer.

But they knew the ascendant as Nym, who appeared to be a teenage boy. Much to Abdun's surprise, when he'd reviewed the data, the numbers did indicate that their research specimen was abnormally strong. Oh, it wasn't ascendant level by a wide margin, but maybe it was deathly-injured-ascendant level.

What really convinced him wasn't the research notes themselves but when he'd started reviewing the timeline and recognized the boy who'd fought the giant ice-worm monster. He followed it backward a ways to see the kid fighting the undead that were roaming the area courtesy of a midsize dimensional void with a badly mangled patch job on it, then forward to see where he was now.

Abdun followed the kid's advancement to the third layer and noted a brief sliver of a second where time seemed to scramble and distort. It could just be temporal interference. That happened sometimes, after all, but this kid was getting more suspicious by the minute. The kid spontaneously teleported soon after, despite giving no indication that he'd learned the spell. It could have been something he'd learned in theory prior to being able to cast it, but Abdun felt the spell was executed too smoothly for that to be the case.

He traced the teleportation to a small cove on the west coast of the continent and watched the boy employ far too many spells for what amounted to fighting off some big fish, just so he could dive into the water. The boy swam down to the bottom, groped around blindly in the silt for a few seconds despite having a water-sight magic active, then gave up and swam back to the surface.

Abdun frowned. The boy's body language was triumphant, like he'd overcome some great obstacle. All he'd done was dive through perhaps a hundred feet of water and come back up again. Surely humans didn't consider that an achievement of any merit. Abdun skimmed backward through the boy's timeline again and rewatched the scene. Down, touch bottom, and up. What was there to celebrate?

Confused now and sensing that he'd somehow missed something, Abdun followed the timeline forward again. The boy flew over to a seaside shack, barely more than a box with more holes than walls, and woke the woman sleeping inside. The two spoke for a bit, and the boy dug a shabby hole in the ground under the shack. It was a painfully slow process, taking hours to do something that would have taken a second for any real ascendant.

Then just before the boy teleported away with the sunrise, the timeline vanished completely. It was like the kid existed one moment, and then never had the next. Someone or something was interfering with the boy's timeline. Everything else was perhaps atypical behavior but still human. Mortals couldn't interact with time though, not like this. They could barely even look ahead, let alone alter it. Either this Nym person was actually Niramyn, or another ascendant had taken an interest in him.

Abdun teleported himself to the seaside shack and looked down at it. Whatever was going on here, he wanted to see it with his own eyes. It was possible someone was interfering with the sensory feedback his spell was giving him. If anyone tried it in person, he'd know.

The woman living in the shack, the one named Ciana, was there right now. Abdun started trawling through her memories, looking for the night she'd talked to the boy. He found it easily enough, but the memory had holes in it. It was subtle, no doubt. He might not even have noticed it if he hadn't come in person. But they were there.

They were talking about . . . something. Whatever it was must have been made by an ascendant, since it was strong enough to cover even the memory of its existence from Abdun's spells. Perhaps Exarch Myzalik himself would be able to uncover more, but this wasn't what Abdun wanted. He'd wanted to deliver Niramyn himself to his master, to bask in the glory and accolades, to claim a fitting reward.

This Ciana woman was an important piece of the puzzle, too valuable to just be left lying around, waiting for something to happen to her. It was best if Abdun harvested her soul now for interrogation whenever he needed. That would help keep the knowledge intact and slow down any other ascendants who found her. Reviewing someone's memories just from their timeline was markedly harder than doing so from their mind in present time.

He'd be damned if he'd let some other ascendant claim the prize after a year of mucking around in mortal minds looking for Niramyn. It was only fitting that he be rewarded fully and singularly for his patience and his tenacity. He reached into the sixth layer and began constructing the spell that would reap the woman's soul from her body and seal it in a soul trap.

It was a good thing Abdun was an egotistical idiot. He spent so much time trying to figure out what his next move should be and refusing to ask for help that he'd given Ferro more than enough of an opportunity to construct his attack. It was a tenth-layer spell, the strongest Ferro knew. Making it fast without being detected was impossible, but Abdun gave him plenty of time to build it slowly.

Ferro appeared behind him just as the weak ascendant was getting ready to reap Exarch Niramyn's mortal companion. He stabbed his fingers into Abdun's back and grasped at his soul well, then triggered the magic that would disperse his victim's timeline. It was a temporary setback, eating away maybe six months of history and pushing him out of time for perhaps a year into the future.

Despite Abdun's relative weakness as a mere initiate into ascendancy, he was still technically an ascendant. It was impossible to really kill him. Ferro doubted he'd broken even a quarter of the anchors holding Abdun's place in time. Not even his own master, an exarch, could fully disperse another ascendant's timeline. Though Ferro was humble enough to admit that Exarch Niramyn could still have banished him out of time for decades instead of a mere eighteen months.

By then, hopefully his master would have fully returned to power. Ferro was doing his best to track the exarch and reach him before anyone else did, but it wasn't easy to pierce the many, many layers of obfuscation keeping him hidden. Those protections were no doubt better than anything Ferro himself would provide, seeing as to how he was only the fourteenth-most-powerful ascendant, and only three of those stronger than him had any sort of loyalty to Exarch Niramyn.

If any of them found his master before he regained his strength, Ferro shuddered to think of the results. Myzalik was perhaps the single greatest threat any ascendant could face, an exarch who specialized in time manipulation. He would have dispersed Abdun for at least five years, and there would be a chain of contingencies woven in to keep dispersing the ascendant within milliseconds of him slipping back into the time stream, effectively locking him out for centuries before the chain ran its course.

As much as it pained Ferro to admit it, his own master couldn't duplicate such a feat. He had far more raw power, enough to disperse an ascendant for two or even three times longer than Myzalik, but he didn't specialize in time manipulation in the same way. And now . . . Now he wasn't even a real ascendant anymore. No doubt many of those who had previously been loyal were shifting over to Myzalik's camp, the treacherous sycophants.

Ferro still believed in his master, and when Exarch Niramyn made his glorious return to power, he would no doubt be rewarded handsomely for that faith. Even better than the reward would be watching his rivals return, groveling and struggling to worm their way back into his master's favor. It would be a delicious scene that Ferro fully intended to immortalize in crystalline memory.

In order to make sure that happened, he needed to do his best to interfere with any other ascendants who were hunting for his master. That meant staying ahead of them, if not finding the exarch himself. This human woman, Ciana, was a potential weak point, but his master's current form had a fondness for the woman. Ferro would not be rewarded for plucking her from the timeline.

So he'd layered the physical area with detection wards and planted more subtle sensors in the timeline surrounding Nym's meeting with her. He was a spider sitting at the center of a gossamer web, waiting for ascendants to touch one of the strands so that he could pounce, all so that he could buy his master more time. As long as no one too strong for him came along, he could keep the hunters at bay.

With Abdun dispersed through time, he reset the trip lines and disappeared again. He'd spent more time than anyone studying the timeline at what mortals called Bloodfin Cove, and even he couldn't figure out exactly what had happened there. It was quite the puzzle, and thankfully it had served as a distraction four times now that allowed him to ambush would-be pursuers.

Sooner or later, someone stronger was going to follow the trail of the dispersed ascendants, and when that happened, Ferro hoped he'd be able to slow them down or that he would have at least found his master first and could whisk him away from danger.

Abdun had been about to reap the woman's soul, and Ferro honestly considered doing it himself. It wasn't like they couldn't reconstitute her existence out of the timeline later if Exarch Niramyn decided he wanted her back. But no, that might serve to draw more interest to the area, and anyone strong enough to overcome him would be able to read her memories regardless of whether she was physically present.

It was better to leave her as bait and ambush the weaker ascendants who came sniffing around. He was just lucky one of Myzalik's copies hadn't shown up personally to investigate. If that happened, Ferro shuddered to think of his master's chances of survival. It had been many, many centuries since he'd been afraid of dying, but this new magic that severed all temporal anchors, it scared him in a way he could scarcely remember from back when he was mortal.

One didn't advance as an ascendant by being timid. Ferro would do whatever he could to become stronger, even take risks like he hadn't needed to take in hundreds of years, not since he was a human himself. He allowed himself a small smile as he remembered his first meeting with the exarch. He'd been a young human of about a hundred years, so proud that he'd reached the level of archmage, so ignorant of what true power was.

Exarch Niramyn had taught him better.

Ferro retreated several hundred miles out over the ocean, wrapped his body in a shell of arcana, and plunged into the icy black waters to sink all the way down to the bottom. He burrowed into the mud a mile below the surface, then slipped into a pocket of pseudoreality to wait and to monitor the situation. He would react when the next threat emerged.

He would give his master as much time as possible.

About the Author

EmergencyComplaints grew up reading fantasy and tried his hand at writing his first novel on an old MS-DOS text editor program when he was seven years old. That story didn't pan out; maximum character limits were a thing back then. Undeterred, he kept writing on other platforms, reading full-time, devouring JRPGs, and playing *D&D*, and he is now the author of the God Machine and Ascendant series. Check out his most recent work on Royal Road.

DISCOVER
STORIES UNBOUND

PodiumAudio.com